Usha Ananda Krishna graduated from the School of Planning and Architecture, New Delhi, and has worked as an architect in New Delhi, Bangalore and Kolkata. In 1980 she began writing advertising copy, interspersing the two careers till she began writing fiction full-time. During much of this time she was a partner at Pause and Effect, an architecture and interior design firm she co-founded in Kolkata.

In 1995 her first novel, *A Turbulent Passage*, was published by UBSPD, New Delhi. This was followed by a biography in 1998, *Minds on Fire*, commissioned by an information technology entrepreneur, and published by Sterling Books. Then she edited/put together two books on Jain philosophy—*Finding Your Spiritual Centre* and *Transforming Your Mind*. After her move to Kathmandu in 1997, she began working on *Fallout* while contributing regularly to *Mirror*, a monthly magazine brought out by the United Nations Women's Organisation. In the last two years she ventured into playwriting, and wrote two radio plays and two for the stage, one of which was shortlisted by Kali Productions, UK, for their theatre festival. In addition to *Fallout* she has completed a collection of short stories. Currently she is working on another novel.

Her interests include reading, theatre, contemporary art and architecture, and furniture design, as well as trekking—she has trekked extensively in the Himalayas.

Fallout

USHA ANANDA KRISHNA

TRANQUEBAR

TRANQUEBAR PRESS
An imprint of westland ltd
571, Poonamallee High Road, Kamaraj Bhavan, Aminjikarai, Chennai 600 029
1 Floor, Praja Bhavan, 53/2 Bull Temple Road, Basavangudi, Bangalore 560 019
1 Floor, 3-5-1108, Maruthi Complex, Narayanaguda, Hyderabad 500 029
Plot No 102, Marol Coop Ind Estate, Marol, Andheri East, Mumbai 400 059
F-5, Okhla Industrial Area, Phase-1, Mezzanine Floor, New Delhi 110 020

First published in TRANQUEBAR by westland ltd 2009

Copyright © Usha Ananda Krishna 2009

10 9 8 7 6 5 4 3 2 1

ISBN: 978-81-89975-97-5

This is a work of fiction. Names, characters, places and incidents are either the product of the author's imagination or are used fictitiously and any resemblance to any actual person, living or dead, events or locales is entirely coincidental.

Typeset in Dante MT by SÜRYA, New Delhi
Printed at Nutech Photolithographers, Delhi

For all those who kept the faith with me

Contents

Overture

An accident, they said. An old man not looking where he was going, missing his step, keeling over. And then toppling, *plunging* to his death. It is the obvious conclusion. Old men being definitively unbalanced—one way or other—and conclusions being notoriously expedient. Nine times out of ten. Anyhow I'm going along with it because it suits me too. So he fell. So be it. An accident? Oh, absolutely. No question. We're nothing if not logical in this family. All excepting me, of course. But I don't think I'm being fanciful here when I say I doubt this was an accident. In fact, I *fear* it wasn't. If it was, it was aided. In effect, he was pushed. It was an accident only inasmuch as he and one other (the perpetrator? avenger? redeemer?) were accidentally there in the same place at the same time. I suppose one could say that life in general is driven by accidents of time and place. And of course that other mysterious force that can turn the coin—reverse time, disappear the place—in a nanosecond. *Fate.*

There is one other possibility, though, which also isn't as far-fetched as it sounds, and which adds the dimension of cognitive action to time and place. I refer to the possibility of wilful self-propulsion—forcing the hand of fate. In other words, he *jumped*. Jumped to his conclusion. (Cheap, cheap, Kaveri!) Anyhow, jumped would be the less awful conclusion.

For whom, though?

The thoughts scrabble round and round, looking for a foothold. Did it happen because he wasn't all there? Or because he was all *too* there? Or because somebody was opportunely there?

I don't say anything. One shouldn't always say what one believes. Nor, for that matter, believe all one thinks. One shouldn't speak one's mind, that is. The mind is such a dodgy tool! And no truth is incontrovertible. So this is not a signed statement. It's a hypothesis. (But death is not a hypothesis!) It's a, what, soliloquy. Who would have thought the old man to have so much blood in him? Only, there was no blood. Just a trickle from his chin. He didn't split open. He fell cleanly and considerately. Like a well-secured mail sack.

But here's the smell of blood still. And all the perfumes of Araby . . . Hell is murky indeed.

Ramu is looking at me. It seems he too is thinking. Although his face is empty as a crater. But I hold back, don't ask him as I'm palpitating to, *have you talked to Jana yet*?

The weirdness grows and grows. The marble is so very white. The light is so very bright. The incense is so very cloying. Everything is so *festive* still. After all, the function had been every bit as grand as Meenakshi had said. The flowers, the ceremonies, the food, the finery. Lilamami's famed diamond necklace. Devimami's brocade sari. Meenakshi's freshly burnished hair.

It was to be a housewarming to remember—and it would be remembered.

The day had begun as propitiously as our astrologer had predicted. Two colourful canvas marquees, pandals, had been rigged in the U court of the building—the yellow-and-red one for the ceremonies, the blue-and-green for dining. Live music, the exuberant pipes-and-drums of the south, had roused the street early in the morning and had been playing without let-up, a tape recorder taking over when the musicians paused for coffee. The lobby floor and the staircase landings were decorated with kolam—the arcane patterns of rice flour and red clay mandatory for auspicious events, and the doors to the new flats daubed with turmeric and vermilion paste. Strings of mango leaves festooned the lintels. Marigolds abounded, draping doorways, curtaining windows, woven in straw to spell 'WELCOME' for the banner over the gate.

At the entrance to the main pandal three small girls, in tinselly, toffee-wrapper finery, pranced around. They were detailed to greet the guests with silver trays of sugar candy and roses, silver bowls of turmeric and silver dippers for scented water, and they were working themselves into hysterics, now force-feeding each other the candy, now splashing the scented water around, chasing after those who forgot their rose or candy . . . Every now and again they collapsed in a huddle of gauze and giggles, and got scolded and shooed back to their duties by their mothers.

Meenakshi, Mani and I had been bidden to come early—Meenakshi to usher in the guests, Mani to engage them in conversation (the worthies, that is), and I, well, because I am part of the package, appended to them as fingernail is to finger, and, as Lilamami stated in her unchallengeable way, hadn't I come all the way from Delhi for this? Although Devimami had sniffed, I was a big shot now, why would I come for a boring thing like *this*. And Uma had snorted that in her opinion I hadn't really come for *this*, I never had a straightforward reason for anything. (But then who's to dispute that, for lies *are* my stock-in-trade.) Then Jana had whispered, oh, Kaveri! Why did you come? They're so angry with you! And the wretched Bharat said, well, this has always been your bolthole. And, I *knew* you were running away from something. But at least he'd been glad to see me. Of course Mani and Meenakshi were glad too, more than, but then their gladsomeness or indeed feelings about anything concerning me is suspect— they're so hopelessly biased.

Anyhow, we were bidden to come early, Mani and Meenakshi and I, instructed to await the guests in the main pandal—which was filling up faster with smoke than with people—and from long-standing habit we have obeyed. So here is Meenakshi, cutting yards of strung jasmine to equal short lengths for the women to wear in their hair, and here I am laying out the bits in a basket. There is Mani sipping pineapple crush and steadily ignoring the conversational overtures of the worthy sitting beside him. He is (ostensibly) interested in the rituals on the platform, although his chair is turned slightly to block them out. He is listening to the mantras, however, with, going by his expression, the exasperated attention that is so typical of him. For Mani, as I like to tease, is a non-practising agnostic. A backsliding sceptic— although he will not admit to that. He has a high regard for the philosophy of the Vedas but it needed more substantiation of its subtleties than the simplistic construal provided by its largely ignorant exponents. Such as these priests. And he certainly didn't care to hear them chant, that is, rattle off the sublime verses as if they were multiplication tables. It was nothing short of sacrilege.

Three priests were mauling the mantras today, on a two-foot-high platform striped white and ochre—the colours of purity and austerity. The platform was cluttered with the paraphernalia of their trade. Silver jugs, silver lamps, silver chalices, silver dippers. Baskets of flowers. Trays of fruit. Incense. Holy water. Dried grass. Coloured rice. A wood fire inside a square of bricks was pumping out the evil smoke that was now choking everybody and irritating poor Meenakshi's sinuses. Mani's uncles, Balumama and Rajumama, were feeding it with ghee from a folded leaf at the end of every stanza while their faithful wives, Lilamami and Devimami, sat coughing and sneezing beside them. But they had to endure it—after all it was their home being consecrated today. 'Suwaha,' boomed the priests. 'Suwaha,' mumbled Rajumama, carelessly flicking his leaf. The priests stared him down; Devimami scooped up a double ration of ghee and thrust it at her husband; Rajumama meekly poured it over the quiescent embers. There was an angry hiss and a fist of smoke made straight for his face. *Damn*, he muttered.

The building of a house is a milestone in a man's life, a rite of passage marking the divide between the responsible householder and the carefree wastrel. It is a proud man who, with his wife in tow and right foot first, crosses the divide as symbolised by the threshold, to take possession of a thing that has possessed him for months, years even. That has sucked up a lifetime's savings, as it had Mani's, and deprived him (and possibly will continue to deprive him for a long time) of the smallest indulgences—till the self-denial becomes a habit. As it had for Mani.

The housewarming of Mani's house-on-the-road had been a culmination of travails, not this effortless, climacteric triumph of his uncles. There was so much left to be done but so little money left to do it! And all those unpaid bills! Some of the contractors were in attendance and he felt their accusing eye—what was he doing with figured glass lampshades when he hadn't paid for the plumbing yet? How dare he buy a rose tree when he had haggled so for the cement? He was less proud than appalled at his temerity in saddling himself with this thing; all he wanted now was to slip in like a shadow and occupy it like the lizards already in residence. Was it worth it? Not taking Meenakshi on the holiday she needed? Not buying Kaveri a pair of party shoes she cried a whole year for? He regrets these petty cruelties now, and wonders if he has been forgiven them.

He smiles sadly at Kaveri when she comes to sit beside him.

She smiles back. My father's feeling his age, she thinks. He's sentimental for the noble old house, his ancestral home, which had stood in the place of this brash new building they are breathing life into. Praying that it will shelter them for many a long year, and keep them in health and prosperity.

But Mani is actually remembering Kaveri shimmering through the echoing rooms of the house-on-the road in her new silk skirt. He'd grudged that skirt, he remembers with shame. And Meenakshi's new sari. Every half-eaten laddoo at the housewarming lunch had made him want to shout, would you waste it if you had to pay for it? He was especially enraged by the priests. Spouting the Vedas from one side of their mouths and talking money from the other! Exuding snuff and oily sweat—the reek of puritanism and fraud! That pigtail on their heads to lift them up to heaven! Those sacred threads draping their bellies like spilled guts! Those were *his* guts! Wrenched from *his* belly! Tradition! Pah!

He had conceded to the rituals because of his mother, and tradition decreed you respect your mother's wishes. 'Tradition has civilised us,' she said to Mani, whenever he threatened to break with it. 'Preserved our culture.' Mani visited his rage on the mosquitoes that kept him and Meenakshi wakeful as they lay wordless and untouching that first night in their new house. In the morning, tired and sore, he almost wept when he saw the angry red blotches staining the newly painted walls.

'Are you alright, Pa?' asks Kaveri, taking his glass from him.

And he is out in the sunshine again. 'Never better, Kaveri! I'm on top of the world!'

Watching her, his beautiful daughter in her peacock-blue sari, he exults, the deprivations, the worries—what were they worth now? Nothing. Not a paisa. The anxieties that had lingered into Kaveri's adulthood, smarting like prickly heat, what did they matter *now*? Not an itch. There was a time the itch had been really bad, as when she stopped her education with an MA (what, no PhD? no MPhil even?) and got herself a job in a bank to be 'economically independent'. It had grown excruciating with the advent of Arya. Was it to this end that he had worked and worried for her—just so she could marry this random sample of the Indian education system? Who'd majored in *business* (not higher math)? From a university nobody had heard of?

Arya was a self-employed chartered accountant. With prospects in a growing economy. (And poor, earnest Arya tried so hard!) It was the most charitable thing Mani could say in the face of Kaveri's obstinacy. 'But I wish he'd get a decent government job!' he said to Meenakshi. 'Instead of this private practice.' As if Arya had set up as a back-street money-launderer.

'He's a finance consultant,' murmured Meenakshi.

'He *fixes* taxes,' retorted Mani. 'Making his living from crooks who diddle *us*! And it's not even a regular income!'

'Kaveri earns a regular income.'

But that was an untimely reminder because, 'She could have done better for herself too!' he mourned. 'And what sort of man is he that he cannot support a wife? I should put my foot down *now*.'

Meenakshi had been unexpectedly firm. '*Don't*.' Then, 'They will support each other,' she said gently. 'It is the modern way.'

'That boy lacks personality. I mean, he lacks enterprise.' No, he didn't lack enterprise—he had shown a little too much of it in making off with his daughter. 'He lacks,' frowning, '*something*'.

Gumption, Kaveri could have supplied, if she had been consulted (years later, of course), but, 'He's our son-in-law,' Meenakshi said, putting the lid on Arya's deficiencies as firmly as Lilamami slammed shut the biscuit tin. *Tup*. That's it for today. No, *no* more. And, 'Stop worrying all the time about Kaveri.'

He can't help it, Kaveri said. He's like a coconut tree. Straight and narrow, and shade for only one person. *Me*.

It was hard for Mani to feel positive about Arya because Mani had never allowed optimism to get the better of him. Only fools did. Mani struggled equally against optimism and complacence—false gods that lured you away from reason. Outwardly he warned against the dangers of scepticism, pessimism, cynicism, and the consequences of succumbing to despair, but inside burned little fires of doubt and disbelief which, in spite of his stamping them out, would flare up again and again. Sometimes the struggle was too much and he would fling down his pencil. Or the newspaper. Or the television remote. 'I give up!' He gave up periodically on the government, Kaveri's physics teacher, Meenakshi's inaptitude for logic. And he became a great provider for the future—the future that hovered over them like a storm cloud of want-and-hardship. That, although miles away, and years—tomorrow never gets to be today, Kaveri said—would now and then send warning flashes of lightning in the form of inflationary economic policies, increased taxes, a failed monsoon.

But the caution, the doubts, were things of the past. The winter of want, that Kaveri used to think would never end, was over. His worries had worked like prayers—they had been answered! Into each life some rain must fall, and *what* a comfort clichés were. At the end of the tunnel, in the middle of the wasteland, on top of the mountain, there was Kaveri.

Above the pandal, in the cloudless sky, the shrewish Bangalore sun snapped and scolded.

Mani suddenly gets up, pulling me up with him. 'My daughter. *My* daughter. *Kaveri Chowdhry*. Who,' he chortles, 'needs no introduction'. And throwing decorum to the winds he hugs me—there, right in front of everybody.

Oh, Pa.

We sit down again to watch the rituals that would ensure the Family safe passage into its new home.

Balumama, as the older brother, is officiating. Like the priests he is shirtless, with his Brahmin thread dividing the hairless flaps of his chest from (right) shoulder to (left) hip. Lilamami, as a proper Hindu wife, is going through the motions with him, but, being Lilamami, three-quarters of her is simultaneously alert for gatecrashers. Rajumama, as the younger brother, has a peripheral role but his visibility is high. Oilcloth bag under one arm, a file clutched in the other hand, he leaps around the pandals, checking and rechecking the arrangements. Someone had to oversee the self-appointed overseers, and Rajumama was that someone. Only Devimami was exempt— nobody could oversee her, least of all her husband! Of course her precious son is an exception. Her son's visibility *and* nuisance quotient are as high as ever but she doesn't tick him off. He's been sneaking around with his camera today, which is how he got a shot of his mother's bum flattening the legs of a stool. 'Yenna, Bharat!' she screeched. 'Cancel it! Wipe it off! Please!' *Please*? Bharat is privileged indeed.

'A classic shot,' he grins. 'You were the butt of my joke. Get that, Kaveri. *Butt* on a stool!'

It's not *that* funny, fool.

'Because *you* didn't think of it.' He trains his lens on my face. 'Any progress with your conscience?'

It's coming along well, thank you. Without *your* help.

I raise my handbag to block out the staring eye of his lens. When I lower it he is looking at me, but not through the lens, and, here is a thing, not with his eyes either. He is not smiling.

The priests continue incanting. The audience continues chattering. The pandal continues to fill up with smoke.

Meenakshi appears to have forgotten the fracas of last

week. It is enough that she has been invited here, given a chance to repossess her position in the family. She is busy charming the guests in her ashes-of-roses sari and her audacious pink lipstick—those Remote Relatives and Friends-and-Neighbours the Family normally dismisses as undeserving of its regard, but have been invited today to make up the numbers required for a 'grand affair'. She has an infinite capacity for people, Meenakshi, and is forever trying to expand mine. 'Come here, Kaveri! You remember Gomumami who came to your first birthday, don't you?'

Of course I remember.

'Mmmm, what a *big* girl you've become!'

Or it is, 'Your daughter from Delhi? The one who recently . . .?' Yes, beams Meenakshi. *Yes. That* daughter. I have only one daughter, you know. One *child*. And they shake their greying heads in wonder. 'So you're the one! Happiness, happiness!'

Meenakshi gushes and flows, but Mani gives everyone a chilly once-over. And who may you be? Do you deserve my consideration? Because these are ordinary people with no hidden complexities or intellectual pretensions (and for this they are to be condemned?), soft targets of lifestyle advertisements, victims of stock market manipulations and land scams, who have no other agenda than to pay their taxes on time and live a decent life, passing their decency to their children, so an orderly world, fuelled by old-fashioned goodness and unspectacular deeds, plain speaking and simple honesty, could keep turning. People, it must be remembered, who had once attracted my grandmother's high-nosed scorn too.

Now Pati's ashes, passing in and out of gaping fish in the river where they'd been scattered, are protesting (but who is listening), *don't waste your time on them! They are not worth your attention!* Her muteness, her remoteness makes a mockery of her entreaty. The immediacy of life is *here*. Colour, music, noise, excitement. This was a time to fritter away in idle conversation. *This* was life, this waste of time.

Mani is thinking of his mother too. 'I wish your poor Pati, God bless her soul, was alive today for this.'

She wouldn't have liked this new building, Pa, in the place of her old home.

'She had reconciled to it. In fact, her last outing was to this place. Just after they pulled it down.'

The outing had been the earth-breaking ceremony. Inexplicably, she had taken a shine to the builders, who'd brought her laddoos from a *Brahmin* sweetshop. And look, they have even sprinkled holy water! The red spots were dried cock's blood (the builders were propitiating their gods in their own way) but nobody had the heart to disillusion her. Not even ghoulish Ramu, the only one I knew who actually enjoyed dissecting frogs in biology class.

'Kaveri, I just remembered Ramu's poem! The cock one!' And Mani, rocking to and fro, recited the doggerel that used to drive us mad with its idiotic rhythm. *Da, da dum, dum. Da, da dum, dum* . . .

He threw a rock,
And killed a cock
What a horrible stink
In the Brahmin precinct!

Up and down Ramu would caper, running the words senseless, till Pati clapped her hands over her ears and begged him to stop.

'But where *is* Ramu? I was told he's coming.'

Right on cue he arrives, Cocksblood Ramu, in a fug of Hamam soap and Jabakusum hair oil, looking as always as if buffeted by an unseen wind. As if someone has just been treating him badly. His too-short trousers reveal battered leather sandals with one broken strap, and his polyester shirt reveals three holes in his vest, spreading like egg yolk. But either he has risen above such considerations or sunk below them—I can never tell which. I don't expect a wife will change the state of his underwear, but she might wipe off the bit of shaving soap under his ear. Over the years he's become quiet—introspective or introverted, I can't tell which. His mother, my aunt Saroja, is proud of his silence—she regards it as a sign of intelligence, and a compliment to herself for having weaned him off needless chatter. 'He is so *quite*, isn't he? Yain, Ramu, romba *quite*, illiya?' Obediently he would nod, and my silly aunt would pass around a smile like it was a hat.

But yesterday 'quite' Ramu had risen like a tidal wave. And made some very satirical comments too.

'Kaveri-a.' He jiggles the change in his pocket. 'When did you come?' When did *you*, I ask back, in the time-honoured family way of answering question with question. Managing to look important, casual, modest, all at once, 'Just now only,' he announced. 'I applied for half-day leave—I must leave *immediately* after lunch.'

'I haven't heard from your mother in almost two months, Ramu,' Mani says. 'I hope she's well?'

'Same as usual.' Jiggle, jiggle. The sameness of his mother cheers him on this unscheduled morning and he grows garrulous. 'Sleeps a lot. She could not come because of Father.'

How's Father, I ask without thinking.

'Same to same.' Jiggle, Jiggle. 'No change whatsoever.'

'So Ramu,' says Mani, 'I hear that rascally Gundu Rao will continue to be your CEO.' Then, as if he's suddenly remembered, he interrupts himself. 'How is Jana?' His face creases with concern, and I find myself wishing he'd just stick to his area of expertise, which is certainly not concern for anybody.

Bharat pops up. 'What-what and all, da, Ramu! Do you still kill ants with hot wax?'

'Yes,' says Ramu. 'I mean, no. Yes, he will,' he nods to my father and, a little desperately, 'No, I don't,' he nods to Bharat.

Devimami comes bustling out of the kitchen shed with a what's-going-on lift of her eyebrows. Followed by an I-don't-have-time-for-whatever-it-is sniff. '*Ennada* Ramu, so you're here at last!'

Ramu smiles weakly.

'I hear your mother isn't coming.' Her eyes dart around, as if whatever Ramu has to say is not worth her undivided attention. 'That pole is crooked ... she needed a special invitation or what? Well, I hope she's enjoying the heat of Chennai. *Forty-four degrees*!' She shudders. 'You'd think she'd want to escape the weather at least.'

Ramu shakes his head in a rotary movement to convey no, she didn't need a special invitation, and yes, the heat was terrible in Chennai.

'What, are you still *quite*? No tongue-a?'

Ramu shakes his head from side to side to convey yes, he does have a tongue.

Devimami isn't impressed. 'If you want tiffin there're some idlis left over. Nod yes or no. Since you will not speak.' She waits exactly ten seconds before turning to me. 'Can you make your cousin speak?'

'I've already taken my tiffin,' says Ramu sheepishly. 'At home.'

'Why? Ours is not good enough for you?'

He's looking hunted now. 'Not like that, Devimami . . .'

'Hmph! Go eat the halva at least!'

From early morning the kitchen shed has been buzzing. Mounds of chopped cucumber, beans, cabbage. Pails of sambar, rasam and buttermilk. Trays of halva, gooey with ghee and thick with raisins and cashew nut. The cooks are cheerful and unhurried, confident that their sense of timing, perfected over thousands of such meals, will not fail them today. Breakfast at seven, lunch at noon. Precisely. They will not burn the milk nor confuse the coconut paste for the sambar with the coconut paste for the chutney as Devimami is convinced they will. The head cook assures her, 'Don't worry, Amma. The food will be first-class, A-1!' But Devimami knows better. No vigilance, no first-class anything. 'Did you finish the sugar in the tin before you opened this sack?' she asks, tripping over the helper boys. 'Isn't that too much salt for these potatoes?' And to the bunch of masochists who do her regular housework, 'This is not a holiday!' If she has no one to pick on she picks on Seena, poor cousin three times removed, who's always good for a scolding because he bungles so. He is trying to count the laddoos now and isn't getting anywhere because she keeps interrupting to tell him he's got it wrong. 'Fifty-*five*! I told you not to move the basket there . . . Are those hands clean?'

Outside the kitchen, inside a tarpaulin shelter, Rajumama is supervising the splitting of banana leaves to eat our lunch off. The paddle-shaped leaves must be split cleanly down the spine, into two halves, without a single tear, or the rasam will leak through. The banana leaf plates are stacked in a neat pile, the discarded strips scattered about, sinuous as snakes and oozing sap. A clean green scent fills the bright air.

Rajumama looks up. Earlier in the day he'd been this side of cool while I had tried to be on the other side of warm.

Hot work, eh Rajumama?

He picks up a leaf, examines it, sighs. 'What I wouldn't do for a beer!'

I can buy you a bottle, Rajumama. There's a shop down the road.

'*Ayyoyo!* With those priests around?' He claps his hand to his mouth. 'I can't even *think* of it!'

Don't think of it then. Just drink it.

That cracks him up. The frail bamboo pole shivers, the holes in the tarpaulin break the sun into dozens of stars. '*Ayyoyo!* Your Lilamami will . . .' he draws a line across his throat with his finger, '*karak!*'

Alright, then I'll come with some tomorrow and we'll celebrate. *If* she'll let me in. Speaking of which, tell me, Rajumama, wasn't that an absurd condition she made?

His smile goes out.

Come on, Rajumama, admit it's crazy. She can't be serious. I mean, banishing me! And dragging Amma and Appa into it too!

'You dragged *every*one into something worse.' *Froop!* He's torn the leaf. He holds the ragged bits, one in each hand. Then he flings them down. Without another word, he stalks off.

'Kaveri! Over here!'

And Jana emerges, that is, sidles out from behind the shelter. She beckons with a hand curled close to her head, bobs her head in furtive invitation. Now what? 'Will you sit next to me at lunch?' Is that all? I breathe again. Her eyes glisten. 'Pleeese?' *Don't beg Jana*, our grandmother would admonish. *Okay, Pati, but can I go and play now? Pleeese?* It's *may I, Jana*, not can I, and no, you may not go and play, you haven't finished your homework. 'Will you?' She pushes me with her hip—another habit Pati hadn't succeeded in eliminating—and expels a cloud of hot moist air. It condenses on my neck.

Of course, Jana. I was hoping to sit with you! (The things one says!)

'Oh Kaveri! I'm so proud to be your cousin!' She digs me with her elbow and I begin walking sideways, crablike, to get out of range. 'I tell everyone you're my *sister!*'

Of course I am, Jana. (The things! But her elbows are all over the place.)

An elbow finds my second rib. 'I thought and thought, whole of last night, Kaveri,' jab, 'and I've decided,' jab, jab, 'to *talk!*' She nods twice, keeping her head pressed down each time to seal her resolve.

Talk about what, Jana, I ask, when something else elbows my ribs. A warning. A flash of unwelcome prescience. But she's chanting, 'Wait and see! Wait and see! *Some*one's not going to be happy!' And there's nothing for it but to wait and see because with Jana you can't do otherwise—reason with her or cajole, bribe, threaten—especially when she's in this mood. At which I get another, sharper jab. *I* am responsible for her mood—and I can do nothing about that either. It's not easy, but whoever said life was?

On the platform the priests are sweating over the mantras, racing each other to the finishing post. But the end is not going to be for a while. Because every ritual in the book has been included. Lilamami will not dare risk the displeasure of a single god and be denied health, wealth and happiness in her new home. Especially wealth. And Devimami is afraid of exciting their envy. As for the audience, it has to sit it out because there is no free lunch. Of course the real purpose we're here, the reason why we cluster below the platform like disciples at the foot of the Master, *is* the lunch. Not Balumama's boring old flats. Nor Lilamami, although she thinks she is the star draw, looking like a wedding present, no, the wrapping paper of the wedding present, in her magenta-and-gold sari and rhinestone spectacles, rather than the bride she imagines herself to be— such melting glances she gives Balumama! (Who is oblivious, alas.)

Joshiyar, the astrologer, is ringed by women angling for a free consultation. He makes all our decisions for us. Whom to marry, what to name the babies, when to undertake a journey. His predictions aren't always reliable though. He crosses and conjuncts the stars till the sky is a cat's cradle but a rogue planet always jumps its orbit in the last moment. He predicted that my Pati would marry a famous doctor and live in Delhi, and that her husband would live to be ninety. (Pati married a lawyer and didn't move from the street even. And my grandfather died at seventy.) He'd predicted Balumama would be a famous scientist and father two sons. (Balumama is an accountant and has two daughters.) But hadn't he, as a callow youth, foretold Great-grandfather's epic voyage across the seven seas? So we didn't argue, didn't even smile when he said, 'He'd have lived till ninety if he hadn't got a heart attack. And he wouldn't have had the heart attack if you'd done the puja I advised.' Or, slapping his thigh to make his point, 'Scientist, engineer, doctor! What difference does it make? All are good professions!'

Lilamami has descended from the platform and is in a heated discussion with a Remote Relative about gifts. Who has given what (or not) and how much (how little) it's worth. Specifically, who had had the nerve to give her a *dented* aluminium saucepan. The audacity of some people, she's snorting, when she catches sight of me. 'Oho, *you!*' She takes a deep breath as if following her doctor's advice to control her blood pressure. 'I've been looking for you for hours! Meenakshi said she gave *you* the sandalwood sticks the priest is asking for!'

Jana, who has seated herself behind my chair, and for some reason is kicking it, says, 'But you only just came down, Lilamami.'

'What do *you* know?' retorts Lilamami. 'You don't have to defend your great cousin.' (Stop kicking my chair, Jana, I tell her ungratefully.) She tilts her head back and examines me from underneath her glasses. 'That's a new sari.'

Illey, Lilamami, it's my mother's.

'Then that necklace is new.'

Also my mother's.

'But *something* is new,' she grumbles.

You just aren't used to seeing me in finery, Lilamami.

Jana leans forward and blows into my ear. 'You look so beautiful when you dress up, Kaveri.' She pats the silk on my shoulder. Her hand smells peculiar. Hot metal or melted rubber. *Snot.* Oh God. Why do I have these unworthy thoughts about poor Jana? Now she touches my earrings. 'Mmmm. I love your earrings.'

I have to exert great control to keep from jumping up. You can have them, Jana, I say hastily.

'Really? Are you sure?'

Absolutely sure. I'll give them to you before I go home.

Lilamami is fingering my sari again. 'This sari, this *sari* . . .' Jana pokes me in the spine. Lilamami's going through her wardrobe, shelf by shelf to locate a sari a) similar to this b) superior to this.

Lilamami returns to earth. She's found what she's looking for. '*Now* I remember.' Her eyes smoulder with an old resentment. 'I had wanted it for Uma but your mother got in first. But,' brightening, 'I got Uma a better one.' (Jana pokes me again—sharply.) 'Thicker silk and *more* gold.'

Of course.

Jana strokes my hair, a cobwebby touch that sends a shiver down my spine. 'Doesn't Uma look like Kaveri?'

'Not a *bit*,' snaps Lilamami. 'Only *you* would think so.'

I find myself getting irritated yet again on Jana's behalf. That's how it is with Jana. She gets you so steamed up, *for* as well as *with* her, that you don't like her or yourself or anybody in the end. It's just not easy. Now I take up for her in the one way I know I can get at Lilamami.

Actually, she's the spitting image of me, Lilamami, I say untruthfully.

'*Who* says so?' Lilamami rolls up her sleeves, so to speak, and Jana looks to me to declare, *everyone* Lilamami, but I don't since I won't be able to qualify it with the names and addresses that Lilamami is even now preparing to demand so she can round up the fools and ask if they're blind or stupid, because as far as she's concerned I'm a sari bought on an impulse and found wanting—*badly* wanting.

Meenakshi doesn't find me wanting. 'This sari suits you so well, Kaveri. You keep it.' She twitches it straight, and the gold threads get caught in the peeling skin of her fingers. 'I haven't worn it much. Thank goodness.'

I took her hand and massaged it. Oh, Ma. You must care for your hands. Cream them. Soak them in glycerine and rosewater!

She snatches back her hands and hides them guiltily behind her back, and then brings them out again to stroke Jana's arms. 'How are you, kanna? I haven't seen you at all today.' Compassion wells up in her eyes in easy tears.

She's been busy all morning, Meenakshi, not in Devimami's meddlesome, bossy fashion, but doing what needed doing without a fuss. She pacified the cook when he threatened to walk out. She found a mislaid silver lamp. She filled the coconut-bags with coconuts, betel leaves and betel nut, to give departing guests . . . Now she's chivvying people to lunch—a job that Devimami jealously appropriates. It is *her* housewarming after all. 'Vango,' she waves her arms, as if conducting a symphony. 'This way, everybody! You, Kaveri! Come here!'

Good morning, Devimami. How are you?

'Hmph! You wished me already. No need to wish again and again! Anyway it's afternoon, not morning. And what do you mean, how am I? Ask how you can help instead! Go tell those people standing there to go in! Really. Some people expect a red carpet or something!'

Jana darts across to take my arm. 'Remember, you're sitting beside me!'

Of course, Jana.

'Kaveri,' she nudges me with her hip, 'will you buy a new car now? And a new house?'

'Perhaps she'll buy the penthouse.' That is Uma who has sneaked up from behind. 'It might *just* do for her.'

Subconsciously, as tradition dictates, we have drifted into two groups. Devimami, Lilamami, Rajumama, Balumama and Uma form one, and at a small but vital distance are Mani, Meenakshi, Jana, Ramu and I. Bharat is in the middle, like sandwich filling. 'Oh, but *you* won't do,' he says to Uma. 'She's very particular about her neighbours.'

'It's a good idea,' begins Meenakshi uncertainly, and, 'It's a good investment,' says Mani, somewhat tactlessly.

'But perhaps not good enough for *her*?' says Devimami, hands-on-hips, so to speak.

'She will never come back here,' Rajumama murmurs, and *she'd better not*, mutters somebody, Lilamami, I think, but the words vaporise in the buzzing heat.

'*Don't*, Kaveri!' whispers Jana, digging her chin into my shoulder. 'Don't come back here! *Don't* buy one of their flats!' She twists her neck to look at me. Her eyes are feverish. *I dreamed of running away. All the time. That time never came.*

The subject of my loyalty or dis- remains unresolved for I'm being driven along by Jana's hip—that has transited from unavoidable to inescapable—into the food pandal, where Rajumama's labours have been laid out in rows on the floor in front of straw mats. Our file fans out, men to the right, women to the left and the devil take the hindmost, to find the largest, best banana leaf to sit behind, and we sink down in a susurration of silk and starched veshti to await the outcome of the cooks' and, nominally, Devimami's toils.

Lunch. At last.

Lunch in the Big House was signalled by the scrape-and-thud of plate-and-glass on the dining room floor. Minutes later, Balumama, wearing a faraway expression, would stroll down the hall and enter the dining room as if he had chanced upon this room and was investigating it. Shuffling to his chair he would sit down and look around him without moving his neck. After this yogic posturing, meant to convey *here is a man who has transcended all worldly concerns*, he would proceed to eat with immense appetite, conveying fingers to mouth in stylish mudras, chewing with a rotary movement like milling grain, and ending each gulp-and-swallow with a broken sigh. *Khoo, khoo!* Two shovels of mushy vegetables. *Khoo, khoo!* A hillock of rice. *Khoo, khoo! Froop, froop, sor, sor!* Sambar, rasam and buttermilk, all gone but for two spent curry leaves and a wilted chilly.

In the Cottage dining room, Kaveri's grandmother, Pati, waited for her husband to finish before sitting down to eat, not out of old-fashioned wifely deference, but because she couldn't stand to eat with him. None of them could. Not that that bothered him. He was as oblivious of his unpopularity as of Pati's sarcasm, and was not one to take offence either. Not even when she said to him, out of the blue, 'Your family isn't known for longevity, is it? Your uncles died at sixty and sixty-six, and your father at sixty-eight . . .' (And here her husband had just turned seventy!) And they were all healthy till the end. The end comes suddenly to you all, doesn't it?'

He replied quite calmly, 'Ama, but some of us lived till eighty.' Pati, looking put out, like someone whose household accounts didn't tally, said, 'Only that lunatic aunt of yours! *She doesn't count!*' Hardly a wifely observation but then, he was hardly a husband. With his sudden disappearances to look for

Truth at the feet of a Master in the Nilgiri hills—just when the bills had to be paid. Truth could be found, Pati said, right under one's nose. In his case, right in his office room. If he only had the sense to look there.

The Cottage kitchen was paved with uneven stone that was cold and damp even in the summer so Pati wore socks with her flip-flops all year round. Cockroaches bred in cracks in the floor and brazened it out all over the room. Spiders vaulted across the walls, dangling their legs in your face. Hairy caterpillars menaced the food cooking on the wood-fed brick stove. (Which was daubed with fresh clay every day and finished with a simple kolam of three lines of rice powder.) During the day a flyblown skylight cut a ceiling-to-floor rhombus that held smoke and dust in its thrall. At night a single low-watt bulb pierced the gloom like the slow comprehension of an idiot. Day and night a brass oil lamp burned in Pati's shrine in the corner. The flame burnished the bronze cooking vessels and glazed the brown-and-white earthenware jars containing gingili oil, rock salt, dried tamarind, pickled mango, lemon-in-brine . . . It didn't light the cast-iron oven by the door in which Pati occasionally, about four times a year perhaps, tried out recipes from *Woman and Home*. Once she made scones and served them with a small pat of butter teased out of the bluish milk supplied by the milkman who, according to family lore, made his cow drink water before he milked it. The scones came out hard and burnt and not a bit like the illustration, but the children ate them anyway. And asked for more.

The children were always hungry. For the good things, not squash and brinjal from Pati's garden. And definitely not rice-and-curds. Brahmin food was laden with taboos rather than nutrients because weak food quelled lust and greed, carnality and venality to prepare you to fight internal wars. And fulfil your cosmic purpose through self-knowledge. It was to this end that the skinny Brahmin acolytes gathered in the temples at first light, wet and shivering and light-headed. And why Kaveri, Jana and Ramu were chased inside by Pati to do their homework, at exactly 6 pm every day, even if they were in the middle of an exciting game. Discipline was the means and the end.

Yearning out of the window for their playtime (fast receding into the sunset), 'Please, Pati,' they'd moan, but, 'Discipline, discipline!' she would intone. And add unfeelingly, 'Practise your singing first. No, no begging.' And they would sit on the straw mat in front of the creaky old harmonium while the daylight leaked from the sky, Kaveri screeching like the wind through the chimney and Jana lowing like the milkman's cow when its udder was fit to burst, till even Pati couldn't stand it. Even so, 'Derive the Remainder Theorem and *then* you can go,' she would say. And that would be the end of playtime, the evening, and even math, for of course, they would sulk and fidget through it. Oh, Pati.

Mani could derive the Remainder Theorem in his sleep. He had Discipline. That was why, even though he didn't hold with religion, he woke religiously at 5 am every day of his life. First to do his lessons, later to do his files (his life's work) and now to read instructive books. Work was worship, not the other way around. But for all Mani's mastery over Euclidean geometry he hadn't learned to count his blessings. So he couldn't teach Kaveri to either.

Bharat is hiding behind the door. He has pulled out his sacred thread from under his shirt and made a cat's cradle with. Now he's making a lasso. A violin string to play on with a knitting needle . . .

Kaveri's giggle rings out.

'*Kaveri*! Concentrate!'

'Kaveri!' Jana is squeezing my knee. 'The boy's waiting! Tell him if you want more rice or not!'

Up and down scamper the server boys, plonking the food on our banana leaf plates. 'Saka, beka, saka, beka?' Enough or more? More for my neighbour, nothing for me. Well, maybe just a *little* bit for me.

Side-by-side and back-to-back we sit, flicking at the hopeful flies. Hot rasam stings our tongues. Sour buttermilk sings in our heads, the dulcet payasam needles our fillings. The payasam's good, isn't it? A *little* too sweet, for *me*. And it could have done with some saffron. Some more raisins actually. I haven't tasted any better than the one at Uma's wedding! That was the hottest summer in *twenty-five* years! Kadavale, the heat! But a sublime payasam!

Meenakshi, the epicurean, tastes first with her eyes, then her nose, then her tongue. *Mmm*! Balumama's bluey-green jowls puff out. *Phoooo*! A raisin sticks in Rajumama's throat. *Ha-humph*!

From the tarpaulin roof a lizard watches the gentle gluttony.

It's poised to fall on Jana's mat. Should I warn her? I think not. She will scream and hop—and why precipitate the crisis?

The shiny black heads bob up and down, up and down. Fingers dip, chins drip. And eyes pop, pop, pop . . . *Splat*! The lizard falls on Jana's mat. And she screams and hops. Shh! Calm down, Jana! It's gone! In the end Lilamami has to slap her into silence—which she does with unnecessary force.

Lilamami (a wad of crumpled wrapping paper now) is peering into the food pails, as if anxious that nothing runs short. Actually she is calculating how many meals the leftovers will be good for. 'Don't keep taking round the appalams,' she admonishes a server boy. 'No need to *force* people to eat.' Devimami, who doesn't hear that, sends Seena (who is still eating, poor fellow) after the server boy to tell the cook to fry some more appalams. Why doesn't she go and ask the cook herself? Since she is outside anyway? Because, being Devimami, she must annoy as many people as possible. The only person she doesn't try it on with is her son. 'Please take a *nice* picture of me, Bhartu,' she says. *Please* again! What is the world coming to? She arranges her features in a leer, slews her head around and tilts her chin in a coquettish angle that unfortunately wrinkles up her neck.

Bharat lifts up his camera, screws the lens into his eye.

I spy with my little eye. Through a hole in the screen in the dining room, Kaveri discovers: who makes little cannon balls of rice and fires them into their mouth. Who builds a dam of rice and floods it with sambar. And who once stuck brinjal under his plate and smuggled it to the dustbin. (*Mani!* Her father!)

I spy with my little eye. But eye cannot explain why I must not peer over the wall, nor gossip across the gate . . . Shut the window, shut that door, don't linger at the gate, and why were you so long coming back from school? No, you may not go to his house. No, you may not invite her home. Friends are for school, cousins are for home . . . Be careful whom you talk to, watch what you say . . .

Years later she understood it wasn't the fear of the outside getting in but the inside leaking out. Preserving the world's illusions about you requires you to steer clear of the world as far as possible.

Why Balumama's dinner so fascinated the children was a mystery. It was just two slices of toast, brown-and-white like a fox terrier, soaked in milk. The climax was the big yellow banana he took out from a cloth bag—his personal banana bag. What concerted interest they paid it! What strong resolve on his part not to offer them one, not even once! Not to break a secret taboo that forbade the giving of even this modest gift!

'*Po po po!*' Balumama frowned at his slavering audience. 'Go away!' If they lingered, 'Which of you monkeys was climbing on the roof this morning? I found a broken tile. Wait till I . . .' It *was* the monkeys, Balumama, the children would whine. Not us.

The Cottage children washed the fine red dust from their feet at the tap outside, grabbed their plates from the dresser—silver christening plates, all different shapes and sizes, and sat on straw mats on the cold stone floor. If dinner was delayed they banged their plates on the floor, *thak-thak, thaka-thak!* Till, 'Stop that noise!' Pati would order.

Pati presided over the children's dinner from her three-legged rattan stool. Her spider's refractory gaze took them all in at once so there was no question of refusing carrot or marrow. Or dinnertime lessons.

As they ate she made evaluatory forays into their school day. What is your arithmetic score? Ninety-nine per cent, Pati. Hmmm. Where did you lose the one per cent? And if it was a hundred per cent, would she say, next time, get a hundred and one? The children were quite sure she would. Stretch finite limits, true knowledge is infinite. Prove to me, recite for me, read with me . . . Not today? Ah, so you don't know it. Go learn it after dinner. Deduce this. Derive that. Measure, weigh, analyse . . . Do you measure iambic pentameter with callipers or a scale, Pati? Don't be cheeky, Kaveri. You want to fail? *Like the others* was unsaid, but Kaveri knew it was there. Serial failure was the leitmotif in the family's history.

And oh, by the way, Kaveri. I read your essay. You must learn to turn an original phrase. Not imitate Enid Blyton.

Pati, we want cream buns and lemonade! Fried tomato! Jam sponge! *Yenna*, you've been reading Enid Blyton again! Those children must have been eternally constipated! Eat your rice-and-curds and learn your twelve times table! It's good for your bowels, it's good for your character!

There was nothing remarkable about Pati's personal milestones. School, marriage, children, grandchildren, 167 knitted items, matinee shawls and bootees included, fifty crocheted, including countless yards of lace, and all the classics of English literature read at least once. All of which had aged her—Pati looked old. Her flesh had worked loose and her skin hung like a bed jacket. Her arms were parched like a famine landscape and scattered with careless grey hairs. Nobody ever said to her, 'My goodness, you have grandchildren!' Or, 'You don't look a day older than when I saw you last!' You're old when you begin thinking you've no more to learn, Pati would say. That wouldn't happen. There was always another mile to go—and she made everyone walk it. She gave up on Meenakshi though.

When Meenakshi was newly married Pati thrust a book at her—*The Story of Philosophy*. 'Read this. It will help you understand life.'

'What for?'

'So you will be happy.'

Meenakshi's mouth made a round 'O' of surprise. 'But I *am* happy.'

Pati wouldn't believe her. Why, Meenakshi hadn't read a single Russian classic! She'd rather make a perfect halva than a perfect sentence! Trying to be kind, Pati said, 'You will understand *why* you're happy.'

'What for?'

It was Pati's turn to stare. Nobody questioned her. 'Because . . .' she stopped, stumped. 'Your wife is rather *ornamental*, isn't she,' she remarked to Mani. In her reckoning to be thus marked by fate was not a favour. 'I wouldn't depend on it if I were she.' As it happened Meenakshi didn't. Others did.

After dinner Mani escaped to the Masonic Lodge, where he walked backwards in a party hat. Kaveri found that out from a book on secret societies. A lot of old men got together and played dressing-up games in a Great Hall, where a Lordship sat on a throne. Mani was very cross with the betrayal of the Brother who wrote the article. Trust *you* to find the book, he said to Kaveri.

After dinner Poor Cousin Seena escorted Jana and Ramu

from the Cottage to the Big House, playing his steel torch to kill the scary shadows. Seena used his escort duty to fill everybody in on the day's doings and comings and goings. He had the makings of a spy, Mani said, but what was there to report? A lot, Kaveri could have told him. Who did what and where and when and to whom. Nothing seriously malicious, only slightly damaging. And discountable—like the shoes in the Factory Seconds store in Gandhi Bazaar. That's what the Cottage people were to the Big House—discounted stuff. Seena didn't mind selling them.

After lunch—Ramu *immediately* after—the guests, including the Remote Relatives, leave. Bharat wanders off to download the pictures from his digital camera, Mani to nap in one of the flats. The rest of us stay back in the main pandal, slumped on the chairs like half-filled sacks. All that is left of the morning's ceremony is blackened bricks and cold ash. And the stale breath of wilting marigolds.

As usual, the invisible historic divide snakes through us. Meenakshi, me and Jana on one side and on the other Lilamami, Devimami, Rajumama . . . It's too tedious. Jana sits next to me, hugging her chest. Meenakshi, as oblivious of the divide as she is of the frost forming on the opposite side, draws one or the other of us into her chatter till Lilamami checks her. 'Meenakshi, the baby is *sleeping*.'

My poor mother looks smacked.

It slept through all the hullabaloo of lunch, I point out. It's been sleeping for *hours*. Something's wrong with it.

'Nonsense,' snaps Lilamami, making a great show of tucking its shawl. 'Babies *need* to sleep.'

Nobody disputes that.

The sacks slide down the chairs. It seems we are waiting for something. Is there going to be another ceremony? No, there is not. Is it going to rain? No, it's not. Is someone expected? No, they're not.

It's time for Mani, Meenakshi and me to leave.

Balumama belches explosively, unapologetically. It sets Devimami off—she turns her belch into a cough. Lilamami does not tell them off, although their belch-coughs are louder than poor Meenakshi's voice. But Uma picks up her baby and stalks out.

Outside, to my satisfaction, it begins to bawl.

Jana clears a fly from her throat. 'There's something I want to say.' She sounds like an insect in extremis. 'I . . . I . . . I.' She licks her lips, shivers, as if a hand has descended on her shoulder. I touch her knee—to encourage her? Comfort her? *Stop* her?

'Don't begin if you cannot finish,' Lilamami says smartly.

Jana opens her mouth again, but Lilamami has taken the floor so she goes back to hugging her chest. 'Two hundred and twenty people ate lunch,' announces Lilamami. The rhinestones flash in corroboration. 'Just think! *Two hundred and twenty!*'

'What, and the rest went hungry?' says Rajumama in mock alarm. His shoulders shake.

Lilamami ignores him. 'This caterer is too expensive. Those laddoos were too big. I mean, food should be good but there's no need for *extravagance*.'

Nobody disputes that either.

Rajumama yawns. Devimami sighs. Jana continues to hyperventilate. The pandal gets closer. And closer. And closer. Through the opening six feet away we can glimpse air, freedom, life. And yet we don't move. Any movement would invite some nameless catastrophe.

A flash of light dances on the canvas wall and vanishes into the whiteness of the doorway. It's a reflection from a mirror or glass. *Rhinestone.* 'What's the matter with *you?*'

Nothing, Lilamami. Just tired.

'Why're *you* tired? *I'm* the one who should be tired.'

Balumama looks up hopefully. Was she going to suggest coffee? She was not. He turns to Meenakshi. 'Aren't *you* tired?'

'Very tired,' says my obliging mother. And, not one to shirk her needs, she moots coffee.

Balumama brightens. *Ummmm!* But, 'It's too early,' objects Lilamami.

'Not for me,' smiles my bold mother. 'Any time is coffee time for me!'

Rajumama appears as much charmed by her as by the prospect of coffee. Lilamami, who is not easily charmed, frowns. 'The cook is resting.'

Then—surprise—Devimami, with a martyred sigh, heaves herself up and—surprise, surprise—you sit, Devimami, *I'll* go, I find myself saying.

Outside, I bump into Uma burping her baby. As if burning one last boat, 'You were my childhood friend,' she says balefully.

One of my lesser roles, yes.

In the kitchen shed the cook puts the milk on to heat, mixes the two decoctions, thin and thick, brewed from Arabica and Robusta roasted and ground this very morning. He's setting the tumblers on the tray when Mani wanders in, groggy from his nap. 'Coffee-a?' he sniffs appreciatively.

Stay for a moment, Pa. Let me look at you. Quick, before anyone catches us! Alright. Got you!

He laughs. 'One of your silly jokes-a!'

Tell me Pa, in all the time you've known her, has Lilamami ever offered you coffee? I mean, without prompting, hinting, asking her outright—if you dare? Think carefully before you answer. Much depends on it.

He shakes his head and laughs some more.

Lilamami picks on us the minute we walk in. 'What is so funny?'

The steam from the coffee acts like smelling salts—even Balumama jerks up from his coma. 'Yenna, coffee-a?'

'*Ama*, coffee,' retorts his wife. 'That's the only time you come alive.'

'Kaveri,' whispers Jana, plucking my sleeve, 'when can you come to lunch?'

Any day you choose, Jana.

Lilamami cranes her neck. 'What are you whispering about?' Jana squirms and tells her—and gets pounced on. 'Oho! And what about us? Have you ever thought of inviting *us*? Eh?'

Poor Jana cringes, but I'm tired of playing champion. 'You come too, Lilamami,' she stutters, showing the whites of her eyes.

'No, thank you,' Lilamami says perversely. 'I can cook a perfectly good lunch for myself. I don't want to spoil your feast. And your *secrets*.' At which Jana loses her nerve and puts out her tongue at Lilamami. Before Lilamami can tick her off she gets up, murmuring something about cleaning the flats, but I suspect she needs the bathroom—Lilamami has that effect on people. Stupid girl, mutters Lilamami, and turns back to her audience. 'Always whispering—these two. Lots of secrets to share, it seems. At least,' she flaps a hand in my direction, 'this one has'.

Devimami smiles thinly. 'Ama, I've never known a child for snooping as much as *this* one. As for *that* one,' she turned around, but Jana isn't there.

'Well, she's done very well out of it.' Two pairs of eyes drive nails into mine. 'Speaking of which,' Lilamami turns to Meenakshi, 'have you thought about what I said last week?'

Meenakshi sneezes. For a long moment there is no sound except the *sroop-sroop* of Rajumama's coffee. Balumama's stomach burbles like the sinking of a boat. 'That was a heavy lunch,' he says. But no one pays heed.

'Meenakshi, I asked you . . .'

'Illey,' says my mother, blinking hard. 'At least . . . no. Not yet.'

'Then kindly do so!'

Mani's chair squeaks. 'Now?' quavers Meenakshi and sneezes again. The smoke has affected her sinuses.

Ma, I begin, when, 'Yes, now!' barks Lilamami. Meenakshi looks to her knitting bag to rescue her.

'You must have discussed it, Meenakshi,' prods Devimami.

Meenakshi casts another desperate look at her bag. 'This is not a good time to . . .'

'*Meenakshi!*'

Mani's chair squeaks again. Why doesn't he speak? *Leave my mother alone,* but Balumama gets in first. 'Does anyone have Digene here?' He sinks another boat in his stomach. Again, no one pays heed.

Lilamami arranges the empty tumblers on the tray as if they are missiles and she would like to fire one at him. 'Well, come on!'

Meenakshi makes a small, useless gesture with her hands. I am getting to my feet when I see she has switched off. She has picked up her knitting and begun clacking her mantra. *Knit purl knit purl, knitknit purlpurl, knit-two-together* . . . It's an Aran pullover for Mani—she's cutting diamonds of blue and maroon in grey dust. Oh, the dignity of her labour! The labour of her love! She labours on.

'Stop pretending to be stupid!' says Lilamami, so loudly Mani starts, spilling coffee on his lap. 'As if you're deaf-and-dumb! Ama, I mean *you*.' She's pointing her chin at me.

'What *I* say,' cuts in Mani, like the whistle of a rescue squad. 'What I say is it's time we went home. Meenakshi, va, polam. Come on, Kaveri.'

But Meenakshi, unable to leave with a bad taste in the mouth, so to speak, comes up with the one thing only she can think of at such a moment. 'Does anyone want tiffin? The cook said he could fry onion bajjis.'

She's a hero, is my mother. She even looks the part, with her orange hair in its chieftain's knot, her war paint of orange and pink. She makes me want to cheer and weep at once.

Balumama perks up but Lilamami looks as if she cannot believe her ears. '*Tiffin-a!* Tiffin . . .!'

'*Yenna*, Meenakshi,' Devimami says primly. 'Really. To think of food after that lunch . . .'

'Perhaps she didn't eat well, Devi,' says Rajumama mildly, but Lilamami is muttering *tiffin-a-tiffin* like a malevolent witch, which means there is going to be no tiffin.

Mani cuts in once again. 'Meenakshi, *polam*. Come on, Kaveri.'

This time my mother obeys. Gathering up her purse, and her capacious cloth bag into which she puts in our take-home coconuts (these observances!), she smiles upon the assembly. 'Poituvaram.' *We're leaving but will return.* The polite goodbye that expects the door to be left open.

Rajumama scrapes back his chair. 'Poituva, Meenakshi.' *Go, but come again. Our door is open for you.* But is it?

Balumama echoes, 'Poituva, poituva'. And, 'Parkalam.' *We shall be seeing you.* Which, optimistically, opens the door a chink. His jowls wobble. 'Lila, why don't you give Meenakshi some mangoes to take home?'

Lilamami's face is a study. I so badly want to laugh I get a catch in my stomach. 'Mangoes-a!' she expectorates. '*Now?*'

Balumama blinks foolishly. 'Well, it *is* the season.'

I can't hold myself in any longer.

Lilamami glares. 'Hiccoughs,' Meenakshi supplies, deflecting Lilamami's glare to herself.

'Mad as ever,' snorts Devimami.

Balumama gets up, his joints crackling like a green log in a fire, shambles to the doorway. En route he puts a hand on my shoulder and squeezes it, which is just so creepy that I jump up. Wha . . . at?

The eyebrows hang over his eyes like loose thatch. From under them he gives me a, whatsit, an old-fashioned look, and, before I can recover, he lowers the lid (sere, stained) of one eye. It's a *wink!* Unmistakably. More creepiness follows. Putting his finger to his lip, beside the single, rakish tooth, he shakes his head. What *is* he up to—distributing mangoes on the sly? But Devimami is asking Rajumama if he's taken his diabetes medicine and Lilamami is muttering a new spell—*mangoes-a-mangoes*—and Mani is jiggling his car keys and Meenakshi has begun her goodbyes all over again, and he slips away and out of the pandal.

'Poituvaram, Lilamami,' Meenakshi is saying in her gentle voice. 'We wish you good luck and happiness in your new home.'

No one can doubt her sincerity. Lilamami nods morosely. 'Who knows what the future holds?' But she has the grace to add, 'Thank you for your help.'

With all the assurance of her ruined beauty (but unblemished goodness) Meenakshi answers, 'Oh, I'm sure you will be very happy in your new home!'

Mani is unlocking the car when we hear a small commotion behind us. Shouting, thudding, the high-wire thrum of a woman's scream. Presently Bharat rushes out of the gate, his face all awry.

'A doctor!' he's shouting. 'An ambulance! Does anyone have Dr Rao's number?'

'For whom?' asks Mani, glancing over his shoulder as if to make sure Meenakshi or I haven't had a heart attack behind his back. 'What's happened?'

'Balumama! There's been an accident!' He begins running down the street. 'Tell my father!' he calls over his shoulder. 'And Lilamami! No.' He skids to a halt. 'Don't tell her.'

'Tell them what?'

He casts about him like a wild man. 'Can someone call emergency for an ambulance? I couldn't get through! I'm going for Dr Rao!' With that he starts running again.

'An *am*bulance?'

'But what happened to Balumama?'

Without stopping Bharat shouts, 'He fell into the lift well!'

What!

Meenakshi makes a strangled noise, clutches my arm. 'Ayyoyo! Ayyo Kaveri!'

'How did he fall?' Mani asks sharply. 'Which floor? Into the pit or onto the lift cage?' But Bharat is halfway down the street.

I pull away from Meenakshi, hoist my sari and run. Catching up with him at the end of the street I grab his belt.

'Let go, dammit!'

First tell me. Is he . . . is he hurt?

The sky is low, heavy, white. It's the kind of light that looks to pick on people—it's picking out every pore and scar on his face. He twists out of my grip and then, unexpectedly, rounds on me, almost knocking me over. 'What?'

Is he hurt?

The sun pours contumely on our heads. Sweat graces his forehead. Sweat trickles into my armpits. A piffling breeze dislodges the dust on the road, sends a leaf scuttling. Suddenly, bizarrely, music shoots out of the loudspeakers—the jolly pipes-and-drums tape—shattering the still, bright afternoon. 'Shut that off!' someone yells. The music stops as abruptly as it began.

How bad is it . . . *say* something, fool!

His eyes are glittering but empty. And cavernous. Like a car's headlamp at noon. He appears to be in a trance. People have materialised out of the building, out of the street, out of the air, and are running hither and thither, in and about, round and round. A car revs up, its brakes shriek, an air horn warns everybody to run for their lives.

I shake his shoulder.

Is he dead then? I mean, is he *alive*?

He turns then, but his eyes are still unseeing. 'What do you think? When you fall from the fifth floor?'

Arrival

The morning sun was still young, a lemon speared on a telecom tower, when the plane skidded to a halt. At this hour Bangalore is awash with molten gold, a light that's special to the city, a divine radiance that greets visitors, dragon-slaying sons, homecoming daughters, and, gracious immanence, even embraces its black sheep—of which I was one, a recent recruit.

After an interminable ride in an autorickshaw with a driver whose passion for speed matched his disdain for speedbreakers, whose skill at meter-manipulation equalled his cunning at detouring to further inflate the fare, I arrived at the house-on-the-road. I paid up without arguing, dragged my bag out and, fumbling in my urgency, unlatched the gate . . . Then, *hold still, my heart*, I checked myself. Not rushing forward (as I strained to), not whooping with joy (as I yearned to), but holding back (as I'd been conditioned to) for a moment's character-building denial. And to savour the modest structure in front of me. To devour its contents. All of me opened to it— eyes, ears, mouth, pores. The blood jumped and the pulse thumped . . . *hold still*! Louder, faster, harder than the traffic pounding behind me in this busy thoroughfare of Bangalore which leads to its outer reaches, where the city spreads its skirts over new housing estates and horse farms and abandoned quarries converted into stress centres.

The occupants of the house-on-the-road, my parents, have struggled with little success against the assaults from their surroundings. To wit, loudspeakers from a marriage hall, flies from food carts, a rotting garbage heap, a clogged stormwater drain. There is no changing this state of affairs, not through the offices of our corrupt municipal administration, says Mani, who has written several letters of complaint and should know. But this is a *middle-class* neighbourhood, defends Meenakshi, as if it is our lot to suffer in silence. Whatever the reason, they've long stopped trying to improve the chances they took when they made their choice of home. In any case, they are not crusaders. Conceding defeat, they have retreated behind their garden wall, and into the house. Here, at least, Mani could maintain law and order for himself and Meenakshi and, nominally, for me.

Over the years this wall has been raised three times. Each time the bougainvillaea was lifted off and rehung, and the aster bed replanted. A fourth raise was mooted and rejected—the house was becoming a fortress! Then the front door was more or less permanently shut and the verandah windows shuttered with bamboo blinds, and we began looking to the small rear courtyard for light and air and life. Despite its edgy situation, this eschewal of the world, together with its ascetic plainness, has imparted to the house an air of monkish introspection, the tranquillity of an ashram. (Meenakshi says the noise of the traffic actually lulls her to sleep!) Inside, the rooms are charged with shared confidences, an intimacy that has grown with the years. Doors and windows open to receive our secrets, and shut them in. Walls and ceilings vibrate, like tuning forks, to our moods. Furniture and floor have absorbed our triumphs and travails, our hopes and hopelessness, acquiring a sheen that no paint or polish can achieve. It is, in short, a house committed to stand by us, do right by us. Even if at times, too frequent for my peace of mind, when the world totters around me and I don't know from one day to the next when it and I will snap apart, the roof seems to be held up only by the incense curling out of the puja room.

Enough. My moment's self-denial was over. I pushed open the gate with its 'Beware Of Dog' sign—although there's been no dog here for ten years—even remembering to latch it behind me. (Oh, the countless times I've left it open and been rapped for the lapse!) And at last I was inside, home and dry. At last I was walking down the cracked-concrete, croton-lined driveway, sniffing the scents uncorked from bottled memory. I was walking . . .

. . . I was floating. My feet scraped the scabby concrete of the drive, but my (disembodied) head hovered on the roof. At the end of the drive, my quick-stepping, sure-toed feet—that claim intimate knowledge of every square inch of this hallowed land—negotiated the chicken-neck between bedroom wall and the carport, inside which crouches the ancient Fiat, my father's faithless and moody steed, muzzled in plastic sacking. It's a mechanical heap that has served us for more years than I can remember, more years than it deserves, and I slapped its bonnet in passing for all the times it has wheezed to a stop at my school gate and refused to budge. Then, squeezing past the lime tree, on which the flowers were sweetly blooming, past the oleander, on which the flowers were gaily cavorting, I entered the walled courtyard. Here I threw my bag on the wooden garden bench and ran into the pantry.

I stopped short at the door. Stopped breathing. Because she was there. In the kitchen. With her back to me. Listening to her transistor radio. To the *Bhakti Geet*, the morning devotional music programme. So rapt she couldn't see or hear what was behind her.

She was standing by the flaking stove where she's stood for years, decades, an aeon. She was standing there, this undisputed keeper of family peace, this guardian of family secrets, this preserver of family pride, and now as always, this maker of angel food. Thirty years of tracing my growth curve with a spoon! Thirty years of sustaining and succouring her child so it could grow the wingspan to fly back and forth to her! Fly through cloud and rain, across desert and sea, to the certain knowledge of her waiting, waiting . . .

The celestial skylight, the earthy terracotta floor. The blue of the gas flame, the gold of the sunbeams. The fire in my veins . . . And the chill in my soul.

Fingers prodded, voices whispered, *go, go, go*! Yet I didn't go to her. Because I wanted to take in some more. So softly, softly, I breathed her in . . .

In the cooking sari I recognised as an ancient throwaway of mine, stained and smelly and rucked over her hips, she was a sachet of spices. A supersaver pack. No, she was a Grecian urn, the ode, that is. For she is beautiful, beautiful. It is a beauty that is beyond sculpted lines and classical arrangement of features. It is inside out, her beauty. You not only see it, you feel it. It's calming, cleansing, ennobling, enabling . . . It holds out hope and cheer and peace and goodwill. And understanding. Forgiveness . . .

She was pushing back the hair, pushing back the years to when there was more hair and less scalp, when her forehead did not take up so much of her face. Streaked orange-grey-black, a parakeet's plumage or a punk's, the dye is her valiant attempt to halt time. As is the pink she dabs on her mouth, although, of course, she hadn't at this hour. In the middle of her forehead blazed a vermilion dot, a satellite receiver of cosmic rays, a symbol of unquestioning faith in her husband, unswerving devotion to him and to the vows she's made for eternity.

Down, down, down to her feet, cracked and crumpling from overuse. Dr Rao diagnosed 'soldiers' foot', a condition acquired from long marches. She must have covered thousands of miles in her kitchen then, soldiering for us. Her feet no longer support her as much as *stay* her, bulwark for the bulk, two sandbags in tarty mauve slippers (where *does* she buy them?), the straps of which bandage the swollen insteps. The feet move with an ancient unstoppable rhythm, the unthinking momentum of a pendulum in a vacuum. She feels no pain from the broken bones, she feels nothing because her feelings are not in her feet, but in her hands. Her hands are her feelers. With them she feels the temperature of this, the texture of that, the rightness and wrongness of everything. Why, they can even feel *my* feelings! Her hands have curved around ladles for so long that in repose too they are handle-shaped. She hides her sculpted hands beneath her sari folds, ashamed of their seasoned, pungent hardness, terrified that somebody important, a VIP (but who?), might shake hands with her, and then how would she live with the shame of that? The feelingful hands are complemented by the seeingful eyes—worn to veiny pebbles by teary onions, fiery chillies, smoking oil. Her busybee hands fluttered about the dappled shelves, intercepting the reflection from the stainless steel vessels lining the walls, and rested briefly on a colander of tomatoes, the chopping of which I would surprise.

Not yet, though. Not yet.

She was turning around! But only to sneeze. A ripe, full-bodied sneeze that set the diamonds in her ears swinging like trapeze artistes. And another sneeze that knocked out her sinuses. Then a sniff—a forthright, no-holds-barred harrumph that I would be able to hear from the four corners of the earth. She wiped her nose with the all-purpose towel she keeps tucked in her waist. What passes for a waist, that is. She is bloated—with love. A love that has no rhyme or reason, no word or symbol, but just *is*. A love that lies coiled and ready to strike. Her dearness, *my* love, soared like a bird to the clouds, like a soul to heaven, to the ripening sun, up, up and up . . .

. . . I couldn't hold out anymore. I couldn't hold *in*.

Amma!

She wheeled around. '*Kaveri!*' Oh, the amazement of her! The blazing joy of her! Her dizzy, delirious disbelief! 'Is it really *you*? Kanna, *kanna!*'

I ran into her arms. Oh, the touch of her! The warmth of her! Her scent—like a new baked bun from the Brahmin's Bakery! My throat caught, my ears sang. And my stupidly brimming eyes flowed over.

She held me at arm's length and gazed as if committing me to memory. Then, peering over my shoulder, 'Alone-a?' she asked hopefully. 'How did you come?'

Yes, alone. (She was hard put to hide her relief.) By the first flight.

'So! You managed to get away after all!'

From what?

'That palace retreat you told us about.'

For a moment I was stumped. Then I remembered. A bit ashamed, oh *that*, I said as nonchalantly as I was able. Yes, I got away. It's not important. So tell me, Ma, is the housewarming going to be a big function?

'Big-*a*? It's a *wedding*! A grand affair.'

They giving you a new sari?

'Ama. A silk one! For you a silver bud vase.'

Good. I needed one. First thing I was going to shop for.

'Oh, why didn't you tell me? I'd have sent you one!'

Oh Ma! I was *joking*!

'Oof! Kaveri . . .' She was searching my face—strip-searching it.

Will I do, Ma? Last for another year at least?

'Oof! Kaveri . . .' She shook her head in happy confusion. 'I can't believe it still! But I'm . . . I'm glad, so glad you're here.'

Me too, Ma. Me *too*.

There was an arrival-day sweetness to the morning, a clarity of detail that I would pick out later in the jumbled reel of my visit. While Meenakshi bustled about making coffee I dawdled on the garden bench in the freshly watered courtyard, which is my favourite spot. The morning had expanded and the sun was everywhere, poking into everything—burnishing the leaves, splintering the glass panes, chasing the smoke from the wood-fired copper boiler around the trees. Glad, I was so glad to be here.

Meenakshi's ginger cat was giving a squirrel the eye, a crow on the roof ledge sawed away at the sharp white air, a distant dog barked—glad, glad!

Last night's rain dripped from the honeysuckle creeper (glad, glad, glad), high in the coconut tree the gardener hacked at the coconuts. Glad, glad, *glad*!

Warm brick, cool jasmine, wet earth. Brisk scent of coffee. The cat pounced, the squirrel fled, the coconuts bounced on the ground. Squawk, rustle, thud. Meenakshi called out. The coffee was ready.

There was a new telephone in the living room (with the out-of-commission old one beside it) and a new brass lamp (which would neither support a wick nor hold oil) in the verandah. Both squatted smugly, sure of their place in this household where nothing is thrown or given away without reason, and where disposable waste is not an acknowledged term. She is the high priestess of the junk cult, is my mother, and I'm her unpopular disposal squad. She caught me eying the lamp and snatched it up. 'Devimami gave it to me for Diwali.'

So? What's it good for? Grinding the coffee?

'Oof! Podi!' She put the useless object into the pantry cupboard and shut the door before I could see what else she was hoarding there. 'You never had respect for money and now that . . . now you're . . .' A switch was pressed. Light spurted from her eyes, her smile, even her crazy orange hair.

As I watched this transformation, the panic surfaced.

She, confused, stricken that she had transgressed *again*, and frustrated that neither her restraint nor her exuberance, not her faith nor her toils, can ever break down her daughter's complexities, change the abstracts to problems-with-solutions, and so defuse her own bewilderment (something she has striven to do for years), resorted to an old whine. A whine that I'd heard times innumerable, in varying strengths of incomprehension and exasperation. 'Yain, Kaveri, aren't you happy? Not even *now*?'

Another *now*.

I am, Ma. Really. Truly.

And I braced myself for the question(s) that were chasing the *now* round and round the living room. She fielded one and lobbed it. 'How did you know about the prize?'

I told you, Ma. From the papers.

'No, really.'

Really. I read it in the papers.

'Oof! Podi! You never give me a straight answer! I *know* it was in the papers! I've cut it out to show everyone! Don't look like that, I have reason to be proud!' Then she got stuck. The role of star-mother was making her coy. 'But I wish you would tell me properly.' A first person, first information report, no less. 'Okay, since you won't, let me guess.' She struck an attitude, a dancer's pose. 'The phone rang early in the morning . . . "*Kaveri* Chowdhry? *Missis* Kaveri Chowdhry? *Congratulations!*" And . . . and . . .'

And her feathers will fall off, I thought, if she puffs up any more.

Open your eyes, Ma. You're way off the mark.

'Okay, then, the *doorbell* rang, someone with a big bouquet . . .' And here, luckily for me, the doorbell did ring. There was a sound as of shoes scraping the doormat, and Mani entered.

For a moment he was transfixed. 'Yaare? Kaveri-a?'

Hello, Pa!

'Kaveri! When did you come?'

Driving home her advantage (he was rooted to the spot), Meenakshi crowed, 'Half an hour ago!'

A tiny line creased his brow. She's had a thirty-minute head start. Then it cleared and he swooped. '*Kaveri! Va, va,va,va!*'

I was a morning miracle; they the blessed witnesses. Two lucky parents, one filial gift. 'Where's Arya?'

Where he is, Pa. Half a country away. I came alone.

As I expected, Mani too did not reproach this desertion. Just the opposite, in fact. This was to be an exclusive treat for them. Thrilling to himself, 'I knew you'd come,' he said. 'My ESP told me.'

Meenakshi and I exchanged smiles. His ESP is notorious for working after the event. It's a fait accompli. But we're accomplices in the fait.

So how *are* you, M&M?

An old silly joke, this nickname. They laughed. 'How do we look?'

Good enough to eat, as always! But it *could* be the light playing tricks. Tell me it isn't.

They laughed again. 'We're just *fine!*'

Now his eyes, with their sailor's reach from years of looking out for me, checked out his favourite subject, contemplating it through his spectacles, and under and over them, searching for any giveaway disloyalties, any signs of decay or dysfunction.

What did he find? What discrepancies? What disappointments? But whatever he found or didn't in my face, I found the complacency in *his*, the triumph too, the surprise of having been proved wrong, the pleasure of having his secret longings gratified at last (after a fashion), I found the pride of possession alarming.

At last, with a grunt, he drew back. 'You're looking a little down. Not quite what I would expect after . . . after . . .' And *wham*! It was back. I have justified being his child at last, redeemed a series of lapses too numerous to be recounted here, paved the way to an easier love ... and, and, and. *How much was I worth now?*

Meenakshi clucked, 'She doesn't seem as happy as she should be.'

I tried not to let this irritate me—this harking at my happiness and the prescriptive exhortations for it that have dogged my life. Then I realised she was upset. It is *her* failure—my failure to be happy.

I'm just tired, M&M.

She perked up immediately. 'And *hungry*! You must be hungry! You need breakfast!'

'A bath first?'

They chorused, '*First* breakfast, *then* a bath!' Then everything else.

Of course it was no use telling them I'd had both, the first on the plane and the second in Delhi. But at least the subject of my happiness, or un-, was shelved. For the moment.

There were idlis for breakfast, and chutney, and spiced oil to pour over it all. There was coconut water from the tree in the courtyard, a hand-span of bananas, each the size of a thumb. Meenakshi positioned herself by the window to chivvy my appetite and cheer me to the finish. Sunlight threaded her hair, spun it into silk. Sunlight lit her eyes, stoked her smile. She can stretch a moment, a sound, a gesture, into a happy ending, and find in it complete fulfilment. She can, on a good day, weave happiness out of air. She can, on any day, wring tears out of the soppiest soap.

She gave me the news, flying her words like flags. Such excitement! Two hundred guests for the housewarming not counting immediate family! Two priests and three sweets! The flats are grand too! Marble in the lobby, granite in the kitchen, teakwood doors—*glass tiles* for Rajumama's bar! They want to call it Silver Oaks! Or Tulip Court! I said, but where are the silver oaks or tulips? Why not Parvati Apartments—after your great-grandmother, Kaveri—but who listens to *me*! Anyway for now we just say The Flats . . . Balumama and Rajumama will be occupying *four* and *still* there isn't enough space for all the things from the old house! Balumama had to give away most of his library—the books were falling to bits anyway . . . Kaveri?

The high wind died. 'You're not listening. And you've stopped eating. Are you alright?'

Late in the afternoon, when I was nodding over the crossword, she came, signalling her approach with a succession of seismic sneezes, and sat on my bed. 'You're not yourself. I knew it the moment I saw you.'

You are yourself, Ma. A Sakyamuni Buddha. Twentieth-century bronze repoussé. That enigmatic smile, those earlobes . . .

She tucked her chin into her shoulder and giggled modestly. 'Podi!' After a bit she sobered up. 'Something isn't right,' she declared, in a manner that conveyed that with me, it could be anything, or everything or nothing. Twisting the bangles on her wrist, she began worrying the lower lip of her famous three-cornered mouth.

The lip was dry and flaking. One of her other famous features, her teeth, was chipped. My beautiful mother was letting herself go. She caught my eye and let go of her bangles. 'Your father's impossible too! He's lying on his bed with his eyes on the ceiling and just smiling when I speak to him! Did you tell him anything that you didn't tell *me*?' A standard grumble, this. That we share jokes, Mani and I, while she and I share problems. She sighed gustily. 'I'm also intelligentsia, you know, even if *you* don't think so.' I opened my mouth, then shut it.

I must have muttered something after that for she stiffened. 'What? What trouble?' She leapt, literally, and clutched my shoulder. 'I knew it!' she cried with half-fearful triumph. 'I knew the moment I saw you!'

Her eagerness would have been offensive but Meenakshi's belief in infinite goodness and in the Infinite Goodness's infinite partiality to her and hers, is so absolute that she is incapable of thinking it might have a flip side. In a minute she would be telling me whatever was wrong would come right tomorrow—after a good night's sleep. Tomorrow, it was possible, thinkable, believable that we'd skip and dance and sing. I wished.

'What is the matter?' She shook my shoulder. 'What?'

Nothing, Ma. Just sit back and enjoy your flight.

Her back slumped. I was discriminating again. Not sharing even my problems now. 'You want too much out of life, Kaveri. And you don't have faith. Get a good night's sleep anyway. Not sleeping gives you *bad* toxins.' She got up heavily. 'Will you eat ragi roti for dinner? Tomato or coconut chutney?'

At breakfast, the next day, she went into a tizzy when I announced my plan to visit the Family that morning. 'Oh, but I can't come today! I have to sort out the coconuts, some are too green, really, that fellow knows nothing, and after that I'm making pickle, the lemons are already cut . . .'

It's all right, Ma. *You* don't have to come.

From behind the newspaper, Mani asked, 'Is it so important to rush off there on your second day?' He rattled the newspaper.

'Now they're saying *bio-engineering* is the next big thing, not environmental science! Why don't you just relax today?'

'Ama, you're so restless! Going round and round that courtyard like a cat with kittens!'

'Every so often they float a new theory and still get it wrong.' He folded the newspaper and thumped on it. 'I think it would be a bit insensitive, Kaveri. Under the circumstances.'

Meenakshi put his coffee on the table and pulled at her lip. 'Maybe I should warn them.' I must have gaped because she hurried on. 'I mean, *tell* them you're coming.' And agitatedly, 'Let me call Lilamami.'

Ma, you don't have to announce me. This isn't a state visit!

Mani grunted. 'You won't get a state welcome anyway.'

That's alright. I don't expect one.

'You could just wait and see them at the housewarming next week, Kaveri.'

I'd rather get it over with before that, Ma.

Mani picked up his coffee mug. 'The point is, will *they* get over it?'

The Family was living in rented accommodation across the road from where their new homes in The Flats were being readied. It is, it *was* a quiet, mannerly road where everybody minded their business, sharing neither their space nor their time with their neighbours. In the last two decades its character has changed—for the worse. Large plots had been chopped into stamp-sized lots, the lyrical details—cornice, pediment, architrave, monkey top—hammered out and masked with cement and glass. Now there was hardly a home left that hadn't been savaged by the times. Civilisation annihilates civilisation. But people had no choice—our family certainly didn't. While inflation and inertia was eroding their capital and the white ants their house, their land was laying golden eggs. Developers may appear like predators but they are, in a sense, saviours too.

Still, it was a shock to see the new avatar of our old family home. The shock, say, of finding an oilrig in place of the Gateway of India. Its featureless newness, rather, its all-too-familiar features, echoed in its cousins and poor relations all over Bangalore, was a negation of history and historical precedent, and a paean to a city that has reinvented itself too fast to forge a new identity. Bland and static and flouting every aesthetic rule, it had none of the old house's dark energy, none of its shifty purpose. Everything was written up on its glass-eyed front—how many bathrooms, for example, and where the kitchen was, and, reading the washing strung in the balcony, the preferred underwear of its residents. There would be no thrill of discovery here, no anticipation of adventure. And no courting punishment.

'What were you punished for?' the insatiable Claire had asked.

All sorts of deadly sins. Climbing, jumping, opening, peeping, listening, asking . . . It was all locked doors and forbidden attics. So much was banned as dangerous—more for them than us, I think. They were a cagey lot and we must have been, who knows, too underfoot.

'But you'd described it as a big place—a place to get lost in.'

That's how it seemed to us. Perhaps it was just gloomy. The rooms were swallowed by shadows. The lights disappeared into the roof. It was always twilight. And always raining.

There was a well so deep you couldn't see your face in the water. And crops of caterpillars on the walls, cobwebs in the corners. Centipedes. The odd scorpion.

'Sounds rather gothic,' commented Chris. 'Was there a resident ghost?'

There was Balumama. My grandmother's brother. His wife hid the biscuits under her bed. I have a cousin who chucked worms at us as a joke. And another who dropped hot wax on ants.

'Sound rather fun—your family.'

'Oh, your family,' said Claire, getting down to business. 'The grandmother, Pa . . . ati. And she had two brothers.'

Yes, Balumama and Rajumama. Much younger than her—there had been several stillborns and typhoid victims in between. And Pati was married off early—before she knew what was what. She had two children—my father and my aunt.

'Before she knew what was what?'

Exactly. They all lived together—not happily ever after, but rubbing along, in a Big House and a little one in the bottom of the garden. Okay, before you ask. In the Big House: Balumama, his wife Lilamami and their daughters, Tara and Uma. Rajumama and wife Devimami and their son, Bharat. In the outhouse: My grandparents, father and aunt. And later my cousins Jana and Ramu. Because their mother, my father's sister, is a little, um, feeble-minded. And their father was a rolling stone. The outhouse—my grandmother glorified it to *Cottage* to elevate our poor-relation status—was given to her out of charity. Lilamami collected rent though.

'Sounds rather feudal. *Dickensian.*'

'I had no idea you were poor!' Claire said admiringly.

Oh, I lived there only for a year—while my father built our house. And anyway, long before that my father had got out of the Cottage and made his way into the world. Because he could derive the Remainder Theorem in his sleep. He was successful—not wildly, but it was enough to annoy Lilamami. And, after all, Balumama and Rajumama had to sell their grand home.

'So nobody stayed rich or poor,' Claire said, as if she had at last got a grip on the situation.

Except in Lilamami's head. Where they were the dress circle and we the stalls.

The terrazzo banister was cold to the touch. From where I stood on the landing, the telescoping canyon of the stairwell was a chilling drop. Fear—on what intimate terms with it we were! Fear was the spur, fear the brakes. Fear gave us wings, fear clipped them. Oh, those portents of fear! Scrape of shoe, slam of door. Eye of skylight, mouth of well. The *or else, wait till I, see me later* . . .

It wasn't *me*, Pati, I wasn't even *there*, Appa. I didn't, I didn't, I didn't.

But you did.

The ants trickled down my legs. I should have heeded Mani and Meenakshi. But it was too late, for the door was opening.

Devimami.

Devimami's door-answering face was first inquiring and then astonished. 'Oh, it's *you!*' After that an odd expression flickered over it—disapproval and outrage and, I think, something approximating anticipation. I didn't have time to work all this out for she was saying, 'So you found your way here, did you?' Sounding as usual as if she was biting off thread with her teeth. Immediately she was off and shrilling down the corridor, '*Look* who's here!'

Who, who, who? A small crowd surged out into the lobby. Lilamami, Devimami and Uma. And two extras—the maid and Uma's baby, drooling on its mother's shoulder.

After a short stunned silence a buzz of self-congratulation erupted. She's come for the housewarming! All the way from *Delhi*? So? Why shouldn't she? People are coming from Bombay and Cochin too! I came from A-merica!

I may be the surprise of the hour, but they owned the surprise because I owed my presence to them. They are proprietary about presences, in this house.

Uma's baby lifted its head and made it loud and clear it did not appreciate surprises, but its bawling was lost in the babble.

I didn't miss the false notes though. They know I don't aim to please, or indeed, put myself out for anybody. As for family feelings, they have sunk to the lowest level yet. But I was happy to play along.

Of course I wouldn't miss the housewarming, Devimami.

'There's no *of course* about it,' said Devimami, striking a true note at last. 'Now that you're a big shot.' She grabbed my hand and shook it as if checking its contents. 'We should be grateful you made time for a boring thing like this.'

'Your mother didn't tell us you were coming.'

She didn't know, Lilamami. I just jumped on the plane!

'And told the pilot where to go, I suppose,' said Devimami-the-wit. 'Where are the sweets?'

Sorry, Devimami, I forgot. I just didn't think.

A brittle smile eased the lines around Lilamami's mouth. 'Do you ever think?'

Uma looked put out. What a fuss! After all she had journeyed from much further off, changing three planes and spending many hundreds of dollars. After all. But she had a Flight Date, a Flight Number, and an Estimated Time of Arrival. She had been expected at precisely the minute she emerged crossly from Immigration, dragging her red American Tourister. 'All rubbish,' she huffed now. 'It's just another of her stories that she's come for this function. She never has a straightforward reason for *anything*.'

To which her baby, bless its lungs, raised another objection. This time everybody jumped to it. *Colic! Constipation! Sleep!* The baby defied all diagnoses and went into a paroxysm. Perhaps it's just angry, I offered, but of course I was not heeded. They patted it and bounced it and made zoo noises at it. 'Give her gripe water!' screeched Lilamami. Give it air, I said, but who was listening? I gave up and just watched.

Uma's high-riding breasts have been humbled by motherhood. Devimami's once proud mane is a ratty ponytail and her singer's voice, that graced many a drawing room in its time, has coarsened from yelling, 'Stand up on the bench!' for forty years in a boys' school. Lilamami's bum has slid further into her thighs, her back's like a Brahman bull's now, and her pestle-and-mortar arms can crush stone. From time to time she would pound her hips, 'Haven't I lost weight?' Perhaps, Bharat would murmur, but if you take a handful of rice from a sackful of rice, is it going to make any difference? Lilamami's figure can e faulted but not her diamonds. They're a family legend. Eight stones on her nose, seven in each ear, a rock on one finger and a band on another. A regular lighthouse, this aunt.

'*So?*' Devimami extended her neck. 'Examination over? How long since *we* saw *you?*' Without waiting for an answer she declared it was two years and eight months exactly. Her precision has rendered everyone slow-witted, and no one ever contradicts her. No one did now. 'Yenge, turn round, let me see you properly!' And she gave me the high chin again. *Ummm!* Her head is a gallery of images, past and present, and she took little time locating mine. 'You've become thin. *Too* thin. You look like a sucked mango seed.'

Uma laughed shortly. 'One would imagine she would have got *fat*. People do, I believe—on ill-gotten gains.' She hoisted the baby to her face and, 'Congratulations!' she flung at me, getting the unpleasant business over with. A safety pin glinted between her teeth. The *congratulations* hung like a burst balloon.

There was a breathless silence. This was a big day for silences.

Then, 'Yennana,' Lilamami barked over my head. 'Why're you hiding there?'

Balumama emerged.

But it isn't Balumama! At least it is, but only partly. This Balumama occupied less space. It had lost a belly and a frown, and had some teeth knocked out too. Except for one long tooth that sat rakishly on its lip. And all this in three years! The change must have been creeping up, but I had been oblivious.

The rubber soles gripped the floor with an unpleasant *pachak*—like the squelching of rotting leaves. There was a rustle, as of a thing creeping in the undergrowth, but it was only the susurration of cloth, a veshti. Trees dipped and swayed in a darkened sky . . . But it was only the fan throwing shadows on the ceiling.

Balumama did a rat-a-tat on my back. 'Yenna! Have you forgotten your Balumama?' His tongue darted in and out of his ruined teeth, alternating pink and black.

'Forgotten-a,' snorted Lilamami. 'She hasn't forgotten *you*, I can tell you!'

'She hasn't forgotten *any*thing,' supplied Devimami.

Balumama worked his blue-green jaws like bellows. An eye opened a crack. There was a knowing light in it, conspiratorial and, if I didn't know him as I did, I would describe as playful. It made my skin crawl. Then, unexpectedly, he held out his hand. Solemnly we shook. Up, down—twice.

Ice-cold lemonade arrived in silver tumblers on a silver tray. Someone coughed, someone gulped. My throat dried to a sticky web. The web got stickier as the questions came, one after the other. Where is your Arya? Why's he not coming— *he's* a big shot now? How long is your visit? And *then* . . .? What're your plans, what're your plans, what're your plans?

Uma was thumping the baby's back as if beating the dust from a cushion. Suddenly, without warning, she dumped it on my lap. All at once there was a powerful smell—which was most certainly not baby powder, and I returned it, nearly dropping it in my haste. Uma sniffed its bottom professionally. *Mpfh!* 'Naughty! I just changed you!' She gave me a miffed glance. '*Enama* sweetheart,' she cooed, stripping off its nappy.

To a man we averted our eyes.

A minor commotion ensued. Uma couldn't find a fresh nappy. She went round in circles. Has anybody seen a pile of dia-pers? Pink with roses? It was a small but vital detail meant to put me and everyone else in their place. Diapers printed with roses. Pants that must be buttoned and unbuttoned ten times a day because Uma's baby was still not toilet-trained. She hasn't the time, Lilamami says, and besides, this is how it is in America. They don't know better, sniffs Devimami (but not too loudly), just look at her nappy rash, I mean, dia-per rash. And carrying around the, um, stuff for hours! Disgusting!

Devimami sniffed now. Uma's baby was of interest only to its mother and grandmother. Crooking her finger, 'I want to speak to you, Kaveri,' she said. 'Come into the kitchen.' But before I could get up, a door at the other end opened and . . .

Jana stood there. *Jana.* My cousin Jana . . . *Hello* Jana!

'Kaveri-a!' she exclaimed through gummy lips, blinking as at an unexpected poser.

Devimami banged the kitchen door behind her.

Jana came in, walking as if the room was swarming with people—people she wanted to avoid—and mediating the gaps between chairs and tables as if touching anything would give her an electric shock. I held my breath as she skirted too close to a glass peg table. She made it at last—getting away with just knocking down a brass ashtray. Her bare feet had left a damp trail on the red cement floor.

So, Jana? So, Kaveri? We greeted each other in a safe clearing, smiling and nodding, clearing our throats, and nodding and smiling again, which is our normal mode of greeting. Then she stuck her hand out for me to shake.

Why does this family so love to shake hands? It is something I have never understood. I took her hand—hot and sticky as an unpleasant secret. *She has been warming it between her thighs.* I don't know why I have these thoughts about poor Jana. It's just not fair.

As usual, she lowered my spirits. A bra-strap peeped out, grey-white and twisted. A wisp of greasy hair stuck to a blackish ring on her neck. Oh Jana! This was such a chancy birth accident—this who should be whose cousin. It's not fair, I thought, for the nth time, and wished she would miraculously morph into something bright and amusing. Tinkerbell, perhaps.

I didn't think I'd see *you* here, Jana!

'Nor I *you*. But see! You came—after all.' She rubbed her face with the end of her sari and studied the cloth for a bit of nose that may have come off on it. She is not easily excited, Jana, as if she is not entitled to excitement, and must check herself in case it turns out to be something else, something underhand or sinister parading under the guise.

Amma didn't tell me you're staying here, Jana.

'I'm not, I'm at Ramu's.' And earnestly, 'I'm setting his house in order, you know.'

This took my breath away. Jana setting anybody's house in order?

A humid cloud wreathed my head. 'Have they said anything yet?' she whispered. 'No?' Her eyeballs rolled. 'They will!' She drew back with a harsh chuckle and hid her mouth with her fingers. Then she leaned forward again. 'Oh Kaveri! Why did you come? They're so angry with you!'

'Jana,' Lilamami called. 'You slept *two hours!*' And, with time-honed insolence, 'Have you had a bath?' I burned for Jana. *Let her be.* But letting *be* is not a family virtue. '. . . the water's still hot. Go take a bath.'

'But I *have* had a bath, Lilamami.' *Don't wriggle, Jana, Pati would scold. Is there an ant on your back?*

Of course Lilamami would not believe her. And to tell the truth she did look as if she'd been dragged through a hedge. 'Look at your blouse—it's disgraceful!'

That's because she lives in Chennai, I volunteered. The whites never stay white there. Because of the dockyards. Soot from the steamships.

Lilamami snorted again. 'The ships are diesel now.'

Devimami stretched her neck round the kitchen door. 'I have lots of relatives in Chennai. *Clean* relatives.'

'I *had* a bath! Just before I came!'

'Change that blouse, at least.'

'But I changed it when I had a bath,' Jana said, desperate now.

'*Your two top hooks are undone,*' Devimami said theatrically.

I was getting irritated now—with everybody, especially Jana, for exposing herself so. Does it matter, I muttered, and to Jana, why don't you just—when she lifted her head. Her expression was one of such intense suffering that I couldn't finish what I was going to say. *Take another bath, Jana.* Wear another blouse. Get another life.

It's just not easy.

There was a new restlessness in the air. It was getting on for lunch, and I was not showing signs of leaving. At last Devimami asked *the* question—in the grand manner she sometimes puts on, 'Are you free to lunch?'

'Maybe she's *had* lunch,' Lilamami said swiftly.

Illey, Lilamami. In fact I've come especially to have lunch with you.

Lilamami recovered quickly. 'Sarisari, in that case you must stay. After all it's not every day you visit us.' Her eyes glazed—she was calculating whether there would be enough left over for the dinner now that I was sharing their meal or, awful prospect, would she need to cook afresh? It is one of my petty pleasures to guess how her budget-balancing will be thrown by such emergencies, and how she will make up for it.

I hope you've got cashewnut barfi for dessert, Lilamami.

'Certainly not. Sitaram has sent us very good mangoes from his garden.'

I conceded defeat.

Then the doorbell rang—two punches and a long peal. There was a sigh of *at last*, and in came the person we'd been waiting lunch for. Rajumama. Bursting in as if the dogs were after him. And shouting to no one in particular, 'That damned contractor has broken the window pane *again*! This time *he's* going to pay . . .' He skidded to a stop when he spotted me, and gave me a harassed look, as if I were the last straw. 'Kaveri!'

'She surprised us!' said Jana, cradling my arm.

'She certainly did,' said Lilamami dryly.

'Ah!' said Rajumama sagely. Then, leaping at Uma's baby, he threw its arm up and whacked its palm. 'Gimme a high five!' It gave a feeble gurgle. 'Gimme a shakehand!' It gurgled again. 'Ha!' He spun around to me. 'Okay, your turn now! Shake!' Obediently I pumped. 'Well! Well, well, well!'

I'm well, thank you. And you?

'A-ha! Being funny-a?' Rajumama shook a finger at me and flung out of the room.

'Pay attention to your plates!' Devimami had squeezed herself behind the too-large table (that once graced the old house's vast dining hall) to ladle out the food. 'Do you want more rice?'

Thump. Rice. *Plonk*. Grated carrot. *Plop*. Steamed beans. Turnip sambar, tomato rasam, soft white curds, in succession. Appalam, gooseberry chutney and pickled lime.

The mangoes from the neighbour's garden turned out to be sour and fibrous, obviously given away because there were no takers at home. Balumama threw down a piece in disgust. 'Yaindi,' his tooth wobbled at me, 'couldn't you have brought Dusseri mangoes from Delhi?'

It was his only contribution to the conversation.

The conversation wasn't exactly lively. Balumama fussed with his gums, Uma fussed over her baby (on her lap right through the meal), Lilamami fussed over all three of them. Rajumama was unusually subdued. Beside me Jana was trying to eat without making a sound, so naturally I was on edge, alert to her every little slurp and swallow. That left Devimami to do the honours. She picked her favourite-of-all topic. Her son. Bharat had become president of the Bangalore Heritage Society. 'He has a regular column in the *Deccan Age* now. On the historic buildings of Bangalore. A lot of people say he writes very well.' She looked to me to challenge this.

I must read them then, Devimami.

I regretted that as soon as I said it—it sounded so condescending. Devimami didn't let it pass. '*If* you have the time.'

After that the conversation completely dried up and we stared at the walls, which were jammed with pictures of gods and goddesses—a medley of sequins, silk, lotuses and gold coins—interspersed with faded sepia photographs of the family, the plainness of our features unrelieved by wedding finery and sash-and-mortarboard. We're plain bordering on ugly. That, if anything, is our inheritance . . .

'Mphf, mphf!' spluttered Jana. 'Kaveri! Look out!'

I was a second too late. A brown arm, wearing a thatch of black hair, had snaked in from behind, lifted a piece of mango from my plate. Juice dripped on my sari. Juice dripped on the table. I smacked the hand down.

'Hel-*lo*,' drawled Bharat, rocking my chair. 'Have you,' he tweaked my hair, 'been walking through a cobweb? No, *it's grey hair!*' He waited for the announcement to throw me into a spin. When it didn't, 'You've lost weight,' he remarked. The first part of a conversation in this family is about how we look.

'She's lost her tongue,' said Uma. Then it is how we behave.

'At least acknowledge him,' said Devimami. Then we're told what to do.

'My humble congratulations,' said Bharat. 'If they are acceptable, of course.' And finally we get the sarcasm.

It's so predictable it's depressing.

Bharat crunched into the space between his father and mother and, helping himself to an appalam, crammed it into his mouth. 'So what-what and all have you been doing?' And chomping busily, 'Too proud-a, to speak to me?'

'She didn't even ask after you,' Devimami informed him meanly.

'Oh, that's because . . .'

'Because?' prompted Devimami.

'Be-*cause*,' snorted Uma.

'Huh-um!' went Rajumama. Which may have been a *because*—it had the right syllables.

'Because,' chimed Jana as if she were about to pin a rosette on my lapel, '*because* she's famous!'

You could have cut the silence with a knife. Lilamami's necklace appeared to be strangling her. Balumama's face was hammered out in pig iron. Devimami bent her head to hide a smile. She was *enjoying* herself.

This, staying to lunch, was really a bad idea.

'So, Kaveri.' Bharat's teeth gleamed in his beard. 'Is this as good as your goat-ball curry?'

'Goat-a! Ayyoyo! Chee!'

'But she makes curry out of goat's balls, Ma. And pig's feet.'

'That's enough, Bharat,' said Rajumama. 'Stop teasing her.'

'Oh, but I must, Appa. For old times' sake. For all the times she teased *me*!'

You didn't do too badly yourself, fool. The worm you put in my lunchbox. And the caterpillar in my bag.

He was delighted. 'Good times, eh?'

'Good times,' Jana echoed dully, her face contorting as if they were times of drought and famine. 'Good times,' she whispered.

Bharat stopped smiling. 'Ah, easy,' he murmured. 'Just breathe, Jana.' Then, leaning across the table, he gave her a piece of mango. 'Here. Try this one.' She accepted it with a watery smile.

The weariness settled on my shoulders. This petty score-off against Lilamami, staying to lunch, wasn't worth it. But I couldn't just eat and run, so to speak. So I continued to sit, a bump on a log—a *splinter* on a log for them.

The afternoon curled with heat, the sulphurous, dry heat of Bangalore that silvers the skin and stiffens the hair. In the living room a languid Devimami snipped the ends off the betel leaves and dabbed them with lime. A lethargic Lilamami rolled them up with betel nut and sugar candy. A morose Jana took them around, dragging her feet. We downed glass upon glass of iced water to douse the acrid aftertaste of betel leaf. Such stillness in the air! Such weighty thoughts!

By and by Rajumama left for his nap, followed by Balumama.

'*Sarisari*,' said Lilamami when I dragged my chair over to her. 'Po, talk to Jana.' Holding Uma's baby up, she began a hectic monologue in baby language. Beside her, Uma held a magazine to her face.

We're not a subtle family.

'So what-what and all are you planning to do?' asked Bharat, stretching out a limp hand. A late greeting—how could I be properly welcomed without a handshake? Remembering past atrocities—burrs pressed into my palm, and dead spiders—I was wary. But this was an open-handed offer, and the hand was as honestly calloused as my mother's, although it didn't move me. It made me want to scream, why, why, *why*? Why just a weekly column for the *Deccan Age*?

His manner, from being friendly, turned combative, and he dropped my hand as if it was a live coal. When he smiled, bared his teeth, rather, there was in his face what wasn't there before. Conditional surrender. Catching my eye, 'How long is your visit?' he asked tensely. 'A week, a month?'

I'm not sure. As of now, it's indefinite.

He nodded distractedly, and hugged his chest as if squirrelling away a toothsome nut. Then, fishing in his pocket, he brought out a chocolate éclair. 'Here, a homecoming present for you.'

Oh, thank you.

My instinct, once second nature, warned me a second too late. A ladybird popped out with the sweet, hopped on to my wrist. I screamed. He laughed. It turned out to be one of those silly toys meant to shut up pesky children. My fickle sympathy evaporated. He deserved his dreary middles.

Well, *you're* the same retard.

He smirked. 'Everyone loves me.'

Count *me* out of your fan club.

'At least I have one.'

'Oh but she has one too!' cried Jana, seizing my arm. '*Me!*'

He smirked some more. 'Ah, but success doesn't always buy love. Only tolerance.'

That's all right. Tolerance is good enough for me.

'I shouldn't be so sure of that even, if I were you. Not here at least.'

'Yenna! *Yenna?*' Devimami was turning from one to the other of us. 'What are you saying?'

Grow up, fool. Get yourself a lady to amuse you instead of ladybirds.

His face changed. Devimami lowered her head and charged. 'Ayyoyo, *lady*-a! Karma! No, no, no!'

He bared his teeth, clicked them at her. 'I *have* one actually.'

She scowled at *me*. 'I know my son wouldn't do such things.' Then, struck by hideous doubt, 'You wouldn't, would you, Bhartu?' she cried.

What *things*, Devimami?

'I don't have to explain to *you*.'

'No,' said Bharat, throwing me a leer. 'Because Kaveri knows. *She's* the lady.'

Jana went mfph, mfph into her hand, Devimami expelled an outraged breath, Bharat walked off, whistling.

'So what are your plans *now?*' said Lilamami from across the room. 'Yenna?' Jana pinched my elbow. *She's asking you, Kaveri!* 'Just sit back and enjoy the money-a? How much is it, by the way?' She rubbed noses with the baby in a show of carelessness—but how she does care! Hectic calculations are going on behind those glasses, I know. Now she is deducting taxes and expenses and commissions. Now she is adding the prize money. But aren't prizes taxed too? A new wrinkle popped up. Of course the newspapers exaggerated. (I can read the wrinkle.) Why, there are no signs of it! I was the same shabby person who travelled in autorickshaws and didn't bring a present even.

She turned the scorn on me—the scorn that hissed and smoked around our growing years, reducing serious purport to farce, dismissing any endeavour not vetted and approved by her as inconsequential and worthless. 'An absurd amount,' she said, sour as sour can be. '*If* one is to believe the newspapers. Which *I* never do.'

Oh, they were very accurate in this case, Lilamami.

'Really?' She looked at me as if she wished she could dock a week of my pay.

Uma took the baby from her and began processing another nappy change. That's the leakiest baby I've seen, I offered, by way of conversation. How many nappies does it get through in a day, Uma?

She took the pin out of her mouth. 'You'd know if you had one,' she said rudely, and to her mother, 'Amma, people calculate in millions these days. Of *dollars*, not rupees. Information technology has changed the *meaning* of money. Anyone smart enough to invest in it at the right time,' she paused for someone, *me*, to ask whether she had, and, when we didn't, said crossly, 'So anyway her booty isn't all that much.'

Lilamami brightened. 'It's not a steady income, of course.'

'One swallow a summer does not make,' droned Devirnami, and they all looked happier.

I thought it time to correct their misconceptions.

Actually, Lilamami, the money is enough for a lifetime of unsteady living. *Two* lifetimes.

'*Really*? Aren't you a clever one.'
And just fractionally, a lid opened.

Kaveri and Uma are tugging each other's plaits and hissing abuse. *Stinky shit. Fat bum. Bugs Bunny* . . . Uma's paper nails make faint scratches on Kaveri's thigh, Kaveri's score bloodily on Uma's arm. Uma wails, a thin but piercing noise, deliberately exaggerated to get help. Sure enough, Lilamami, never too far from trouble, shoots out of the back door, and grabs Kaveri (whose nails are a guilty red). Kaveri wriggles away but stands her ground. Lilamami thrusts her face into Kaveri's. '*Glaring* at me! Who do you think you are? Who do you think *I* am?'

Which is a stupid question, as any child can tell. Sure enough, 'The lady who hides the biscuits,' answers Kaveri, entirely sincere, if not exactly innocent.

Lilamami's striking head withdraws with a hiss. '*How dare you!*'

Meenakshi arrives, with her unfortunate sense of timing, just when Lilamami is giving Kaveri's cheek the five-finger. Meenakshi, to her own surprise, does the same on the other cheek. And sends Kaveri *wham* into Uma. *Husha-husha, all fall down!*

Uma snivels and examines her torn nails as Lilamami bears her off to safety and first aid. Kaveri is stood under the tree by Meenakshi to atone. She stands for hours, days, months, years—twenty minutes by the clock—trying to understand her sin. What had she done? She'd only told the truth!

Meenakshi explained: Children must know their place.

They mustn't step out of line. Or speak out of turn. Even if it's the truth.

Balumama has told Jana (and Jana told Kaveri): You have been loaned to us by the milkman. The goatherd. The one-eyed coolie. You'll be returned if you don't do as you're told. You want to disappear? Then ... That was the fear that threatened to knock them off the edge of their handkerchief-sized world. Of being reduced not only to a nonentity but non-existence. You aren't who you think you are, you aren't even *are.*

It was years before Kaveri understood what really infuriated her aunt was the upstaging of them all by Mani. Balumama, for all his father's influence and money, had no proper vocation, and no regular employment, and Rajumama's job was too modest to contain Devimami's sense of grandeur. But Mani had won scholarship after scholarship and carved himself a respectable career. It was the ultimate insult for privilege—to have to concede to presumption. If it was shameful to fail, it was insupportable to succeed, over and above your betters. What were the acceptable terms of success? Lilamami spelled them out silently, clearly. Cottagers must defer to landowners. Stay a pace and a half-beat behind them.

Uma's paper nails were shining ovals now, toughened by years of treatment in the US. Her husband had defected there when sent on a training course by his company. Lilamami had tried to quash the gossip. '*Everybody* is an immigrant in A-merica.' But we continued to tease: What's it like to be an illegal immigrant, Uma?

Uma was condescending. 'Well, to begin with, we're not *illegal*. We have a green card, and we've applied for citizenship now. Our house will be fully paid up in ten years. We've started a savings account for Baby's college and we've bought into a pension scheme. *And* booked a place in a senior citizens' home.'

It seems rather a long way to travel for these future joys, Uma.

Oh, but they lived a very good life now too, thank you. And she produced evidence of it. Glossy pictures of herself and her husband, the Defector. Posing inside their refinanced house and their fully paid-up Nissan. Making a V-sign at the Niagara Falls in yellow raincoats. Peering into the Grand Canyon in Red Sox caps. Shaking hands with Mickey Mouse in coordinated sweatshirts. (Shaking hands there too!)

Every other summer Uma sat in front of her red American Tourister, dispensing Mars Bars and hair ties and cute magnets to stick on the refrigerator. From time to time she pulled out a surprise from the lucky dip. 'A night-dress case for you, Kaveri! Look, it's shaped like a lipstick!'

Thank you for adding value to my life, Uma.

Uma was giving me her sideways glance—the one that slides out like a dagger from a sheath. She was about to be funny. 'Look,' she nudged her mother. 'She's dreaming of being on the Oprah Winfrey show!'

They were still going on over my head as if I wasn't there. Who is *she*, I muttered. The cat's mother? But, 'Oprah Winfrey!' breathed Lilamami, hugging the baby to her chest. '*Oprah Winfrey!*'

Uma snorted. 'You won't be so thrilled when Oprah

Winfrey gets her to talk. They have a way of ferretting out things on those talk shows.'

The bulb fused. 'I never thought of that.' Agitatedly, 'We mustn't let her, Uma!'

Calm down! I'm not going on Oprah Winfrey, for heavensake! In any case nobody cares.

Uma looked down the edge of her nose. 'I was joking.'

Lilamami forgot herself and shook the baby hard. 'Nobody cares? *We* care! *You* don't care about anything! That's always been your problem!' Her mouth worked up and down, the baby began mewling. 'It's all lies! Lies, *lies!*'

'It *is* lies, Ma,' Uma said impatiently. 'It's cheap gossip.' Well, that's one way of looking at it, I suppose. She pulled her mother's arm. 'Va, Ma. Help me fix Baby's feed.' (The baby was rioting now.) Her mother stumbled behind her. Help *me*, she seemed to be crying. *Help* me.

I did want to help. At least tell her, don't take it so hard, Lilamami. Nobody remembers, you know. Nobody gives a damn even if they do. People move on. I started after them, but was pulled back. An arm encircled my waist, a hand fumbled for mine. There was the familiar adenoidal breathing, moist, hot. My skin prickled and popped. 'Va, Kaveri. In *here*,' she pointed me to a door, her face flickering with a private urgency—secrets I was unwilling to share.

She rushed me through the door and slammed it shut behind us as if expecting to be mowed down by bullets. 'We're alone now!' she said with a happy sigh.

She gets her kicks from such odd things. What *are* we doing here anyway, Jana? In this house?

'You're visiting and *I'm* helping to clean the new flats,' she said seriously.

They don't need *you* Jana, they need a broom. Don't you be one.

I was about to deliver a little homily on the subject when, 'It's okay Kaveri,' she stayed me with her hand. 'I *like* cleaning. But never mind *me!*' She grabbed my arm. 'I saw your picture in the papers! And in Star News! I told everyone you're my *first* cousin but they won't believe it!' I wanted to say something happy, something like, one look at us and anybody can tell we're cousins, Jana! But her hand was hot and clammy and she was puffing clouds of water vapour. 'If I have a daughter I'll name her after you!' She patted the flat stomach that should, by now, by rights, have pouched an embryonic Kaveri. Come on, God, fill it. It's no big deal for you to send down another mouth to be lovingly, devotedly, obsessively overfed. Do it with spores or lightning or something, but *do* it. What's the idea of sitting on it?

The bedroom was like a left luggage department in a railway station. A pair of rosewood cots pushed together, and half the area cluttered with clothes, books, folders, toys, plastic bags of stuff, baby paraphernalia and, bafflingly, a steel tiffin carrier. A chest of drawers was jammed in a corner, its surface crowded with English china and Venetian glass. Trunks and suitcases filled the corners. On a wingback chair behind the door, half-hidden by a pillow, was a pile of nappies. Pink, printed with roses. Uma wouldn't be able to spot them unless she sat where I did. Should I tell her, or not? Life throws up such interesting moral dilemmas. Not, I decided, losing this one.

Jana had cleared a space for us on the bed. 'I didn't mean it, Kaveri,' she muttered, staring at the bedspread. 'About . . . those being . . . good years.' Her hands clutched the bedspread.

'They were bad, bad, bad! I'm glad that old house has gone! I hated it!' She subsided into a spell of noisy, angry breathing.

Oh Jana. Try, try and think of the fun times. Climbing the roof and raiding the mango tree and . . .

'There was no mango tree,' she said firmly. Which was just so surprising that I dropped the subject.

She was sitting hugging her stomach, her head bowed. I'd lost her. Or she'd lost me. It was in times like these I wondered whether we really are bits of each other. But the bit of her that is like the bit of me must surely remember the garden. At least its duplicity. Tricked out in light and colour during the day and sinister shadows stalking us in the night. They tried to laugh away our fears. It's the same garden, the same trees and bushes and squirrels—aren't you the same, night or day?

Of course we aren't. We aren't what we appear to be. There is a night and day to all of us. An inside and an outside. A lie and a truth. We knew better even then.

A jerky yellow finger of light pokes around the vast wilderness, the *garden*, that divided—or connected, depending on your outlook—the Big House and the Cottage. It wobbles over the buffalo grass, disappears into the caves of trees. It wakes a crow from its slumbers, alerts the snakes in the hedges. The watchman is on his nightly round. Thieves are afoot at this hour, although he hasn't spotted them. They're invisible, and their thieving is untraceable. Like his torch, they just gouged holes in the darkness. 'Get down from there, you monkeys!' Balumama shouted, a noontime thief, black against the white sunlight. 'You'll break that branch!' Ebony-skinned Balumama barking obscenities that even Lilamami objected to. But he heeded nobody, not even the whimpers of his daughters, Tara and Uma, stuck high in the mango tree (that Jana had denied the existence of), too frightened to come down. *'I'm going to beat the shit out of you!'* He emptied his spleen as he would his bowels. Regularly.

Needlepoints of light prick out a new constellation in the night sky—the Big House and the Cottage. A moon like a comma sits on a ridge, to fatten the jasmine buds for Lilamami. She always got the first pickings, except the time Kaveri beat her to it. Setting the clock for a predawn hour, she raided the bushes before Lilamami arrived, hiding herself to watch Lilamami emerge in her crumpled night sari, swinging her silver basket.

That was a bad year for Lilamami. One day she found dog turd on her kollam, 'Right in the *middle*—Blondie would never do that!' Another day her petticoat strings were tied together. *'Ten* of them with *reef* knots!' Then the lefts of her footwear disappeared from the Big House verandah. 'Kaveri—who else?'

Pati gave the children a lecture: You should not fritter away your study time.

One night Balumama's mosquito net mysteriously slipped its moorings, entangling him, and he woke up shouting and swearing. Lilamami conceded *that* could not have been Kaveri. Then who was it? Kaveri knew but she wasn't going to tell.

Light from the Cottage windows rolls down the steps on to the earth. Two yellow squares divided lengthways by four bars. Each bar holds a different smell: fried cabbage, tomato rasam, steamed rice, chillies-in-sesame oil.

The smells shiver and dissolve. Kaveri turns to stone. She

is alone! Lured by the fireflies, she has strayed into the garden! Her throat is cracking, she cannot cry out. Then, 'Dinner, Kaveri, come inside!' Meenakshi calls. Her mother's fat, comfortable voice, moving in concentric rings around the danger, exorcises the ghosts.

Pati, when consulted, told her it was all in the mind—fear and the getting rid of it.

But it wasn't. Even Pati didn't know that. Fear was something you could see and feel and taste.

Kaveri knew many things Pati didn't. She knew Bharat had found Lilamami's secret hoard of biscuits under the bed. She knew where Mani went on the first Saturday of every month. (It was a house with a Great Hall in which a Lordship sat on a throne and old men walked backwards wearing comic hats and making secret signs.) She knew why Jana and Ramu hated sleeping at the Big House, which they had to when their parents visited and there was no room in the Cottage. She knew when Ramu was being stupid and when stubborn, and that when Jana looked lost it meant she had found something she didn't want to find.

Jana was running like a motorised starfish. Down the garden path. Cutting the air with her elbows. Running, running but where was she going? There was nowhere to go.

Sometimes Kaveri wondered whether grown-ups really didn't know what she knew or only pretended they didn't. Pati said nice people didn't have secrets. So perhaps they didn't know, after all. Or perhaps they didn't tell.

But what was one to do when the secrets weren't nice? Weren't tellable?

Forget the past, Jana. Think of now. Think present tense.

'Yes.' *Yesssss.* She tilted her head so the eyeballs rolled. 'But the past was also a present once. So where does the past stop and the present begin? Or the present become the past?' She blinked slowly, like a tree-bird. Once again she left me speechless.

Presently she gave a little shake to snap out of the past. (Or the present!) But her face was torn with strife. She had crossed over and hadn't returned. She passed her hand over her eyes to drag herself back to the here-and-now (so soon to be consigned to the there-and-then). 'Your mother said you went to Bombay, Poona, Delhi.' And as if I've been condemned to this unhappy fate, 'You're going to the US too.' She tried out a smile, didn't succeed. 'Your mother said the wine ran out in Delhi,' she said sadly. 'Then the cheese ran out.'

Then everyone ran out. And that was that.

She laughed. The room brightened—a curtain had been pulled back. In my relief I laughed too, immoderately. 'The British high commissioner was there, your mother said. And the French ambassador! Everyone was there.'

That's not *every*one, Jana. *You* were not there.

'Oh, *I* don't matter! There were three hundred other people! *Important* people!'

Well, if she's told you so it must be so. Anyway people have to go *somewhere* in the evenings. The movies hadn't changed and the wine was free.

She laughed again. 'Kaveri, you are so funny!' Her eyes swam. The brief pleasure had left her beached. 'I wish I were *you*.'

My throat contracted. *No*, Jana, I said, and she drew back, startled. I mean, you wouldn't like that at all, Jana.

'I would *love* it.' She jumped up, walked to the window, pressed her face to the grille. 'You're *everything* I could wish for. You're so lucky.'

I was consumed by her longing. Am I lucky? I suppose I am. I've never had to wait on luck, if *that* is a marker. Or work for it. Luck is blind and deaf anyway, and just so ham-handed at times.

She spun around and hooked her arms to the bars behind her. 'But it wasn't just luck, Kaveri! You deserved it! People deserve what they get!' She shook her head, confused. 'What am I saying!'

We hadn't heard Devimami enter. '*Yenna* Jana, philosophising-a?'

Poor Jana froze. She looked exactly as she used to when Balumama caught us at our tree games—hanging from a branch, motionless as a chrysalis. Her mouth had fallen open, and I found myself wishing she would shut it and breathe through something else. Her ears perhaps. Or her belly button.

She was giving me a weather report actually, Devimami. I hear it's been unseasonably warm this summer.

Jana went *mphf, mphf*, in her nose, and Devimami went *ummmmm* in her throat, like water gurgling through a pipe. It's supposed to convey one part non-comprehension, one part disbelief and a third of grudging appreciation. '*Ummmm!*' The water drained out. 'Lilamami wants to talk to you, Kaveri. She's waiting in her room.'

Then Rajumama charged in, almost knocking his wife down. 'I'm off to The Flats! Kaveri, you wanted to see them! Want to come now? Okay! Be a good girl and I'll take you home in my new Honda City. It's a *gas guzzler*, you know,' he said proudly.

'Yenna, Lila's waiting to see her.'

'Later, she can see her later! Come on!'

'That man has no sense,' Devimami grumbled. 'Come back here before you go home then, Kaveri!'

Rajumama's short stride was at odds with his face, which had lengthened with end-of-day weariness. It had elongated too with time, and it didn't have such a great start either.

We crossed the street. The trees were thick with wet crows, the pavement splattered with their droppings. It had rained in the last hour—one of Bangalore's sudden downpours that catches the sky unawares. A grey cloud was still chasing the renegade sun. The Flats, a tightly stretched banner across the horizon, appeared insubstantial—they wouldn't be real even if completely occupied and the windows were lit from inside, not as just now by weak sunlight. A single TV antenna propitiated the sky. On the gate a fearful mask warded off the evil eye.

'Well? Impressed-a?'

Impressive, I answered, thankful that its size overrode all other considerations. It certainly was big.

Rajumama's mouth did a U-turn downwards. He's not stupid. 'At least you've allowed it's big.' At the gate, 'Orient yourself,' he ordered. 'Can you tell where we are?'

The garage was over there, wasn't it? And the watchman's house about there. And *there* the courtyard, the garages, the path to the Cottage ... And this is where the front steps were—right?

Right. We sat on those steps every evening, the children sliding down the cement rail, Lilamami plotting to buy the new coffee tumblers with false bottoms to fool visitors shameless enough to arrive at coffee-time, and Pati knitting and wondering if she could substitute jaggery syrup for treacle in a recipe for gingerbread she'd found in *Woman and Home*, and Devimami practising her wit on the neighbours. 'Yenna, Kamala, won a lottery-a! *Buying* mangoes! Your tree is not good enough for you?'

The gulmohur, the cassia, the gooseberry and the lavender . . . All the trees of our endless games. I was pointing randomly but Rajumama was pleased. 'That is absolutely right.'

That is absolutely wrong, I think. It can't be right to chop down one's childhood friends. Not to build *this*.

They cut them, one by one, beginning with the grandfather jackfruit in the Cottage garden, trussing and tying it to the mango, its neighbour of sixty years and now a stake for its execution. Then the hacking began. *Ack-ack-ack*, like the rasping of a diseased lung. The broken limbs bled resin, the knots wept gum, the leaves rained down on the hard red earth. Late in the evening it keeled over with a terrific crash.

For days Pati stared at the sightless eye in the ground. Mani tried to comfort her. 'It's only a tree, Amma.'

Pati snapped upright. 'Only a tree? *Only?* That only-a-tree was there long before you were born!'

From the Cottage windows Pati tortured herself with the devastation of the rest of the garden. On the second day the mango was felled, then the gooseberry and guava and chickoo and grapefruit . . . Pati's prized collection of crotons was next to go. Scabs of bleached-white worms wriggled under the pots, mats of black ants with stings at the ready, and hairy caterpillars, kin to those in the privy that scared the children into constipation.

Pati transferred to Mani's house-on-the-road, taking with her only the silver idols from the puja. The few pieces of furniture that had been provided by the Big House went back, every stick accounted for, to Lilamami, including the broken gate-legged table. Everything immovable was contracted to the developer. He didn't have Pati's feel for history, but a very good sense of geography. Where to get the best price for old tiles, where to melt scrap iron, where to reuse the seasoned rafters.

Rajumama's new home in The Flats was spacious and luxurious, and fitted with many a convenience and luxury. Chandelier in the living room, etched glass in the dining room, Shiva–Parvati ceramic tiles for the puja. Blinding chrome and brass everywhere.

Rajumama was worshipful in his temple. Stroking a hideously racy granite counter, 'I chose this myself,' he said. 'You absolutely cannot rely on contractors for the finer details.' From the balcony he pointed out Balumama's flat across the U-court. 'I can hail Balu from here. Watch this.' He clapped his hands and there was a resounding echo—proving what I had suspected. That the U-court was less a light well than a sound box. 'So, you know, it's really one house.'

That's nice, Rajumama. It'll be like the old days!

A tiny vertical line appeared between his eyebrows. 'Stop putting on an act.'

Back in the flat, someone, a painter, came to consult him. 'I must go now,' he said, still distant and unsmiling. 'You can get an autorickshaw at the end of the road.' He rushed off, followed by his pack of dogs. Without excusing himself from the promised ride in his gas-guzzler. Without a wave even.

I decided not to go back to see Lilamami. I'd had enough for the day.

When I reached home, 'Was it too much for you, Kaveri?' Meenakshi asked, worrying her lower lip. 'Were they okay? Would you like coffee?'

Mani put an arm around my shoulders. 'Have a beer with me.'

Targeting my happiness as always.

Oh, M&M.

The kitchen was warm with food vapours. A grey cloud floated over the skylight so it was confidingly dim as well. 'Kaveri,' Meenakshi quavered. Don't, please don't, I implored silently. *Don't* say it. But she did. 'Kaveri, please understand. We *are* proud of you. Except . . . just that . . . if only you hadn't . . . Kaveri, you hurt them!' *Is this what you learned from me in all these years?* I was getting dizzy—a novel sensation for me. 'I *wish* you hadn't . . .' She began receding into a void. There was a buzzing in my ears, like that of a hive upset, the skylight dimmed and the terracotta floor heaved. Into an echoing tunnel she was saying, 'I don't always like what they do but . . .' when the buzzing drowned the rest of her words. Where are the *bees*, was my last thought, before the floor knocked me down.

It was late evening when I woke, to find myself in my bed, covered up to the chin. The window blinds were throwing striped shadows on the wall opposite and in the bands the guava leaves shifted and smoked. Meenakshi, who was standing guard by the door, heel-toed off immediately to announce the good news to Mani—clattering a saucepan to hail the miracle. In seconds she was back, bearing a mug of cocoa, which she waved under my nose like an incense burner. 'You're not eating enough! And I told you to wear a sweater!'

She'd brought something else to wave under my nose. It was *The Subcontinent Quarterly*. Drawing my attention to a pencil-marked portion, 'Did you really say this?' she asked in a troubled voice. '*My single most significant creative input is instability.*' 'You said it's *inherited*! *I'm* unstable now?'

The single-mindedness of parenthood!

It wasn't you, Ma!

'If not me, then your *father*?' If anything, this agitated her more. 'Your father won a gold medal in physics!'

Right on cue, he materialised.

Listen, it wasn't either of you! I didn't *mean* it, I tell you! I was just joking!

Mani joined us on the bed. 'But if you didn't mean it why did you *say* it? It is a very irresponsible comment.' *Yes, it was! It was!* 'As a joke,' sternly, 'it is in very poor taste'. *I agree, I agree!* 'Don't you have any higher ideal than this cheap wit?' *I'm sorry! I'm sorry!* 'Well, you're not especially celebrated for wisdom.'

An old grouse this—that I feel more than I think. Heart ruling head, and not too wisely either.

'She has the artistic temperament,' murmured Meenakshi.

'*Tcha*! I hope it hasn't gone to her head.' That the money hasn't addled it. I know, I know. The cash component of realised ambition causes moral dissipation. And money doesn't buy discernment—it only gives you more choices. Yes. And when people make the wrong choice they squander both money and their life. Yes, yes, yes.

He calmed down. 'You must be careful what you say to these charlies, Kaveri. The media does not understand your brand of humour. And it's notorious for misquoting. As it is, I mean, bad enough that, um-ah.'

He looked at me. They looked at each other. We all looked at each other. He began winding tape into a cassette with a pencil, making painfully slow progress. She began tinkering with her gold bangles, cleaning the filigree with a hairpin. She made no progress. Shadows were gathering in the room. Under the bed, small, invisible activities were taking place to mysteriously transform air to cobwebs and fluff. Outside, the fading light was sending the sparrows scuttling into the trees. Murmuring, 'I didn't realise it's so late,' she got up to switch on the overhead. Its dusty illumination tweaked shapes into objects, deepened the lines on their faces. The comforts of drink–dinner–television were beckoning but we were being detained in this detention room, to do the history homework we had forgotten.

I can't understand, Pa, why people can't take the long view about this.

'What do you mean, *we* take a long view? *You* should have.' (Of course. I got it the wrong way around. This was about *me*, not *them*.) '. . . should've thought what you were doing to your family.'

How strange that nobody thought of that before.

Mani raised his eyebrows. 'Strange?'

I mean, that you should bring it up *now*.

'And when else, if not *now*?'

Years ago. When somebody *in the family* got away with some rather strange behaviour. No, not strange. Shameful. Immoral. Criminal, I would say. And nobody said anything. Did anything.

'You're overreacting, you know.'

I had bumped into a wall.

I don't believe you're saying this, Pa. That you care so little.

'And you care so much you had to do *this*.'

He had manoeuvred me into a corner as he had countless times before. There was a long pause. Enough to fit in three cars and a bus. At last, 'Kaveri,' Meenakshi said weakly. 'Your father and I want the best for you. But,' she dropped a hairpin, bent to pick it up, came up with a bit of fluff. 'This,' she puffed, 'is our *family*'. She looked imploringly at Mani. 'We're an old family. Respected and . . . old. People *still* talk of Thatha.' Her breath juddered. 'He brought the first lavender sapling to India. From France.'

Mani grunted. 'He was a member of the Asiatic Society. And your great-great-grandfather was a Dewan of Mysore. The Maharajah's right hand. The British Resident was his good friend. And . . .'

'I believe he loved dosai! And liked the chutney really hot! (Thus is our family history scripted.) And there was that Mr Murray, who used to come to tea! He painted the cassia tree!'

'A fine painting . . . wonder where it is. And your great-grandfather, I was going to say, Kaveri, was a Civil Servant in the British Government.'

Another chain-hugger. He also serves who stands and waits—especially on white people.

He frowned at this manifest instance of my shallowness.

'Anyway, Kaveri, whatever *you* may feel, in *my* opinion we cannot be dismissed as nobodies.'

While we're about it don't forget we're descended from Balumama too.

He turned on the Stare, my grandmother's Stare, and parenthetically, her father's and *his* father's, and all the great-grandfathers, going on and on like parallel mirrors.

Nobody cares about bloodlines anymore, Pa. Except dog breeders. We're just a bundle of outdated traditions.

There was a doleful sniff from Meenakshi. 'I have no one else but them. I'm an orphan.' And, to my dismay, she began crying. Crying in a frightened, helpless way, face tucked into her shoulder, hiding her tears behind her arm.

Mani and I were aghast. She didn't seem like a wife-and-mother now, or the still-beautiful lady the world admired (with all the privileges it granted to beautiful women as a matter of course) but a tired old woman with dyed hair inside whom still lingered the lonely, motherless bride, so grateful for a readymade fold. That was now threatening to turn into a wolf's lair.

Ma, you have us! Oh! This is too absurd. You aren't an orphan at sixty!

She raised a cross, wet face. 'Once an orphan, always an orphan. What do *you* know?' She honked mournfully, and dabbed her nose with the edge of her sari.

I was pierced with guilt. I had done this to her. I had scratched a line in her softness, the unmarred softness of a woman who has had to take her chances in a man's world, in Mani's world, specifically, but who had miraculously (or because of her ameliorating beauty) escaped the rougher experiences of what this might ordinarily involve. She had handled life's knocks with tact, grace, even humour, to have to deal with this? A knock not from the man's world she has spent a lifetime in surviving, but shockingly, from a woman, and unforgivably, her child. Her face was full of this betrayal.

The traffic had the low and indeterminate howl of a distressed animal. A headlight punctured the curtains, broke a mirror into shards.

So tell me, what do you want me to do now? It's too late for loyalty.

'And the *royalty*!' Mani cracked up. 'Too late to return it!' Gusts of laughter streamed out like bunting. 'You c . . . a . . . n't return the . . . returns!'

Meenakshi touched his knee. He stopped, wiped his eyes, had a minor coughing fit.

A solution. We were still in need of a solution. Laughter and tears notwithstanding. Problems must have solutions—usually found at the back of the book or upside down on a page—but this one was proving elusive. For all her thoroughness Pati had omitted to impart a vital bit of instruction. Or we'd been inattentive.

The bed sheet stretched white and unnegotiable. Meenakshi had tucked me up again so I could just about wiggle my fingers and toes. Having got me in a straitjacket, where they could get at me any time, they could safely withdraw. 'I'm going to bed,' Mani said. 'My eyes are gathering darkness.'

'Sleep well, Kaveri,' Meenakshi murmured. *Don't let anyone mess up your life*, she used to say to me when things went wrong. As if I wasn't the agent of my undoing. It always cut the strings. She said it now but it failed to do the job.

Her orange-black plume waved a cheery goodnight from

the door. His shoulders fell marginally but his step, the heel-first, splayed-toed tread of the elderly, was as firm as ever.

The days were bright as a new-minted coin, and hot and clammy as if clutched too long. Every morning I sluiced myself with scoops of smoke-and-chlorophyll-scented water from the copper boiler and dried my hair in the courtyard, pacing it the while. Thirty feet to the oleander, turn right, twenty feet to the honeysuckle, turn right, thirty feet to the mint tub, turn right, and back to the oleander. I could never have enough of that courtyard. They watched me with fanatic fortitude, my mother from the kitchen window, my father from the dining window across. There was no jollity in us, no joie de vivre. No esprit de corps. They appeared to have their backs to a wall, not rooms, trying to fathom this woman, their daughter-in-absence, now an absent daughter. Fathoming her has never been easy, and now it was near impossible.

He raised his glass—but not in a toast. She raised her ladle—*that* was a toast. To life.

In that seductive quiet I clung to a few objects of sanity. Meenakshi's gold butterfly hairpin perched on her carroty knot—with what unflappable calm! Meenakshi's twiggy ankles holding up her bulk—with what unshakeable faith! And Meenakshi's first letter, written when I was newly married and installed in a one-room Delhi barsati, struggling with a single electric stove in the cupboard kitchen:

> 'My dearest Kaveri, I hope you and Arya are doing well in your new home. Is the saucepan useful? Here Appa and I are doing well. Lilamami and Co and Devimami and Co are doing well too. Saroja and Co are not doing well, but don't worry.'

Midway it veered off like a cross-country runner exploring a side lane. '*Did you watch Sampras thrashing Becker? It was a thrilling match.*' And swerving on a hairpin bend, '*I've thought of a menu for your housewarming party.*' Oh God, Ma! This house needs no warming—we're roasting in it! But the instructions follow—in inexorable detail. '*Lemon rice, vegetable korma, onion sambar, carrot salad, chutney, pickles, and payasam. (For recipes see attached pages.)*' It ended as all Meenakshi's letters, '*With hugs and kisses, Your ever-loving Amma.*' The hyphen conveyed eternity. Ever-loving. Never-ending. Love to the power of infinity.

Arya laughed when I read out the letter. 'Serve the hugs-and-kisses for dinner. At least we wouldn't have to throw *that* out.'

I preserved her love-letter. Preserved too (in their original packing) the two follow-up gifts of love of a porcelain coffee set and a crystal cream jug. Where would I store them even? More hallucinating.

'*Always make coffee with fresh, full-cream milk and equal proportions of freshly ground Robusta and Arabica. Never boil coffee.*' Spoon Nescafe and sugar into mug. Pour boiling water. Add milk. (If it hasn't soured or been finished up by the maid . . . Meenakshi can never grasp how precarious our existence is.)

Dearest, dearest Meenakshi,

I fear for your stability. I fear your ankles will snap one of these days. That your knees will buckle. I can't ask you to eat more, dearest M, because you eat far too much as it is, and it all goes to the wrong places. You're now a balloon on a string, and I'm afraid the string will give way. And then where will we be, Appa and I? For we are holding on to the string. To your ankles.

Declension

The first email came in the afternoon of 28 April. I remember the date clearly because it was the day the newspaper article appeared in *The Times of India*, on the second page, with the nation's news, under an inch-high headline:

Big-time Literature Prize

The National Civic Foundation, a three-year-old establishment for human betterment, has instituted a new annual literary award—the Dharma Ratna—intended to be on par with the National Book Award, the Man Booker, and other prestigious international literary prizes. The Foundation, it may be recalled, also awards the Dharma Ratna to high achievement in public service. This year's beneficiaries were Mr Trilok Singh, MP, for staying the Sindhu Hydel Project, and Mr K.K. Abdul, municipal commissioner, Secunderabad, for his role in slum clearance and rehabilitation. Short-listed for the first Dharma Ratna for literature is A Forgery of Love by first-time novelist Kaveri Chowdhry. Described as a novel upholding the highest Indian literary traditions and at once perspicacious and compassionate, AFL is also a fine example of fiction as a medium for social reform. Through its treatment of a thorny subject . . . etc . . . etc.

I had brought the paper to read with my tea, to the dining table, which is really our worktable—my computer sits on it and Arya's files, and I shell peas here and it's also the place where we keep Fevicol and clothes pegs, car keys and (half-opened) packets of chips. We usually eat straight off the stove, so to speak, or, when we're feeling posh, off a tray on our knees. We are immured in these loose domestic arrangements, Arya and I, not only because we're disorganised as well as inveterate procrastinators but also because our flat turned out to be long on promise and short on delivery. That is, it looked like a playboy's penthouse in the film presentation but the non-virtual version is its junk room. We could be faulted too, for heeding with ill-judged haste the war cry of the 1990s: *Invest in real estate now* and the blandishment *before prices escalate*, and not being strong enough, or smart enough, to resist the malevolent forces that drive this city (Delhi). So for two years now we've been living from instalment to instalment, not so much living as camping, more or less (it always surprised friends we slept in a bed and not in a hammock and that we didn't subsist on Maggi noodles cooked on a Primus stove), postponing such ordinary comforts as specific furniture for specific needs, and acclimatising ourselves to the discomforts of a place built neither for summer nor for winter but the brief in-betweens. We hadn't indented for chilblains and heat rash—those were extras thrown in with the coloured tiles and the chrome.

But the email, the email:

You constantly overwrite your life, said the Guru, and still get it wrong. You believe your troubles will hatch and fly away—although not one has done so yet. Time and again you call upon superstitions to deliver you, and they in turn prod you into foolish mental tradeoffs that serve no purpose other than

> *to offer you succour (meagre, spurious, temporary) when what*
> *you need is faith and surrender. Time and again you have*
> *been told with all the disappointment that can be loaded into*
> *that exasperating voice, the voice of reason, 'This isn't worthy*
> *of you . . .' V*

It was a quotation from my novel. The address was groovyman@viamail.in. Which didn't mean a thing to me. Neither did the signoff *V*. I decided to ignore it.

I couldn't ignore it. It hovered around the whole day like a pesky fly.

The next day there was another email—another quotation.

> *So to cure the blight in your soul, to buy a spurious peace, you*
> *resort to deviousness. Because as the highest—arguably the*
> *lowest—living form, only human beings exercise self-deception*
> *as a means of survival. The survival of the whole, that is, and*
> *not the pieces, for isn't that a special attribute of human*
> *beings too—that the fusing of one wire does not blow out the*
> *others? We must, smiled the Guru, be the only species to be*
> *able to live on with so much of us closed off. V*

Spite mail, I believe it is called. Except there was nothing spiteful here. There was . . . Then it came. In a flash, in an apocalyptic, hot–cold shiver of recognition. I glimpsed the why-and-what. I sat down, holding my head tight to stop the yammering inside.

I spent the day wondering whether or not to tell Arya. He had been so elusive, so remote of late. Almost as if *he* had authored *AFL*, and had a hundred and one exigencies to follow up. He had also turned, well, shy. As if it had compromised him in some way, not me who had peeled my soul for it.

To do him credit he did read my gift of the first copy, traversing ant-like over the difficult terrain, looking up now and again in a puzzled way. You? Us? *This*? Where *did* you do your research? And we had even laughed. Poor Arya! It *was* hard on him. But he tried, was generous even. At first.

With every passing day he'd got increasingly belligerent, even hostile. I read it as impacted humiliation. He, with star billing, had been upstaged by an extra. And when the extra is a woman, who is also his *wife* . . . It is easy to subscribe to the principle of equality in theory, specifically gender equality, but, as most theories, it fails in practice. Charity doesn't begin as much as end in the home. Nine times out of ten.

However, I did tell him about the emails that evening. He did me the courtesy of removing one earphone and suggesting that I should consult Pulin Grover who, he was sure, had contacts in the underworld. (Arya can't stand my publisher.) After that he replaced his earphone and that was that.

Well. Our ten-year-old relationship has not been distinguished by many concessions. Nor has it been altogether marred by the stand-offs. Fairly early we admitted that whatever we had got together for, *this* was not it. *This* was something we had talked ourselves into so we had only ourselves to blame for the duping. We were always at different points on the happiness graph. When he was down, I was up and vice versa. Perhaps his gripes, heaven knows, are more valid than mine. I'm not a restful wife. No solicitous enquiries, or hot cups of tea or cosy chatter. He alleges I take out more from our marriage than I put in—always have my hand in the till, metaphorically speaking. And it irritates me that he was always checking entries and withdrawals like the accountant he is.

Anyhow, having cast our lot—defying the naysayers and doomsayers—and unable to come up with alternatives, we carried on. People choose to believe in each other because it makes them feel safe. They will endure unhappiness if they believe it's a shared human condition—they find solace in being a participating principle of existence. We comforted ourselves with the spurious logic that millions of couples were running this very same three-legged race, and so thinking, hobbled away on our course, balancing on common courtesies and incidental kindnesses. Which is not to say the resentments didn't flare up. If your married life is as duplicitous as this, they do. They *do*. But our overriding grouse was boredom. Tertiary boredom. Arya and I simply *bored* each other.

So then. Did I look *away* from Arya? Did I, that is, seek an alternative relationship outside our sacred union? A non-common law alternative that might, conceivably, subdue a few of my unrests? *Of course* I did. Much of my creative energy was dissipated in dreaming it up. I imagined a face, a voice, a manner, although without specifics. Just that it was a yogic face, a seraphic face that would leave its imprint—nose, eyes and mouth—on a white hotel towel. (White hotel towels feature prominently in my erotic dreams. Perhaps there is a Freudian pointer there.) Attached to the face was a contortionist's body, outstripping my most frenetic longings. I would go limp sometimes, imagining this cosmic energy.

And Arya. Does he look outward too? As to that, I cannot say. He purports to be committed to this union, not in the morally feeble way of women (he says) but with manly honour. It's unmanly to waver, whatever the provocation, and, as he has reminded me many a time, he *has* been provoked. So, among my other uses I'm his trial of strength. Actually I believe he quite enjoys flexing his spiritual muscles at me.

In the main we have hung together because there has been no major imperative to stay apart. Also we've grown lazy. For the first few years we deluded ourselves that we were scripting our Great Romance in a barsati, a room-on-the-terrace, where, had we known, more Great Romances break than are made. Then we moved into this Great Indian Middle-class Dream in a prematurely aging building, one of thirty-two in a mouth of decayed teeth, to live cheek by jowl, head to toe, bum to crotch with our neighbours, and aspiring like them to move easterly and southerly, upwind from the seedy west side of the city. Ours is a two-bedroom flat, one bedroom initialled for the baby that has still not made an appearance. (Perhaps this baby possessed a prescience we didn't.) The room houses, instead, Arya's hysterical mother, who visits every November to cook fish for her son, and my parents, who arrive every January to chase the smells out with incense.

Sometimes I think it is the flat, this joint commitment to the only concrete thing in our lives, which has kept us together. Perhaps we continued to dream of a thrilling finish to our disappointing start, optimistically a surprise climax. Perhaps we were afraid of going it alone in a predatory city that neither of us belonged to, but that threw up enervating daily challenges. My own take is we were victims of the bookends syndrome— each needed the other to hold together the circumstances common (and frustratingly unalterable) to both.

Speaking for myself, the flat was a sign that my adulthood had finally begun. But I often found myself wondering, in the last year especially, if, in thus purchasing independence, I had not instead trapped myself. For one thing there was the loan to repay. And in addition to the lack of space there was the absence of spatial cohesion, the delicate meld of privacy and expanse essential for spiritual wellness. There were the randomly cast rooms measured out like parking slots. The shower stall that bruised your hips. The balcony with the art deco railing that grudged two (small) chairs. Windows with ill-fitting shutters—and far too many of them. (We were spoiled for light—the glare kills us in the summer.) Pretensions galore, low tricks played by developer and realtor in their equivocating sales pitch. They had omitted the main point, which was that this was just a walls-with-a-roof slab, and not a soul's refuge, which is what we craved here, in this city of crude distinctions and runaway excesses. A city in which Arya and I struggled to find meaning—without getting drawn into its crass commercialism, its strident subculture, its frantic endeavours to stay ahead in the game, not by fair means but as foul as its collective deviousness could devise. So far we've avoided the bullying and intimidation, the cringing and whining, the climbing of backs and scratching them, all of which is necessary, indeed imperative for survival here. We've been less successful about not getting disheartened by the mistrust that deprivation fosters, the ugly urgencies brought on by shortages and circumvention—a desperation that jumps queues, ignores decorum and ordinary civility, and pokes and intrudes relentlessly.

As a result we have become two of a tribe of hangers-on, both vulnerable and refractory in our little world, which, because of our passiveness, we have colluded in creating; so sometimes we are the prey, sometimes the predators. Of course our quiescence, our observer standpoint, is a cowardly acceptance of immorality as a way of life—but what is the alternative? Weary waiting, the futility of stasis.

Whatever it was that had kept us together and *here*, I had stuck with my State Bank of India job, year after tedious year, waiting for Arya's dream break. The break was to come in the form of a fabulous client embroiled in a giant income-tax snarl who would arrive in a puff of smoke like a genie. This much I can and do say for Arya: he has faith. The six-mile ride to his airless cubby in Nehru Place, every day but Sunday, is surely a pilgrimage?

That the break should happen to *me*, not him, was something neither of us had foreseen. Nor had I foreseen it was to be a break in every sense of the word. He hadn't voiced it, but I sensed the anger, and the loss. It had broken *him*, my break. I felt badly but what was I to do?

That evening I again broached the subject of the emails to Arya. In that moment the phone rang. I jumped, but it was for him. When he returned he was muttering son-of-a-bitch, son-of-a-*bitch*.

Arya, about these emails.

'Not now, Kaveri, *please*. I have other things to worry about besides the shenanigans of your shady associates.'

He wasn't going to give me a hearing then. Serious, sympathetic or helpful.

Well. This non-participation was perfectly in keeping with the rancour of this period. Still, it was hard to accept in full and final resolution, that there was no future mapped on his face. Once its sparseness had, God forgive my girlish fancies, led me to believe he was an aesthete. It had *moved* me. But now it seems that the wide brow was not a mark of intellect but vacuity. It has gone on too long, the non-ness of Arya.

In the morning we still hadn't got round to discussing the emails. I stayed clear of the computer and prowled about the house. Waiting, watching, listening. *Brooding*. It's too much, I thought, as I broke an egg into the pan. It's too little. He doesn't care. The egg curled up at the edges but stayed stubbornly phlegmy in the middle, and I jabbed it. The yolk broke and stuck to the pan. Damn.

Arya walked in, spotted the egg, turned glum. I had a bout of remorse. The egg was so snotty, so yellow. Perhaps *I* was the cause of Arya's inconsequence. I had shrunk him with, among other things, this unspeakable breakfast. It's not fair, it's not decent, and, oh Arya, I said sorrowfully. I am *so* . . .

But he was scraping the egg into the sink, pouring the gritty coffee to flush it down the drain hole. Then he left, banging the door behind him. Damn, damn.

When I couldn't bear it any longer, I accessed my email. There was this:

Man believes in the truth of belief. He will believe in anything that is seen to be believed. All that's needed is a critical mass of belief. That is what tyrants depend upon. The provenance of tyranny is truth, not the truth but a truth—a single twisted fact. V

And another:

The Guru scoffed at citing the valency of good and evil in the meting out of divine reward and retribution. Irrational as faith in such a process is, he said, it was even more absurd to confer divinity on a force that arbitrates men's affairs like a lower court magistrate. There is no eternal damnation or salvation, he said. Only earthly forgiveness.

After a long while I called my friend Gita, who's an English professor at Miranda House. Gita, I've had a couple of anonymous emails. Really? What sort? Abusive? Indecent? No, no, nothing like that. Just some . . . stuff quoted from the novel. Which bits? Anything controversial or offensive? Do they mean anything to you?

All at once I was unequal to her curiosity. It's probably some prank, Gita. *But you sounded panicked* . . . Did I, really? Must be the egg I ate for breakfast. It's hatching or something.

I tried to laugh but began coughing. *Kaveri, are you alright?* Yes, thanks, Gita. Just a bit out of sorts. Sorry I bothered you . . . meet me for lunch on Friday?

The sink smelled appalling. Holding my breath I turned on the tap and dialled my second number of the day. Caught unawares when it was answered on the first ring, I gasped. Pulin? *What? Who?* It's me, I wheezed. *My dear, my dear. Is anything the matter?* At which I felt unequal to *his* curiosity too. Nothing, Pulin. Just . . . how's it going? *How is what going?* Oh, everything. The book sales, plans for the book tour, all that. *Oh, fine, fine.* Off he went on a happy tangent. Then, predictably, *so my dear, when do I see you?* What? Oh any time, Pulin, you know where to find me. *By the way, there's mail for you. Quite a few letters, in fact. I'll send them across* . . . No, don't! *I beg your pardon?* Yes, of course send them, Pulin. Thanks.

We wound up making a needless lunch date—for Friday again, I realised after he rang off. I replaced the receiver, thinking it was strange how everyday words could suddenly take on a fearful significance. Anonymous. Transcript. Life-support. Morbid interest. Eventuality.

What next?

What I did next was crazy, even for me. After a whole day spent in fruitless pondering, I printed out the letters, shoved them in my bag, hailed an autorickshaw, and gave the driver an address about which I had no clue. That is, the address (from the visiting card in Arya's card index) was right but I hadn't a clue if this was where I should go. Before I could change my mind we were bumping along, at a pace that scrambled reason and prudence.

After nearly an hour of racketing through Delhi's traffic, across flyovers and under bridges, past yellow government housing endorsing socialism and tall glass boxes promoting capitalism, past browning greens and greening browns, we entered Defence Colony, a tony suburb in the south of Delhi. No. 43, Block C, was one of several similar houses that lined a shady street. Like its neighbours it was a plain cream two-storeyed cube that covered its narrow plot, with french windows giving to a scraggly pocket lawn, an ornamental wrought-iron gate, a short driveway to the garage, and a side entrance for the ground and upper floor flats.

Feeling as if I was at the start of something, something that was pointing me in a direction—perhaps even prodding me towards my destiny, I rang the doorbell to the ground floor flat.

He opened the door himself. 'What a, um, pleasant surprise!' He *looked* pleasantly surprised too. Stepping aside for me to enter, 'Is Arya parking the car?' he asked.

I've come alone, actually.

For a moment he blanked out. He recovered quickly and shut the door behind us.

We sat on two armchairs in the living room—an airless place that looked as if it was dusted each day and locked up for the night. The curtains were inadequately drawn against the evening sun. The furniture, which was symmetrically arranged around a square of carpet, could have been a floor display in a shop—it gave the impression of plastic wraps just whipped off to clinch the sale. The illumination from the ceiling light, needlessly switched on, was dim but not cosy. It was a room for conducting an interrogation rather than a conversation.

He was looking at me with polite inquiry. 'Tea? Coffee? Something cold?'

Nothing, thanks . . . well, tea perhaps. Tea, please. Tea's fine. Thanks. That is, if it isn't trouble or anything. I didn't mean to barge in but . . . (But what? What did I mean?) I'm sorry, I hope you aren't busy or anything . . . I just needed to talk to someone, and I thought perhaps, I thought possibly, I thought of *you*.

He nodded. Feeling a bit foolish I blundered on. You see, I tried talking to Arya, and he wasn't helpful. He wouldn't, um, cooperate. And I wanted to talk. To someone. You see, I think I may have a . . . problem.

He was very still and very, well, *there*. His wide chest looked safe, dependable, resourceful. Like a bank vault. One could take shelter in those hands too. I took out the printouts and gave them to him.

I got these—yesterday and today. By email. Anonymous—I don't know anyone whose name begins with a V.

He read them quickly. 'What are these lines?'

They're from my novel.

He rubbed his chin. 'Oh. Ah. Anonymous, eh?'

Yes. Squalid.

'Puzzling, actually. Perhaps it's just a stunt by an, um, appreciative reader. Who especially liked these lines.'

There was an anticipatory silence, as if there was a third presence in the room that I had brought with me, and, if I minded my manners, should introduce to my host.

My host was Arya's Client. This is how I always thought of him, initially because I couldn't be bothered with any details of a person whose provenance was Arya's profession, and later to mitigate my guilt about a relationship that was (for me) overcast with disrepute—an inevitability if you are brought up, as I am, to believe the institution of marriage is respectable even if not sacrosanct. So Arya's Client was who he was and who he would continue to be even when he ceased being Arya's client, and when, as seemed imminent, Arya ceased to be Arya—for me. He had first visited us a month ago, showing up one evening, without notice, in the middle of an argument, which I was set to win. To drop in his bank statement. Or tax returns. Some paper or other. Hadn't he heard of the post? Courier service?

It was obvious he liked Arya. People generally do. Arya is non-threatening in addition to the other nons. Adept at reductive logic too, which is comforting, especially when you are dealing with large figures. Becalmed clients stayed with him long enough to find out that over-simplification has a price to pay. A cumulative price that no logic or reworking can reduce. Then they fled, often without clearing their bill—I think they felt justified—leaving Arya to make desperate phone calls like the yap-yap of a puppy snapping at booted heels.

Well, this man spent the entire evening with us, drinking rum-and-coke with the concentration of a superannuated clerk at a freebie. *And* he stayed on to dinner, helping himself liberally to the egg bhujia and rice-and-vegetable curry. Arya encouraged him, interjecting sly remarks such as, 'We enjoy these impromptu evenings, right, Kaveri?'

I gathered from that evening that 1) he lived alone, a bachelor, 2) he was a research scientist—working on something that wasn't the stuff of dinnertime conversation apparently and 3) he was one of Arya's few clients who actually paid him. And Arya told me he didn't have air-conditioning in his car. On principle. That impressed me.

What also stayed with me was his person. He was tall and

big—possibly a size 13 in shoes and, who knows, in gloves as well, because his fore, middle and ring fingers had four phalanges. His features were prominent and irregular—a fleshy nose with a dent, a strong jaw, a knobbly forehead, a smile that revealed large, cared-for teeth, and hair that sprang out like a tangle of broken guitar strings. His eyes, behind black-framed glasses, were attentive but without the sticky familiarity, the tiresome up-down-turnaround speculation that characterises male interest in this part of the world. He seemed prone to spells of stillness—as if he was reigning in energy that might, because of his size, cause havoc. Perhaps he was suppressing wayward impulses. Perhaps he was balancing an equation. Perhaps he simply and completely lived in the present.

He had come again, this high-minded giant, to take us to a restaurant in Nizamuddin, a little-known but obviously distinctive eatery. We left him to do the ordering, and he made a careful choice of steamed seaweed with oyster sauce, glass noodles with shitake, broccoli with roasted sesame, red snapper with chestnut . . .

Halfway through this feast we both looked up. He raised his beer glass. 'To happiness. From unexpected quarters.' We held eyes for a long moment, oblivious of Arya, who was paying court to the red snapper. All at once we laughed—caught in a private joke that carried a significance beyond the present and outside this room, and that excluded Arya as if it were *he* who had brought about my ill humour that other evening, the possible cause of our present mirth, and *he* the spoilsport who might blight our future fun. After that he, Arya, grew progressively morose. It would seem that in displaying a taste for self-mockery to charm this stranger, a side of myself I denied him, my husband, I was devaluing him.

And when Arya thinks he's being devalued he feels unmanned. Locked out of our electrified field, suspicious and suspenseful, he sulked for the rest of the evening.

Something extraordinary happened that evening. My life, I thought, in a daze of euphoria, was changing in ways I couldn't guess at as yet but would be revealed soon. And—this was my certainty—this man would have something to do with it. A lot to do with it. I imagined something of the sort was happening to him too, for he looked at me as if willing me to see it. And share it.

It was that serendipitous moment I presumed upon in coming here today.

The tea arrived, brought by a manservant. On a painted tin tray were two thick china mugs, an earthen sugar pot, a glass plate of water biscuits and a small glass bowl of dark jam. The tea was the colour of amber and smelled of wet leaves burning. And autumnal mist and drying peat. If longing had a scent this would be it.

We drew our chairs up to the tea tray as if it were a fire, warming our fingers on the mugs. He spooned the sugar in (How many spoons?), spread the jam on a couple of biscuits (Do you like jam?), proffered the plate. The jam was delicious, nothing I'd ever tasted. Dried apricot or perhaps it was fig. And ginger, lemon peel and nutmeg.

'How can I help you? Has Arya seen the letters?'

He didn't want to.

'Ignore them.' He folded the printouts, handed them back. 'So you drew a blank with Arya.'

Didn't you?

He laughed. 'When I first met you, I thought you were

impulsive.' He looked thoughtful. 'Are these quotes critical to the story?'

The table was stained with overlapping white circles—old markings of wet glasses. He set his mug on one—and I on another. It was the start of a game. His Knight to Bk2 and my Bishop to Wh3.

'I haven't read your book. Since Arya has, perhaps *he* could . . .'

Look, can we keep him out of this?

'Sure.' He smiled easily. 'You need someone who's read your book—knows it well.'

Like the critics—they know it better than I do.

He missed, or chose to bypass the irony. 'So you heed the critics.' His smile was condescending.

I wanted to get up and leave then. But I gritted my teeth and hung on.

'Perhaps you should just go to the police.'

No! I mean, it's not life-threatening. And I don't want the publicity.

'Isn't it a bit late to worry about that?' Despite the smoking leaves and misty autumn the room began closing in on me. The air-conditioner gave a groan, stopped briefly, whirred again. 'So. Not Arya, not the police, not anyone who knows the book.' He shook his head in a puzzled way. *Why me?*

I couldn't think of anyone else. Oh, I'm sorry! I didn't mean to be rude! You see, I have nobody, nobody I can trust.

'That seems to me a worse predicament than the letters,' he said gravely.

That's when I did the second inexplicable thing of the day. I began crying. Crying properly, not the glycerine simulation of soap heroines. Crying in gushes of gob and saltine streams—

emotional slop that is, historically and histrionically, a woman's last resort. It was humiliating. And of course it altered the mood in the room.

'It's alright,' he muttered, fidgeting. 'You don't have to explain anything if you don't want to.'

But I do want to! I came only because I want to. You see, you have . . . a face one can talk to.

He laughed. 'Let me get fresh tea and then you can talk to it.' He got up, unfolded himself, that is, leaving me to wipe the slime from nose and cheek.

He returned with the tea and once more we went through the pouring-spooning-stirring routine. Then, 'Suppose you begin at the beginning?' he said. Leaning back, tea mug to chest, he fixed his gaze on me as if it was the most fascinating thing in the world to watch someone scald their lips.

The book launch had been an event—well publicised by Phalanx Publishing, generously sponsored and supported by the Indian Council of Cultural Relations, gratifyingly well attended by Delhi's culture-seekers. The venue was the boxed-in sculpture court of the British Council. The time was evening. The setting sun had stained the pink sandstone walls crimson, deepened the red of the lilies to burgundy, augmented the green of the lawn to the intensity of chemical spill. Taped Vedic chants heightened the mystique of the East.

The air grew torpid with laughter and wine. Hyperbole rose with the smoke—up, up and up. The head of the British Council put an arm around her and informed her she was a lovely woman. The director of the Indian Council of Cultural Relations said, 'Nothing significant that happens in the country passes us by, you know!' And loped off to fetch significant people to meet her, who, obliged to buy *AFL*, stood twisting it in their hands as if it were a greasy hat. The mayor of Delhi—normally a woman of restraint—heaped such fulsome praise on *AFL* it stretched the limits of credibility since, clearly, she had not read it, but nobody minded since it was such a civil occasion with everyone dressed up and being gracious. Pulin Grover spoke for twice his allotted time (in an accent that had been manufactured in a Ludhiana factory and vended in an American supermarket), wooing potential customers with fine words and cheap wine, and not enough wine at that, which was a mistake, Kaveri thought, because that must reflect on the contents of the book, and surely a book launch should have more wine than books to ensure its success? She was about to tell the barman to stop hiding the bottles under the counter when she heard Pulin announce, '. . . ladies and gentlemen, let us give Kaveri the clap!' Fortunately, nobody caught on that he had just urged them to give her the disease of the kings, except the British Council head and Chris—the UK publisher's representative—who clutched each other and laughed for a full five minutes.

Still, the signing queue was flatteringly steady—even if it hadn't snaked into the street. But these weren't readers, these were autograph-hunters! Her heart skipped a beat for Mani and Meenakshi. *They* had read *AFL*. They had memorised it. They would have returned again and again for her signature, till she had covered every single page. It was dedicated to them, of course. *To M&M, whose criminal indulgence of me made this book possible.* But they had been downed by the flu a few days before the event, and were stuck in Bangalore, chafing in body and spirit.

Arya, who was present, was chafing too. He was burning in fact, his self-immolation palpable. In his eye, curved like a scythe (to cut her down), she glimpsed the end of the beginning. An end and a beginning. There is a price to pay for everything and for once this was not going to break the bank. Whatever else it broke.

Reporters, reviewers, readers. Scepticism, cynicism, sarcasm. A hundred and one questions. What was its central idea? Love and Loss? Suffering and Survival? A Voyage of Self-Discovery? A Rite of Passage? How would *she* describe it? In a sentence? In a word? In a *syllable*, then? Give us a lead. Throw us a line. Chuck us a crumb, *come on!*

At last, 'Rape,' she answered hollowly. 'Incest. Suicide.'

'*Now* you're talking. Is it a slice-of-life? A, um-ah, first-hand experience? Could we sit and discuss it?'

That was the beginning. She didn't want to talk about her novel.

Then spotting Chris, and Claire—the American publisher's representative—she excused herself and hurried over to them. They were listening to the inaccurate explications of India supplied by Pulin Grover. Chris from London was asking for a guide to explore the Civil Lines where his forbears had fought in the Sepoy Mutiny, and Claire from New York was asking for directions to a Vipassana ashram to replenish her spiritual reserves. And Pulin Grover (from Delhi) was masterfully diverting them to a 'wonderful restaurant that serves the best Ethiopian food in town!'

Kaveri could have told them it was the *only* restaurant serving Ethiopian food, take it or leave it; that Pulin Grover had no cultural affiliations, so everything foreign was 'wonderful'; but she and Chris-and-Claire weren't on gossiping terms yet. She could have also told them that although he appeared to be an irresistible force they could easily neutralise him by asking him his golf handicap—except that would have been ungrateful because, really, it was because of him that *AFL* was going to be read by snipers behind sandbags, refugees in tents, lifers in prison . . . So he should have his day. Although, in her opinion, he was having far too many days these days. 'Have you eaten Chicken Wat?' he asked Claire.

'I'm vegan,' Claire replied. She shut her eyes and began to count her beads. Rude thing, Kaveri thought. On the other hand Pulin Grover would drive anyone to counting beads.

'So Ka-ve-ri,' Chris cranked up his eyebrows. 'Another book by a beautiful Indian woman?'

Claire opened her eyes. 'Another beautiful book by an Indian woman,' she said, firmly establishing the rules of their relationship.

They were full of plans. Book tours. Meet people, you know? And do serious readings in serious places. London, New York, Washington DC, Sydney, Toronto . . . 'Next week?' asked Chris, fingers on cellphone.

That brought on a second reluctance. 'I haven't asked my bank for leave,' she said cautiously.

They looked a bit startled at this allusion to a life outside the book. Claire counted three beads. 'The week after, then?'

She was gripped by a cold panic. 'Let me think about it.'

'What's the matter, girl?' Claire said. 'Don't you want to go?'

'Not much.'

'Very laudable,' murmured Chris.

'I mean it's too soon.'

'It's not a day too soon,' declared Claire.

'I would imagine it's never too soon to get away from Delhi,' murmured Chris.

'For some of us Delhi is home, Chris,' said Pulin Grover huffily, 'We can't all live in Kensington, you know.'

Sorry, muttered Chris. Claire's retroussé American nose turned pink. 'You have obligations, Kaveri. There is,' she said with an un-Buddha scowl, 'a lot of money involved, after all'.

'I know! You don't have to remind me! But I *can't*!'

Claire missed a bead. Chris switched off his cellphone. Pulin Grover had a small choking fit.

Kaveri climbed down. 'I'm drained,' she whimpered, fingers to forehead. And, despising herself, 'I'm so *tired*.'

Chris and Claire decided she was on the verge of a breakdown. They were very understanding. Nervous breakdowns they were familiar with, reluctances they were not. Chris told her to take a stress pill. Claire advised a spiritual workout. 'You'll learn to breathe, *seriously* breathe, and life is all about breathing, isn't it?'

Pulin Grover swallowed his anger. 'Take up a *cause*, my dear. AIDS or child abuse or something. You'll feel better. More positive about life.' His eyes narrowed. 'Perhaps global warming. Too many people are in this AIDS business.'

Chris intervened. 'Let Kaveri tell us when it's convenient for her.'

When pressed for a commitment the reluctance returned, like a small tidal wave.

'Reluctance.' He turned the mug in his hand, considering its possibilities. *'Reluctance.'* He looked up, shrugged. 'Nerves.' He smiled roguishly. 'Or a bad conscience.'

The room was simply not one by which you could make out anything about its owner. There were no books or personal touches—it was wiped clean of fingerprints, so to speak. The ancient hi-fi system appeared to be there only to provide a resting place for a black Buddha head. On one wall there was a clock with gold lettering, which had stopped at 2.30, am or pm. The curtains (red poppies on a blue background) and the upholstery (porridge with black specks) reminded me of the state government guesthouses where Mani used to take us for cheap holidays. The yellowy polish on the wood invoked travelling salesmen drowning their anxieties in rum, and scoffing biryani in newspaper wrapping.

I'm sure my father would say a bad conscience is a tool to realise your potential.

'And you'd have heeded him.'

Pulin Grover on the other hand believes a conscience per se is a party-pooper. He told me to get rid of mine.

'You'll be much happier without it, believe me! Just live freely! *Abund*antly! Get a decent car to start with! Get an *image*! Stop going around like a hippie housewife!' Bending over as if to steady himself he took a quick peek into her blouse. 'Come on, think big! Think *global*, yar! A bed-sitter in Bayswater, how about that! You could borrow cups of sugar from Vikram Seth!' He laughed hugely at his joke, which was not his joke but Chris's. 'I will show you how to spend!' Before she could protest he dragged her off for her first lesson—to a revolving rooftop restaurant. '*Beer?*' he shrieked. '*Beer?*' As if she'd asked for a hemlock julep. 'You can't drink beer! You deserve wine! A . . . a Puilly Fuisse!' He jerked his head imperiously at the waiter. The waiter murmured. Pulin Grover frowned. 'No? A Nuit St George then!' The waiter bowed his head and fussed evasively with the water glasses. Pulin Grover flung his napkin down. 'What sort of establishment is this? Don't you have *any* French wine?'

Indeed they did, said the waiter, offended. She watched the elaborate uncorking-pouring-and-tasting ritual—Pulin Grover peering into his glass to read his fortune there—amusing herself at the continued antics of her host during the meal (so emphatically French there wasn't enough of it) and the play of light on the faux waterfall. To his disappointment she wouldn't—couldn't—rise to the occasion. At last, taking pity on him, she ventured the hope *AFL* would live up to the wine and the food.

'Of course it will, my dear!' he said. He sipped, threw his head back, swilled as if it were mouthwash. Then, lowering his head, his eyes scrabbling at the neckline of her blouse, he touched his glass to hers. (It clicked like Pati's false teeth and she could hear Devimami snort, '*Moulded* not cut!') 'To the book!' Click. 'To money!' Click. 'To you and me!' The horror peaked.

He laughed. 'So was the guilt about making money or not spending it?' A tiny line dented his forehead. 'Somehow it doesn't fit in. Guilt, I mean. Whatever I know of you.'

The room rebuffed any attempt to relax. The chair was knifing my back. The curtains let in sharp slivers of light but skimped on privacy. The gunmetal ashtray on the coffee table looked as if there would be a light patch under it, like grass that's never seen sunlight.

He was leaning back, legs stretched out and hands behind his head. 'Nerves,' he said, after a while.

Ingratitude, is what my father would have said.

'And you would have agreed with him of course.'

Naturally. He's older than I. That isn't a circumstance that's going to change.

He laughed. The telephone rang somewhere in the recesses of the house and presently there was a knock on the door. 'Excuse me,' he murmured and went inside.

When Mani flashes on the screen, could his helpmeet, his queenly consort be far behind? Lo and behold, there she was, exactly seven steps behind (oh Hindu wife!), in all the glory of her tawny feathers. On the sunlit plumage hope rose. *We are there for you, Kaveri. Always, always. Just think of us* . . . Swiftly the hope faded. The screen blanked out. Why don't you appear, my faithful genies? Where is your nagging omniscience? *Why don't you come to us, Kaveri?*

I didn't want to go to them. I couldn't face their complacence, much less share it. (*That* is ingratitude!) In fact they had asked if they could visit me in this thrilling time but I had said, I think you'll be bored here just now, Ma.

To which Meenakshi replied, a little sadly, 'You mean *you'll* be bored with *us*, Kaveri.'

And I didn't have anything to say to that. Because I didn't want them to come. Didn't want Meenakshi thanking goodness over and over, didn't want Mani vetting the manuscript as he'd offered to, especially as he dismissed novels as opiates that dulled the senses, and a form of entertainment on par with circuses. Except Dickens. And Shakespeare had written some fine stories too. Once, he called just to quote the great man: *'But when I tell him he hates flatterers, he says he does, being the most flattered.'*

But Mani was a thousand miles away and the flatterers were crowding my door.

At last, they wrote. At last no circumlocutions and perambulations, no allusions, alliteration or catchy cadences. At last a narrative style unhampered by tiresome rhetoric and arcane references. At last a story with immediacy and prophecy. That addresses the two questions weary readers are increasingly asking: So what? Then what?

AFL, they wrote, is a seminal disquisition on the dissonance and harmony of a civilisation more ancient than Greece. At once portentous and provocative, it is cast in fabulist mode with realistic underpinnings of ancient Hindu caste divisions as ballast. Its noetic peregrinations explore the theatre of the absurd, but without the mindless capers of slapstick comedy— *AFL* is nothing if not noble and exacting. In its reflective if epigrammatic style, written with a pen dipped in ichor, it has the evocative economy of a Mondrian and the wit of a Dali.

And in one strange review: *AFL* is a moving spirit that will haunt itself.

Of such flights of imagination are myths created. The danger is when you begin to believe in the myth of *yourself*. And become blinded by your belief.

But I had banished Meenakshi from my door, and invited the idolaters in.

The door opened. He shut it behind him, sat down, lifted his shoulders in a movement that appropriated a shrug. 'I don't know how to help you, Kaveri. Because I don't know what to make of this. What you want me to make of it, that is.'

I began collecting my bag. But he stayed me with his hand. It felt good, his hand on mine. It felt very good.

'There's more, I think,' he said quietly.

He was wearing finely corded cotton corduroy pants and a white cotton shirt with the sleeves folded up to his elbow. The shirt was very white, very creased. His leather sandals were worn but of good quality. He looked like someone who cared for his person but not lavishly. Not slavishly.

The air-conditioner coughed discreetly to remind me this was an interrogation, and I was there to tell, not hide. My lips must have moved for he leaned forward, frowning. 'What's that? A *basin*, did you say?'

The party at Gita's flat in Gulmohur Park was the kind of Delhi entertainment that begins long after normal people go to bed and goes on till everybody is too drunk to eat, and after that too drunk to go home. Just before midnight a late guest arrived. He looked familiar, or at least a type. Beard, sandals, kurta and the brash confidence of one who will be welcomed— even if he's three hours late. Gita, who was the kind of hostess that never stayed longer with her guests than it took to ask if they needed a refill or tried her garlic dip, dragged him across to Kaveri but forgot to introduce him so *Bhasin* was all Kaveri caught when, with a mock bow, he said, 'Bhasin's the name . . .' The rest of his words wound up in a spool of music and Gita was exclaiming in her hectic party voice, 'He's the *most*

widely read man I know!' As though the magic words would open vistas for Kaveri in the cramped room.

'I read your novel is what she means,' smiled the scholar, lifting a glass off a passing tray.

'Try my garlic dip!' Gita flung over her shoulder as she churned off.

He was, it transpired, a literary historian. 'I like to think of myself as a champion of a lost civilisation, but *you* represent a civilisation recently excavated. Tell me something.' He combed his beard with his fingers. 'So much of today's fiction seems to me a slick packaging of superficially assimilated facts. Unsound premises. Without any meaningful mediation of truth.' He frowned at his drink as if he'd spotted an insect floating in it. 'There's an *absence*. Of what I call the four Ps. Point of view, philosophy, plausibility and plot.' He tossed off his drink, grimacing as if he had swallowed the insect. 'There's too much *din*. Well, it seems to succeed. The noise gives it credence. What do you think?'

'I don't,' she said shortly.

'Don't take it personally!' His laugh fluttered the petals in the vase, and a few people looked at them curiously. 'Tell me instead what you think of stream of *conscience* as a genre.'

There was a sudden quiet in the room, as if everyone had wound down simultaneously. Gita was stranded in a corner, casting about her as if wondering how and where to restart her party. Kaveri took a step towards her in the same instant she gave a little cry and swooped on a timid-looking woman clutching a glass to her chest. Meanwhile the bearded one whipped around to face Kaveri, giving her no room to manoeuvre. 'I've made you cross!' he cried.

'You've made me hungry, actually.' She edged past him to

the dining table where a basket of bread had been kept as emergency rations. But he followed her, so they were caught in a bizarre circling of the dining table.

Cornering her, 'I wasn't attacking your novel, you know,' he said. 'Just asking for your um, considered, opinion.' ('I don't have one,' she muttered.) He picked up a roll, examined it, and threw it back into the basket. That annoyed her. She chose one that wasn't touching it, and moved away. But he followed her again. 'Let's change the subject,' he said in a placatory tone. 'Do you believe in the power of the subconscious?'

'I'm not superstitious.'

'I meant as a centre of influence. The past as a stratification for the present.' His eyes narrowed. 'Because it's funny you know, but there was something in your novel that woke *my* subconscious.'

The bread worked into rubber in her mouth. 'That's not so remarkable,' she said thickly. 'The subconscious goes back several lifetimes, I believe. Any run-of-the mill mystic will tell you that.'

'Perhaps I'll get it by and by. Meeting you here like this must be a sign.' He flashed his teeth. 'Don't look so alarmed! Perhaps it just means our paths will cross again.' And still grinning, 'You must have been a gifted liar when you were a kid. Now don't get prickly! I only meant childhood liars make good novelists.'

'I should think they make unreliable witnesses.'

This time she laughed with him.

He hadn't moved a muscle during my (bowdlerised) recital. Now he shook his head. 'I haven't got the point of the discussion. Is it the bit about the subconscious?'

The sofa legs were ebony ovals tipped with purple rubber—exactly like the paps of tribal women. I wondered idly if he was aware of this, and if some day I would point it out to him. I picked the last biscuit off the plate—just for the jam. It had gone soggy and tasted like a stale teacake.

The silence lay between us, a game bag oozing something sinister.

It's not important. Nothing substantial. Nothing . . . critical.

'I wish I could make up my mind about whether you're enigmatic or just evasive.'

Oh, enigmatic will do fine.

But my heart was not in the backchat.

'Do the quotes wake *your* subconscious in any way?'

Look, let's just drop it.

His face changed.

I'm sorry. That was unfair. I'm *sorry*. Perhaps I should leave.

'Look, Kaveri. *I'm* not the one who's got bothersome emails.'

Rubbing the grit from my eyes, I sat down again. Through the chinks in the curtains I saw that night had crept up upon us. Gate lights had come on in the house on the other side of the street, yellow globules with the house number on them.

I had overstayed my welcome. The visit had disintegrated into one of those tedious affairs that no one will terminate because that would deny it purpose, imply we suffered from a paucity of ideas. We were straining to give the dribbling minutes shape and coherence, pretending (without mentioning it) that it was the letters (flickering at the edge of our consciousness) holding us to our chairs when really it was unwillingness to consign the past hour into limbo, and ourselves too, as if people would drop dead if they ran out of speech.

He asked if I would like a drink—wine, vodka, a beer . . .? But I guessed it wouldn't lighten the mood. Besides, I was awash with tea. Besides, we'd used up all the air in the room. Besides, it might push me into confidences that I at least would regret because already questions doubting my sanity were crowding my head, and two of them would nag me, I knew, in days to come. Did I talk too much? What was he thinking of me? There was a third, too, the answer for which depended on the answers to the first two. *Would I see him again?*

When at last I mooted going home, he was hard put to hide his relief. Straightaway he offered to run me home in his car. Of course, that didn't improve my spirits.

Jai Hind Colony, where Arya and I live, is indistinguishable from hundreds of look-alikes classified as MIG (Middle Income Group) housing built by the DDA (Delhi Development Authority). This one's boast is its size. It's like a huge slab of diced cheese, the cubes separated by streets that skirted the minimum requirements for light and air. All the dreariness of urban middle-classdom is represented in it. The newly discovered recourse to bright colours to cover design deficiencies. Staircases that bridged levels but not social gaps. Badly hung doors leaking gossip during the day and light in the night.

Looking up as we crossed the parking lot I spotted Arya on our balcony. Watching us. To my dismay I immediately began to feel—and act—surreptitious. Surprisingly, so did my companion. I walked as if my neck was held in a vice and the rest of me was cast in cement. He walked as if his spine was braced with steel rods.

Without any preliminaries Arya offered his unexpected guest a drink. Politely, it was refused. I sensed a frisson in the room, a shift of gears. Then, wordlessly, Arya picked up his glass, marched to the bedroom—and shut the door.

We sat on the sofa that once supported Arya's and my frenetic exertions but now sags sadly with the memories.

He looked around the room, which we've treated as a box, filling it right up to the top. A patchwork quilt canopy hangs over the sofa. Stuffed parakeets swing on a trapeze hooked to the fan. A palm supplicates the ceiling in the corner. 'It has, um, personality,' he volunteered doubtfully.

We like it here, I said, obliged to defend it. One can live life first-hand. Second-hand, that is. The big advantage is nobody bothers us here. We're not in films, and our neighbours aren't interested in any other, um, art form.

'You could always move,' he said, glancing at a windowpane from which the putty had worked loose. The dirt held it fast but he couldn't know that.

Not all of us can afford Defence Colony. (That was uncalled for!) Nor, perhaps, do they like it. (Sour grapes, my dear!) They just might be happy where they are. (What was I thinking!)

'*You* don't sound happy.'

And you sound like my mother.

This was bad. But, perversely, I went on. Bungled on. You're like my mother too. She used to prod me all over when I fell down, to find out exactly where and how much I hurt. She made it worse.

This was very bad. 'You know,' he said mildly, 'I'm getting just a little bit tired of your family.'

Of course that terminated the evening, which, although I despaired would go on and on, I didn't want to end. I walked him to the door silently screaming, *don't go!* Don't, *please* don't go!

On the landing I tried explaining.

It's not jealousy, you know. It's just that he can't bear exclusion.

He nodded. 'Will you be alright?'

I didn't ask whether he referred to the letters, now receding into the night, or the invisible Arya who was advancing swiftly.

Yes, thanks. And I'm sorry for intruding on your evening.

He looked a little startled. 'I don't have *evenings.*'

Then he was gone, leaving a large hole behind. I stood for a bit, the doorknob in my hand.

In the bedroom a snoring Arya and an empty glass were classically deposed, the one on the bed, the other under it. In the living room the parakeets continued to swing gently in the mock breeze.

Next morning, accessing my email before I set off for work, I found another note.

> *I trust you have got the message by now. Or do you want me to spell it out?* V

That night I once again appealed to Arya. Before I even unfolded the printouts he held up his hand. 'No. I don't want to hear about it.'

The next few days he took off early on his journey to his

cubbyhole, before I left for my bank, and returned after I was in bed. A few nights I stayed up for him, but he offered neither apology nor explanation. When I questioned him he said he was 'catching up with things'.

Why is Arya forever *catching up* to move forward? Life always seems a jump ahead of him. When he chases an opportunity it usually turns out to be just a hope, swiftly replaced by hopelessness. Arya is seized with fits of hopelessness as people are with fever. He *shivers* with hopelessness. He gropes around in his darkness looking for hope or a bottle of rum—which for him is the same thing. Then his clients get restive, his peon insolent, and everyone else predatory.

As for me, I just want to flee.

The next couple of days I lived on a knife's edge. From time to time I considered asking Arya to help me choose a new car, look for another house for us—only to pull up short. This was the future I wasn't, suddenly, sure of. There was so much I wasn't sure of.

One evening I couldn't find the TV remote. When at last I did—behind the stove where neither of us could have 'misplaced it'—it was too late for my programme.

Arya returned late as usual. I barred the door to the bedroom.

Arya. It's not working.

'What isn't?'

Us. Our marriage.

'Oh?' He lifted his head. 'Since when?'

Since a long time. Since years.

'I don't buy that. We were quite happy till . . . that *book*,' he spat out, and then the coward hurried off to the stereo.

I haven't been happy for a long time! Do you hear? Not for years and years! (Cruel *and* mendacious but war had been declared.) It's time we faced up to things, Arya!

Fiddling with the knobs he muttered, 'Faced up to what?'

I sighed. This was going to be uphill.

Look Arya. There are *lots* of perfectly intelligent couples who've split amicably. Just shaken hands and gone their separate ways.

He spun around. 'Where? *Where* are these intelligent, *amicable* couples? I don't know any.'

Secretly, I agreed with him.

But, they are there, I said firmly.

'Only in books.'

Secretly, I agreed with this too.

Perhaps, Arya (look at the silver lining Arya, the other side of midnight, come on!), we'll be exceptions. *We'll* make sensible divorcees.

He went back to fiddling with the knobs. The stereo coughed up some rock music. He shouted over it, 'You've never been sensible about *any*thing!'

Try me on this. Look. We don't have to stick together because of . . . just because we don't have any better ideas. Things change, Arya.

'How adaptive you are!'

Truthfully, Arya, I don't see a future.

'No, you *do* see a future! For *you*!' And banging on the lid of the stereo, he yelled, '*I'm* not agreeing to a divorce so *you* can get cheap publicity!'

That was Spat No. 1.

There were no emails or calls that week. This unnerved me. Tactics to wear me down, I thought.

Then one morning there it was.

Time to talk, I think. V

And soon after, the phone rang. Before I could answer, it stopped. An hour later it rang again. Again it stopped. When it rang for the third time I let it ring. The rings went on and on and on.

After that my jumpiness got so bad that even Arya noticed it. 'Whose call are you expecting?' he asked when I leapt to answer the phone for the fourth time.

Nobody you know. Nobody *I* know.

'Oh, yes? Who're you fooling?'

The time had come, I decided, to consult Pulin Grover about some discreet legal recourse.

The next afternoon, a Saturday, when I knew he'd be in by 5 pm after golf (I now knew his routine), I set out for his house. It is located on the fringes of Shantiniketan, hanging on to but not quite making this fashionable address. As I expected it turned out to be a house with a frontage, as we say in Delhi, which is all about fronts and frontage. Exotic palms, orchids looped on trees, birds of paradise poking through clumps and a doorbell chiming the first bars of *The Marriage of Figaro*.

The door was answered by a young girl dressed in a parachute, with a hundredweight of sequins sewed into it.

Hello, hello, is your father home?

She looked startled. *'Ji?'*

Oh, Lord. Is your *sahib* home?

He wasn't but the memsahib was. I was shown into a chilly emporium where a vast woman was sunk in a sofa, watching a Zee movie. She was also wearing a sequinned parachute. All became clear—it was *her* hand-me-down the slave was wearing. But this one was rather better filled. Flesh festooned its owner's hips, flesh ringed her neck. Flesh was corded, gathered, humped and folded about her person, even her too-red mouth was redrawn to look like a full-blown poppy. Upon my entrance she lifted herself a few inches, and gave me the old up-and-down—placing me in a context in those few moments. Geographical and social. Then, looking as if acting against her better judgement, she beckoned me to sit.

However, when I told her who I was, she quickly recomposed her features, switched off the television, fluffed up her black-as-black hair, and grimace-smiled. Then she reached for a bell push and pressed it twice.

It must have been a pre-arranged signal for soon trays appeared—huge plastic things with plates of food floating like lily pads. Kachori, samosa, gulab jamun and assorted pastries. Tall glasses of sweating sherbet. 'Bete,' my hostess rebuked her slave gently, 'is this *all*?' When it became shamefully clear that this was indeed to be all, 'The choice is yours,' she said to me, with a grand wave. 'Take, take, you look so weak!'

I reached for a lily pad, happy to comply. It was part of the treatment.

Then followed another of those unfounded, confounding hours that had been crowding my life of late. Mrs Grover talked. Talked and talked and talked. And I, feeding as hectically as a silkworm larva, listened. Listened and listened and listened. Pinned as I was to the cushions I couldn't do otherwise. There was no sign of Pulin Grover and his wife seemed in no hurry to end the visit.

Presently the food I'd consumed began getting its back on me, and I started losing vital information in the grumbling inside. I'm sorry to hear that, Mrs Grover, I commiserated, at one point.

'Don't call me Mrs Grover! I am your sister-in-law! Your *Bhabhi*! Pulinji is your big brother!'

I toasted our new relationship with a sip of sherbet, wondering what insecurities Big Brother Pulin subjected this poor woman to. Come to think of it, I had never seen her with him. Perhaps she was too huge to move.

My musings were brought up short. '. . . ninety-five years old . . . four daughters and a son and I the youngest . . .' The kohl-ed eyes were shedding jet beads. She belched loudly and uninhibitedly. I had become family.

I struggled to connect, struggled harder to get up, but my body, my mind, my entire life had sunk into the cushions. The sofa, the room, its occupant, her relatives, all her associates had become absolutely necessary to my survival. The shutdown was so complete that I drifted into a trance.

Hard times, Mrs G, I heard myself saying. Sadly, time itself does not stop for anyone.

'Yes, yes, that is exactly my thought on the matter! You are so correct! Time is a great healer, the only healer!' Then, digging me in the thigh, 'But Mother is Mother!'

I have a cousin who says that. Only he also says Mother is Father too. And vice versa.

For a moment she looked puzzled. Then she brightened. 'Very true, very true! That is exactly my feeling too! You are so intelligent!'

Wriggling like the worm I was, I drank up the rest of my sherbet in one big gulp.

Then she asked me, and not so subtly either, exactly how much time I spent with her husband in this business, and where. For some reason I found myself inordinately eager to prove my innocence. So desperate did I get that I began blustering, repeating and contradicting myself in silly little ways that took on a sinister hue the minute the words left my lips.

It dawned on me at last that Pulin Grover had changed his schedule. Extricating myself from the sofa, I said, I must run. I've kept you too long. Could you please tell Pulin, I mean Mr Grover, I mean Bhaisahib, that I wished to . . .

But I didn't wish to. Didn't wish anything. It's not important, I said at last, and, my limbs waving like seaweed, crawled to the door.

Bhabhiji plodded behind pleading, 'Stay *ji*, please stay. He's late, very sorry for that, but he will come back for dinner.' And a little desperately, 'I'll show you photo albums of my daughter's wedding! Best photographer in Delhi, best decorator, reception in Maurya Sheraton! She married a very decent capitalist family, you know.'

But I, who till now had no count of the hour, suddenly heard the seconds chirping like crickets in the monsoon. Loud, rhythmic, without a let-up.

On the doorstep, she grabbed my hand, and held on to it as if it were a safety strap in a crowded bus. In a paroxysm of remorse I returned the clasp. Surprised, gratified, she squeezed hard. For a minute we stood in a clinch, she listing to starboard, both of us playing a game of who-blinks-first.

She did. She pulled her hand away—only to reposition it on my shoulder. Her eyes were moist. 'Thank you for giving me company. And your advice.'

Was this a rebuke? I'd hardly got a word in edgewise. 'Maybe,' she regarded me with sad longing, 'we will meet again. I go to the Sheraton first Tuesday of every month for our ladies club. You can join for tea if you like, and our ladies club also.'

At last she let me go.

At a loose end once again, I walked to the main road and hailed a scooter. 'Arrey, kahan jaoge?' the driver asked, thwacking his horn. *Aarey, paaarp, kahan, paaarp, jaoge, parp-parp?* Where to, *now*?

I directed him to Connaught Place, to Book Nook, to which I paid surreptitious visits, to see if *AFL* still had pride of place in the window. It had, I was pleased to observe, and actually counted the stack. The more successful you get, I'd discovered, the more jealous you become of your success. I was gazing, a new parent at the hospital's nursery window, when a pair of khaki chinos emerged from the door, an arm (encased in white) took mine in a no-nonsense, come-quietly-now grip, and I found myself being marched off.

Coincidences are not always providential but this was an instance when it was. I hadn't spoken to him since that evening a week ago. I wasn't planning to, even. And now here he was, delivered to me. By the evening post. Who was I to question providence?

Connaught Place is like a slice of orange cut transversely. Its classical buildings are wedged between an inner and outer circular road, around a green core, and the streets separating the wedges give to Delhi's older neighbourhoods. Once a fashionable shopping promenade, Connaught Place now suffers the fate that all once grand places in these parts do—that of having lost face as well as hope of recovering it. But in spite of the litter and the pavement stalls and the mutilation of its noble details, its deep, shadowy arcades are still good for an amble. So we ambled along, paring the segments.

Just as I was wondering how long we would be peering at the window displays (as if we might find our afternoon's agenda there), he stopped at the entrance of a coffee bar, and held the door open.

'Tea or coffee? Something cold?'

My recently abused stomach lurched but rather than fuss I asked for tea. He ordered coffee for himself and two of their special cakes, the rum balls, for which the restaurant was famous.

Ordering done, he stretched his arms across the table. 'What've you been doing? Besides gazing into shop windows?'

I showed him the last letter.

'Do you, um, carry them around everywhere?'

I'd gone to my publisher to ask for help. Legal help.

'Will he help?'

He wasn't in.

'Lucky *I* was out, eh?'

Very lucky.

'You could just stop accessing your email, you know.'

That isn't a solution.

Pushing away his cup he unwrapped the paper parcel he'd been carrying. 'Look what I bought.'

Oh, I'd have *given* you a copy.

'I thought I'd push up the sales figure.'

That is kind of you.

'Perhaps,' he tapped it, 'I'll find a clue. After all, it's all in the reading, isn't it? As the Zen Buddhists would say.' He grinned. 'Perhaps my subconscious will do better than your friend's, the one you met at the party.'

My stomach heaved. A brackish brew filled my mouth. I rushed to the bathroom—just in time.

A light was on in the living room. A chair was pulled up to the light. A man was sitting on the chair under the light. He was reading *AFL*, apparently, but not really, for he was humming as well. An indeterminate tuneless hum, to keep time with the footsteps tapping in his head. All of him was alert to those footsteps—eyes, neck, and shoulders. The instant Kaveri pushed open the door, he sprang to his feet. The rug humped, and he tripped and fell.

Stumbling across to her he asked, 'Are you okay? Are you alright?' As if it were she who had taken a toss.

'How did you get in?'

He straightened up. 'Your maid was just leaving and . . .'

'You broke in.'

'What rubbish, Kaveri.' She flung her handbag on the kitchen-dining-work table, poured out and drank a glass of water. He righted the rug with a foot and went back to the chair. Of all the nerve, she muttered.

'So. Why did you run away?'

'I suddenly remembered I had to let out the maid.'

'She's not a dog. She can let herself out. She did too.'

'You don't have to make it your business to pry into mine.'

'That's a bit much. Under the circumstances.'

'I was counting on you.' Her voice shook just a little. '*Counting* on you.'

He was squinting at the iron Bastar horse-and-rider on the table. 'What were you counting on?' She didn't answer. He picked up the horse and examined it. 'What *is* bothering you, Kaveri?' He put the horse down, taking care its tiny hooves didn't scratch the surface.

She looked at him imploringly. 'I can't,' she whispered. 'I can't . . . go on.'

'It *is* serious, then,' he said slowly.

She gazed at the rug as if it might help her in some way. Fly her out of the window, perhaps.

'My dear Kaveri, we *are* trying to establish the cause, aren't we? Not do away with the effects. Which are bothering you quite a bit.'

'And you're wondering why,' she said sulkily.

'Because *you* were wondering why.'

'Look,' she said, meeting his eyes at last. 'I'm tired. Can we do this some other time?'

'Sure,' he said cheerfully. 'Perhaps after I read the book.'

At the door he said, 'You could always move out for a bit, you know.' His lips twitched. 'You could move *in*.' And laughed at her expression.

She shut the door behind him. But a tiny flame flared inside her.

She stood for a while with the doorknob in her hand. He had left a hole again—a bigger, deeper hole. And where was he, the one who pledged, before a posse of witnesses, to plug the holes in her life? Suddenly it didn't matter any more. Each one to each-each one, as Mani would say. Cheered by this flash flood appearance of Mani (and if Mani was here, could Meenakshi be far behind?), she went into her room.

And there, frozen in an attitude of stealthy joy, stood Mani and Meenakshi. She was squashed against him, the top of her head pushing his nose out of joint. He, square-shouldered, square-jawed, was frowning at something in the distance as if he would, if he could, change it. Shoulder-to-shoulder, arm-in-arm, they solicited their daughter's love. *Their* love (for her, indubitably) was gilding the non-reflective glass. *We're there for you . . . always, always.*

She smiled at this sudden deliverance. If only her mother knew the number of times she had delivered her after that first wriggly emergence in Bangalore General Hospital! How many times Mani had fathered her after initiating that first miraculous journey whose destination had been her! Stretching her arms upward she s-m-i-l-e-d. Oh, M&M. Then, still smiling, she made for the bathroom, regressing as she walked, from imperfect adult to the perfect infant that Meenakshi had trundled, gaping and goggle-eyed against her bosom, for a steaming, therapeutic bath.

Back in the living room she was greeted by Cole Porter on the stereo. A glass idled on the table, and Arya sat protecting it, humming in doleful off-key. Another ham humster. *Every time we say goodbye I die a little . . .* What a gag! *Every time we say goodbye I wonder why a little . . .* Small wonder, when you think about it.

'Arya, where is the Nescafe? I looked for it all morning.'

'Arya. I'm asking you . . . I know you've hidden it. It was there last evening and . . .'

'*Arya*. Look at me. I'm talking to you.'

Look at her. Average, regular, medium. Not fat, not thin, not beautiful, not plain. Just *even*. This evenness, a precision of features and clear skin, wide brow and wide-spaced eyes, accounts for the overall impression of prettiness. Of course there is the smile too. It reaches out, pulling up the corners of her lips, arcing her cheeks, lighting her eyes . . . But there are hidden mores to this woman. Those tuned in can thrill to the elemental carnality in her, the hint of recklessness. On the surface of it, however, she looks as if she takes home stray dogs and cats. She's credited with (erroneously, God-help-us) compassion. People zoom in on her the way small children do on the one person in the room who does not welcome their advances, and she gets chatted up. Before she can count ten, strangers have locked eyes with her, and she has become the unwilling recipient of their confidences. Regrettably, she is not unaware of her charms. Lamentably, she exploits them.

'Arya, look . . .'

'No. *You* look at *me*.'

Look at him. Mark the circles. From head to belly flap, from the contours of his cheeks to the moulding of his buttocks, he is a study in orbs. In the roundness, read good nature or, as Kaveri does, a lack of direction. These are catenaries rather than curves.

'*Answer* me,' said this Shape of the Universe. All the circles jumped to take note. '*He* was here, wasn't he.'

Then followed one of those passages of domestic strife so familiar and predictable that anyone can sing along, as it were. Midway something happened to change forever their equation. Her hair worked loose from its knot and tumbled down. When she raised her arms to re-knot it, two dewlaps, two moons in the first quarter, popped out from under her blouse. Indifferently, but to him, the watcher, heart-stoppingly sexily, she flicked them back, pulled her sari across her breasts. Curtain.

After an interminably agonising moment his blood ran again—only to flood him with a crippling ache. He ached for those breasts, to touch them, press his face to them, gather them to him. He ached to pull her hair down so she would have to put her arms up again, let down her defences. But, with an instinct entirely off the mark (only he didn't know it), he willed himself not to. He *must* not. Staring bleakly at the floor he swallowed his pain. And she, despite the calm of her brow, wanted for him to pull the pin from her hair so she would have to repeat her manoeuvre (the effects of which she was only too aware) so he would encircle her with his arms, tuck in the straying breasts . . .

When he didn't go to her, she concluded, wrongly, that he had so sickened of her that he was unmoved by this, surely the most erotic signal, the most wanton invitation from a woman. And she hardened her heart.

After that, Spat No.2 twisted, turned, and ended at last in a volley of spitfire.

'What does he have that I do not?'

Gumption, she almost said, but it was not that. Goodness, she tried, and her breath caught. *Wholeness.* 'He has a sense of me,' she murmured, and smiled to herself. He could be a running mate.

'What is he to you that I'm not? What does he *give* you?'

Ballast, she thought, and smiled again—ruefully. What *was* he to her? What was *she* to him? 'Look, Arya, let it go. It doesn't matter.'

'Doesn't it matter that I . . . I love you?'

She sighed. 'Arya. Loving me *is* having a sense of me. Yours is, has been for a while now, off centre.'

'And his is so bang-on it becomes *love*? Two-and-a-half meetings, and bulls-eye, it's *love*?'

She felt a little foolish. 'Let's just say he's sensitive to my needs.'

'*Needs*? Have you ever considered *my* needs?'

'I admit I haven't. Not much.'

'Does that mean you don't love me?'

She did not answer.

His shoulders sagged. His deflation would be pitiful if she didn't feel so pitiless. Not for the first time did she wonder whether this, this bringing out the worst in each other, was his fault or hers. Without meeting her eyes, as if confiding a shameful secret, he mumbled, 'I love you and I need you.' Two licks of flame flickered behind her blouse, engulfing him. Burning his flesh. Singeing his hair. Melting his gonads—oh God! 'I need you,' he groaned as the molten heat poured down his legs.

She just looked at him. Humiliated, 'Don't fool yourself about this man,' he snarled. 'You're only a curiosity for him. A research specimen. As for *you*, you're just feeding your damned ego! I bet he's flattering your book! Isn't he? *Isn't he*? He is! I knew it! I *curse* it!'

'Don't bother. Somebody already has.'

'What? Who? What do you mean?'

'Oh, hell. Forget it. I'm going to bed.'

He found her lying on the edge of the bed, with three inches to spare, face pressed into the pillow. Beside her was no man's land, an expanse wide as an ocean and empty as a desert, and planted with mines. The ultimate exclusion, he thought savagely, balling and throwing his shirt into a corner. Why had the bitch consented to marry him? *Condescended* to him? He should fling himself on her. Tumble her off the bed—that would be easy enough anyway. But he would not. Could not. That didn't make him feel better about himself.

She heard him stumbling and swearing. His rum-and-water would be lapping at the edge of his consciousness just now, but in an hour it would rise like a high tide to drown him. Another half-bottle would be flung down the garbage chute. Half-bottles, for godsake! Buy your drink like a man, not a bloody half-man!

In the night she slipped into his dreams—she as him, to dream in his head. Bloated with his drink, stupid with his stupor, she lurched in and out of the blackness that was his headache. And she lusted after her smooth-supple femaleness. The pliancy of her thighs. The swell of her belly. The pucker in her nipples. The sweep of her back from shoulder to buttocks. The back itself in repose, in tension . . . She wanted her-as-him to ravish her. Hardening and softening in the glutinous dark, she yearned and yearned.

Three times she woke, unhappy dreamer. Once it was the wail of an ambulance, and she sat up to glimpse through the square of window the flaky lightness of a sky that never slept. Then it was the doorbell, which she staggered out to answer— only to find nobody there. Perhaps it was a jangling in her head—an alarm, a siren, a knell . . . The third time Arya, mumbling gummily in *his* dreams, flung a wrathful arm over her.

Near daybreak she was lying on a high, carved bed, covered with slippery cretonne, in the middle of an empty room with a tilting floor and green walls. A four-leafed fan trailed long strands of cobweb in the sluggish air. A fluorescent light burned her eyes. Her head buzzed with fireflies. Through her eyelids she saw a shadow move over her.

She woke in the morning, dry-mouthed and disoriented. 'Who was I?' she asked him. 'And where were you?'

He brought me tea in bed, and toast and honey. Calm and considerate, he was almost, almost, the man I had married. The man whose measured articulation I had mistaken for erudition—an arbitrary judgement that cost me dear. But now, in his sudden concern, I suspected treachery.

He spooled honey from the pot, licked it with relish. 'Something has gone wrong with your book, right?'

I can't bear it. I can't bear the slime coating his voice, the gleam in his eyes. He is so pathetic I could cry.

'This is exactly why you'll never be happy,' he said, with another lick of honey. 'You're so secretive.'

I jumped out of bed. Let go, will you, I yelled. I'll bloody well be what I choose!

The next two days we played a game of waiting for a) one of us to strike and b) an intervention (divine?). Trapped in a space that seemed to have shrunk even more in the past week, we bumped into each other even when we were two rooms apart. We would have crowded each other out if we were *miles* apart.

On the evening of the third day he came home early—to Spat No. 3.

Arya, this has to stop. You've hidden the cupboard keys now.

'Is he your email fan?'

What are you talking about?

'Your *boy*friend, my erstwhile client.'

You're mad. You *must* be mad.

The bags gathered under his eyes. 'He calls you, writes to you, visits you . . .'

Thought, word, deed, eh?

'Shut up! Shut *up!*'

But for gross inaccuracies, Arya, this could be funny.

He picked up a heavy crystal ashtray (another of Meenakshi's impossible gifts), weighed it like a discus. The pinhole of light in his eye was a point of no return. 'Betrayal.' He grinned maniacally. 'Adultery.'

Adultery. He is so absurd, this man, with his stuffed cheeks, and his stuffed shirt, and his belly flowing from his belt. *Adultery.*

I think, Arya, we should make some ground rules for our discussions.

'Such as?'

Stop making low-down accusations, for one.

'They are based on observation.'

On imagination. Inflamed. And please put that ashtray down.

'*You* said he has a better sense of you than I do . . . sense of what? *Touch? Feel*—is that it? Does he feel you up? Eh? Tell me, damn it! *Tell* me!'

Your mind is just so . . . squalid. But forward-thinking. I grant you that.

'Don't try to get out of this with your damned cleverness!'

What am I trying to get out of?

'I *told* you!' He struggled to recompose his face—matter over mind. 'Adultery.'

If that's what you read into a visit or two . . .

'For once admit the truth! It's not just visits! It's more!' His features contorted. 'I'm never around—so who knows what goes on here?'

Weariness stole over me. Who would be like this if they had a choice? If his visits bother you, Arya . . .

'They do.' He moved his neck in his collar, turtle-like. 'I'm old-fashioned.'

The top of my head lifted. A white-hot glare poured in. What *do* you want, Arya?

'I want . . . I want . . . I just want you to go. Or me. One of us.' He cast around wildly, seeking escape.

Then he ran to the front door, wrenched it open, banged it behind him. It opened again. His face was ugly with anger, the mouth a figure of eight. 'Whore!' he hissed.

Big moment. Of truth and revelation. Off he rushed, clattering down the stairs. Wouldn't even wait for the lift.

I chased him to the landing. Go tell it on the mountain!

I tottered back, flung myself on the sofa. Feel my feelings, why can't you! Feel what I feel! We quicken to the same sounds and sights, open and shut our wings to the same heat, we march to the same drum, so why can't you *feel*?

He hurled the answer up the silent staircase. *Because you shut me out from your feelings.*

After long minutes of gazing at nothing I packed a small bag.

'Dilli railway station?' inquired the scooter driver astutely.

Light-head with recklessness, I gave him the address of the house I had visited just once, not the countless times of Arya's tortured imaginings.

He stood aside to let me in. Just as he was about to shut the door, he spotted the bag. 'You travel light,' he commented mildly.

I left the livestock behind.

The smile went out.

Oh, come on. You owe him no loyalty—you are no longer his Client.

'And evidently he's no longer your Arya.'

The bag sat on the path, waiting, a runaway tale, no ending in sight. I kept my eyes on it—we both did—as if it was a thing that, if not watched, would dissolve on the screen, and then what would be the meaning of this scene?

When I was at school, I said, I had to carry so much stuff—satchel, tiffin box, water bottle, gym shoes, sweater—that my father would tease, 'Where is your sleeping bag?'

He was listening intently for the point in this autobiography.

I didn't have a sleeping bag then, and I don't now.

He nodded gravely as if this was the sort of thing one must be prepared for (or guard against) in these uncertain times. Then he carried the bag in, and shut the door behind us.

Inside we were again at a loss for words. This time he spoke. 'Tea? Coffee? Something cold?'

We pounced on this momentary relief.

Dinner was a tense business. Looking over each other's shoulder at an uncertain future rather than at the uneasy present comprising bhindi sabzi, dal-rice, peas-paneer and all the etceteras, they both longed to get it over with, whatever *it* was. The *it* bristled with possibilities. The *it* stuck in their throat with the food and got in the way of the conversation. (Another chapatti? Hmmm? Yes, thanks. Pickle? Hmmm? No thanks. Salad? No. Yes. Thanks.) The recent past, the only time they had shared, had been unpromising in its auguries, but who could tell? *It* could just happen.

This is the place, she thought, where we put in a bookmark and suspend reality, because from now on unreality will be the order of the day. Arya, as Banquo's Ghost, was hovering over the congealing banquet. Arya, as hell's angel, breathed hellfire. Arya, as soothsayer, was tearing his tongue out. Would he be proved right? That really was the question hanging over them, and getting in the way of the tomato salad, dal-rice, peas-paneer and all the etceteras.

In a way Arya had ordained this visit, the mother of all visits.

They went up to the terrace, pulled out two ancient rattan chairs from the landing, and a pedestal fan, and dragged them to the middle of the rough cement floor that the streetlight crumbled into glittering sand. He plugged the fan into a power point in the parapet wall, and, presently, a hot little breeze dried their damp faces.

The powdery sky pulsated with criss-crossing airplanes. Shadows flitted across the roofline. People had come to take in the moon, drawn out by the potent, potable light. Insomniacs were afoot too. Perhaps lovers. And thieves. The thieves were everywhere.

They laboured on with their small talk, discussing, of all things, the airlines that serviced Delhi. Eight flights every day to London, did you know? Really? As many as that? This place is on the flight path, in fact. Yes, I gathered as much. Look at that one, I mean, just hear it! I bet it broke the sound barrier! Right. Did you see the cockpit? Indeed I did. All lit up. The windows too. Portholes. Whatever. Right. Diwali in the sky! *Right.* Wonder what they're getting for dinner?

They fell silent. The moon, thirteen nights old, had a bit torn out of its edge, and she drew his attention to the small imperfection. But he seemed abstracted. Discouraged, 'I'm sorry I'm imposing on you,' she said stiffly.

His face broke into a smile. 'But I'm delighted you are!'

'Delighted you're party to betrayal?'

'I haven't lured you here,' he said reasonably. 'And what betrayal?'

The word *betrayal* started in her a minor turbulence, and she grabbed the arms of her chair to steady herself. 'Well, um. It's not exactly a betrayal. Only relatively. I mean, only apparently . . .'

He laughed. 'I love the way you set out your definitions in non-absolutes. And the way you hide behind them.'

'I don't understand.'

'Kaveri, if you keep having to justify yourself to yourself, you can't afford a conscience.' He took both her hands in his, his workman's hands with its four-phalanged fingers. 'I read your book. I enjoyed it.' He gave her a sheepish, almost humble, smile. 'I had no idea . . . It has some great ideas. That I, anyone could identify with. Universal. Like a collective principle.' She got up and went to the parapet. 'Is that too simplistic?' he asked anxiously.

She was looking over the parapet. With the dust haze the lights looked ethereal. A saintly glow. A city of saints? Hardly. 'Universal ideas,' she murmured.

'You know what I mean,' he said eagerly. 'Ideas that belong to time, not just persons. At least, to everybody.'

'Or nobody.' She turned around. 'A cooperative farm of ideas,' she mused. 'That's a thought.'

He looked puzzled. 'Are you trying to codify a new value

system? Communal ownership of ideas? People do take out patents on their ideas, you know.'

She clutched the edge of the parapet behind her. 'Well, they shouldn't. Ideas are *abstract*. They shouldn't be treated as a commodity—to be bought and sold. I think that corrupts the ideal of free thought.'

He pushed up his glasses. 'Freethinking is quite different from giving away your ideas for free.' His chair creaked. 'A perfect world would be one of non-transactional coexistence, I suppose. But this isn't one.' He stood up. 'Anyway, your book most certainly is a commodity.' He stretched, stifled a yawn. 'You own it. *And* you've done well out of it. Not someone else.'

She picked at a loose bit of cane on her chair. 'I sometimes wonder about that. How it would've been if it hadn't been successful.' The cane came away in her hand.

'You could have blamed that on your cooperative farm of ideas!' He laughed. She turned away. 'This isn't making sense, is it? All right then, would you rather it hadn't been successful to experience *that*? You're such a fraud!' She laughed with him. 'By the way, I found those quotes in the book. Not that I'm any the wiser.'

She covered her face with her hands. 'Oh God. Those emails.'

He pulled away her hands. 'Relax,' he said gently. 'Nobody can get at you here.'

She shuddered. 'I can't, I can't get away.'

'From whom? Your father?' He cupped her chin and turned her face to his.

She thought her face would burn his hands. A plane swooped down, dangerously low. Involuntarily she ducked. 'Kaveri? Are you alright?'

'*I don't know! I don't know!*'

In a flash, in a leap-and-bound, he had his arms around her. From there it was but a step to draw her up—to him. And from *there* but another to bring his face to hers, to put his mouth to hers, his whole self to hers. To her willing, waiting self, that is. By and by they walked down the stairs and into the colluding darkness.

At midnight, when day turns on night and darkness concedes to light, where prose becomes poetry and rhyme informs reason, at the point sea gives to sky, in that watery territory, at witching hour (as it's called), the witch rode. Rode the skies and the heavens. In the few seconds of insane clarity or lucid insanity, in the moment she breached the clouds she thought, this is what I saw that day in the restaurant. We began moving to this then. It was written in the instant the stars and the stones and everything in between—all the laws and principles and equations that Pati taught me—came to be. This man, me, Arya, Pulin, the book and the emailer—we're in one cosmic bind. For all that it still is a miracle. A fork of lightning picked me up from a biblical wilderness, dropped me here. For me to be with him tonight.

The neon lighting of the twenty-four-hour payphone booth across the road squeezed through the chink in the curtains. The bed glimmered like a moonlit sea, their bodies burned blue. Propping herself on an elbow, she considered the slim hips, the long legs, the hands fisted loosely on the belly. With her forefinger she traced the whorl of hair on his chest. Her fingers flickered over his thigh, brushed the curled innocent-in-sleep of that which Pati coyly called a conch shell. It *is* a conch shell, she thought. A trumpet. A seahorse rearing its head. If she put her ear to it, she would hear the sea. She tried it, ear to shell, mouth to conch, blowing gently . . . He woke groaning and reached for her. Oh woman!

Then it was his turn to pry, with tender impudence, the mystery that was she. To discover the origami of *her*. Petals, sepals, stamens . . . His body gave hers a beautiful new purpose. A brand-new meaning.

Breathing his gingery scent, so alien yet so familiar—this must have been there in her, else how could it be so, so *wantonly* cognisable—she exulted, *it can't be, but it is*. The wonder is that we imagine this, the reiteration of the oldest truth of all, is a new invention. Ours. A breakthrough, no less. She wriggled down his belly, down and down, to kiss the tiny, puckered lips, taste the infant drool—the libation. Her tongue was but the graze of a butterfly's wing, but it knocked him senseless. Aaargh, God! He said God, but he did not think God. He had little use for God just now. Or prayer. *This* was a prayer. This grace.

Holding her face in his carpenter's hands, he drank deep from her eyes, a draught of liquid sunshine. Oh woman!

Afterwards, she circled the room, touching lightly one object after another. As if in learning these shapes she would comprehend the newness of her. The realness of him. Dreamily she parted the curtain. The payphone booth insinuated itself further into the room. He drew a sharp breath. 'Kaveri! Get back! Somebody will see you!'

She laughed—such proprietariness about their impropriety! She was still laughing when a car burst into the lane. Its headlights pierced the telltale gap, and she gasped, flung an arm across her face. In that apocalyptic moment she was revealed—hair alight, breasts stark and staring, spine a catapult drawn. In a trice he was beside her, crushing her nakedness to his. They were one crackling flame. A single burning breath. Long after the car's roar died down the brightness of its slipstream lingered in the room.

Back on the bed, back to where they had been and back, back, back ... He was overwhelmed by a rush of completion. Of satiation and lightness. As if he'd been stuffed with feathers and tossed up. This is it. *This is it.* It can go no higher.

She was first to wake. The moment of consciousness was paralysing. The light seeping through her eyelids had a different, otherworld quality. The morning cheeps and caws were in a foreign tongue. Her worst nightmare had come about—she was in a time–space she could not comprehend, with a stranger beside her. *She had been abducted.* When comprehension kicked in, she sank back on the pillows, slack with relief.

The bed was an odd size—too wide for one, not wide enough for two. A bookcase covered an entire wall. By the window was a table with a brass telescope, a globe and a dictionary. There were pictures on the wall, of the kind printed on the sleeves of mood music CDs. His modest toiletries occupied a small, tidy space on one side of the chest of drawers. In this scheme the lifeless sitting room was a small and meaningless mystery. He could as well have put in a pool table there. Or a prayer rug. Or a punching bag.

He was compact in sleep, his limbs neatly dispersed on his side of the bed. The unruly hair—she resisted an impulse to twang one of the guitar strings—was threaded with grey. Hair sprouted uninhibitedly on his chest, even on his shoulders. A winged beast. On his ankle was a red bump, a sore or pustule, a mosquito bite impatiently scratched. She was surprised that it should move her, that she could actually vest in it tenderness she didn't know she possessed. She touched his shoulder with the tip of her finger.

Without stirring he murmured, 'Are you admiring my back?'

'Do you always wake so wakefully?'

His laugh took the edge off her shyness. 'Only when I have something good to wake to.'

Wresting himself out of the sheet that had wound itself between them, he pulled her legs up, locked his head in her knees, drew slow, widening circles on her belly, breaking the rhythm to kiss her—wildly, fiercely, from limb to limb. In her eyes he saw—and accepted with gratitude—the gift of eternity.

Your face, he whispered, your face. I wish I could print it on my hands. Then I could look at it forever.

Your hands, she whispered, your hands. I wish I could take them with me. Keep them as a pet.

She stayed the hands. She had to ask, was afraid to, but she had to. Is it . . . is this . . . are you . . . because of my book?

Oh love, he sighed. Oh love. It is *you*. But the book *is* you, isn't it?

When he emerged from the bathroom he was relieved at the neatly made bed, her orderly face, the absence of hysteria. Two mugs of tea steamed on the table, filling the room with the scent of smoking leaves.

He stopped to stroke her hair, then picked up his tea, went to the window. Parting the curtains, 'It's going to be a scorcher,' he reported. Through the condensation on the glass the brown and scabby lawn was already radiating heat waves. The chandelier blooms of the laburnums lining the street glowed in the hot white light.

'Can you stay in?' she asked. 'Just for today? Plead sick as they all do?'

'Of course I can't. I'm not sick.'

Her spirits dived at this government-clerkish rectitude. 'What shall I do while you're away?' she asked, a little peevishly.

'What would you do if I stayed?'

Flopping back against the pillows, she raised a mischievous eyebrow. 'As to that, I have ideas aplenty. I *am* in the ideas business, you know.'

The indigo kaftan glowed against the white of the pillows and sheets. Her face glowed against the indigo. Now her hair, live black filaments, picked up the radiance. Very nearly, he stayed back. Especially urging him to countermand his sane self was her throat. The slender stem and what it connected ... He wasn't yet completely familiar with the form obscured by the kaftan. There was some recall, though not enough. But there was time yet to rediscover it. Time enough to know her. All of her, inside and out. To unwrap all her wonderful secrets.

She smiled at him—the smile that pulled her face up. Up and up.

Kaveri. Love. Stay with me forever. Never go.

By the time I bathed and dressed he had eaten breakfast and was gone. Outside, the sun had struck a higher note, and the street was fully awake. Sparrows peppered the laburnums. Crows were going at full throttle. Women, still in nightwear, their baggy morning faces alert to the small-time villainies of plumbers and milkmen, leaned their untethered bosoms on garden walls to bargain with the hawkers. Old gentlemen limped back from their morning walk, greeting children on their way to school.

Old gentlemen, in plaid shirts, corduroy berets, blue-and-white Nikes . . . My finger, ever on the hair trigger of memory, twitched.

But old gentlemen everywhere look the same. More or less.

Later, the manservant, as noiseless and incurious a being as one could hope for, more a sprite than a being, served me breakfast, which in this house at least, was eaten at the dining table. With it he brought me the *Times of India*. Idling through its pages with the toast-egg-banana-coffee, I spotted it. Headline and six inches of column space.

Oh! Oh, oh, oh, oh! And oh!

Ten minutes later, when I could control the trembling in my legs and hands, I sent out for the other papers. They repeated the same thing, except in the details, and in the speculations about my whereabouts. One paper knew for a fact I was discussing film rights with Channel 4 in the UK. Another quoted my chartered accountant-husband Arya Chowdhry as saying he was only the husband enjoying the ride. This was outright fabrication. Arya is not one for modesty—modesty for him is mediocrity in reverse gear. And he never goes anywhere for a ride. He was going to be furious at this incursion on his privacy. A liverish reporter in yet another paper wondered why a book, a *novel*, should merit all this attention. And who exactly comprised the National Civic Foundation and what was the source of its funds?

Let me know too, I muttered, when you find out.

He sounded distant and small on the telephone. As if he was speaking from under a microscope. Listen. I put gargantuan lips to the mouthpiece, to the eyeglass. Did you read the *Times* this morning? (Stupid question. Of course he hadn't.) *I've won the Dharma Ratna!*

'Um?' And, swift upon that, '*Oh*! Wow!' Hardly inspired, but it was music. 'Congratulations!'

I crawled under the microscope with him. Do you think the papers have made a mistake? (A lifetime of expecting low returns for high investment mistrusted this fortune.)

'Of course not,' replied he with an assurance based on years of experiencing the opposite. 'The press is quite responsible.' (But *was* it a responsible press that reported Arya was basking in his wife's glory?)

We emerged from under the glass, to position ourselves, ear to ear in a split frame. 'What now? Don't you have to acknowledge it? Communicate your acceptance? Something?'

I don't know. I suppose I must do *some*thing. Sometime.

'That is decisive and specific.' He laughed. 'We'll celebrate in the evening.'

'Where *are* you?' demanded Pulin Grover, after spluttering his congratulations. 'You haven't been home since last night, I believe. Your bank said you reported sick and will be on leave indefinitely. Kya mystery hai, ye?'

There's no mystery, Pulin. I was tired and took a break, that's all.

'Tired? When it's just begun? It's a great honour, I tell you, my dear, a *great* honour! The papers are looking for you! They want interviews . . . so when, *where* do I come and fetch you?'

You don't.

'*What!*'

I'm not ready to meet anyone, Pulin. I need more . . . time for myself.

'But the Foundation is *asking* . . . Whatever,' he ground out painfully, 'you say. Call me when you are ready. But make it soon!' And, as if he was giving away his life's savings he added, 'My dear.'

Poor Pulin Grover. He was sorely tried.

Arya's voice had a cottony texture. Have you been drinking, Arya? (He squawked.) Have you seen the papers?

That brought on a coughing fit. After which he wheezed that they indicated neither my whereabouts nor my whatabouts, what the hell was I about. Prepare to be surprised, I muttered under my breath.

'Don't bother to lie!' he cried. 'And *don't* sell me your artistic temperament! I know where you are!' Another squawk. 'Dharma Ratna! HAHA!'

Then he enquired if I was planning to give myself up for it. Whether I would still qualify—disgrace to Indian, Hind-oo traditions that I had become. That brought on another coughing fit. I felt a prickle of regret. He was hurting, and hurting badly. 'What if you lose this because of no-show?'

I shall forgo it then. Anyway, this is not a lottery.

'Grown that big?' Then, 'I can't believe this is happening to us!'

I said I thought the prize was happening to *me*. And felt a bit of a low-life after I said it.

'This other thing. What you are doing to *us*, to our *marriage!*' And, 'I knew this would happen,' he whined. 'That you'd leave me.'

That shows how little faith you have, Arya. People who don't have faith *will* get let down. It's a natural law. *I* am only an instrument.

He grunted dispiritedly. Then, in the manner of someone who has kept the best to savour at the end, he informed me that the National Civic Foundation members were hoodlums of the first order. Everyone knew they had underworld political connections. (Everyone except me, in other words.) 'One has a number of tax evasion charges pending against him. And the other made his pile in the sugar scam. *As* I told your father when he called.'

Not for the first time did I think that this, what we do to each other, is just so degrading. I hadn't left a minute too soon. '. . . your father wanted to speak to you'. And sounding as if he was sucking on a piece of candy, 'I told him you'd gone away, I don't know where.'

A trick opening yawned. I stepped around it. That's all right, I said. *I'll* tell him where I am.

At which, so vindictively it knocked the breath out of me, 'Next time those hoodlums ask where you are I'm going to say you're not interested in the prize.' Oh, say what you like, silly fellow, I muttered. 'By the way, some guy called for you. Three times since last night. Wouldn't give his name. Another of your admirers, I suppose.'

I sat chewing my lip for a bit, and then, when I couldn't sit any more, rushed out of the house and began walking up and down in the street. The laburnums, hung with their chandeliers, offered little shade. A hot little breeze blew dust into my eyes. The city thumped in the distance. Turning at the corner one last time I walked into the payphone booth.

The dim booth was like an aquarium. Through its heavily tinted glass the burning street appeared misty, as if tumbled by cool monsoon clouds. To give the lie to this illusion, it was stifling, and the man manning the thingummy, the call-recording machine, was steaming up the room with his leers. An urchin outside crossed his eyes and pulled his cheeks out with his fingers, studied the effect in the glass. The man stopped leering and raised a threatening fist to the glass, cursed. *Ullu-ka-pattha*.

That broke the ice, so to speak.

'You like walking, I believe so?' he asked, undoing a button on his shirt. 'Visiting No. 56, I believe so?' I gave him my number to dial, but, 'Friend or relative of No. 56?' he wanted to know. 'Staying long?' He undid a second button to reveal a very shiny, very gold baby Krishna pendant nestling in a bed of curly black hair. He began playing with it humming a film song the while.

I was furious with myself at being caught staring, and at my unnecessary scrupulousness in not making this call from the house. The goose pimples popped on my midriff. It required superhuman effort not to pull my sari over my shoulders. To do so would be to admit defeat.

After an interminable wait the customer emerged. 'Your chance, madamji,' bowed Mr Hotshot, easing his crotch. I shuffled into the booth, ducking to avoid bumping the ceiling.

After incoherent congratulations and phone-grabbing by my two biggest admirers in the world, 'Where *are* you?' demanded the male half of the duo. 'Arya didn't know. We called several times at the flat.' The other half shrilled, 'We were so worried! We even phoned your bank!'

I was wondering how to deal with this, when I had a Eureka moment.

I'm at a retreat in the Neemrana Palace! (Speaking in Tamil to frustrate the listening post outside.) Some miles out of Delhi! We're not supposed to make calls! They're teaching us gourmet cooking! French Provincial and Provencal! (It's easy once you start. And Meenakshi was always complaining I short-changed her on the details.) The first day we were taught Quiche Lorraine, today it's Crepes Suzette . . .

Mani cut in. (*Stop babbling! It's a long distance call!*) 'Why didn't you tell us you won the *prize*? We read about it in the *news*papers.'

I too found out from the papers, Pa. Just today.

'I see.' He didn't, but he calmed down. 'Hmmm. It's very creditable.'

Creditable. My spirits floundered. *Creditable.* 'The family will be flabbergasted,' he went on gleefully.

So that's what my prize was. A sock in the nose of the family. My spirits dropped some more. 'Have you met these people?' he asked next. I was forced to confess I hadn't. 'Arya says they're a bit shady.' But just as he was about to expand on that, I heard Meenakshi shush him. Then she came on the line. 'When are you coming here, Kaveri? Why don't you come for the housewarming? Have you received the invitation?'

Not yet, I replied cautiously. I haven't been home for a while, Ma. This is supposed to be a retreat.

What useful tools lies are.

A slow afternoon floated by. The manservant, that soul of discretion, served lunch at exactly 1.30. I read a little, slept a little, prowled around the house . . . My curiosity getting the worse of me, as usual, but then weren't we insane with it last night? I didn't find anything, though. No photographs, no inscriptions in books, no *I love you* coffee mugs. (Kaveri, you snoop!) Only a poster of a girl playing a flute, indeterminately naked waist upwards but with a saintly expression, as though she had simply forgotten to wear her blouse. I stopped by the computer in the study. After only a minute's deliberation I switched it on—I had no business to, but when had that stopped me from doing anything? However, it required a password to operate so I couldn't access the Internet.

The sun came to a white-hot boil, reddened, and sank beneath the windowsill. The laburnums deepened to canary, then cadmium, and then, when the evening wore on, paled to lemon. The street changed its tune. The vendors' voices were hoarse now and the housewives' whiny after the day's unsatisfactory score-offs. The old men in Nikes were back, but to talk, bunching together on the street corner, as old men do, to berate the government.

At 7 pm he returned and stood hesitating at the door to the study—where I was watching television. You've got it right, I assured him. This *is* your home. He laughed and went into the bedroom. *His* bedroom where I may not follow. That is the difference between wives and well, the others. Wives can presume. I presumed too much with Arya. Perhaps that was my problem.

'Did you access your email?' he asked when he emerged, smelling of soap. 'Oh, I forgot, you need a password. I'll do it for you.' Then he found the Internet connection wasn't working. He raised an eyebrow. 'Just as well?'

Just as well.

In all the time I was there he didn't have it fixed.

We gave the soul of discretion the evening off and shared a bottle of wine over Chinese takeout from Yew Chew, eating the spring rolls and the sour-hot straight out of the greasy containers. Later we went back to the terrace. The rattan chairs appeared to have unravelled a bit more since yesterday. There were more moon-worshippers too and the moon had filled out.

Yew Chew, specifically the mushrooms, was making itself unpleasantly felt. Although my discomfort wasn't entirely Yew Chew's fault. I was having trouble adjusting to my present situation. It didn't help that the payphone booth manager was lolling by his door, shirt opened to the *fourth* button, rubber-necking the street as if he was the President's bodyguard. Any moment the red eye would pick me out.

He continued to guard his silence as jealously as I did mine. At last, 'It's all right Kaveri,' he said gently. 'Treat this as time-out. The anxieties will not be forever.'

I am afraid there may be a time when I will look back and wish this *was* forever. That this time was where I needed to be—and couldn't.

'It could be—if you wished.' He covered my hand with his. His hand. My shield.

How I wish! But it cannot be . . . unless I get out of this bind.

'What bind?'

It's hard to explain.

'Try.' He pressed my hand. His hand. My lifeline.

It's like this. You spend the first three-quarters of your life investing in happiness for the remaining quarter. You spend the last quarter regretting lost investment opportunities. You learn to be cautious, not happy. In any case you'd be tempting fate if you gave in to happiness.

He laughed. 'It seems rather self-punishing.'

It's a family trait. You started life with an unspecified debt. It never got paid—only bigger. There was always something owing. So you always felt incomplete. And then you couldn't expect rewards. Or returns. It seems contradictory, doesn't it? You were expected to succeed, but when you did, it was . . . an impertinence. So you hid . . . oh, this is getting weird, even for my family.

'Hid what?'

Your worth. You see, it wasn't done to let it all hang out. You were expected to succeed but not chase success. That's how you kept pure. And anyway money doesn't buy happiness—you're only as rich as you're happy. But happiness wasn't the goal either. I think, um, to keep going was. For my father at least. He'd wound me up to run, and hopefully, I would till I wound down.

'What a strange upbringing.'

I used to think it was so for everybody.

'Oh, Kaveri. It's *not* so for everybody.' He pulled his chair closer and, unmindful of the spying antennas, held my face. His hands. My refuge. 'Your father was the wrong handler for you. You should have had someone who was light-hearted and, well, quirky.'

He *was* quirky, I replied. I could do no wrong because I was me, and for the same reason I could never get it right either. I suppose he believed it was character-building—to keep me guessing. But he was a *good* father. No question. He just wanted the best for me—and that meant for himself too. It's just that . . . that he couldn't spread himself a bit more. You see, when you're an only child you're expected to be something of a Swiss knife for your parents. All in one.

The terraces were emptying. 'I think what's happened is that you have so little faith in yourself that anyone can shake it. Like this emailer. Although it's not clear why.'

Not clear why. 'Is something the matter?' he was asking, from a long way off. From even further away I heard myself reply I was tired. He jumped up. 'I'm dead beat too. Let's go down.' If you're tired, his eagerness seemed to convey, then so am I. I'll always be tired for you.

The familiarisation with my new circumstances was not easy, with the practical details coming up, the details that preserved civility and decorum. The situation couldn't be allowed to deteriorate just because of the 4 x 6 bed. (I measured it.) But I could not suggest a wider bed. I could not do anything about that sitting room either—apart from giving it mouth-to-mouth resuscitation. That would presume permanence on my part. He once remarked it was the transient nature of affairs that made them romantic. Perhaps he was a romantic. Perhaps he was shy of commitments. Perhaps, like me, he had been raised on cautionary tales. Perhaps he lived intensely in the present.

And how easy it was to live in this present! In the feverish nights, and in a simulacrum of darkness with the curtains drawn against a nosy sun (for there were matutinal engagements too, pre- and post-prandial—matins and vespers, a hallelujah chorus, glory be!), how I rejoiced in my first real freedom! After years of stifling inhibitions, this was heady indeed. Not to factor in consequences and conscience! To throw cause and effect to the birds! To know that somewhere out there Pulin Grover was baying for my blood! And, a thousand miles away, while I was redrawing the moral boundaries of my life, Mani and Meenakshi were worrying about the rain spoiling the roses! And across the Atlantic Claire was frantically teaching her beads a new mantra!

Meenakshi was right. It is people who give us a sense of ourselves. People measure our consequence. Or in-. People mark our characteristics.

I marked a few of his in that time. Not a whole lot, not phobias and allergies but what made him angry (deceit) and what made him smile (I did). He liked Chinese food of course. Music? He was tone-deaf. A deficiency but hardly a fault. And clearly he had never bought flowers before. He would bring me those hideous—and hideously expensive—arrangements with speared blooms and teased greens. He was easily conned, I gathered. Not like Arya. (Damn! I'd sworn to myself to keep off this comparison!) Well, not like someone I knew who filed his bills, all his bills, including the cleaner's. And he was not prejudiced like someone I knew to believe that real men ate meat. And that fish grew you brains, especially the small fish bought live in a bucket and clobbered one at a time, so Baby could become a chartered accountant one day.

Sensing my fugitive's need for seclusion, that alternated with claustrophobia, he'd take me out early morning, and under cover of dusk. (Yes, he did take time off after all.) We walked in Lodi Gardens, Purana Qila and Feroz Shah, in and out of bat-infested tombs, and gardens quivering in the April heat. We drove around the city, ate in restaurants he'd look up in food guides, poked around places that sold unusual things. He bought me an opium pipe, an enamelled silver screw pencil, a tiny jewelled leopard pendant. We saw a Hindi movie—he hadn't seen one since college and, 'It's as bad as I remember!' he exclaimed in delight. We were two people who had time on our side and each other. Just that. No peering into the future and no digging into the past. And certainly no questioning the present. Happiness in unexpected quarters. We looked at the couples around us, bored, bickering, indifferent . . . Not us, not us, we told each other wordlessly. Not now. Not ever.

The right handler? Absolutely. But I had to make sure. And at once.

Wake up!

Blinking at his wristwatch he groaned. 'Three o'clock! Oh God, Kaveri, you do pick your time!'

Sorry, I didn't think. But tell me. Why am I here? Am I mad? Are you? Or are you a foil?

'A what?'

A foil. For my madness. Am I here because any normalcy just now would finish me? Is this, are *you*, a madness to prevent that?

He sighed. Completely awake now, he shuffled to the bathroom, drank a glass of water on his return. Propping himself up on his pillow, 'That's a good try,' he remarked pleasantly. 'To justify *this*.' He thumped the bed. 'That you are not in your senses. But,' his voice cooled, 'I do not appreciate being a figment of your insanity. Even temporarily. Or your delusion. However grand.'

But I am yours too. Aren't I?

He snapped on the lamp. 'No, dear Kaveri, you're not.'

Well, that's how it is for me. It's quite cosy though, this craziness, isn't it?

'Quite crazy, this cosiness.' He swung his legs over the side of the bed and stood up. 'Why do you LIE to yourself?' he said in a voice that frightened me. 'Lie to *me*, and that's it with us!'

What did I say wrong?

'Your prefixes—in spite of, because of, therefore . . . and now insanity. Listen.' His eyes, without the cover of his glasses, were cold and unfamiliar. 'You are *not* insane. You're as sane as anybody.'

Well, don't make such a big deal about it. Isn't everyone out for what they can get?

'For what they can give too. But you wouldn't understand that, would you?'

I believe pure love is a neurosis.

'Oh, it's specifics now, is it? *Pure* love! Kaveri, you're comic!'

Pure as in absolute. I mean, outside of parental love, *I* haven't experienced it. And that is most certainly neurotic. So love is either a selfish need or an expedience or madness. Take your pick, I muttered. I really *was* mad to have started this.

He snorted. 'Madness. Indeed. Poor Arya. To figure out every bloody day whether you're there with him or in some loony land. Whether your responses are actually ravings.'

I knew it! I knew Arya has been bothering you all this while! What he was to me, and I to him! What we were together!

I was triumphant, I was wretched. It was inevitable that Arya would be an issue. The living with him, the leaving of him. The, not to put too fine a point on it, *sleeping* with him. Deserters are not trusted, least of all by their new allegiance.

'You're wrong,' he said coldly. 'Arya, poor chump, never had you. Nobody can. At least I don't suffer from that delusion, whatever else. I'm not that crazy.' His eyes narrowed. 'You haven't really left Arya, have you?' I turned my face away. 'If it's not Arya breathing down your neck, who is it?' I buried my head in the pillow. 'The emailer?' After a pause, 'Your father?' And, entirely without irony, 'Your God?'

I don't know! I don't know!

In the morning we were tired and out of sorts. On the verge of a good old-fashioned tiff. It was there everywhere. The same forebodings, the same delirium, the same discontent. The same quantification of exchanges. In the how much I love and how little you, how much there should be, how little there is. In the I-ness and the you-ness, the this-ness and that-ness. Oh, it was there alright. The madness of believing happiness is a function of change. All of a sudden I was a long way from home. And my pillow, my hook on the bathroom door, my tea mug. The eccentric tap that only I knew how to close. And yes, even my computer—with its sinister contents.

After he left I set out. At a traffic light, which was taking forever to change, I jumped out of the autorickshaw and walked the two kilometres to Jai Hind Colony. It was late morning when I finished the unpleasant journey, wiped out by the heat, which in this instance also had the happy facility of wiping out anxiety.

The place was like a tomb. This was the stillness that halts time, repels human agency, turns bones to dust. My person was an aberration in my own home! The refrigerator yielded a tomato that oozed pus, a sliver of cheese like a nail paring, an uncovered bowl of dal wearing a collar of fur. In the balcony the African violets were wilting, the leaves filmed with soot. All the signs of abandonment were there—my last-worn sari on the bedroom chair, the socks balled up in my walking shoes, my water glass on the bedside table. Arya was preserving my relics for a private reason. Perhaps he was proclaiming my treachery to friends he gathered around his plight. Perhaps he had set this up as a memorial. In that he had succeeded. I'd never felt so dead. Almost, almost I could smell the incense. And the tuberoses.

There were two letters on the telephone table. I opened the plain envelope first, which had the address written in the dearly familiar writing. The letter had the usual poetic touches.

> *... I hope you and Arya are doing well. Appa is recovering from a cold but otherwise doing well. He goes for his walk as usual. It's been hot and chilly here—hot in the day and chilly at night. It rained last evening and may rain again today. Typical Bangalore weather! We haven't heard from you—are you very busy? By the way, your school is having an Old Girls day. Of late we haven't seen much of Lilamami and Co. Only Bharat phones and gives us some news once in a way. Do write soon. And call if you can. We miss you! With lots of love to both of you, Your ever-loving Amma.*

As always I was folded in Meenakshi's embrace, but there was a touch of melancholy in the face I conjured up. Of late she hadn't seen much of Lilamami and Co. She had to hear their news from Bharat's once-in-a-way phone calls.

The other letter was in a gaudy gold envelope, with red turmeric daubed on its four corners. It was the invitation to the housewarming.

> *My dear Arya and Kaveri,*
> *How I wish I could avail the twin pleasure of meeting you and inviting you in person for the Housewarming Ceremony of our new house! It is a proud occasion indeed for us and we will be honoured by your gracious condescension in joining us to celebrate the restoration of our glorious heritage.*
>
> *However, what with the time drawing to a close before the great day, making the clock my closest rival, and with the unseasonable rain clouds shedding their divine tears profusely and hampering all tie-free movement, may I humbly request you to understandably treat this postal invitation as more than a personal call, and participate in our joy? I look forward to receiving your direct advance greetings for the success of the ensuing function, and the honour of your presence enlivening*

the auspicious event with members of your family in full complement.

With sincere best wishes,
Yours truly and brotherly,
S.G. Balan

Compliments of:
Shrimathi Lila Balan
Shrimathi Devi and Shri S.G. Rajan
Shri S.R. Bharat
Shrimathi Tara Nataraj
Shrimathi Uma Raman

At the bottom, as a thought for the day:

Honour thy Father and Mother

I was enormously cheered by the extraordinary missive, and read it three times. How little I knew Balumama! To think that all the while he was peeling us off the trees there was *this* flowing in his veins!

At last I nerved myself to switch on the computer. There was a note from Pulin Grover, asking me to give myself up. Or words to the effect.

'I understand your need for privacy, my dear, but privacy can become an obsessive self-enforcement . . .

Chris priming him, for sure.

And yes, there it was.

He looked into the vertical tunnel. Only a few seconds between is and was. Not enough to experience the transition. He wasn't about to consult his feelings anyway—they were too subjective and fugacious and erratic. Besides, if he did, he would never . . . He shut his eyes and, purposefully, let go of the last of them. The feel of rough stone under his feet.

And a postscript too.

I tried calling you several times. You seem to have gone underground! Get in touch with me—26678402—we need to talk. V

The building's internal rumblings grew louder and louder. In the din a single thought shrieked. *Water the violets.* But I could not stay a moment longer. Throwing the pots into a plastic carry bag (and how lovingly I tended each leaf, cherished each blossom!), I staggered out.

The tombstone clanged behind me.

I told him about the email. That it, whatever *it* portended this time, was closing in on me. I had to leave.

'But to *Bangalore*? That's a long way to run, isn't it?'

At this point I can't think. At least not linearly. Or even laterally. I'm considering it holistically. (He raised his eyebrows but I didn't give him a chance.) It could be one of the family, is what I'm thinking. There are no pointers, I know, but there is the history. (He opened his mouth but I rushed on.) I have a cousin who used to throw worms at us. And another who used to drop hot wax on ants. An uncle who looked up our skirts when we climbed trees. So you see, the field is open.

He laughed. 'I don't see what you're getting at but I'm beginning to understand where you come from.'

I straightened a picture, sat down. Jumped up again and straightened another picture. Now the first didn't align with the second.

'Kaveri. Stop that.'

I sat down, but the jumping didn't stop inside me. From the kitchen came the clink and clatter of dinner being readied, the strains of Bollywood music. The aroma of frying onion and garlic. An ordinary world of feeding the cat and winding the clock and locking the door against the night. It was as unattainable as the remotest star.

'Kaveri. What *is* the matter?'

I want to go home. I *need* to go home. Please let me go home.

He stared. 'But I'm not stopping you. If that's what you want, go ahead.'

He went to the sideboard to open a bottle of wine. We drank in not very companionable silence. When we climbed into bed, 'Things may look different tomorrow,' he said. Which was a feeble stab at comfort. He must know that that never changed what they are today.

Their lovemaking was distracted. Although they had not spoken about changes, change was in the air, tightening a cord around them. When she could stand it no longer, she threw off the sheets. 'You think I'm crazy, don't you?'

'A bit overwrought, yes.'

She laughed harshly. 'It runs in the family—we're all overwrought. Wroughten through and through.'

'For heavensake. You don't want help. You just want to go halves on your craziness.'

'And you, you want a research sample. A live *specimen*. Delusion, dementia, de-degeneration. I . . . have . . . it . . . a-a-all. Oh God. I can't. I ca . . . n't go on.'

To his dismay she began weeping. This was the third time,

the *third*, that he has made her cry. It didn't augur well at all. She sat with her head bowed over a tightly balled body, rocking with grief.

But. He couldn't find it in him to pity her. What was it about her naked sorrow that so repelled him? 'Damn,' he muttered.

She froze. His heart lurched. 'Kaveri, I . . . I'm sorry. I didn't mean it. It's just that I was . . . I can't bear . . . the thought of you leaving me.'

She lifted her head. 'And *I*. And *I* *you*.' Her face, damp with tears, glowed with a special radiance. 'Listen,' she said shyly. 'I read this somewhere. A Tamil verse.'

'Look my bangles
Slip loose as he leaves
Grow tight as he returns
They give me away . . .'

He picked up her wrist, kissed her bangles. (Meenakshi's love encircling her day after day.) 'I shall look out for your bangles. I shall learn to read your bangles.' He kissed her wrists, her palms, her fingers, her forehead, eyes and mouth. Her neck. Neck to breasts was just a handspan, then another to the waist and one more to the belly . . . He was spanning her. Measuring her length and breadth with his stonemason's hands. Covering every square inch of her with his lips. His tongue made cool silvery tracks on her fevered skin. His mouth, full of tender promises, pledged itself to her.

'Oh Kaveri. Soul of my soul. I am as insane as you are. *All* of me gives that away.'

Day was breaking when his eyes opened to hers. He said, 'I thought, I hoped, this was your home.'

She took his hand and held it to her cheek. 'It is—for now.'

'It can be—forever. Remember what you said about finding a time without end? This could be that time.' And when she didn't reply, 'Running away again,' he sighed.

'Please.'

'In search of truth now. Armed with doubt, anxiety and fear.'

'Please.'

After breakfast I rescued the African violets. Eight pots tumbled out of the carry-bag, their puce, purple and pink blossoms broken and bruised.

He stared. 'Where did *these* come from?'

We set them up on a windowsill. 'Just once in four days? And we're watering them now?'

That's right.

'Well, then,' he brightened, 'I don't have to bother remembering. You'll be back to water them.'

I don't reply. I cannot reply. He bent to straighten a stem. 'How many,' his voice was muffled, *'multiples* of four will there be?'

He raised his head. And there it was. The face on the towel, on my pillow. The face that showed me my soul.

It was sad. So very sad.

Patrimony

Mani and Meenakshi peered out of a silver frame, from the same photograph (black-and-white) that graced my dressing table. It was taken on their honeymoon in Mysore. Behind them are the plumes of the famous fountains of the Brindavan Gardens, their loveliness eclipsed by the bride's. Less remarkable but presenting a critical contrast, like stone for stained glass, or lode for lodestar, is her new partner-for-life. Both glow with well-being; with wellness and being. The sun stars Meenakshi's hair, silvers Mani's, makes bottomless wells of their eyes. The black-white light has cut Mani's mouth into two parallel lines, and ringed Meenakshi's with a penumbral O. Eyes and mouths are unfathomable but the chins are eloquent. Tilted upwards and outwards they arrow towards uncharted space. The world is too cramped for these two, so they must seek the skies— where the gods are. They *are* the gods. A god-couple. Shiva-and-Parvati. Krishna-and-Radha. A couplet from a thousand love poems.

Their open-and-shut faces, the surreptitious bliss in their stance, point to the obvious conclusion. The only logical one for that long-ago iridescent morning.

They have risen from a love bed.

That early elation has been tempered by time, tampered by events, but the hope is a lifetime's undertaking. The hope that coloured that black-and-white picture, those stars they were shooting at, the life in their expectancy, was for their as yet unborn child. How do I know? Because they've told me so. 'I prayed to have you, Kaveri,' Meenakshi said, touching folded hands to forehead and heart.

Me as me?

'You as you,' said Mani. 'Just as you are.'

I believe that. I have no reason not to.

Mani and Meenakshi peered round the door.

'Busy-a?'

Not at all, M&M. Only doing the crossword.

They darted in, as if late for the show and the doors would close, and quickly perched on the sofa (Meenakshi) and on the chair (Mani).

For a minute nothing happened—just we three Druids sitting in our magic circle. Then Mani leaned forward and screwed his eyes at the paper. 'How many have you solved?' He has no patience for crosswords.

'I like the easy one,' offered Meenakshi. She attempts it once in six months.

M&M. You don't want to talk about crosswords.

'Ha-a-hum . . .' Mani pulled at a non-existent beard.

'Um-ah-ah . . .' Meenakshi pulled at the pendant on her necklace.

I get it. It's an *anagram*.

'It's your *book*, Kaveri,' Meenakshi said in a rush. 'Yesterday we didn't, we couldn't . . .' She stopped, then lowered her head to impart the unpleasant diagnosis. 'That Guru who, um.

What he did to those children . . .' She rubbed two betel leaves together, summoning a genie to her aid.

The genie cleared its throat. 'What your mother is saying is it was too close to, ah-um, what happened that time . . . The incident of, um.'

'Not *exactly*, but a bit. *Quite* a bit. No, just a little bit. I mean, it reminds one of . . . it seems as if you'd used . . . Kaveri! Balumama is, *was* a lot like that man!' She fanned herself with the betel leaves.

I put my hand on her knee. This must be so hard for her.

Balumama doesn't have a conscience though, Ma, and the Guru did—in the end.

'But that doesn't make it better! This Guru committed suicide!'

'It seemed a bit, um, *suggestive*, you know.'

'People are superstitious about death, Kaveri,' Meenakshi said earnestly. She picked the stem off a betel leaf. 'And you can't kill your own family.'

Mani threw her an impatient look. 'The point is there's been a lot of talk. *Loose* talk. About what happened . . . that time.'

History, in a manner of speaking, *is* loose talk, tightly bound. A careful extrapolation of careless facts.

I revisited history, eh Pa?

'You did.' After a small pause, 'What other explanation is there for your plot? And your villain's resemblance to Balumama?'

None at all. Balumama *was* villainous.

'Don't talk like that, Kaveri! He's changed since then . . . and anyway he wasn't like that Guru.'

But if he wasn't, Ma, then why all the fuss?

'But he was . . . stop laughing. Oof! You're confusing me.' She folded the leaves, tucked the ends in, popped the sachet into her mouth.

Ma, people talk too much. You mustn't listen to them.

'*You* did,' Mani said. He massaged the back of his neck so the hair stuck out like a white ruff. 'You were so inquisitive.'

So what did I hear?

'*Half*-hear. The rest of it you imagined.' He looked at me expectantly.

Meenakshi brightened. 'Kaveri has a colourful imagination,' she said, reciting from a school report card.

Oh, riotous. *Stratos*pheric. She sees a clown's nose in every tomato. But imagination, wild or tamed, does not prepare you to deal with life. (Meenakshi's Lesson for Life: Life is *not* a Dream, row, row, row as you will.) And it will not do here. Imagination originates in, is substantiated by, is given credence through, experience. Nine times out of ten. And the subconscious works through the conscious—you cannot understand colours if you were blind at birth.

We were moving through the last hours of daylight. The evening sun trickled in through the parijata outside the verandah window, the sacred white-and-vermilion coral jasmine that must be shaken off the tree because it is forbidden to pick it. The traffic had shifted gear to frenetic, but the pedestrians had lost their morning ebullience. Things had gone right and things had gone wrong during the day, but scanning their tired faces, who could tell? They would deposit their troubles in their porch, along with their shoes, shelve them for the night. That is what porches are for. A transition between the chaos outside and peace within. Between day and night.

So what was to be done now? The Bureaucrat's Dilemma.

Should I be cashiered, or fined, or let off with a warning? Would any leniency be construed as that deadliest of bureaucratic sins—nepotism?

Mani rubbed his jaw. 'You don't know how difficult it was for us.' His skin had the texture of much-washed flannel. There was greyish lint where the razor had been careless. 'Your mother and I tried to minimise the damage. But it was not easy. Especially because we were so proud of you.'

I could imagine the pride! The shouting from the rooftop, the muezzin's call to worship, the town crier's summons to come hear the news.

'To give them their due, they *were* happy for you. Till they read the book. After that . . .' They looked at each other helplessly. After that everything went downhill—with the brakes off.

'Even Bharat was angry, Kaveri.'

Mani snorted. 'He said it was therapeutic puke.' He snorted again. 'He *would* use a cliché. Comes of being a newspaperman. But it wasn't in the least therapeutic, as it turned out.' Then, jocularly, to soften a blow, or suddenly mindful of his lifetime's role, 'But therapeutic puke has its uses, eh Kaveri?'

The silver lining. The success-at-any-cost. Never mind the process violations—they're justifiable in this case.

Streetlights had lightened the sky to a predawn milkiness, gilded the parijata leaves. Windows were bluing up with cathode rays. Mosquitoes fizzed out of the shadows, squatted fearlessly on ears and nose. Meenakshi switched on the wall light. The room appeared bleaker in the feeble pinkish glow.

Mani shifted in his chair. 'Funnily, Balumama didn't say anything. Just sat and let everyone talk for him. Almost as if,' he frowned, 'he was biding his time'. He shifted again. 'I argued it was quite common, what you, um, described. It didn't convince them.' There was a second's hesitation. 'It didn't convince *us.*'

Meenakshi continued to look bewildered. Common enough perhaps for the rest of the world, but we're not common. We're *Brahmins.* We're arbitrators, never perpetrators. Negotiators, never instigators. But we're colluders, Ma, I muttered. Famously sympathised with the British. And apathy is collusion too. *And* instigation. Bystanders are accomplices.

She was giving Mani an imploring glance. I tried, *we* tried. Where did we go wrong? '*Yein*, Kaveri? Did you have to write *this*?' Then, with more faith than conviction, 'You didn't mean any harm! You just didn't think!'

Kaveri doesn't think? Kaveri doesn't mean what she says? Mani's scepticism took his eyebrows all the way up to his hairline. She mayn't have meant harm, and sometimes (very rarely), she looks before she leaps, but she has a thinking mind, thank you. After all *I* trained it. No, her problem is she lacks judgement. And tact. And she tends to obfuscate—which is such a disadvantage for calculus.

Deep lines parenthesised his mouth. 'But she has principles,' he murmured. He waited for me to acknowledge his part in instilling them. When I didn't, 'It must have been a coincidence,' he said grumpily, and swatted at a mosquito. '*As* we told them.' The mosquito escaped and Meenakshi cupped her hand around it, let it out of the window. ('Tcha! Don't do that, Meenakshi, it'll come back.')

The coincidence angle was the weakest defence. It was, in fact, a straw.

Lilamami didn't clutch at it. The so-called coincidence was not incidental to the plot—it was central to it. That wasn't indicative of oversight or innocence—but how committed Meenakshi was to my innocence! Then Lilamami had gone off on a new tack. Mischief, she cried. It is mischief, as usual! It is money, said Devimami. Money talks, *she* talked. 'She *used* us!' stormed Lilamami. Without their permission. And for this use, or misuse, I must now pay.

But in what coinage? A puff of wind agitated the parijata. Meenakshi shivered, rubbed her elbow, saved another mosquito.

Things, it appeared, settled down for a while. But they came to a boil with the announcement of the Dharma Ratna. There were two enquiries from the papers and a photographer came round.

So close to fame, yet so far. Eh, Pa?

Our eyes locked. His don't-talk-back-to-me glare, my so-what-will-you-do stare. I was first to back off. Naturally.

Dried cells flaked the loose muscles of his arms. A defeated, old-man smell rose from him. He was being forced into a corner to defend an exposed flank, being pushed back into the hole from which he had, years ago, by dint of resolve and application and mastering the theory of relativity, crawled out, in his single pair of shoes (resoled with a bit of rubber tyre) and the cable-knit sweater his mother had made with recycled wool. Another dreary instance of history repeating—like undigested radish. 'Hmph. You go too far for your own good, Kaveri. That's always been your problem.'

'Kaveri,' Meenakshi said, biting her lower lip. 'That first day, the day you came, you said something about a problem.'

Mani pounced. 'What? What problem? You're keeping something from me!'

Headlights screamed through the guava leaves. Drs Mani and Meenakshi turned on me. How can we prescribe any degree of cure if you don't tell us everything? Hold nothing back. *First*. Did your bowels move this morning?

The air snagged in my throat.

It's not important, Pa.

But they wouldn't let go—gave me the third degree, in fact, so, I've been getting anonymous email, I confessed at last.

I wasn't entirely honest about the emails. I said I didn't have them, when all the time the printouts were burning a hole in my bag. But I had to tell them—they nearly pulled out my tongue—the gist of their contents. Of course they panicked. Would I come to harm? The word 'police' popped out, but I squashed it. Do we, I impressed upon them, wish to force this madman's hand by calling the *police*? After all (I tried to reassure them), this is only email—you can't send a letter bomb through email. Which unfortunately agitated them afresh. A letter bomb! Would that be next?

In the end it was the anonymity that calmed them. It made it unreal—surreal. The messages could have been from outer space. Mani tried to sell me the logic that only cowards wrote anonymous letters, and cowards didn't bite—just barked from afar. Or laughed, in this case. Then Meenakshi, pleating her lower lip, said it seemed an odd prank to play when the prankster wasn't there to watch the fun. (Her instinct scoring a bull's eye as usual.) Whereupon they again got so agitated I had to promise to go to the police at the first sign of trouble. Whatever shape *that* might take.

At last they withdrew. But they were not at all happy. They hadn't been allowed to make free with me as they are accustomed, and they couldn't bear that. After all, naked I had arrived into their world and naked I must proceed. I had signed away my secrets with my bare bottom and all the other indignities.

At dinner that night we got into an argument, Mani and I. It was inevitable. His interest in my affairs has always been inexhaustible, and he hadn't yet spent his curiosity on *AFL*.

'So tell me, Kaveri,' he smiled toothily, 'how many countries has your book been sold to? What *exactly* will you net?'

I decided to tease him. You mean in terms of readers, Pa?

'Tcha! *Money*! Net of expenses!'

He wanted a balance sheet. How much in and how much out, how much the operational (or frictional) losses.

What expenses, Pa? Midnight oil? The interest payments on my computer? Tax deductions on my house loan?

'I've no idea. All this is new to me.'

It's new to me too, Pa. I did not write anticipating *this* result—just enjoyed the process.

This was unpardonably patronising but it pleased him. There are unexpected air pockets in Mani. 'That is exactly the attitude I would wish for you.'

You wouldn't say that if I hadn't been successful, Pa. (The greyish irises widened.) What I mean, Pa, is you are not one to take failure philosophically. Failure as defined by you, that is.

He pounced. 'What do you mean, take it *philosophically*? There is no such thing as *a* philosophy. There are only *schools* of philosophy.'

Well, the school that teaches you detachment from rewards. Negates the reality of success or failure. Or at least downplays it as illusion.

'Ah.' He flicked his hand and went back to kneading the

rice into his sambar. 'Vedanta. Half-baked at that.' I gritted my teeth.

I mean, whatever *school* of philosophy teaches you to step lightly. I'm sorry Pa, but you came down heavily on me. You could never accept my limitations.

'Tcha! It was for your own good—that I raised the bar for you.'

I would have preferred you to leave it where it was, Pa. Accept me as I was. Instead of constantly trying to improve upon what I was not.

His brow creased. 'I have tolerated a lot from you. If that's not acceptance, what is?'

It was futile. I couldn't get through. *He* couldn't get through.

Why's it so hard for you to give in to the inevitable, Pa? Why don't you see it as a grace—to be able to give in? Gracefully?

'I'm a survivor. You don't survive by giving in. You survive by fighting the odds. It's a lifelong battle. I believed,' dolefully, 'but perhaps I'm wrong . . . I liked to think I *equipped* you to do this.'

You equipped me to manipulate the odds. And not just for survival. For success—at *any* cost. Because you wouldn't let *me* give up, Pa, and *you* wouldn't give *in*.

'I believe you must go on till you're satisfied you've done your best.'

What a volte-face! And what a con! Because, of course, I had to satisfy *him*. And that was an impossibility.

That implies, at least I inferred, that compromise is unthinkable, Pa.

'That hasn't prevented you from compromising, I notice.' And in case I didn't get it, 'Compromising your family.'

I checked my temper. (It took more counts than ten.) Perhaps I saw no other way to achieve my purpose, Pa. *Your* purpose. And guess what—I made compromises before this. I stand guilty.

'Well, don't hold *me* responsible for your guilt. Guilt is personal.'

Personal! When it's you who makes me feel guilty!

I couldn't go on. Neither could he. He was looking so stricken I wanted to rush across, put my head on his shoulder and cry, it isn't you Pa, it isn't you! It isn't me either! It is our legacy! Like the warts that pop on our neck, this too was in store for us—the burden of each other's guilt!

Meenakshi clattered a spoon or something. It was her water tumbler. She had tumbled it to the floor. There was very little water in it, fortunately. The clatter cut the wires, gave us pause to breathe. Fortunately.

I'm sorry, Pa.

But he would not leave well alone. 'I would never consciously inflict guilt on anyone, Kaveri.' His face crumpled in sad bewilderment. 'Not for anything on *you*.'

I cringed. But I managed to smile—for him and for me.

I'm sure you think it's another path to self-knowledge, Pa. Examining a guilty conscience now and then. But I have no desire to know myself. I'd rather get a good night's sleep. For that you have to dodge your conscience.

'I'm sorry if that's all you got from me in all these years.' He sounded very sorry at having squandered his precious wisdom. 'I intended you to aim higher.'

Anger flared in me as the years of his proprietary bullying came rushing back. The devil goaded me to take on this old man who, in his agitation had begun to belch, gulping mouthfuls of air in dry, hollow gasps. *Chh- chh- chh.* A chequered history of love, submission and slavery drove me as much as the devil. And we were off again and running.

For which you drove me, Pa. Of course you never *intended* to make me feel . . . inadequate. But you did. Because it had to be the best for you, nothing less, and my best wasn't *your* best!

'Well, we know now what *your* best is.' He gave me a faun-like leer. 'It's this book.'

That was the closest I had ever come to hating him.

You saw my inadequacies as failure, Pa. You even reviewed them. Quarter-yearly. So I learned to manipulate them—to serve your purpose. I couldn't fail you, could I?

'And for this . . . this *deceit* you blame *me*?' His fingers dripped sambar on his vest. I felt a pang. 'Is there nothing you can *thank* me for? All the encouragement, and the support? The *love*?'

I could not speak. Then recalling my adolescence, his captious omnipresence, my confusions, I hardened. The encouragement was extortion. He had charged an extortionist's fee for the support. *Hmmm. Surely you can do better than this, Kaveri. Try again. Try, try, try again.* As for the love, he expected returns on that too. A disciple's homage.

It was emotional blackmail, Pa.

'I don't want to hear that expression in this house.' His eyes were pebbles. In an instant he had grown, from a rice-eating old man to a monster crunching bones. A Jack in the Beanstalk miracle had taken place before my eyes. As it had done times without reckoning. '*I will not tolerate those words in this house, do you hear?*' The pebbles started out of his head. Ping. Ping.

And it was back, the sensation of a train thudding between

my ears. It was back, the helplessness, the hopelessness. Approval, love, safety had been withdrawn. I was going to die. I'd been thrown into this giant's maw. Because I had gone too far.

We went through the motions of eating. Slowly, reality returned. The light warmth of the summer night, the incandescence of the terracotta, the scent of jasmine. Meenakshi crunched an appalam, stifling the crackle with water so her eyes bulged. (Poor Meenakshi. This was a quarrel. Tricked out in fine phrases and looped with bafflements, but unquestionably an unpleasantness.) Reality was articulated too in the tangerine streaks in her hair, the fireball lily in the crystal vase. The child grew, the giant shrunk. Where a fearsome mask was only seconds ago there were pouches of hollow skin and swallowed air. *Ch-ch-ch.*

I must go then, Pa, mustn't I? Since I won't take it back. Emotional blackmail.

My tongue wrapped itself around the words. *Emotional blackmail.* Unwholesome and glutinous. Caramel filling.

'Oh-oh. *Look* what I have done . . .' In her distress Meenakshi had poured water over her rice instead of rasam. But father and daughter did not heed her. The father looked at *her,* his child, as if *she's* turned into a monster—which she has—and he is afraid of what it can do to him. It will leave him, it will go away, never to return. It is the end of everything. Oh, the power, the power! The rice congealed in a sad lump on his plate.

But he stood his ground. (I admired that.) 'I can't stop you from doing whatever you wish. Now that you have no use for my approval.' He pushed his plate away, rice and all. Meenakshi's face fell. I felt another pang. Pang after pang!

A hard light ricocheted off the dishes. The crystal glittered, the fireball lily blazed. I ran out of the room.

I lay on my bed, face in the pillow, my heart racing miles to the minute. My heart was full of beats but empty otherwise. Like a drum. My stomach was empty too but it was weighted with rocks.

'Kaveri.' She was standing by the door. 'I have brought you some curd-rice.'

Amma. Please. I *can't*.

'For *my* sake, Kaveri.' She held out her begging bowl. 'Don't argue with him, Kaveri. And I've told him not to talk about your book.'

I took the bowl from her and ate the pledge of faith.

The next morning all was as it should be. He was back to stalking me. There was no doubt who *this* heavy breather was. 'How about walking in the park with me, Kaveri? Instead of eroding the courtyard?'

His voice was jokey but his face was crossed with doubt. Ordinarily, there would have been no question about my loyalty, but there's no telling now. 'I'm feeling a bit dull,' he pressed his case. 'A little exercise will do me good.'

An exiguous excuse but a command too—it had an unignorable resonance Meenakshi's supplications lack. My base instinct, the one I try to keep clamped, cried *no*! I want to grate carrots in the kitchen and gossip about whether Balumama really would have been diddled of fifty thousand rupees if Lilamami hadn't spotted the discrepancy, or was it just a calculation error. I wanted to find out how Jana's marriage was doing. I wanted to . . .

But when he turned his face up to mine, like an empty dinner plate waiting to be filled, I was struck with panic. The kind I had known in his brief illnesses—illnesses that threatened to orphan me. (*All* his illnesses threatened to orphan me, even at the height of his vigour.) The old fright returned. I must obey or I would regret it one day. I must put down this rebellion, my heart's betrayal, or there would be a karmic reckoning. Was it out of love I did it, or fear that one day I would be haunted by this small instance of disloyalty?

'Pollama, Kaveri?'

Pollam, Appa.

He was all dressed up for our modest outing, in a red-and-blue plaid cotton-flannel shirt and a green-and-yellow striped beret. A festival of colours. But the usually clear eyes were dappled with misgiving. Knowing well my selfishness—it was bred by him after all—he doesn't entirely trust my compliance. I just might, for all he knew, unlace my shoes, shrug, say, forget it Pa. Some other time.

What could he come up with to prevent that? 'Let's go to our secret garden, Kaveri. There is a magnificent bauhinia I want to show you.' And he whistled a snatch through the window. Ah, so that is today's special offer!

Give me a minute to change, Pa.

So I put on my sweatshirt, pushed my hair through a rubber band, tied my shoelaces. What did it matter that it rained last night and the bauhinia show would be a washout? That our secret garden has long been public knowledge? It wasn't much to give up, this half-hour out of my useless day. *But it is! It is!* I had to heed this martial call because green-and-yellow beret took precedence over rust-and-orange hair. That's the way it was, has always been. That's the way it will always be.

'Ready-a Kaveri?'

Ready, Appa.

Waving off the autorickshaws that came panting up for our custom, we crossed the road to the safety of the greens. And thereon to a side street leading to our 'secret garden'.

It was one of those perfect golden mornings that made you ache with unspecified longings. The blue of the sky had the clarity of a temple bell. The sun was bursting with goodwill. The earth teeming with potential. Hope was the order of the day.

The rain trees lining the road were loaded with flowers, canary yellow contrasting with the almost black leaves. ('Tcha! Not *rain* tree, Kaveri, *Peltophorum.*') Snowy drifts of sky jasmine had fetched up on the grassy verge. ('*Cork*, Kaveri, if you can't remember *Millingtonia hortensis.*') But we didn't linger. Our walk had a purpose, and purposefully we marched through the avenue of Ashoka trees, standing tall and straight and true. Two rows of soldiers presenting arms.

As I feared, the magnificent bauhinia was somewhat dishevelled. And four walkers and a courting couple had tumbled onto our secret. Yet all was not lost. Sheltering under a branch, Mani located five perfect blossoms, magenta beaded with silver. And, after all, the garden was large enough to contain all of us in our solitude. It was a time of perfect acquiescence. *Look here, Appa. Look there, Kaveri.*

By and by our soles became crusted with gravel. Some day, back in Delhi, I would shake out a red flake, wonder where it came from. Then, when I remembered, it would light up the room, this transcendental fleck, flood it with the evanescence of this morning. It would, for just a moment, dispel the brassy harshness of that city. But that time seemed too far away now—an impossible time. For now it was enough to find an unsullied bauhinia to gift Meenakshi, who deserved better than gravel on her mirror floors.

'Kaveri, how do you propose to invest your advance, and the prize money?'

Evidently, he had been brooding over this. The wonder was it had taken this long for it to surface. I considered telling him it was stashed under my bed, then decided not to tease him.

'. . . you must plan, you know. It's not small change to leave idling.' He tucked in his chin, tried to look stern, failed. Instead there was a flash of teeth, a dazzling display of his gratification. 'Also, what about the rights—cinema, TV, translation, etc.?'

It was all delightfully unfamiliar, and he was loving it. Hitherto, earnings meant modest remittances on the first of every month, and modest, predictable, annual increases. Not munificence on this scale. 'You must invest *wisely*. And *soon*.' Before the fatal midnight hour strikes and all that gold turns to hay. 'Remember what I always tell you. Save one-third of your income.'

Oh yes. But which third? The third we spend on eating out because I'm too tired to cook? Or the third that pulls us across Arya's troughs? What about the third that went in restocking the house when a maid cleaned it up a little too well? My father's excellent grasp of finance makes no allowances for our fragile ecosystem.

'You can laugh all you like but you'd be a fool not to heed good advice.' I held my breath. 'Remember what Mr Micawber said.'

I do, I *do!*

But it was no use. 'Income one pound. Expenditure nineteen shillings eleven pence. Result happiness. Income one pound. Expenditure twenty shillings and *one* pence. Result misery.'

Right, Pa. Income one crore, ten lakh rupees. Expenditure one crore, ten lakh and *one* rupee. Result misery.

The sun squinted through the leaves. An itinerant ray lit his face. His eyes were clouded and the skin had worked loose around the mouth. I smiled and took his arm to show there could be no hard feelings between us. But his features still looked bruised.

I was just pulling your leg, Pa. The income's nowhere near that.

He sighed. 'I realise that, my dear. My sense of humour has deserted me.' He looked so dejected I squeezed his arm.

We'll restore it, Pa, I said, shaking a fist. We'll fight for it!

He lifted his face, such a sunny face, to mine. 'It *is* being restored, Kaveri. With you here.'

Oh, Pa.

He lowered his head confidingly. 'I'll let you into a little secret. You remember the times I used to talk to you about destiny? I never let on but I often had doubts about this business of a Grand Design. *Serious* doubts. Especially when things went wrong.'

The 'things going wrong' was a sideswipe at my frequent non-compliance. Naturally any course of destiny ordered by him and evaded by me couldn't have been the machination of a rational agency.

Good heavens, Pa. And here I believed every word when you said there is logic and order in everything that happens! A *grand* logic and a *grand* order!

His laugh rang out. 'Oh, I must have believed it too—because I wanted to. Subconsciously.'

For a moment, the sun dimmed. *Do you believe in the power of the subconscious? I could have sworn there was something in your book that woke my subconscious.*

We stopped by a small hill of watermelons. A single broken head had spilled gore on the pavement. Wicked black seeds winked in the sunshine. It's all right, I said silently. In the Grand Design we're just dots, and to the Grand Designer we're *invisible* dots. The headlines shriek, the ambulances scream, humanity weeps—and yet the sun continues to rise. *And* shine.

'. . . just *some*times, I wonder if the alternative is not more alarming.' He flicked a seed off the path with his walking stick. 'Chaos, you understand. Arbitrariness as a natural law. The doctrine of caprice, not cause and effect. Mind you, I don't think there is malicious intent. I just can't subscribe to the idea of omnipotence, much less a *fair-minded* omnipotence. But I must admit,' twinkling, 'your book has converted me. I feel . . . vindicated. All those hard years of trying to do the right thing, not thinking of rewards or returns . . .' He sighed, then smiled. 'I enjoyed reading it, especially the tussle between conscience and intellect and your analogy of a mountain and a river. Mind you,' a little sternly, in case this extravagance might dilute his holdings in me, 'some of the arguments were undigested, but still . . . you could even have stumbled upon a couple of original ideas there.' He nodded at a pigeon perched on the kerb. 'Who was your muse? *Me*?'

Alerted by a secret warning device, the pigeon took off with a squawk, disappeared into the clairvoyant blue.

He bounced along as if the earth had lost several units of gravity. 'To be frank, I never thought you had it in you!'

I didn't think you did!

'I said I never thought *you* had it in *you*! Not me!'

Oh, lord. I MEANT, I DIDN'T THINK *YOU* THOUGHT *I* HAD IT IN *ME*!

But my words were borne off by a yammering autorickshaw.

'It wasn't *me* I was talking about! It was *you*!' The cords in his neck stood out.

This is crazy. I KNOW!

'What?'

Oh lordy-lord. I'LL TELL YOU AT HOME!

I had bellowed into a sudden vacuum in the traffic. He jumped, rubbed his ear. Sorry, Pa.

'*Nobody* can hear a thing in this noise,' he said stiffly.

Exactly.

I was committed to walk with him every day. He collected me at the gate as if it was his due (I was happy to pay) and we proceeded to play our conspiracy of make-believe. While he didn't actually take my hand before we crossed the road it was there. It was there in the '*Wait*, Kaveri,' and the 'Go *now*!' But his invisible grip was less a safeguard for my incompetence than a prop for his frailty. His failing eyes perceived amorphous shapes, creatures on mysterious migratory trajectories. Trying to gauge their position and getting it wrong, he shied away from a car on the other side of the road, even as he advanced into a dreaming cyclist. I rescued him each time, pretending he was too fast for me. 'This road is *impossible* to cross if you're not used to it. Just stay beside me!'

I happened upon him once, gripping the arms of his chair, his expression murderous. As if he was about to swoop on a mosquito.

Where is the mosquito, Pa? *Pa*? What's the matter—what're you looking at?

Meenakshi dragged me away. 'You don't understand. He's imagining the . . . the end.'

This is spooking me, Ma. I must ask him . . .

'No, let him be, Kaveri. He's at peace.'

That he's most certainly not.

'He's old, Kaveri. He's afraid. Don't get into arguments with him.'

We're *all* afraid of death, Ma. Why, when I'm in a plane I'm afraid I'll fall from the sky.

'This is different.'

She was right. He and I were at different points in the continuum. He was afraid of falling from anywhere—even his chair. The earth could give way beneath him at any time.

Standing behind his chair, I space-gazed with him. What did he see? Death in different guises. But no guise is the right fit. No cues are timely.

Oh, Pa. You don't have a choice. Not even you.

Two days before the housewarming I received a summons from Lilamami for the talk we hadn't had that first day. The summons came via Devimami (naturally she offered her services) to Meenakshi.

'Don't go,' said Mani promptly. 'Make some excuse. Say you have a headache.'

'But,' faltered Meenakshi, pinching her lip. Nobody defied Lilamami. 'But we don't want any unpleasantness at the housewarming!'

Perhaps I can read Bharat's scrapbook when I'm there.

She looked relieved but, 'Whatever are you encouraging

him in that for?' growled Mani. 'It's high time he got into a proper career, instead of this bit work for the newspaper. How much is he paid, do you know?'

I've no idea, Pa. Does it matter?

He harrumphed. 'It may not matter to *you*, but some of us have responsibilities.'

In that case Bharat is free to do what he likes—being free of any responsibilities.

'Well! Someday he'll realise the futility of such a life, and the waste of a good law degree.'

In the scheme of things Pa, in your Grand Design, perhaps it's as meaningful to preserve useless buildings as it is to preserve the laws of the land. Of *this* land, at least. What I mean is, perhaps he's happy doing what he does.

Mani snorted as if to say, what has happiness got to do with making a decent living?

Everything, Pa, everything.

Meenakshi decided to come with me. She packed a dozen coconut barfis to take as a peace offering. Although she didn't say that's what they were. 'Rajumama likes them,' she said.

The car wouldn't start and she began unpacking the barfis, humming to herself, when I mooted an autorickshaw. 'But it's going to rain!' she cried.

You don't *have* to come, Ma, I said for the nth time, but, casting a longing look at the kitchen, she turned her back on the house as if she knew where her duty lay. While we waited outside the gate, 'I don't know . . . I really don't know . . .' she kept saying in a hand-wringing sort of way, when an autorickshaw puttered to a stop and put an end to her dithering. She bent down to rescue two jacaranda flowers from the kerb and then climbed into the vehicle with a come-what-may sigh. I scrambled in after her.

'It's not that I am *scared*,' she said, biting her lower lip. 'There's nothing to be afraid of. I've known them for forty years.' She sounded as if she didn't know them at all. The autorickshaw speeded up, her sari billowed out. She pulled it in and tucked it under her legs. 'They can't do anything. They'll *say* things but they always do that anyway. I'm used to it.' Her back slumped. 'Anyway, they may not be home. If they aren't,' she sat up again, 'we can go shopping. If they are— Kaveri! I *wish* you hadn't . . .' The sari escaped from under her legs. She grabbed it, tucked it back. 'I have enough problems. Did I tell you the cat is pregnant? I had thought it was male!' And all this time I hadn't made a sound.

Cheer up, Ma. I've got my handy-dandy revolver in my bag.

That earned me a smile. In the early afternoon sunlight her still-pretty teeth glinted. She had applied—with a liberal hand—her favourite rose-pink lipstick. Now she glazed the rose petals with the tip of her tongue, straining towards the driver's mirror to check the effect. The driver caught her eye and grinned. Flustered, she withdrew. But the damage had been done. Sticking his leg out of the side of the auto, he crooned, 'Juuulie, I love yooouu!'

'These fellows are such loafers! No respect at all for ladies. Can't he see I'm old?'

I prodded the roll of fat squeezed out by her blouse. Not with that sexy lipstick, Ma. He's paying you a compliment. After all, you were once a schoolgirl's dream. Ms Roselips '76.

'Have some respect for me, Kaveri. And don't call me by that name.'

It's better than calling you Fish-eyes, Ma. ('Meenakshi' literally translates to 'eyes-shaped-like-a-fish'. Which isn't the same as Fish-eyes—as my mother never fails to point out.)

'You don't have to call me that either. And it's not *fish-eyes*, you know. It's eyes-shaped-like-a-fish.'

Anyway Ma, your beautiful mouth was my only claim to fame at school.

'Now, you're getting very silly.' She leaned back on the loose plastic seat, which, if you're not careful, can tip you forward. Sure enough it did, and we scrabbled to right it.

It's true though, I resumed when we'd settled down. By the way, I met one of your fans at Nilgiri's yesterday. Kausalya. She asked after you. Very fondly.

'Really? She actually remembered me?'

Kausalya was my house captain and star shooter of Sophia's basketball team. How I worshipped her! How I yearned after her as she stood foursquare and perspiring on the basketball court! Those sturdy legs in their tight shorts, those brawny forearms! Those dewy droplets on her forehead! And in the middle of the generous exudation *a perfect pimple*! This goddess actually descended to speak to me one magical day, at the annual inter-school basketball match. At half-time, flushed and sweaty with eight epochal goals, she walked up to me, *me*, Kaveri, water dribbling down her chin from a bottle she'd lifted so stylishly to her mouth, to ask me, *me*, Kaveri, 'Have you a safety pin? My damned blouse button's burst.' Her damned blouse button! Her button be damned! She spoke to me! 'Can you get hold of a pin?' demanded the superwoman impatiently. 'It's nearly time!' And I got a pin from heaven-knows-where and, in a daze of love, handed it to her. 'Oh, thanks.' To this day I cannot recall how I pulled off the miracle of the pin. Why, they won that match because of that pin! An epic battle could have been lost but for me!

How did you know my name, I dared to ask the goddess afterward. 'Oh, we all do,' she said, looking bored. 'You're the one with the beautiful mother. With a mouth like a rose.'

Meenakshi cheered up vastly after this narration. Tucking her chin into her shoulder, she giggled. 'Podi!'

As we turned into Gandhi Bazaar her giggles ceased. 'Kaveri, can we stop here first? At Sari Emporium? I've picked a sari for you. I want you to see it.' She leaned over to speak to the driver.

Oh, Ma, not *now*! Let's get this other thing over with.

'But I've *told* them to keep it!'

It won't spoil if kept for another hour.

'But we're—oh! Oh, oh! We've passed the shop!' She crumpled into the seat.

We'll stop on the way back, Ma. And have a coffee at Nilgiri's too. And chocolate cake. With chocolate sauce!

But she would not be comforted. 'You're so *bossy*, Kaveri. And I really wish,' she puffed as we climbed the stairs to Lilamami's flat, 'you had written a happy story. With happy people. After all, there are so many happy people around.'

A perfect non sequitur had bloomed again.

Stop worrying, Ma. They aren't mad at *you*.

Which wasn't the smartest thing to say. She clutched my arm. 'Kaveri, don't upset them further. Just be . . .' But here the maid opened the door and I never learned what I should be. Not myself, for sure.

There was no sign of anyone. Bharat was out, apparently. So were Uma and her incontinent baby. Rajumama was probably supervising a painter. Balumama had done one of his disappearing tricks. Jana, I presumed, was busy cleaning her brother's flat—doubtless using a toothbrush to do it.

Suddenly we turned shy, Meenakshi and I. Years of familiarity vanished into the plastic-covered jacquard sofa set, and the lacquered centre table displaying old issues of *India Today*, *Business Today* and *Femina*. High on the wall hung a blue-and-gold clock, and another, black-and-bronze, on the opposite wall. This was a waiting room. We waited. And by and by the maid arrived to take us inside.

Lilamami's bedroom was as determinedly pink as Meenakshi's lipstick. The walls were salmon pink, the curtains cerise, the bedspread magenta and the laminate on the dressing table fuchsia.

Like entering a uterus, eh Ma, I whispered, to shore up her spirits. But her attention was elsewhere. On Lilamami.

Lilamami was leaning against the bed's headboard in a queenly pose—neck aslant, feet elegantly crossed at the ankles, hand smoothing hair. Devimami sat at the foot of the bed, Rajumama in an armchair in a neutral zone. Upon our entrance the ensemble rustled, as if an invisible conductor had lifted a baton. The maid dragged in two straight-backs for Meenakshi and me, and left the room. The inescapable line slithered between us.

'So,' opened Lilamami. 'Here you are.'

Second fiddle Devimami struck up. 'Why didn't you come back that day?' she said to me, and, 'Where are *you* going now?' to Rajumama, who was sidling out of his chair. He sat down again and began cracking his knuckles. She spread out her hams as if she'd wangled a ringside seat and intended to make full use of it. If there were a funeral with only three people in attendance you could be sure Devimami would be one of the three.

It was not exactly a rousing welcome. Still, we hadn't been shown the door.

'So, Lilamami.'

'So, Meenakshi.'

'So, Rajumama.'

'So, Meenakshi.'

'So?' Lilamami inclined her head in my direction.

There's not a whole lot one can respond to that. Where's Bharat, I asked.

'He'll be back in half an hour,' Devimami answered. 'Till then you will have to put up with us.'

Lilamami drew herself up. '*She* put up with *us*?'

'How's the interior decoration coming along, Rajumama?' Meenakshi asked nervously.

He looked at his wife. 'Well. It's coming along well.'

'Is the painting finished?'

'More or less.'

How many flats have been sold, Rajumama?

'None since we last met.' Stupid me. It had only been three days since we met.

'You think it's as easy as selling spinach?' said Lilamami, sarcastic as you please.

'Or books?' said Devimami-the-wit.

'Kaveri doesn't do the actual selling, you know,' explained my good mother. But since no one asked who actually did, she fell to shredding her lips with her teeth. I put my hand on her knee.

With this address, Rajumama, and with the kind of finishes you've used, marble and all, it shouldn't be too hard to dispose of, I mean, sell the flats. Also, with our family's standing . . .

I could have kicked myself. Lilamami had found her

opening. 'Our family's *standing*,' she boomed, 'is *mud* now'. And in a tone that shot home the bolts, 'Thanks to *you*.'

Well, the business of the day had begun. The silence was broken by a tiny yelp from Meenakshi. 'My foot got knotted,' she explained apologetically. This is an old complaint. Various joints in her body suddenly, inexplicably and painfully 'get knotted' as she calls it. She flexed her foot. I knelt down to massage it. To my fury, neither of my aunts offered sympathy.

However, 'Devi, get Meenakshi some hot coffee,' Rajumama said. 'And for Kaveri of course. Sarsari, for *all* of us.'

'We've *had* coffee,' Lilamami reminded him.

'Just a thimbleful,' he pleaded. 'With fresh milk. That coffee was so-so.'

'The old milk isn't finished yet.'

Rajumama's face fell. 'You should not be drinking so much coffee,' Devimami told him and, 'I've kept the fresh milk for tomorrow,' Lilamami said and, 'It'll keep you awake,' Devimami said and Meenakshi protested she didn't want coffee and I began wondering why it was that in this family a simple request engendered a parliamentary debate when, looking ill-used, Devimami cranked herself up and padded out, and, even before the door closed behind her, could be heard bawling instructions to the kitchen.

After a bit the maid brought a tray of steel tumblers and a plate of murukku. Devimami sent her back for a spare tumbler. When it came she poured a teaspoonful into it from each of the others and handed it to Rajumama. Nobody commented on this uncouth behaviour, not even her husband, who received his tumbler meekly. 'Dip your murukku in the coffee,' she ordered us. 'It tastes very well.'

Obediently, we dunked. It tasted very strange.

'So, what is your great daughter going to do?' said Lilamami, addressing a point in the distance.

Meenakshi fidgeted. 'Nothing much, Lilamami. Just rest, I suppose. She's tired. After all the . . . um. She needs to rest. Because she's tired. From all the . . . um . . . you know. It's tiring and she's, um, resting.'

'*Tcha*! What is she going to do about the . . . *book*?'

I don't have to do anything, Lilamami. It's there for anyone who wishes to buy it.

Lilamami turned to Meenakshi. 'Is she stupid or what?'

'She is not stupid,' returned my mother with spirit.

'She's being funny, then. This is not the time or place to be funny.' Lilamami flashed her rhinestones, first at me and then back at Meenakshi. 'Haven't you talked to her yet?'

'I . . . no. I mean, yes.' Meenakshi gave me an anguished glance.

'Really, Meenakshi,' said Devimami.

Lilamami slammed her coffee tumbler on the tray. 'Didn't you tell her she must cut out some of the passages? Change them?'

She couldn't be making sense even to herself, but I owed it to her to explain.

That's not possible, Lilamami. It's already out.

'For future editions,' said Devimami crushingly.

There's a contract. I can't break it—not without reason.

'Of course you can—it's your book, isn't it?' Devimami again.

There *is* a reason. Tell your book people it's causing a scandal.' Back to Lilamami.

'Ama.' Devimami's neck was going up and down like one

of those spring-necked dolls. 'It's affected your parents too. Ama.' Nod. 'See how sad your mother is?' Nod, nod.

Meenakshi blinked. 'Oh, but.'

Book people love a scandal, Lilamami. (*How exciting, my dear! Which one of your relations is scandalous?*) You can forget about appealing to their sensitivity. They have none. My book person would say a scandal is a route to market capitalisation. (*Can we get a good media story out of it?*)

Two lines popped up on either side of the pottu on Lilamami's forehead, gripped it in a vice. Red powder sprinkled her nose. 'Say you had to do it for family reasons.'

She was making less and less sense. Beside her, Devimami nodded away.

Lilamami. Once it's out there's nothing I, or anyone, can do.

'You can. You can put in something like, "This is fiction and the characters don't bear any resemblance to any living person."'

'Ama. For future editions.'

'That's a sure way of telling readers the opposite,' murmured Rajumama. 'They'd smell a rat.'

'They already have,' said Devimami. 'They smelled *us*.'

'Kaveri . . .' Beside me Meenakshi was busy trying to make her large person small. She was crunched into her chair, her arms and legs entangled in her sari. I worried briefly about her feet. All of her would be knotted before the afternoon was over.

Our silence roused the bully in Lilamami. She rapped the bedstead. 'As for this prize. You have no moral right to it. Anyway, how can you accept anything from these people? *Civic* Foundation? Who *are* they? Traders and contractors.'

Devimami made a face as if she'd swallowed castor oil. 'Ama.'

In some circles they'd pass as decent capitalists, Lilamami. Anyway, *I* don't care so long as their cheque doesn't bounce.

Lilamami's forehead was a fishing net of wrinkles. 'But the publicity! The newspapers have already come here several times.'

'Ama.'

There was a pins-and-needles silence. Meenakshi, alternating between two different pains, touched my arm. I bent down to massage her foot again. '*Pollam*, Kaveri,' she whispered. 'Please let's go.'

I straightened up. We'll have to leave now, Lilamami. Amma isn't well.

'You can't go! I haven't finished! I . . .' She slumped against the headboard as if the air had been let out of her.

And now I did feel sorry for her. It was an ennobling emotion. But I also knew from old it would not last long.

Lilamami. Just shut them all up. Tell them it's just a story.

'Nobody will believe that,' said Devimami. Her eyes glistened. *How* she's enjoying herself. 'There are too many similarities. And nobody can mistake the setting—it's the Big House exactly.'

'It isn't there anymore,' murmured Rajumama. He reminded me of the spare in an orchestra who hits a triangle suddenly and vitally, as if he's just remembered to.

Devimami shook her head at him. '*We* are still here.'

She began with the inconsequentialities. The description of the road, the old tin-roofed school down the road, the neighbourhood. The woodshed where Blondie once had her puppies. The staircase with the missing treads. The privy at the bottom of the garden, lit by a lantern in the night. The disused well choked with algae—that I'd found a use for. It had come in very handy, in fact.

It got closer. Hotter. Bumpier. The Austin (which had been Balumama's first car), the Parker pen that Balumama clipped into his pocket. And the Panama cigarettes he used to smoke were, damningly, the Guru's choice too.

'Lots of people smoke Panama,' Meenakshi offered, trying to get a handhold on this slippery exchange.

Devimami quelled her with a glance. 'Meenakshi, we're not stupid. Why *Panama* when there are a dozen other brands to choose from? It's a mischievous detail.'

'It's her sense of humour,' quavered Meenakshi.

Lilamami held up her hand to block any more transports of humour. 'You think it's funny when a troubled man jumps into a well?' Then she took the bull by the horns. 'Balumama had enough trouble with you children. Always plaguing him.'

'*You* were the worst,' contributed her faithful ally.

Rajumama stirred uneasily, hit his triangle again. 'Let's not get into this now.'

But Lilamami swept on. 'And he was always looking out for you. He had such concern for your safety.' Yes. He pulled us off the trees. Dragged us off the roof. Chased us off the well. 'And this is your thanks for that? It's all because of your indulgence,' she turned on Meenakshi, who looked so guilty I wanted to shake her.

Devimami bounded behind in full cry. 'Ama. You didn't control her, Meenakshi. Didn't *discipline* her enough.'

Meenakshi's head drooped. It was her fault I was so wild. She had paid out too much rope. 'She has the artistic temperament,' she murmured, but without much hope.

'Tcha!' frowned Devimami. 'She has no *respect*.'

They encouraged me to respect myself first, Devimami. So I could stand up to people.

'*Well!*'

Meenakshi jerked up. 'Don't speak to your aunt like that!' She could never be at the helm here—traditionally we were the deckhands—but could, with diligence, become the lookout. 'Say you're sorry. At once.'

Sorry, Devimami.

Lilamami was slowly puffing up. 'That court scene she wrote! That man who was tried!' Then her face went all dented and queer.

'Like Balu . . .' began Meenakshi. '*Oh!*' She clapped her fingers to her mouth.

Sometimes I wonder about my mother, I really do. But a bell jangled in my head. *Trial?* Was Balumama tried?

Lilamami looked at me with near hatred. Devimami started forward. Rajumama was finding his nails an inordinately interesting study. Meenakshi flattened herself against the chair. At this rate I would have to scrape her off.

'She's pretending,' grated Lilamami.

'Ama,' nodded her true friend. 'Putting on an act.'

Pretending about what? What act?

It gave me no pleasure to prod Lilamami into the confession booth. My eyes felt gritty, and there was a sour taste in my mouth.

Rajumama frowned. 'Don't play the innocent. Of course you know.'

What are you all talking about? I tell you I *don't* know.

'He was wrongly accused,' said Lilamami fiercely. 'And he was a freedom fighter!'

'He still wears khadi although *I* stopped long ago,' mused Rajumama.

'A true Brahmin. Simple living, high thinking. Why can't people remember *that*?'

Devimami, sensing the pace flagging, rushed to shore up the argument. 'They *do* remember. That's why they have begun gossiping.'

'*I* haven't heard them,' said Meenakshi, rather pluckily.

'Nor I,' Rajumama seconded, giving Lilamami a sympathetic look.

'But *I* have!' Devimami was frantic now. The contretemps, shaping up so well, was dissolving. 'All my friends have been asking me about . . . about *it*!'

And I thought, not for the first time, it's not Lilamami but Devimami who is the niggardly one. She can't spare anyone the smallest respite.

Lilamami, who had gone off into a small daydream, suddenly woke up. 'He went through untold suffering. Untold suffering,' she repeated, liking the sound of it. 'He suffers even now.'

This was the first I'd heard of Balumama's untold suffering. Meenakshi's puzzlement informed it was news to her too. She was also looking a bit peeved. People were several moves ahead of her—again.

'He has been functioning on only one kidney for years,' continued Lilamami. 'He's not out of the woods yet. Not out of the woods,' she repeated, liking the sound of this too.

'A dysfunctional kidney and an overworked one,' nodded Rajumama. 'The doctors want to remove it but Balu keeps putting it off.'

And I wondered if we were to discuss Balumama's kidneys for the rest of the afternoon.

But *that* was not his sickness, Rajumama. His sickness, as *I* understand, was . . .

Rajumama coughed twice. Lilamami's devouring mouth quivered. Meenakshi smothered a sneeze. But, but, but. In Devimami's eyes there was an instant, just a millisecond, of triumph. She dipped a bit of murrukku into the bottom of her glass and crunched. She let out a discreet coffee-belch. *It tastes very well.*

The aunts went off into a whispered consultation. *She could. She should. She must. She has to. She. She. She,* popping like sesame seeds in hot oil. Meenakshi looked at me anxiously. Is it over? Can we leave now? 'It's getting late, Lilamami,' she said in a hesitant voice.

This halted the confabulation on the bed. It also arrested Rajumama's hand inching towards the murukku.

Then, 'In forgiveness there is salvation,' announced Lilamami, confounding us all.

Understanding dawned. Television! Lilamami's search for a guru had ended in a small-screen goddess from the US. Now her opinions are anchored by Oprah Winfrey.

Meenakshi's relief was palpable. 'Yes. Kaveri didn't mean to . . .'

'I didn't mean forgive *her*, Meenakshi,' snapped Lilamami. 'I mean *him*. You never get the point of anything.'

I got pretty mad at this and was about to hit back when, 'Hello, hello!' said a new voice from the door, and Devimami's face lit up as if she'd sighted a shooting star. 'What's going on?' Bharat entered, taking off his jacket as he came in. 'This looks like a trial in progress!'

Lilamami froze. Devimami gasped and Meenakshi looked at me as if I'd sprung a trap on her. Bharat didn't appear to notice anything amiss. 'What-what and all have you been up to, Kaveri? What's the parleying about?'('Yes, ask her,' snorted Devimami, and, be *quiet* you silly woman, I muttered.)

Then Lilamami made another announcement. 'If Kaveri refuses to edit her book she will not be welcome here. Neither will Mani and Meenakshi.'

And Meenakshi nodded as if she agreed to this damning condition!

Devimami exhaled a coffee-flavoured sigh. *It tastes very well.* As for Rajumama, he completely distanced himself.

Bharat looked from one to the other. 'You're nuts. All of you.'

Devimami sat up. 'Why are *we* nuts? *She* is nuts!' She frowned. Something wasn't right. 'She is *a* nut.'

'Anyway I can't stop now,' said Bharat. He nodded in my direction. 'I'll see you some other time.'

At the door he just missed colliding with Balumama. 'Yenna, yenna!' grunted Balumama. 'Conference-a?'

Nobody answered. Balumama shuffled in and pulled up a chair. 'Bedroom conference-a, boardroom conference-a? Or b-o-r-e-d room-a?' Still nobody answered. '*A-ham,*' he cleared his throat in a disappointed way. 'What were you all discussing?' Nobody had an answer to this too.

The sun had moved around the building. Late-evening light, low and livid, poured through the window, caught Balumama full on the face. His face was so ordinary! Stripped of the angles that once gave it fearful purpose, it lacked its old menace. The eyes were no longer beetles tunnelling to the back of his head. The foul tongue lay curled, not coiled, inside the snapping (now sagging) jaw. This new blandness called the old bluff. There was nothing here to fear. Or flee. He scratched a white flake in the corner of his mouth and glared at me. 'What are you studying in my face? The Koran?' Then, surprise, he smiled. It was his old smile, something between a smirk and a sneer. He was about to pounce. But he didn't. He just nodded, as if concluding some inner dialogue to his satisfaction, and plonked himself down in an armchair.

Devimami stirred. 'I must get dinner ready. Will you stay . . .' she turned to Meenakshi, when Lilamami cut in. 'They said they were leaving, Devi.'

We had said no such thing but who was going to argue?

Then, out of the blue, that is, out of the depths of his chair, Balumama said, 'Lila, give Meenakshi some mangoes to take home.'

Lilamami was rendered speechless by this new outrage. Meenakshi gave her a sickly smile. 'Don't bother.'

Lilamami found her tongue. 'There aren't enough to give away,' she said shortly.

Even I was ashamed of her.

Meenakshi faced them as if they were a firing squad. 'Poituvaram.' *We're going but we'll return.* Was it a promise or a plea?

Rajumama said, 'Poituva, poituva, Meenakshi.' *Go, but come again.* 'Soak your feet in hot water. Put some rock salt in it.' And with a jovial smile, 'Must stay well for the big day, eh?'

Devimami said, 'Come early to help out.' Another conciliatory move. Or perhaps, who knew, it was a sly snub for Lilamami.

'We'll be there exactly at seven,' Meenakshi promised fervently.

But she walked out of the room as if there was a gun pressed to her back.

We were back in an autorickshaw, rattling along the main road of Gandhi Bazar. There had been no offer from Rajumama to run us home in his gas-guzzler—perhaps he hadn't dared to offend his sister-in-law. It was raining, the mild, disruptive rain that typically begins just when schools and offices give over, and we huddled together against the chilly breeze blowing through the open flaps of the vehicle.

Meenakshi was upset on so many counts that she found it hard to articulate any of them. *Now what*, she kept moaning. *What will we do?*

It will pass, Ma.

'Lilamami will expect me to grovel.'

Grovel then, I very nearly retorted—I'd reached snapping point too—but, on no account, I said. Hang on to your pride.

'You've hurt theirs.'

Alright, Ms Roselips. What is all this about Balumama being tried? What was he charged with?

Night was advancing on the heels of the Bata sandals of the work details returning home. Dusk and rain clouds had leached the colour from the buildings, and low-watt lamps perforated the dense foliage in the gardens. In the main square, cyber cafes and coffee bars spilled light and music on pavements crowded with fresh produce and flowers. Meenakshi was too upset to ask to stop at the sari store and I didn't remind her.

Ma. What was Balumama tried for?

Meenakshi scanned the faces on the streets as if seeking one from which she could draw the wherewithal for her story. At last, reluctantly, 'The mechanic's child,' she said. 'Do you remember the mechanic who used to look after Balumama's Austin?'

I do. Vaguely. A snotty brat. He used to pester us for sweets. They left rather suddenly, didn't they?

'It was a scandal at the time.' She corrected herself. 'It *would* have been a scandal but it was hushed up. Thank goodness.'

Oh, so Balumama molested him then.

The autorickshaw bumped over a speed-breaker and Meenakshi clutched my arm to steady herself. 'That's what they said. But why did you say you didn't know?'

Because I *didn't* know. I guessed. Just now.

'You couldn't have guessed something like that, Kaveri.'

Well, I did. So that was it! Well, well, well! It explains a lot.

'It explains nothing, Kaveri,' she said crossly.

Look Ma, it's not a brilliant deduction. We *knew* what he was like.

'He was not like *that* at all.' So doubtfully, I gave her a hug. She shrugged off the hug. 'You heard gossip.' She pulled her saree across her shoulder. 'Really, Kaveri. You're *always* . . .'

Here, there and everywhere. Nose pressed to the glass. Okay, you don't have to use *every* opportunity to lecture me. Get on with the story.

'The mechanic took him to court. But he lost.'

God. What a coincidence. That I should be his Nemesis! 'Who?'

Nobody you know, Ma.

Meenakshi went into a sulk. I was using grand words that

excluded her but, conceivably, included Mani. In absentia, even. I gave her another hug.

It's not important, Ma. Please go on.

Balumama's trial was in-camera. Although the petitioners weren't to know that. Their idea of a court came from the cinema. Justice and injustice were meted out by black robes and thundering voices. They were regretting heeding their local Congress party member who had brought them here—mainly for the political mileage in the next elections. The mother took heart from her son, but the father's eyes wandered frequently, uneasily, to the tall windows overlooking the court gardens and the freedom and safety there.

From across the room, Balumama surged with new confidence. These weren't adversaries, these weren't even *persons*. Just a backdrop. They were the *masses*. They looked as if they had strayed from the fields for a day's outing in town. His shirt appeared to have been pressed under a mattress. Her rayon sari still bore shop creases. Put a broom in her hand and you wouldn't see her for the furniture. Stick him under a car with a spanner and where was the case? From here he could even smell them. Garlic-sweat, betel leaves, oil and toil. Years of scrubbing with Lifebuoy soap could never rid them of it.

Then he spotted the little boy—and his bravado shook. He was so grave, so wide-eyed, so *believable*. He was like candy. Sugar-pink fingernails, caramel eyes, chocolate limbs. *Suffer the little children to come unto me.* Casting about for something to pin his courage on, Balumama picked on his father's position—and wealth. He sat straighter.

It was a disgraceful proceeding—even the court clerk kept his head down. The evidence seeped out like a noxious gas.

Balumama's stained teeth and yellow fingernails told of the rot within.

Defence used intimidation tactics. 'I put it to you,' it thundered at Prosecution, 'that your clients have been priming this boy to obtain money by blackmail'.

'That is speculation,' bleated Prosecution.

The Judge overruled the objection. When it was explained to her, the mother burst out, 'Why would we teach him to say such shameful things? We don't need that kind of money!'

'Well?' said the Judge to Balumama. 'What were you doing with this boy?'

'I practise yoga,' said Balumama. 'Yoga teaches children are flowers. My yoga teacher says a child can make you forget a hundred sorrows. The boy was a . . . a yoga practice.'

Defence looked fed up. 'Produce the yoga teacher,' said the Judge, setting a date for the following week. Prosecution looked fed up.

In the Big House the air turned blue as Balumama took to cursing the judiciary system, the audacity of non-Brahmins and other low-class people who didn't know their place, and the perfidy of Brahmin judges who ought to know theirs. Lilamami was beside herself with fury, and showed her heels when he tried to talk to her. She gave him his tiffin as if tossing him a bone, and locked her bedroom door against him.

Years of the disciplined life had imparted to the yoga teacher a demeanour of contemplative calm. The law and its machinations were not his concern. Neither was the world— not this one at least. 'Yes, he is my student,' was all he would say of Balumama.

The court clerk rattled his typewriter. The plaintiffs fidgeted and worried. More promises were broken than kept here, would they get justice? At this juncture the Judge admonished the father to sit properly in court. (He had crossed his legs.) Balumama, encouraged by the admonition and the presence of his teacher and a secret escape clause he appeared to be hugging to his chest, announced he was interested in Tantra and had been experimenting with it when the defendant happened upon him.

'Obviously, your client has surprised you too,' the Judge said caustically to Defence. 'Perhaps you will be so good as to enlighten us.'

Balumama went into a complex explanation of the profound metaphysical concept of the coiled serpent of spiritual energy at the base of the spine. The divine merging of male and female energy in a cosmic medium, which union had the sanction of the gods. The spiritual release that was as different from gross copulation as gods are from beast . . .

'But this is a *boy*,' cut in the Judge. 'Not an energy. Which are *you* anyway—a Tantric or a Yogi?'

'Actually I'm a theosophist, your honour,' said Balumama, as if he had this ace up his sleeve all along.

'Silence!' rapped out the Judge although no one had spoken. The court clerk glanced up nervously. Defence looked startled, then dismayed, then furious.

The prosecution lost the case. (Although the Congress party member got his ticket for the Assembly elections.) Rather, it was dropped for insufficient proof. The way things turned out, there had been an intervention—and even the Judge was powerless against interventions. And of course Balumama's contribution to the freedom movement was factored. Then, the feudal country, newly freed, hadn't resolved its confusions. Indignation was rife and rhetoric reverberated. All men are equal, we'll all feast together at one laden table! But at the laden table there would be those who would not allow their neighbour's plate to touch theirs. They were the ones who couldn't be touched by the law either.

Meenakshi supplied the broad outline. Mani filled in the details later. Including Balumama's exit line. 'Blow, blow, thou winter wind, thou art not so unkind, as man's ingratitude.'

'Singing to the gallows,' snorted Mani, taking out his whisky bottle. 'Kaveri, kindly get me a soda.'

Meenakshi turned from the stove, frowning as though piecing a jigsaw puzzle in her head. 'You knew *something* about all this, Kaveri. It's not possible you didn't.' The saucepan missed the gas ring, tipped over. A stream of water rushed to the edge of the counter. 'Oh, oh, *oh!*'

When all was under control she resumed carping. '*Always* poking around. Such a bad habit. Look where it's got you now.'

Don't be a scold, Ma. You'll become like Devimami. My bad habit got me a prize and more money than we could have dreamed of. We can go for a holiday to the US—to the North Pole, if you like.

'This isn't a joke.' Angry tears sprang to her eyes. The tensions and humiliations of the evening had finally overpowered her. She was about to have a jolly good cry. All the indicators were there. As a prelude, 'You're never serious,' she wailed. 'You always see the worst in people! Like a, what's it your Pati said, a drain-inspector . . .' Her hands flew to her cheeks. 'Oh, Kaveri! I didn't mean that! If only you had just omitted or changed . . . you *could* have, you know. Sister Burque used to say you are so good with words. And Sister Britt-Compton said . . .'

Oh, Lord, the Sisters now. We're calling upon ghosts to our aid.

The cooker gave a shrill whistle. She let out a shriek. 'I forgot and put the weight on! The rice will be a pish-pash!'

Don't worry, Ma. You just think of the wonderful holiday you, Appa and I are going to have in South America.

She darted like a lizard's tongue at a fly. 'What about Arya?'

Oh yes, of course. I forgot him. I'm so used to just the three of us, you know.

'After *ten* years of marriage? Kaveri, what *is* going on?'

Relax, Ma. Don't give such a keen ear to everything.

But she was not comforted at all—she was on a different time zone *again*. And, while we were laying the table for dinner—her eyes shining as if mooting a special treat—she ambushed me. 'Kaveri, why don't you have a baby?' (Why don't you—and I—go to the movies and eat dinner at Paratha Point?)

What, *now*?

'By *now* is when you should have done it. *Then* is when you should have thought of it. But it's not too late. *Think*.' She trained her eyes on me, concentrating a stream of energy from her brain into mine via her popping irises. It was hypnotic. 'You will settle down with a baby.'

A cure for vagrancy, eh? Only you could think of it, Rosy girl. But you know what? You could be right.

She started puffing up. I took the air out. But for all the wrong reasons, Rosebud.

'*Oof!* What are the right reasons for having a baby? What are your *clever* reasons? *I* can tell by looking at you . . .' this was going to be more fantastic than I had thought, '. . . it is *exactly* what you need. I have told you so before.'

You certainly have. You can't be faulted on neglect of duty.

'. . . if you were a normal girl I wouldn't have to tell you these things.'

Not now, Ma. *Please* not now. Don't let's talk of my abnormalities. Then I relented. Look, Rosy-posy. You have a mothering instinct and a nesting instinct. *I* have been short-changed on both.

'O . . . h?' She was not sure whether she should continue the dialogue (would it be any use, that is) or console herself that I wasn't being serious as usual, and that I actually was heeding her advice. 'You don't understand what you're missing,' she said wistfully.

What *you're* missing, Rose of Sharon. For years you've been getting ready for it. Grandmotherhood. Fattening yourself. Studying babies' clothes—aha! Colouring your hair in amusing stripes, so you can leap out from behind the sofa. *Rrrrrrr!*

'You're *never* serious, Kaveri. Shall we have idli or dosai for breakfast tomorrow? Or would you prefer upma? What do you mean a bit of everything? I can't make everything! You can't *eat* everything! Oof, be serious now!'

At dinner, coincidentally or perhaps they'd been talking, Mani remarked (good-humouredly enough), 'Did you know Oscar Wilde said children begin by loving their parents and end by judging them?' He chewed, swallowed, and on a note of surprise, 'They never, ever forgive them, it seems. Eh?'

The corner of his mouth crinkled. I wasn't fooled. The byplay was really a plea for reassurance, my denial of such an outrageous declaration. The plea was also there in the plate of halva he inched towards me. A bribe. *Judge me kindly!* Haven't I been a good father? Oscar Wilde was an unhappy cynic, *and* a queer to boot—what sort of father could he have made? An indifferent one at best, is what I would reply. He had no idea about parenting although he did know a thing or two about words. And, *that's right*, my father would respond. We will concede Mr Wilde's wit and damn his other impertinences. *We* know all there is to know about parents and children. Ours is a sublimated experience.

All of him was straining for that all-important confirmation. But, but, but.

We're on track then, aren't we? Following the leader. (*The power of words*! Although I'm quailing.)

'Hmmm. Hmm. Are we?' He doused the shock with a gulp of water.

But tell you what, Pa. It's those who have loved most who are most unforgiving.

It didn't help. The ghee congealed on the halva. He continued to look routed. Oh, the power, the power!

With breathtaking irrelevance Meenakshi pitched into an explanation of how to make good halva. 'The secret is really ripe carrots and really fresh ghee and really first-class saffron . . .'

After dinner there was a power cut. We put aside books and knitting and huddled in the candle-lit gloom. The darkness was total, primeval—even the streetlights had gone out. Mosquitoes danced and sang, undaunted by the smoke from the mosquito repellent. Meenakshi was abstracted as if still working on the tricky V-neck in Mani's Aran sweater in her head. Giving up suddenly, 'I do wish, Kaveri,' she sighed, 'you hadn't used Balumama in your story. He isn't a pleasant man, but he wasn't mean to *you*. He *liked* you, in fact. And,' putting her finger on it as usual, 'he's the only one who *still* hasn't said anything to you. Although he has the most reason to.'

That's no reason to forgive him, Ma.

'Forgive what? That mechanic's boy business?'

The candlelight was suddenly too bright. It has come to pass, I thought. The circle has been drawn. It's moving in to its centre. And, after all, I've been hurtling towards this from the moment I tapped the first key for the first word.

Ma. That episode in my story had nothing to do with the mechanic's boy business. I really didn't know about it.

'It was nothing to do with Balumama then?'

It was everything to do with him.

'Stuff and nonsense,' snorted Mani. 'Riddles and riders.' The candle guttered, the flame leapt. 'I mean,' he muttered unhappily, 'you must have been mistaken . . .'

Oh no, Pa. There was no mistake.

Meenakshi was following every word with her finger. 'You *saw* something.'

'Tcha! Behind a door as usual.' *Ch, ch, ch.*

The fumes of the mosquito repellent hung in the air. Meenakshi sneezed, staggered to the window, gasped, sneezed again.

I *was* behind a door, I finally admitted to the two oil drillers, but it's not what you think.

'What was it then?'

At last. At *last*.

'Go away!' cries Jana, running down the garden path. 'I don't want to talk to you!' Her skinny legs scissor the yellow ribbon of the path, the too-short chintz pavade slapping at her knees. Her arms will slip out, worries Kaveri, if she beats them about like that. Doesn't she know they're a ball-in-a-socket?

'Get away from me!'

But Kaveri gives chase, all the way to the back of the Cottage, into Pati's vegetable patch, where they sink down in a heap, panting.

The kitchen garden was a dank place mobbed with buffalo grass and brambles and the nastier kind of weeds with sharp edges and poisonous sap, all of which flourished in the sluice water from the kitchen. Pati's vegetable patch was an island of doubtful specimens, buffeted by the undergrowth and preyed upon by every bird in the neighbourhood. But it was a hallowed place nonetheless. And they've flattened three tomato plants! Kaveri swallows painfully—her throat has dried out—and waits for her heart to stop. For the sky to crash. For the tomato plants to grow back.

The sun rains down straight and hard. A caravan of black ants dribbles out of an anthill. Insects like dust motes hang motionless. The smell of stagnant drain water is nauseating. Jana opens her mouth, gulps. (Breathe through your nose, Jana! 'I can't, Pati, I have *adenoids!*') Her upper lip is dotted with droplets. A fly begins feeding on the sweat. She swats at it. It buzzes around and settles on her forehead. She swats at it again. 'Go *away*,' she hisses at Kaveri.

'But what exactly happened, Jana? You said he came in the middle of the night and woke you up.'

The fly, back on Jana's forehead, rubs its forelegs in abject supplication. Kaveri tries to brush it off, Jana beats her hand down. 'I *said* I don't want to talk about it!'

'Tell your mother then. Or Pati.'

'*NO!*' An animal's bellow. Startled, Kaveri pulls a tomato off a vine. She looks at the tomato in dismay—Pati's tomato!—drops it quickly, kicks it away.

'I can tell *my* mother if you wish.'

'NOOOO!' bellows Jana. She grabs at Kaveri's dress and thrusts her convulsed face into Kaveri's. Her eyes under iridescent eyebrows are fathomless holes. 'If you weren't here I wouldn't have to go there! I'd have my room! I *wish*,' she quivers, 'I *wish* you'd go away! I wish *we* could go away!'

'You can share my bed. I'll ask Pati.'

'*No!* There's no place! Your parents are in the room too! And she'll ask why and I'll be punished!' Her face is desperate and ugly and dangerous, all at once, like the caterpillars Bharat caught and tortured.

Kaveri, filled with pity—pity but also relief her offer has been rejected—reaches out to touch the thin shoulder under the printed cotton blouse, the pavade, any dry and clean part of Jana, but as always, is repelled. What if one day I have to be her nurse? What if I have to give her, oh heavens, a *bedpan*? She withdraws her arm (encased in red-and-white polka dots, clear-starched by Meenakshi). 'Let me tell my mother at least.'

'Nooo! If you do, if you do, I will . . . I will kill myself!' Jana grabs Kaveri's hand. (With fingers that had just wiped her nose.) Kaveri shrinks but doesn't withdraw it. She shuts her eyes and throws her arms around Jana, then and there committing to her cousin a selfish goodwill, an expiatory concern, an undefined allegiance that has, despite irritations and bickering, endured to this day.

Jana drives her nails into Kaveri's palm, straining the goodwill. Then, in a sudden turnabout, 'You want to know what he does?' she says fiercely. 'I'll tell you!' Her eyes glitter with awful purpose. Dread and revulsion prickle Kaveri's spine. *Don't tell me!* But a peculiar thrill runs through her too— as if she is about to open a forbidden door. 'He *touches* me. He touches me all over. Here and here and then . . .' *Don't! And then?* Then a spew of water rushes out of a spout in the kitchen wall, flooding the carious drain. 'Makes me touch *him*,' Jana whispers.

'Where?' Kaveri whispers back.

Jana thinks for a bit. 'All over,' she mutters, staring vacantly at a cockroach clambering out of the drain.

Grey scum sticks to the moss on the walls of the drain. Bits of food float in the greasy water, looking like vomit. Kaveri is afraid she will throw up. Her hand closes over the leaves, and, *pachak!* She has crushed a tomato! She looks down, horrified. Two tomatoes gone! The scent of tomato juice stabs the still air. Forever she will remember it. The smell of guilt and shame and corruption.

Jana buries her face in Kaveri's neck. Goose pimples pop on Kaveri's skin. 'Promise me. *Promise* me you'll never tell anyone.'

'But Jana . . .' Just then their Thatha comes out of the Cottage, winding his sacred thread round his ear. He is going to visit the privy at the bottom of the garden. Like a good Brahmin he has to get his sacred thread out of the way. It always made them giggle but now Jana gives the inside of Kaveri's elbow a warning pinch. Ouch! Shh! They drop down again.

Leaves poke at Kaveri's crotch. An ant crawls over her bare foot but she doesn't dare brush it off. A tiger moth flutters down on a dandelion, terrifying her with its violent colours. But she doesn't move.

From inside the privy comes the sound of a bucket being filled. Smoke shoots out of the black nostrils of the kitchen chimney, sullying the liquid light. The ant climbs off Kaveri's foot, leaving behind a tiny red spot and an itch.

Thatha bangs shut the door of the privy, and, unwinding the thread from his ear, walks back to the Cottage.

Jana puts her mouth to Kaveri's ear. '*Promise!*' The spittle hits Kaveri's cheek.

'I promise, Jana,' Kaveri says hastily, before Jana can spray her again.

Kaveri rubs her sore foot. Jana mops her face with her skirt. Her eyeballs roll to the corners. 'He does it to Ramu and Bharat too.' There is a discordant note there that puzzles Kaveri. Is Jana boasting? She understands the awful truth of it years later.

Jana was establishing a secret society that would exclude Kaveri.

At dinner that night, 'Who trampled on my tomatoes?' Pati asked. And now Kaveri's heart did stop. Beside her Jana made a tiny noise. Her eyes held Kaveri's as if it was a handhold on a cliff. Kaveri turned to Pati and shook her head. (Shaking your head wasn't the same as lying.) Then she crammed grated carrot into her mouth. (Pretending to be busy was also not lying.) 'Hmmm,' said Pati, training her spider's gaze at them. 'Those tomatoes were just beginning to ripen.'

The beast was cunningly selective. Just as in any fairy story. *You and you and you.* Kaveri began making small connections. Why did Balumama keep following them with his eyes? Why did he stand under trees? Concern for their safety? Protecting the garden from their innocent play? What was he—a *tree guard*?

The mosquito repellent was a heap of ash. The candle, put to use during the power cut, had burned to a stump. With the clarity that comes in the wake of a fever, I observed the unnatural angle of Mani's neck. Meenakshi's knuckles were pressed to her cheeks as if to staunch bleeding. Her eyes brimmed over. The shock had breached a dam.

I thought you knew. That everyone knew. I thought it had been pushed under the carpet because of this great family feeling you keep on and on about.

Mani's neck was still straining in a peculiar angle. 'We didn't know. If we had . . .' His nostrils flared—he was going to explode, I thought, and then his mouth and throat convulsed in an unmistakable way. He was swallowing a yawn.

'Ayyo pavam,' Meenakshi moaned. 'Ayyo pavam.' Her sobs splintered into sneezes.

'Poor Jana,' echoed Mani. 'Poor, poor girl.' But his hands were busy with the whisky bottle.

For a while there was only the sound of Meenakshi's sniffs and Mani's sips. The lights came on suddenly, a blinding miracle. We palmed our eyes, protesting its officious intrusion into our circle.

Mani blew out the candle. 'When was this?'

Where was I, is what you should be asking, I thought. The year we stayed in the Cottage, I replied, with difficulty, for he was crunching murukku now. When this house was being built. There was no room for Jana and Ramu in the Cottage, they were sent to the Big House to sleep—do you remember?

'Ama. I remember.' Meenakshi shut her eyes and folded her hands on her chest. 'O Shiva. Shiva, Shiva.'

'You should have told us.' Crunch, crunch.

I'd given her my word I wouldn't.

'Not even tell *me*?'

I'd promised her, Ma.

How could one even speak of such things to them? How would they understand the child's fear of exposing grown-ups to its world—a world ravaged by a grown-up? How would they understand the fear of being punished for stumbling upon, for breaking and stealing into the grown-up's secret world? We were wrong and they were right. Always. Because we were we and they were they. They'd blame us for being there. For *being*.

Mani jerked up. 'Did he ever touch *you*?' The tendons in his neck stood out. And his nerves. His thews and sinews. Every cell had been alerted.

No, I answered, but with what strange guilt! He didn't touch me.

The cells retracted. His shoulders slumped. I hadn't been touched.

Why was I spared and she not?

'Are you crazy, Kaveri? Just thank your stars you were!' Immediately, he was contrite. 'It should never have happened to anybody. What a terrible thing!' With what tenderness did he stroke *my* cheek! 'Poor Jana. Poor, unlucky child.' He heaved a huge sigh. It blew my mind. 'If he had touched a single hair, if even his *breath* had touched you, my God . . .'

How about Jana? She was touched! Touched so it left her touched!

'Kaveri, kindly control yourself. Of course we'd have done something if we'd known. Taken action.'

What action?

He stiffened. 'I don't like your tone, Kaveri. *Ch-ch-ch.*
You're forgetting she had a father too.' His mouth turned
down. 'And I don't see what you wrote in your novel as
showing especial concern for her.'

Something went off. A Polaroid explosion of instant colour
and poor resolution, extravagantly vulgar. *Don't bring my book
into this!*

It's enough. I can't stand it. Not for another minute. I run
out.

I lay on my bed, tired and angry and terribly, terribly depressed.
He's as selective as the other beast, only he didn't hunt. He
would lay down his life for me, this man, but only me. And to
think I had rejoiced in this very particularity! Now I know it's
just another face of selfishness. The measure of his love is
fear—for my life. His sorry childhood has this too to answer
for. It has immunised him against other people's sorry
childhoods.

'Kaveri?' Meenakshi came to sit on the bed. She put a
suffering arm around my shoulder, twitched my sari straight.
Years of slights and blights had whittled down that arm but its
fingers were nimble as ever. 'Please don't argue with him. It
makes him so unhappy.'

I'm not in the business of spreading light and cheer, I
muttered, and was instantly sorry. *She* was in that business,
heart and soul, and it looked as if she'd failed—again. Her eyes
were tearing.

'Don't be angry with him, please, Kaveri. Do you think he
would have kept quiet if he had known?'

I couldn't give her the answer she wanted. Some years ago
I could have, and all would have been well between the three

of us. We don't know our parents, not entirely. That's why we're always afraid of them. First, because of what they might take away from us (approval, love, safety) and then of what they might have given us. Darkness in some form. Darkness in *this* form.

I *wish* he'd spare a thought for other people, Ma. Just once in a while. It won't incapacitate him, Ma, it won't deplete him! He won't be a lesser man for it!

Her brow puckered. 'He just doesn't think that way, Kaveri.'

Is that a flaw or a failing? A birth defect?

'He's old, Kaveri.' She picked a strand of hair from my cheek and, with infinite tenderness, tucked it behind my ear. 'You can't change him now.'

I wish, Ma, that occasionally, just *once* in a great, great while he would look outside of me. I wish he'd just once concede we have separate destinies, he and I. It's so oppressive sometimes. Being his daughter.

I didn't say it aloud though. My mother had enough to bear.

My established equation with Mani had altered in the past year. The old constants still held but there were new variables to deal with. I had to balance his past domination with my present, hard-won, independence, but do it discretely, incrementally. He must not guess at my growing disillusion (although he must surely see his time-worn gambit of *I'm right, you're wrong, so don't argue* has run its course) and he must not know that the day was not far off when *I'd* be tucking *him* into bed. I owed him that at least. So I kept the pretence while he kept the tradition. Together we maintained the delicate peace.

'Kaveri, can you pour me a wee tot?' *(A wee tot!)*

I pour, hold out the glass.

'A wee bit more.'

I oblige again, and pick up the water jug.

'Isn't there any soda?' *(Of course there isn't. We don't buy soda in crates or even half-dozens. That would be an extravagance.)* I offer to buy some. *'Just buy one bottle,' he instructs. 'One, mind.'* As if such moderation would minimise the trouble. And I am wrenched with exasperation. Why not six sodas for six days?

I do not argue, however. Such importunities are the stuff and substance of our life. One bottle it is, from the little shop down the road. Back again for another tomorrow. The shop is used to our funny ways.

'Keep the rest of the soda in the fridge—I'll use it up tomorrow. Ice, yes. Just one cube. That's a nice sweater you're wearing, by the way.'

You bought it for me, Pa.

'So I did! You know, I had quite forgotten it!'

Oh, no, you haven't, Pa, I say silently. You remember every single munificence. You have them itemised. Year 1988. Item. Shetland sweater. Pearl grey, crew neck. Year 1980. Item. Scottish kilt. Red and green plaid. 1976 . . .

We embark on a voyage of discovery of all the things he has bought me. From London and Frankfurt and Washington DC . . . trips marked by humiliating deprivations and self-denials to indulge me. Such noble sacrifice, for so short-lived a gratification! A lifetime, even two, would be inadequate to express my gratitude. I am unbearably burdened. The time has come to repay those debts. I would need a king's ransom to do it.

There are opportunities after all. Late in the night, when I am nodding off, 'Can someone make me a salt water gargle?' he enquires of the room at large. (*I'm the only occupant.*) *'I feel a cold coming on. That buttermilk at dinner was freezing.'*

Meenakshi pops in with her impeccable timing, to say it wasn't the buttermilk, it was the ice in his whisky. Buttermilk does not cause colds—it never has in her entire experience. On the contrary, it cures them. In her experience. It's also known to cure stomach upsets, headaches and hives . . . She's getting carried away beyond the pale of credibility, when he interrupts. *'Sympathy is also known to cure. Kaveri, just heat this up a little, will you? (By now the salt water gargle has grown cold.) Your mother,'* in lowered voice, *'won't let me enjoy my one drink'.*

Once I would have spoken up for him. But now we two women, two halves of a pod, two clangs of cymbals, two palms in a prayer, we are an act. And he is merely the spectator.

'It'll get cold,' he grumbles, when we conspire to store his coffee in a flask to save making endless half-cups.

It can't, Pa. According to the principle of heat retention in a flask that you taught me.

'Still. The outside temperature does affect it.'

'It is quite hot outside,' murmurs Meenakshi. *'Thirty degrees, I believe.'*

'Twenty-eight degrees in the shade.'

'We're 3,000 feet above sea level,' she says mystifyingly.

'Three thousand two hundred,' corrects the Passion-for-Accuracy. *'How is that relevant?'*

'Anyway they give you a flask on all the trains now.'

'But it tastes awful.'

In the end we capitulate. All day she fusses around with hot drinks and mushy food (for a cold!) while he huddles in bed, smoking his thermometer. All night she lies awake while he saws away at his cough. But she makes no such allowances for herself. When she has *a headache she ties a handkerchief around her head to keep it from splitting, to stop it from spreading to her hands, and getting in the way of her work. Getting in his way.*

Such exasperating love, this! It's a mystical journey—with no beginning and, it seems, no end.

The summer wore on, Bangalore's hard-hitting heat that cracks the earth and shoots stars into the noon sky. Each day I scoured the sky for a sign, but it stayed empty. Give me time, I had said. I will come when I'm done. Don't call me. Now, although each day I yearned to reach out, a little tug at my sleeve held me back. Is he being tactful, is he sending me a message? Because had *I* been *him* I'd have risked more than a snub to heed my instinct. I'd have picked up the phone.

The summer wore on. Meenakshi's cat made her a handsome gift of a rat—a prime specimen in every way, all nicely dismembered and scattered about in the puja room, to delight Meenakshi when she went in to light the lamp. Chirruping its triumph it was quite taken aback by her hysterical ingratitude.

The summer wore on. We sat in the verandah, the three of us, evening after evening, teased and tormented by the mosquitoes, with our books, knitting, questions and answers, questions with no answers. When I couldn't sit any longer, couldn't confront my thoughts, that is, such as they were, I'd go out into the exercise yard. Thirty feet to the oleander. Twenty feet to the honeysuckle. Turn left . . .

A week after my arrival a small news item appeared in the

Deccan Age. It said that owing to unavoidable circumstances the Dharma Ratna award ceremony had been postponed to the end of the month. Pulin Grover had bought time for me.

And the same morning Meenakshi brought me a letter. 'For you!' She waved it playfully.

He's written, I thought. He's missing me, he's asking me to come back, he's . . . Stop knocking, my heart!

Meenakshi smiled coyly. 'He's missing you!'

It isn't him, I managed to bring out. It isn't Arya, I mean. It's Pulin Grover.

It is now more than a week since you left Delhi. How are you? You were not looking too good when I saw you last. You must take care of your health for the busy time ahead. Speaking of which I enclose the final itinerary for the UK and US. As you can see it gives you less than a week after the British Council readings in Bangalore and Chennai to prepare.

Claire and Chris are wondering about you. I have managed to convince them you needed this break. However, it would help us all if you return soon, and begin your promotion tour. Warmest regards, etc.

P.S. There is a Writers' Conference in Tel Aviv in December. Will let you know the dates.

P.P.S. Some man called and asked for your number. Said it was urgent. Since he didn't give me his name I didn't.

'Is everything alright, Kaveri?'

'Kaveri, you're not looking alright to me.'

Please, Ma. Can't even my face get some privacy here?

She withdrew, her back stiff with hurt, and that whole day I was circumvented. Suddenly, I'd become large and invasive and out of place in this household, a stool for everyone to knock over. It got so unnerving for all of us that it was a relief when, in the evening, I cried off the violin concert we were to attend.

Soon after they left, the doorbell rang. 'What's the matter?' Bharat greeted me. 'You look as if I'm a ghost! And why're you barring that door?'

I waited for the thumping to subside—my pulse was kicking with the relief.

What do you want?

'Huh? That's a nice thing to ask! When I've come to see you!'

What about?

'What *is* the matter with you? I came to ask if you wanted to buy an elephant! There's one going cheap.'

Come in, you fool.

'It costs less than a car and so much grander, don't you think? We can go halves on it. I'll use it to commute to work and you can have free rides when you come down. We'll buy a coconut plantation to feed it. Aha, at last she smiles.' He shut the door, and handed me a folder. 'Meanwhile, something for your reading pleasure. My scrapbook.'

We sat in the glass-fronted verandah, which at this hour was infused with a green-yellow light from the garden. 'So,' he leaned forward, hands on knees. 'What-what and all have you been doing? The persona non grata in person!' He shook with laughter. 'Those crazy women!' Recovering, 'I say, how about a drink? From that bottle your father doesn't offer anyone?'

He must have his reasons for not offering it to *you*, fool. And he'll know at once.

'Marks levels too-a?' Wickedly, 'Let's doctor it with water so he won't know.' He jumped up. 'Come on, I know where he hides it!'

Pouring the whisky we were caught in a moment of roguish excitement. 'Oh, if he finds out!'

He will, I assure you.

He was convulsed. Holding his glass up, 'So!' he said. 'Here's to you!' Then he thumped his glass down without drinking. The merriment had gone. 'Actually, here's to an insensitive, manipulative opportunist.' And he picked up his glass again.

Cheers. Always useful to get the dirt about oneself.

Without further ceremony we gulped Mani's whisky. I winced. Must my father be drinking this? Daughterly neglect!

'Dirt. Ha! You know what you get when you dig dirt? *Worms*. A can of worms.' His eyes were the colour of coffee grounds. 'You know what I'm talking about. Don't act dumb.'

I can make an educated guess.

'Educated! Ha! *You* weren't the one who got educated. *Princess*. Whiter than white.' He uttered a snort of a laugh, tossed off the rest of his drink and, without even setting down his glass, tipped the bottle into it, filling it halfway up. I was going to have a lot of explaining to do.

So that's your grudge.

'An old grudge, but I haven't let it get in the way.'

In the way of what?

He threw some more whisky down his throat and stood up. I stood too, I wasn't sure why. Perhaps to take away the bottle, or perhaps to pre-empt something else. As I lurched to the table, a little dizzy, two arms encircled my waist. A hairy cheek scratched mine. He whispered, 'In the way of *this*.'

I should have known what was coming—I'd glimpsed his expression, and you learn to read a leer pretty early in life. I took a deep breath prior to blowing out the words like bubbles, which is the way to talk to a lunatic fingering a knife.

Why, fool! (*Careful, that knife might hurt you!*) I didn't know you weren't inclined this-a-way!

'What?'

I thought (*let me see it, then, just for a second*) you weren't, um, like us. I could be wrong of course, I added quickly.

Pft! A bubble broke. The knife glinted. This was dangerous. I inched my hand towards my glass—God knows I needed to—but he slapped it down. '*What did you mean by that?*' Then he was pinning me to the table, his arms crushing my ribs. I couldn't move, I could hardly breathe. 'Just what did you mean by that? I know,' through clenched teeth, 'there've been rumours. I know what they're about—I'm not stupid. But,' he tightened his grip, 'it's not true. *This* is.'

Stop that! What d'you think you're doing?

What he was doing was pulling at my blouse. Easing a finger into it, he scrabbled around, found a nipple, and pushed it. An impatient caller. The hooks snapped, and he slipped his hand in, his mouth experimenting with my neck the while. In addition to all the other discomforts, his knees were pressing into the backs of mine. I got a whiff of unwashed jeans/pencil shavings/tomato sauce-and-bread-and-butter—the odour peculiar to college canteens. He hadn't graduated from canteens yet, for godsake.

You *idiot*! Let *go!* Take your knees off mine! Are you *insane*?

'Oh, come on. You're a woman of experience. Lots of experience, damn it.'

Great. A reputation now. Okay, you've made your point. Now shove off.

But he didn't. He took it as an invitation to wrestle with him. I stopped struggling and went limp. (Resistance excites aggression. It didn't work. Another theory busted.) 'Don't you feel anything? *Anything* at all?' *Feel my feelings, why can't you!*

No. Nothing at all. Except you're . . . annoying . . . me . . . and I'm . . . not . . . enjoying it. Not one bit.

'You're lying.' The arms tightened another turn, the lips were not kissing as much as suctioning flesh. I feared he'd bite off my ear. I managed to push him away at last—an inch. He laughed. Squeezing harder, he panted, 'Then admit you do care.'

This . . . is too . . . much! And in my mother's house too! Stop that! *Stop* it, I said! I *don't* care, get it? I never have. *Now* let go.

'Hear this first,' he said fiercely. '*I* care. For years it's been you. Only you.' Giving me one last push on the *you* he set me free.

Back on the sofa he pressed his fingers to his head. 'I've never been able to look at anyone else.' He sounded as if it cost him his entire life to say it. Suddenly, I was sick of it all. Sick of the dishonesties, the pretences, and, most of all, the unsanitary conditions of our relationships in which even simple affection has a smell. I wished I could give him a hug, tell him, I'm not worth it, nobody's worth suffering or sacrifice—except that that isn't true either. Plus, the hug would be taken for a truth it wasn't. 'I thought you felt the same too. That stuff you wrote—the cousins who loved secretly. I thought it was *us*.' The shadows under his eyes were spilled Coke.

Oh, come on, fool. It was only a story.

He leapt up. 'Oh yes? Who're you fooling?' His shoulders slumped. He walked to the table, poured. (I would have to buy another bottle.) Suddenly, he wheeled around so the whisky spilled out of his glass. 'What *is* real for you? What *are* you true to? *Who* are you true to?'

Just don't think so much, fool. It's bad for you—especially when you're drinking. Speaking of which . . .

'It must be liberating to be so without feelings.' He returned to the sofa. 'For anybody but yourself.' Strings of hair were sticking to his forehead. He flicked them away as at a bothersome fly. Or me, perhaps. 'Have you,' he said savagely, 'ever been *humiliated*?'

Once. I got a haircut like a cross between a tea cosy and a Zulu hut.

'One day,' he glared at his glass, '*one* day you'll wake up screaming'. Then, abruptly, 'Do you remember the time we went to see *Lord Jim*? When we were climbing into the car and you turned and your breast brushed my arm? It was *deliberate*, wasn't it?'

This was really depressing. I mean, to fantasise over a brush with a breast. A *cousin's* breast, not to labour the point.

How wanton of me, I said, trying to keep it light.

'You sat next to me in the hall. Your knee was against mine. You put a popcorn in my mouth.'

And you put one down my neck.

But he'd gone very quiet. 'You *chose* to sit next to me— you changed seats with Ramu.'

Worse and worse. He needs psychiatric help. At least, regular workouts at a gym. I reached out to touch his arm. He flinched. 'Ah, don't,' he murmured, closing his eyes. '*Don't.*'

Perhaps I changed seats because I couldn't see properly, I suggested, and he slammed down his glass on the table— precariously close to the edge. Have it your way, I said hastily. If it makes you happy. I'm sorry you misread it, though. And, um, that glass. It's part of a set that my mother . . .

He jumped up. 'Shut *up*! You're not sorry! You're not sorry about anything! You're a *cheat*!' He grabbed my shoulders. 'You married Arya only to get away from home!'

And that, of course, makes me a cheat.

'You use people!' The spit bubbled in his mouth. 'You think they *exist* only for you!' He let go of my shoulders with a push.

Well, nobody's complained yet. Except Lilamami. But then she complains about everything.

'You don't care about *anybody*, not even your parents.' The eyes were spent cinders. 'One day you'll regret it, you know.'

I already do.

'What d'you mean?'

The lamplight dimmed and brightened. A nimbus with a white epicentre, charred blackness beyond. In the middle, nothing. A black hole. A vanishing point. Without seeing, without thinking, I picked up my glass. He caught my wrist. 'No. First tell me what you meant.'

I've had anonymous email, I was forced to admit *again*. Naturally he asked what they said, but I wasn't getting into that, of course.

Oh, nothing much, really. Nothing threatening anyway. Just annoying. Insinuating.

'I don't believe you.' A sparrow flapped frantically against the windowpane, knocked itself out, fell, caught its fall before it hit the flowerbed. 'You wouldn't have mentioned it otherwise.' He peered at me with bleary eyes. 'I was right then,' he nodded in a pleased manner. 'You *are* running away from something. Well, this has always been your bolthole.' A moth fluttered down, glued its wings to the windowpane. I watched its antics, thinking it's annoying the way the family jumps into my affairs. It's ruthless, their concern. 'So what do they in-sin-u-ate?'

I *said* it's nothing. Forget it. I wonder . . . do moths sleep? Or hibernate? Or just die?

'Desperate too, it seems. Have you been to the police?' Two flies lit on the windowpane now. A lot of activity in the garden tonight. A regular nightclub. 'So you *haven't* been to the police. The point of which is you don't want them in on this.'

Because I think it's just a prank. Or spite. You'd be surprised how much spite there is in the world. Actually, for a while I'd thought it was . . . *you.*

'I see. I'm part of the spite going around.' His mouth twisted into a half-smile. 'You said that as if you *hoped* it was me.' All the life seemed to have drained from his eyes. 'Why— because I'm envious? Sorry to disoblige, but it wasn't me. I don't write anonymous letters.' And ruminatively, 'But I'm missing the point. Which is, you *don't* think it is me.' Not as muddled as I thought. He finished his drink—his last, I hoped— and bounced on the springs. 'Anyway. What do they in-sin-uate?' He narrowed his eyes. 'I see. Not something nice. But,' he lifted a limp hand, 'she won't tell. Her lovely lips are sealed. And the point of *that* is, why?' He leaned across, frowning in an effort to focus. 'Have you been neglecting your conscience again?'

I wished he'd leave, just *go*, but he drew his legs up on the sofa, folding them in the lotus position. Without taking off his dirty sandals. I was going to be in trouble with Meenakshi now. 'One can track this person's email identity, you know. There's a fellow in my office who's an ace at cracking the Internet.'

No! I mean, let me think about it. It's not important. Not critical . . . big night for insects, hah? See that bumblebee?

'So it *is* important.' He shut his eyes and assumed an intense expression, as if focussing on some divine show going on behind his eyelids. 'Important enough to rattle you.' He opened his eyes. 'What have you done *now*, I wonder.' Your eyes are going to pop, I muttered.

He unfolded himself and scrambled up. 'It's a bit late for regrets, whatever it is,' he said severely. 'Sorry I can't help you. Go sleuthing elsewhere. Dig up more worms.' At the door he turned around. 'You touched nerves, not chords, you know.'

After he left I dusted off the sofa, rinsed the glasses, picked up the bottle to put away. It was quite empty.

Late next afternoon, a Sunday, I searched for almost half an hour in the slip roads behind Gandhi Bazaar's main thoroughfare before I found Ramu's home. It turned out to be a small independent house, one of the last of the old ones in that area that hadn't been renovated, razed or knocked into flats. Painted cream with green windows, it had a high granite plinth with five (unpolished) granite steps rising to a verandah enclosed in diamond-patterned wire mesh and hung with half-curtains. Terracotta pots of crotons lined the steps. The rest of the little garden was tamped earth dotted with tubs of flowering bushes. From a crack in the curtains I could see right through the house via open doors, through the verandah into the 'hall', dining room and rear verandah, all the way to the backyard to a whitewashed brick planter with the sacred tulsi. An oil lamp burned in a small triangular niche set in the planter. Jana would have lit it after her morning puja.

I rang the bell.

Jana peeped over the half-curtain. Her mouth fell open,

then burst into a frenzy of delight ('Kaveri-a! *Va, va, va!*'), and she ran in to deposit a steaming saucepan that was in danger of slopping over. Finally she thought to open the door.

Jana's excitement drew Ramu out. Sister and brother stood together, beaming, beaming. I gathered they did not get many visitors.

She ushered me into the tiny, chappal-strewn verandah, pushed me into a wicker chair, darted off to bolt the door in case I took it into my head to run away, pulled out two more wicker chairs for herself and Ramu (who stood cracking his knuckles), and at last the three of us were seated, crunching in our legs to avoid kicking each other.

So how's the cleaning going, Jana?

'Cleaning-a?'

Didn't you tell me you were cleaning . . . I mean, organising Ramu's house?

'Yes! There's lots to do still. I scrub and scrub but the cockroaches come back anyway.'

Ramu shook his head mournfully. 'No use whatsoever.'

It seems a hopeless project to me. When do you have to go back to Chennai?

Jana's smile slipped. Too late I remembered that her malingering was as much for herself as to help her brother. She is married to a brute whose one glance would shrivel the lushest greens. Who, I suspect, has killed all her ova.

By and by she brought us coffee, in shiny steel tumblers with the price stickers still stuck on them. The coffee was fragrant, frothy, just the right colour, and not over-sugared either. Jana is reputed to be a good cook. Apologetically, she proffered a plate of biscuits. 'Shall I fry onion bajjis, Kaveri? It'll only take a minute!'

No, no, Jana this is fine.

I helped myself to a biscuit, then another and, dismayed at my greed, ate three. 'Oh good, you *like* Glucose biscuits, Kaveri!' She scrabbled up to replenish the plate.

No, no more. Sit and talk, Jana.

She was pleased to obey—would she kill for anyone too? Killers are made of such undemanding compliance. Such blind allegiance. Such honest intent. Usually, her devotion annoyed me, but sometimes, like now, it frightened me too. It made me feel I possessed a secret power. I searched her face for a clue as to how far she would go, but it was blurred—overcast with a pinkish fluorescence from face powder applied with a heavy hand. There were no overhangs here, no overwriting, no comings and goings, no searchings and findings, nothing that gave the features relief, or the viewer a respite. It was like this in the keen morning sun, or in the unforgiving glare of afternoon, or, as now, in the twitchy evening light. One could read nothing there.

Ramu was using all his concentration to dip his biscuits into his tumbler, and snap up the soggy triangles before they disintegrated. Crumbs floated in his coffee. Crumbs stuck to his cindery moustache, even his nose. His nose anticipates mine but his mouth is his own, indeterminately his father's. Wiping it, 'Want to see the house?' he mumbled.

The house comprised a passageway of a 'hall' with a corner for a tiny dining table. There were two small bedrooms, a smoke-stained kitchen, and a scaly bathroom redolent of the waste of generations. Ramu's room looked like the scene of a police search. He opened his cupboard for me as if it were an album of a memorable vacation. In the kitchen two cockroaches scuttled out of the floor-trap and a lizard darted across the wall. We beat a retreat to the verandah.

I thought your company had offered you a room in the Intercontinental, Ramu. Since this is a temporary posting.

'I gave it up. Too expensive.'

But *they* were paying for it. At least you won't have cockroaches there.

'It's still a waste of resources. Whosoever pays.' And he looked to me for approval.

But I didn't hold with needless parsimony, however nobly inspired. What're you saving *them* money for, Ramu? Somebody else will enjoy your benefits.

Brother and sister appeared faintly shocked at my moral turpitude. 'Ramu has *principles*, Kaveri.'

Naturally, I rose to the bait. He's a stand-alone then. You'd be surprised how few people are ruled by their principles, and how many by their entitlements. Consciences are a luxury.

'Ramu is not like them.'

And, 'I *like* it here,' Ramu said, shaking his head from side to side.

I gave up. This was not the occasion to tell Ramu it was likely his company would view his stand as an eccentricity or worse. But it made me uncomfortable, and not a little irritated, that these two should take this high moral stand.

Oh well. I wouldn't save somebody else's pennies for them for anything.

They smiled uncertainly. They weren't going to believe that.

Passing clouds dimmed the verandah. Passing thoughts shadowed our mood. Jana switched on the overhead. Almost immediately, a flutter of light-moths clustered around the bulb, colouring the light a streaky cinnamon. She fetched a pan of water, stuck a candle in it. The light-moths, eashels we call them, rushed to the flame with suicidal fervour. In minutes the water was thick with gauzy corpses. Jana studied them pensively. 'It's going to rain tonight.' *Eashels ride the rain winds.*

It certainly points to it, Jana. The clouds were looking pretty sodden when I started out. God, look at that candle! Eashels are flame-throwers, eh?

'Eashels are suicide squads,' Ramu contributed, modestly pleased at his wit. We all smiled and pondered awhile on the self-destructive tendency of eashels.

'Do you remember how we'd find their wings in our homework, Kaveri? They never learn, do they?'

No, they don't. They haven't in these twenty-five years. They won't in two million years.

Jana poked a struggling specimen into the water to put it out of its misery. 'When are you getting the Dharma Ratna, Kaveri?'

Sometime now . . . You know what, Jana? (For I've had an inspiration.) I'm going to buy you something to celebrate. A pearl necklace. And a bracelet to match. Earrings too. *You* choose them. I know you like pearls.

I had happened right, for she was ecstatic. 'I love pearls!' And clapping her hand over her mouth, 'But it's too much, Kaveri!'

No, no, Jana. It's too little.

'Little-a?'

It's the least I can do for you, Jana.

'Least-a?'

Then I asked it, I had to, it was there, the question, a stone in my shoe, a boulder on my chest. And the answer was there too, the dread of it and the dreadfulness.

Floating like turd in a sewer, crawling like a roach in a

dustbin, I asked it. Did it . . . were you troubled by the book, Jana?

The happiness faded. 'I don't know.' She turned her shoulders this way and that—a caterpillar in the final throes. I resisted an awful impulse to check if she was shamming, like some caterpillars do. 'I try not to think about it,' she said, staring at the floor. 'It's . . . it's only a story.'

Exactly. It *is* only a story, Jana.

Ramu pushed back his chair. 'It wasn't only a story. Lots of it was true too . . . it was real. For us.'

'No. It *is* a story.' Her voice was stifled, as if her mouth was stuffed with something. I felt hot and stifled myself.

'It's *our* story,' Ramu said fiercely. 'She took it.'

Not all of it. The ending is mine. No one can connect it to that other, that business, nobody knows about it.

Ramu pulled me up short. '*We* connected,' he said huskily. The ceiling began pressing down. *Nerves, not chords.*

Jana lowered her head. Her hair was stiff with grease, snowed with dandruff. Live white powder clung to the parting as if it would never let go. Oh Jana! I took her hand, squeezed it. It felt like squeezing a wet sponge. It's not easy. Just not easy.

I owe you an apology, Jana. (How hopelessly inadequate. Sorry has never done anyone much good at any time.)

Their faces were rubbery with incomprehension. Nobody has owed them anything before.

Look, I came so we could talk. It will help you to . . . to . . . come to terms . . .

'I don't want to talk about it.' She snatched her hand back, hunched into her chair.

'Is that why you wrote it?' Ramu asked. 'To *help* us?'

Ramu and irony!

I wanted to come to terms with it too, Ramu. Work it out of my system.

Ramu reared up like a tidal wave. '*You* want to work it out of *your* system? It wasn't even there.' (Ramu and opinions!) Although he hadn't moved he had drawn closer to her. 'It was there in ours,' he said, with lips cut from cardboard. 'It still is.' The floodgates had indeed lifted.

'You don't know!' Jana burst out, 'You don't know how it is to feel dirty! Even after a bath!'

Two pairs of eyes drilled mine, grilled mine. No one would dare sully you, Princess. You were special. Your parents' golden girl. While we—with a shiftless father on one side and a foolish mother on the other—fell into the gap. Pati took us out. Took us in. But then you arrived, you and your parents, and we fell into it again.

Everything, it would appear, led to me. Atone, atone . . . For being you. For your mother's beautiful ignorance. For your father's love. His singular, consummate, blinkered love— that kept you pure.

I'd have felt like *killing* Balumama. I might have, too!

Jana smiled. That she could find it in her to smile!

Ramu wasn't smiling. 'That only happens in stories. Like yours.'

'But Ramu, she didn't kill anybody in her story,' Jana said seriously. 'That man killed himself.'

If he hadn't I would have done it for him, Jana.

Now they both laughed.

The wax continued to drip into the water, the eashels to dive into the flame. *Suicide squads.*

But why didn't Bharat tell somebody? Devimami? Rajumama?

'He was scared. Because he . . . stole biscuits. Balumama knew that.'

We fixed our eyes on three different corners of the verandah. Was it stealing, though? To help yourself to biscuits in your own house? Lilamami had deemed it so—a punishable offence. And he was always so hungry. We all were—for the good things. But not *you*, Princess. Not for long, anyway. Your parents stole you away to live in your castle-by-the-road where you had everything you wanted—without ever having to ask. Atone, atone—but how?

I should have told someone, Jana. Promises or not. I could have stopped it—and I didn't.

Jana scraped her chair closer. 'You mustn't blame yourself, Kaveri!' Her anxiety added to my wretchedness. She looked at me with something so like compassion that for a moment I was confused.

Unfortunately that also sparked off the old familiar irritation. Why does she assume that sacrificial stance? As if tied to a stake? Why does she allow fate to exact its due? *Get them off your back!* When Jana extended the biscuit plate her elbow stuck out like a coat hanger. When Ramu took my coffee tumbler his fingers curled like an anemone's tentacles. It was congenital, her penurious elbows, his predatory fingers. Stand straight, Pati would hector, how often must I tell you to keep those shoulders up?

It's not easy. It's just not easy.

The candle had become a lady in a ball gown. Eashels clustered around her Medusa hair.

Jana lifted a head weighted with lead. 'I dreamed of running away. But I was afraid of getting lost.' She covered her mouth with her hand. She was still afraid. Oh Jana. When people run away they are lost before they take a first step.

'Me, too,' Ramu said. 'I thought of it all the time. That time never came.' Absently, Jana held out the biscuit plate to her brother. Absently he took two biscuits. At least the deprivation was a thing of the past.

It did, Ramu. You grew up.

He shook his head. 'Too late.'

Too late for what?

'To be . . . normal,' faltered Jana, fixing parched eyes on mine.

This is normal, Jana. This, what you, *we*, all are now, is normal. That horrible . . . business is not.

She was clinging to the bars in a cell. Wrongly imprisoned. Caught in a world I would never enter. And for the first time it occurred to me that all the noble ideas in the world were nothing if they could not save one troubled soul. 'But it happened, Kaveri,' she whispered, her eyes imploring me to deny it happened.

Well, I said feebly, it's happened to hundreds, thousands . . . Worse has happened. You aren't alone.

Sister and brother peered resentfully through the bars. Excuse me, they seemed to be saying, we're not plotting standard deviation here. Only *we* were deviated. *You* weren't. Anyway, what care we for hundreds and thousands? Alone is alone—what would you know of such isolation?

Perhaps, I said, without much hope, the book will be a release *some* day?

Brother and sister considered.

'I don't think so,' said the sister sadly.

'Never,' said the brother, emphatically.

I failed, then.

I was completely unprepared for their distress. Oh no, Kaveri, you didn't! Don't ever say that! We didn't mean you to think that! Only . . . why did it have to happen at all?

They were waiting. Why us, why us, why us? I had no answer to that, of course. All I knew was fate had its ways of keeping us in line.

Jana. This didn't happen because you were you but because *he* was *he*. And because *you* were there. In the wrong place, wrong time.

'But you were there too, Kaveri.'

Their eyes did not accuse but did not exonerate either. Suddenly (this was so strange) I felt isolated too. They were so sealed in each other's fate. I didn't belong there. They were part of the larger world, the hundreds and thousands, while I, I had no cause or country. Alone was alone.

I did know isolation.

That night I lay awake for a long while, looking out of the window. The oleander was squirting colour into its buds, the parijata tree was readying itself for its morning shake-out, coconut fronds were combing the clouds. All was as normal as normal could be. What was normal?

In the morning the mosquito nets lay over the beds in sugary drifts. I looped them over their stands, made the beds, kicked the dead mosquitoes into the corner. It is my duty too to plump up the cushions, fill the water jugs and dust Meenakshi's curios (including the lamp that holds neither wick nor oil). I finished my chores quickly, for this was the day of the housewarming and we had been bidden to come early—Meenakshi to usher the guests, Mani to engage those worthy of his attention, and me, well, I'd be there on sufferance, but I had come all the way from Delhi for this, hadn't I?

So I wore the peacock-blue silk sari Meenakshi had loaned me and her ruby pendant-and-chain and my own gold sandals with the slice-of-potato heels, and Meenakshi wore her ashes-of-roses crepe de chine and her favourite too-pink lipstick and the gold butterfly pin in her freshly burnished hair, and Mani wore his best veshti with the green-and-gold border and a starched white jubba that stood out like a tent, and we wrapped our gift—a low relief carving of a silver Ganesha in a blue velvet box—and set off in the ancient Fiat with the balding tyres and the faulty fuel gauge, in good time and good spirits, to warm the new homes of my granduncles Balumama and Rajumama. And their faithful wives Lilamami and Devimami.

Requiem

Requiem

The whole world seems to have landed up outside The Flats, summoned by the invisible wire that buzzes loudest with bad news. About a hundred people at the very least, surging like milk boiling over, and more pouring in every minute. Many of them are guests returning for this unexpected anticlimax to the morning's festivities. A police jeep is blocking the gate. The caterer's truck has backed into a flowerbed. Somebody's blue van is occupying Rajumama's Honda City's prime spot, and Devimami hasn't chased it off! Motorbikes, autorickshaws, cars . . . clogging the street, leaking into the main road. Already! A Bollywood starrer premiering at the Rex is nothing to it.

The parking lot is a mash of humanity. Jasmine hair oil overlays the incense, and sweaty polyester, chewing tobacco and garlic. It is the familiar reek of Bangalore's street orders. The street orders are pushing at the building, eager to get at the kill. Policemen begin poking them with batons. Angry murmurs rise and I fear a riot. The police, however, have intuited we are family and allowed us through. Meenakshi, after one scared glance at the thing on the floor, has scuttled off, sari end to mouth, to join a cluster of women on the staircase. Mani stood over the white heap for a minute, hands folded, eyes closed (praying?), before proceeding to a caucus of worthies in the corner.

Rainbows bounce off the bevelling in the glass doors of the lobby. All the lights are on inside—the wall fixtures, the pendants, the stars in the ceiling. The chandelier, Rajumama's pride and joy, is wearing a sulphurous halo, its artificial illumination incongruous with the fanlight's mercurial glare. And that is the atmosphere generally. Incongruous. The flowers, the kolam. The scent of sandalwood, incense, rosewater. Everyone still in their finery. The just-consumed feast still on tongue and fingers. Incongruous.

In the middle of the floor, directly under the chandelier and surrounded by a knot of people, including two policemen, Rajumama and an officious elder, so it is barely visible, is a white bundle. It could be, for all anyone can tell, the laundry waiting to be collected.

I had imagined a huddle at the bottom of the lift shaft, a pool of blood seeping into the concrete. I had imagined telescoping darkness, the echo of machinery cranking in the underbelly of the building. I had imagined broken limbs tangled in steel rope, a rag doll sprawled on top of the lift car.

I had watched too many late night movies.

And now I'm afraid of what I will see. A garbage bag burst open? A cracked watermelon? Ooze, spill, matter? What matter?

I don't want to look.

I must look.

The legs first, which the sheet does not completely cover. They're seasoned ebony, with a dusting of dead cells like sugar on a chocolate biscuit. Deep-scored lines, like the squamous tracery on Jana's legs (so we inherit that too), erupt in a delta of cracks on the soles. The cracks silted with dirt, the toes sheathed in snail's shells. Dignity in death has been denied Balumama. The world is witness to his unsavoury feet.

Now for the head. The sheet has slipped off here too, but nobody has thought to pull it up. His face, resting on the creamy floor, is fire-resistant clay, graven in high relief. Although it's no work of art, this, and the marble too elegant a mount for such an exhibit. But life, *death*, is full of ironies. Balumama's Bata chappals, sitting side-by-side and ready-to-walk, is an irony. The bright blue sky is another. As is the distant crack of a cricket bat, the trill of a sparrow, the toot of a car horn. Life is being lived full throttle elsewhere but here it has stopped mid-cry. Here it has seeped out from nose, eyes, mouth, ears, orifices. Like stuffing from a torn mattress.

But there *is* no stuffing in Balumama. He's a furled-up flag. His tumescence is an empty sock.

If a referee counts ten and blows a whistle will he jump up? And ask, in that nasty put-down way of his, what we mean by crowding him in this uncouth fashion? Is he a street drama or what? The absurdity is that he *is* a street drama. A one-man show. With lines to speak too—delivered in his growl: Get off my face! Get off my body! (*Get off that tree! Get off the roof!*)

But the circumstance, the circumstances. The fall. The plummet into endless night. The flight of wingless bat into lightless hell. The crash landing. Had he thought in the moment after the fatal stumble that he would land on his feet? When had the panic set in? It couldn't have lasted more than a millisecond but it must have seemed like an aeon. Such time is incomputable. An instant, a lifespan, not much difference between the two here. Had he screamed? Or had the shock knocked the breath clean out of him? He has fallen cleanly alright, like a well-secured sack. Nothing has spilled out. The outer covering has held. How fortunate he has, *had* such a thick skin.

The women have snaked up to the first landing and are leaning on the railing, stifling their hysteria on each other's shoulders. Their pottus bleed on their foreheads, their flowers smell of sweet decay. Already, this is a house of death. Devimami, in the forefront as usual, waves to someone. No, she's just shaking out her handkerchief. Just for a second her expression slips, and near-pleasurable expectancy shows, like brick through flaking plaster. But hark! A sniff. A great big harrumph. That is most certainly Meenakshi, who is always first with the tears, and must clear her sinuses before she can properly give way to them.

The wail of a siren startles us all. It's the ambulance. Activity intensifies in the lobby. The ambulance attendants run in followed by Dr Rao, our family doctor, and a doctor from the hospital. The murmuring gets louder, although nobody can see much because the 'team' has surrounded the body. Not that anything can be done now. Still, black bags are being opened, instruments brandished, and someone actually takes his pulse! After five minutes of such uselessness they give up and go into a huddle.

All at once, as if it has received a secret signal, the landing-watch turns and swarms up the staircase. Behind me there's activity too. More people have arrived. An osmosis takes place as the latecomers squeeze through the lobby door and ease out the early birds. What is it about an accident that makes everyone behave as if it's a banquet and there's a run on the food?

In Lilamami's sitting room there is standing room only. Devimami, who is state-of-the-art, refers to it as the *living room* but it looks dead to me. The white bed sheet that covers the sofa (to preserve its newness) is an unfortunate metaphor. Rigor mortis has set into the Sheraton chairs. Lifeless eashels paper the lampshades.

In the doorway, looking at home in this inhospitable non-home, because she is a product of mood, not place, and this gloom is ineluctably hers, is my cousin Jana. Her arms hang down as if she has no more use for them. Her head lists to one side as if she's listening to something going on in her head. A requiem, perhaps. Or an anthem for a veteran freedom fighter. Her eyes skid across the room, stumble when they collide with mine. She twitches as if touched with a live wire.

Lilamami is lying on the sofa. As First Mourner, she is leading the lamentations. Ayyo! Ayyo, Ayyo, Ayyoyo! The Remote Relatives and Friends-and-Neighbours chorus the refrain. *There, there, Lilamami. Dhairyam, dhairyam, Lilamami.* Be brave. Be strong. Death is the only certainty of birth. He is now at peace. He is with God. God is with you too. 'I'm with you, Amma,' says Uma, patting her mother and her baby in turn. Lilamami clutches Uma's hand, the baby howls, Uma muzzles it with a pacifier, whereupon it begins choking. Uma shakes it hard (she must be very stressed), slings it on her shoulder, resumes patting her mother.

'O Shiva!' wails her mother. 'He didn't live for a day in his new house! Gone, gone!' It's all her fault, of course. His fate had been linked to hers through the moon and the stars, and it was written she would bring him to this. That she, the Black Widow, would one day cannibalise him.

Pavam, pavam. Poor man. Poor, poor man. So fine, so kind, so brave, so blind.

Cathartic tears flow, a summer storm. They're for the unfairness of life, the perverseness of Fate that gives only to take away. And so soon, so soon! Because it's always too soon.

Uma's baby, its face ugly with baby rage, lunges to grasp a clump of Lilamami's hair. Lilamami lets out a screech, Uma pulls away the brat, Devimami takes over the ministrations. Bending over Lilamami, *ummmm*, she gurgles *Ummmm*. There's a promissory note there too—but what can Devimami offer her sister-in-law at this juncture? She produces a bottle of Amruthanjan No Pain Balm. She rubs the pungent unguent into the suffering forehead, and hoists the sick head onto a pillow—a manoeuvre that looks as if she's trying to strangle her.

'Dhairyam,' murmurs Meenakshi from the sideline. 'Be brave, Lilamami.' And she promptly gives way to tears.

Lilamami struggles against Devimami's no-nonsense grip, and, with one mighty heave, sits up. Abandoning her First Mourner role, 'Tara,' she raps out. 'Someone must tell her. Devi, *you* do it.'

'By phone?' Devimami asks, but we've all been rendered stupid.

'What else,' snaps Lilamami. 'Sea mail?'

At which I do something so inexcusable that even dear, faithful Meenakshi is hard put to condone it. I burst out laughing. I tried to change it into a cough but the damage was done.

Eyeballs bulge, mouths open and shut. Hands flutter like fins. The room's turned into an aquarium! Suddenly my head is seized, held as if it were a football in a tackle. 'Hysteria,' Meenakshi explains to the outraged assembly. 'The poor girl is terribly upset.' Knowing my mother, she could even believe it.

Nobody else does, though. Lilamami finds her voice first. 'Did you see that? She *laughed*!'

'She's crazy,' declares Devimami. 'I've said so before and I will say it again. She's raving mad.'

Meenakshi will not take this lying down. She shoves my head into her bosom to squeeze out the remnants of hysteria. 'It is the artistic temperament. Writers are sensitive.'

Meenakshi's unfortunate sense of timing couldn't have been worse. Sure enough, 'They are *completely* insensitive,' says Devimami.

Beside her, Lilamami makes a choking noise.

Devimami gets busy telephoning. First Tara in the UK, then, because Uma is busy with her baby, Uma's husband, the Defector, in the US. In Maidstone, Kent, it is 10 am and Tara's microwave is beeping that her coffee is ready. In Dustville, Arkansas, the Defector is rudely roused from a dream of the NASDAQ going through the roof. The chaos of the Third World is disrupting the order of the First.

Devimami, keeping her voice low to spare Lilamami, keeps repeating herself in a sonic metre that unluckily sounds thrilled. Precious minutes tick on. Lilamami is marking them, getting more and more tense. '*Yenna*, Devi! Why do you whisper? They're thousands of miles away, not at your elbow!' The First Mourner act is slipping.

'He fell into the lift shaft!' Devimami shrieks. 'He's *dead*!' There's a collective gasp and, 'He's no more,' she qualifies decorously.

I catch a blur of movement from the far end of the room. Jana has broken out of her trance and is weaving her way between the mines hidden under the carpet. She's heading for me! 'Come, Kaveri,' she murmurs, tugging at my arm. 'Inside. Let's go inside.'

Why? Let's go outside. There's more air.

But she gives my arm another tug. 'No, *inside.*' Stumbling behind her, all I can think of is she's reeking of onions.

As she pushes me into a bedroom we hear a commotion behind us. Lilamami is flopping about the sofa, screaming. I turn around to get the full measure of her face. It is wild—contorted, streaked with tears and vermilion powder. '*She drove him to it!*'

She is pointing at me.

We shut the door. I walk to a chair, more shaken than I care to admit. The smell of onion retreats to the window. Jana is standing backing it so her face is in shadow. 'I saw the accident, you know,' she remarks, conversationally.

In an instant I'm up—up and across and clutching her wrist. Oh my God, Jana. What did you see?

'The accident. Him falling.'

How did it happen? You must tell—come, let's go, the police are asking questions, everyone is guessing what ... Jana! Come on!

'No,' she shuts her lips in the mulish way that so annoys everyone. 'I shan't tell them anything.' Her features are smudgy, but her voice has an edge—a warning edge. And, I think, she will not tell, too. She'll clam up the way she used to when we were kids, when she had something to hide. Hide!

I don't like this at all, Jana. Exactly what did you see?

She puts her head to one side. 'Do you believe in karma?' Before I can answer, '*I* do,' she says.

You mean Balumama falling into the shaft was because of his *karma?* Jana, it was carelessness. Just bad luck that he didn't look where he was going.

'Bad luck.' She smiles without mirth—pulling her lips over her teeth. 'He deserved it.'

Jana, people don't always get what they deserve. It doesn't work that way.

'It does so.'

I want to say, surely *you* deserve better after that unspeakable time—you don't deserve the boor you married! You deserve children, children whom you will not leave to chance, whom you will protect from every passing fearful chance, as you had not been protected in your chancy life. You deserve children to right your childhood, so you can breathe through them—free and joyous breaths.

There's no justice in this world, Jana. You should know that.

'Well, there is. There's karma.' She drums her fingers on her thigh, keeping beat to the tune playing in her head, her eyes rolling along with it, as it were. The old exasperation bubbles up in me.

Why do you keep on with that, Jana? You *know* it was an accident. He was in the wrong place at the wrong time.

'But he was the right person.' She stretches her mouth again in that dreadful smile.

Pay attention, Jana. *There's no right or wrong about this*. It could have happened to anyone. He lost his footing. He believed he was stepping into the lift. It was an *accident*.

She gives a cheerless cackle that chills me. 'Is that what the police think?'

What does it matter what the *police* think, you silly girl? What other explanation can there be for an old man falling into a lift well? Logically?

'Anyway, he's gone.' She squeezes her eyes shut and tautens her body as if about to dive off a high diving board. 'We're safe now. *You* too, Kaveri.'

Safe, you funny girl? From Balumama? He's been out of our lives a long time.

Her eyelids flutter but stay shut. She smiles again, a smile that shuts her in. I know then that she will not come out. Perhaps never. Still, I keep on—I have to.

Jana. Why *safe*? And why *me*?

She opens her eyes but they're blank. 'He's dead,' she says wonderingly.

Jana, there's something more to this. What am I safe *from*?

But she just shakes her head.

Jana. I don't like this. Did he say anything before he, um, fell?

She gives me a look in which distress and puzzlement are pleading for clarification. 'He said that you ... you ...' And here the door flies open. I could write a thesis on doors opening (or shutting) at crucial moments in my life.

It is Meenakshi, and she comes straight to the point. '*Yenna*, Kaveri, how could you *laugh*? What got into you?'

It was too much for me, Ma.

'Why should it be too much for *you*? And why must you *laugh* if it's too much? Why not *cry*?'

Good question. Ma, Jana was just telling me we can't fight our karma. (Jana's eyes are wandering, lonely as a cloud, over hill and vale.) She thinks Balumama was so weighed down by his bad karma that he toppled over.

'What a thing to say! I know you children didn't like him but now he's ... Pavam. You should remember the good things about him.'

There aren't any.

Meenakshi bristles. 'Show some respect, Kaveri. Now that he's ... ayyo pavam.'

Oh Ma. Ever one for protocol. The dead take precedence over the living.

'Well . . .' She worries her lower lip with her teeth. 'At least respect his memory. Remember him for what he was.'

That's not a good idea, Ma.

She's figuring it out (that lip will need first-aid) when, 'He loved cake,' Jana says dreamily. 'He'd wake from his sleep if you said *cake*.'

This is so unexpected, even for Jana, that Meenakshi and I are speechless. Then, 'I didn't know that,' Meenakshi says. In her voice there is regret at her ignorance of this pathetic instance of Balumama's nature. *She* would have baked for him had she known. She would have baked for Satan himself, my mother would. 'How did *you* know, Jana?'

Her face is a death mask. 'I used to buy it for him.'

I'm struck by a dreadful doubt. Every rupee was stretched to snapping point. There was no such concept as pocket money—there wasn't any money to pocket.

Did he give you the money for it, Jana?

'No. I . . . stole the money.' She begins bumping the wall with her bottom. But *stole*? With every rupee accounted for every night and tallied over and over?

'Where did you steal the money from, Jana?' Meenakshi asks, looking upset.

'From . . . the . . . Shiva temple. The dhanam plate.'

Steal from temple offerings! Meenakshi looks at me, aghast. 'Why, Jana, *why*?'

She stops the bumping. 'I hoped he wouldn't . . .'

'Wouldn't what, Jana?'

Sometimes, no, often, I wonder at my mother. I really do. Shout and scold, Ma. I scowl, willing her to catch on.

Meenakshi's rosebud mouth is about to bloom again.

Think, Ma. I *told* you about his charming ways, for godsake. I direct all my energy into her brain, which, it seems, has suffered an overload. She nods, but it's still touch and go. *Ma!* He used to frighten us, remember?

'Some of us more than others.' Jana's eyes hook into mine.

I turn away from the awful knowledge contained in those eyes—but I can't shut out her thin fingers scrabbling in the coins and flowers on the offerings plate. Perfecting the give-and-take operation with each attempt. And getting patted on the head for it too. *Good girl. That's right. Give to the poor Brahmins.* She would have hidden the coins (in her blouse?), run to the bakery, bought cake—coconut, jam, chocolate, iced pink or green—run back to the old house, dodging and hiding, for who knows whom she might run into . . . 'Here, Balumama.' Here, Balumama, and what else? Would she have pleaded with him to leave her alone? And would he have heeded her plea? Shared the pitiful bribe with her? Would it have been business-as-usual after? I feel I'm breathing through a pipe thick with sediment. Oh God, I *wish* I didn't have an imagination.

The swine. The rotten, perverted bastard . . .

Meenakshi is furious. 'I will not have any more disrespectful talk about Balumama, do you hear? Jana, that was wrong, that you had to steal for him, but the poor man is dead now.' She folded her palms and touched them to her forehead and heart. 'The dead are one with God.'

Not *this* one, I begin, irritated at this show of piety—in a minute she'll be conferring sainthood on him—when Jana chips in. 'Not him. He'll come back. To wipe out his karmas.' Her face is a death mask. 'He has to go through several rebirths for that.'

My cousin-the-prophet. Etched in black and white by the harsh afternoon light, she appears older than my mother at this point of time, older than Pati even. As old as time. What a prospect, Jana, I remark, annoyed with both of them now for all this God-talk. How long will it be before his first coming?

Pat comes the surprising answer. 'Three years. Till then his soul will wander around the earth.'

I must say you're well informed, Jana. (Where does she get her religious instruction?) Do you have his itinerary mapped out too? Tell us where he is in the birth-death cycle. Is this a fourth or four-hundredth incarnation? He has a long way to go, judging by his record in *this* life.

'Kaveri! Porum. Behave yourself.'

But I can't take Jana's karmic comedy seriously, Ma. So, Jana, tell us. After flitting about the universe, when and where can he be expected to alight? Not *here*, I hope. That would be too morbid a fantasy for even this jolly household. (Meenakshi looks fed up.)

'It depends what he does in his next birth,' declares the sage. 'This was a *bad* one. He has to pay for it.'

It seems to me a lot of other people have paid for it.

'That is because of *their* karma.' Her body shudders—rattles, that is.

So then, will Balumama enter a better cycle or a worse? Will he be a slave or a master? A hammer or a nail? Sage or a satyr? Cause or the effect?

'Kaveri,' moans Meenakshi.

'You can't really tell with karma,' says the wise one. 'It is carried over many lives. Like Lilamami's leftovers.' She tries on a smile. It doesn't work.

Aha! An imponderable then. If we can't answer the eternal

question we shouldn't speculate on the outcome of it either. We can contemplate it, though. If that's any comfort. So according to you, Jana, Balumama's fate was inevitable. One way or other. Deserved or un-. Since we don't know how he led his ten thousand past lives.

'*Kaveri*! This is *not* the time and place for such a discussion!'

'I know Balumama was preparing to leave *this* one. The signs were there.'

'What were these signs, Jana?' Meenakshi asks, in spite of herself.

'He gave me mangoes to take home,' Jana says dreamily.

So? He offered us mangoes too.

'He's never given me anything before.'

Meenakshi pinches her lower lip. 'It *is* odd—him giving away mangoes.'

You make it seem like they were his worldly goods, Ma. Perhaps they'd started rotting. I can't think of a single reason why he'd part with *any*thing. Certainly not to pay off karmic debts.

'Kaveri! Mind what you say!'

I would imagine anyone with a premonition of death would cling to things, not give them away. To take to the next life, you know. Like the Egyptian kings.

'Porum. If you don't stop this,' Meenakshi's voice is ominous, '*I shall tell your father.*'

Oh, please! *Please* not that! Anything but that! (She frowns. Was I being funny?) But just consider, Ma. Jana's theory would be more convincing if he was giving away *cake*.

'This is too much! Wait till your father . . .'

'He wanted to make peace with God,' says Jana. She stares at a point on the floor. 'He wanted to be released from his bonds.'

Convenient that, eh? So many of us are simply *begging* to be released, but are not. And Balumama escapes. And that, too, he doesn't go screaming or drivelling or drooling. Rather unfair, actually.

'Devimami is right. You *are* mad. Stop it at once or I'll send you home.'

At this point something comes over me—impatience, unease or sheer devilry. Jana, I wag my finger. *Beware*. If you don't tell us what really happened, Balumama will come to haunt you forever. Then, opening my eyes as wide as I can, I point to the door. *My God!* He's already there! Just behind you! Look out!

I am completely unprepared for her reaction. Clapping her hands to her ears she takes a running leap to the bed and buries her head in the pillow. Her shoulders quiver, and she makes small whimpering sounds.

Meenakshi rushes across to comfort her. 'Are you satisfied now?' she hisses at me over her shoulder. 'Are you *happy*? You'd better go home. You're *no* help here. Go home *at once.*'

The living room is poignant with dying jasmine. Lilamami, who's lying comatose, bridles as if my reappearance is one more affront in a history of several. Devimami gives me a brief glare before turning to my mother, who has followed me out to ensure I don't linger. 'Can you ask the cook to make coffee, Meenakshi?'

Lilamami sits up. 'No, not coffee! Tea.' Even in her distress Lilamami does not forget that tea requires less milk than coffee. '. . . eleven, no *ten* cups. Neela is leaving.'

Meenakshi pinches my arm. 'What are you smiling at *now*? Go *home!*'

In the lobby preparations are being made to remove the

body. The crowd has more or less dispersed. An accident, they murmured, clicking their tongues as they walked out. An old man who didn't look where he was going misjudged his step, tripped, keeled over. Into a lift cage that wasn't there. I have my doubts about that, but now's not the time to voice them.

Balumama is on the stretcher, properly covered so nothing of him is visible. He's a neat package, ready for clearance. Already. Two ambulance attendants wait for instructions. A policeman slouches, picking his teeth. Dr Rao has his arm around Rajumama's shoulders. 'Death was instant. Don't worry, Raju, your brother didn't suffer.' Rajumama, too dazed to register anything, just cracks his knuckles. A grisly sound. He looks smaller than ever. The lobby appears too large for him— as the new flat will be for Lilamami.

Bharat comes up to comfort his father—practically standing on his toes to do so. 'Kaveri,' croaks a voice behind me, making me jump. It's Ramu—when did he come? He's looking harried. Perhaps his rascally MD will fire him for extending his leave of absence. Or perhaps it's something else. I'm dying to ask him, *have you spoken to Jana*? Now is not the time to ask, however.

The weirdness grows and grows. The marble is so very white. The light is so very bright. The incense is so very cloying. Everything is so *festive* still.

The ambulance attendants pick up the stretcher. Bending as if to pay my respects, *cake*, Balumama, I whisper. Coconut, jam, chocolate, pink-iced or green, take your pick. And I wait for the lightning to strike. It doesn't. Meenakshi was being needlessly sentimental as usual.

Balumama leaves, escorted by Rajumama, Mani and Dr Rao. They are going to do a post-mortem on him, although I can't imagine what they expect to find. Perhaps what he ate for lunch addled his judgement. They'll bring him back though, for the cremation rites. The policeman who was picking his teeth has graduated to his nose. With them is a little man, nervous and aggressive at once. It is the builder. 'The lift company is responsible!' he shrills. 'We should sue for criminal negligence!' He wipes his brow with a large stained kerchief. 'I advised another brand but Mr Balan insisted on this cheaper one.'

Balumama must have been forced by Lilamami to buy cheap. Another of life's ironies. Or the machinations of karma.

A lengthy explanation follows—about original equipment manufacturers, architect's responsibilities, contractors' terms, insurance . . . The builder gets more and more agitated. Finally, 'Well, sirs, Mr Bharat, Mr Ramu, Mr Inspector,' he offers a conciliating hand all around, 'I will take your leave.'

Only Bharat and Ramu are left now. The three of us walk outside and stand by the entrance canopy so recently occupied by the welcoming party of the little girls. By the left gatepost, next to the banana stem that's still holding up, a clay pot of faggots is sending smoke signals into the sky. *Somebody here has passed on*. The world is being notified. Already.

Bharat tells us the lift will be sealed off till the police investigations are over. They suspect faulty electric circuitry. The external door shouldn't have opened when the lift cage was not there. Balumama, believing there was an unlit cage there, stepped into it. To complicate matters, he had cataracts in both eyes.

Well, sirs, Messrs Bharat and Ramu, for your information, Jana has a different opinion. She says Balumama was pushed into the pit by his misdeeds. Cause of death: Bad karma.

Ramu's mouth falls open. Bharat snorts.

And Lilamami thinks *I* drove him to it. Meaning he *jumped*, not fell. Because of the book.

Bharat snorts again. 'What nonsense. Balumama is not the suicidal type.'

'Or an accident type,' murmurs Ramu. But Bharat and I are too busy arguing to pay attention.

Well, anyway, that is what Lilamami thinks. Because of the book.

'You'd better stay away till all this hysteria dies down,' Bharat says. 'As it is . . .'

As it is there're two schools of thought here. The push may have been bad karma—or a prod from Balumama's bad conscience. But karma or conscience, it resulted in the same end.

'Shut up. This is not funny.'

'He has never had an accident,' mumbles Ramu.

'So? Accidents happen accidentally, Ramu. You'd better tell Jana not to shoot off *her* mouth either. She'll be pulled in for questioning. The clowns will begin to think *she* pushed him in or something.'

I think we're all struck by the same thought at once. Struck is the operative word, because for a few seconds we stare dumbly—I at Bharat, Ramu at me, Bharat at Ramu. Then we reverse the order. Idly, I consider their expressions—Ramu's is a rabbit caught in a headlight, Bharat's the half-lidded mask of an Assyrian, and, 'Why're you gawking like a half-wit?' he asks me irritably, so I know how I look as well.

Because, fool, the same stupid thought occurred to me that has obviously occurred to *you*.

I don't add that it had, in fact, occurred to me a while ago.

Dangerous enough, the mind monkeying around. There was no need to rope in the tongue. Better to rein it in.

'I'm not thinking anything,' snaps Bharat. 'And I'd advise you not to either. Not to put your thoughts into words either.' Quite. He marches off without, as they say, a backward glance.

It is late afternoon. Crows, winging home, heap scorn on our heads. A pack of dogs have dragged out the banana leaves from the garbage and are busy eating the leftovers. The decorators are dismantling the canopy—pulling down the flowers, unhooking the WELCOME banner and packing up the fairy lights that were to light up the night.

Ramu touches my shoulder. 'Kaveri,' he croaks. 'It . . . it could have happened, you know.' And miserably, 'That Jana . . . that she . . . could have . . . what you talked about the other day. What you would have done to him if . . . if you were us.' He rubs his mouth as if he can't believe what just came out of it.

I take his arm, more to steady mine—I'm very frightened myself but I shouldn't let on I am. Listen, Ramu, don't worry about it. You know Jana. She just says things. For, um, effect.

In the features retracing mine (tipping the scales in my favour, I think, but only just), hope and hopelessness alternate like sun and shadow. He wishes he could trust me but does not know how. I shake his inert arm to press my case.

Pay no attention to her, Ramu. She didn't see anything, she . . . what was she doing in the building?

'Helping to clean Rajumama's flat.'

What is she—a cleaning service? Why couldn't she have gone home? Why was she there at all?

Ramu eases his neck from his collar.

I'm sorry, Ramu, I didn't mean that. I just wish she hadn't been there.

'It wouldn't have made a difference,' he mutters, avoiding my eyes.

You mean because ... Oh God, Ramu, you don't really believe ...

'It could have happened any other time,' he reasons, this astonishing cousin of mine whose tongue has worked loose—tragedy has cracked *him* up too. 'Or,' pensively, 'any other way'. This was the best way as it turned out, is what he's not saying and, he believes it, I think. *He really believes it.* This is her brother. He should know. What else does he know?

Ramu, listen. I spoke to her just now. She was very ... strange. Among other things she told me *I* was safe now—but wouldn't say why. And this morning she said she was going to *talk*—but not about what. She did try after lunch, but Lilamami didn't let her. Then she left and nobody saw her till after ... Nobody saw *him* either. (I'm beginning to feel queasy.) Where is she now?

He swallows, pushing a golf ball down his throat. 'She's gone home.' He looks at his feet. 'She was planning to tell the family about ... that business.'

Ramu. Listen. *Don't* repeat this to anybody, and *don't* encourage her in this karma business. Do you, I look hard at him, want *trouble*? He swallows again and shakes his head. Do you want her to be questioned by the police? Go to *jail*? He shakes his head again, with rather more energy. Then listen, Ramu. She's fantasising. She's just making up stuff to get attention—that's our story. (Poor Jana. It's a story that will stick only too easily.)

He brightens. 'Because she does not have children!' Then he looks stricken. 'Sorry, Kaveri.'

That's alright, Ramu. Not all of us mourn our childless state. Some of us live in thankfulness for it. But perhaps you're right. It could be she's suffering from delusion brought on by frustrated motherhood.

He seems satisfied with this explanation, which, in these parts, serves as an excuse for any abnormality from kleptomania to dementia. 'I will persuade her to go to Chennai to mother and father.' And a little doubtfully, 'To her husband.'

Yes, you do that, Ramu.

Anyone but to brother. He's giving me the willies.

Mani and Meenakshi stay behind to help with the funeral arrangements. There's something about a funeral that perks people up. It's an event, requiring as much planning and execution (as much hustle and bustle) as any other. From time to time Meenakshi calls to fill me in, sounding as if she is sorry I am missing out on all the excitement, but also apprehensive I might show up to partake of it. To pre-empt this she keeps assuring me that everything is under control and I needn't 'worry'. She also slips in detailed instructions about what is in the fridge and what's on the stove, and what must be taken out and what put in.

I'll manage, Ma. I run a home too.

There's a short and telling silence. Then, 'Tara is not coming,' she continues chattily. 'She has exams. After everything's over, Lilamami can visit her, I suppose. Go there six months, then go to the US for another six . . .'

Lilamami's future is being chalked out. Already. Well, it all sounds rather hopeful. She could never have done this when Balumama was alive—he hated to travel. Meenakshi rattles on and on about who has been informed and who is yet to be informed, who is coming and who isn't, and who is already on the way ... She's the chief of protocol, I gather. Lilamami, with reckless regard to expense, has commanded her to sound the bugle, call relatives in Mumbai and Delhi, Minneapolis and Staten Island ... Sanity will return when the phone bills arrive, but just now everyone is too caught up in the little drama to think straight.

Just a minute, Ma. Did Lilamami say anything more about me, my book, driving Balumama to, um ... *it*?

There's a pause. 'She did say ... something. But she's not herself. Okay, now I must go. I have to see to dinner. I'll phone again. Don't forget there's rice in the fridge.'

A lot of people in this business aren't themselves, I think, as I replace the receiver.

Towards the latter part of the evening I call Bharat—only to be told Lilamami is getting more and more hysterical about Balumama jumping to his death, so I had better not show up.

Oh Lord. Surely even *she* can't seriously believe that. Surely there's no reason to ...

'This is it. You see, that lobby was not so badly lit that you couldn't see there was no lift.'

But what about Balumama's cataracts?

'Yes, that's what we explained. But Lilamami insists he could see perfectly well to read a book yesterday. And he was an alert man. All there, all the time. Perhaps he wasn't himself this afternoon.'

He certainly was groggy. We all were. The ladoos were too big, remember. Listen, fool. *I'm* not the problem, don't you see? *Jana* is. She must be kept out of this. She must go back to Chennai. *You* make her go.

'I'll talk to you later.' His voice is frazzled. There is a lot of background noise that sounds like a teashop. Clatter and shouting and Bollywood music. 'They're taking the body to the crematorium now.'

Mani and Meenakshi return late at night from the electric crematorium in Wilson Garden. Meenakshi's sari sighs to the floor, revealing a yawning petticoat and a blouse that has popped a hook-and-eye. Meenakshi's clothes never quite make it across her. Threading her arms into a housecoat that has only three buttons left so it is hardly decent (daughterly neglect here too!), she says mournfully, 'Poor Rajumama is hardly speaking. And Uma was inconsolable after you left, Kaveri. Pavam. Delayed shock, it seems. They had to give her a sedative. One forgets he was a father.'

One didn't forget that, Ma. It made him all the more sinister.

'*Don't* keep speaking ill of him. Can't you keep quiet for at least today?'

Sorry, Ma.

After a bit she unbends. The autopsy revealed nothing so the body was released for cremating. The crematorium was crowded but they managed to jump the queue thanks to Rajumama being a friend of the inspector-general of police's nephew. 'He looked very peaceful,' she says reminiscently. 'It didn't show on his face, the accident. He died of internal injuries.' She shudders, then sighs. 'Who knew when we woke this morning this would happen?'

I don't have Appa's keen ESP but I *thought* something was wrong when Devimami said *please*. Twice.

'Be *quiet*, Kaveri.'

Although it is long past 11 pm they take a ritual head-to-toe bath (Meenakshi making Mani do it), carefully soaking their clothes in a separate bucket. They scrub away the defilement of the corpse, and their exhaustion and the confusions of the day. Now they have nothing left of Balumama on them. Tomorrow his ashes will be scattered on a river. Death is a great tidier.

Their heads are full of the cremation. They're in a high old mood to talk. I make Bournvita and get the biscuit tin, Meenakshi cuts an apple, and we consume our midnight repast, light-headed as people are after a tragedy that doesn't really touch them. Although Meenakshi's emotions tend to overpower her, her recovery period, like her attention span, is short. Now, the funeral, rather than the events that caused it, occupies her.

'A Neighbour-Friend brought dinner,' she said, 'because the kitchen fire cannot be lit in a house of mourning. Terrible food some people eat. Unfit even for a funeral house. Beetroot and cabbage cooked together. *Pink* cabbage, can you imagine ... and full of chillies! I gave your father rice-and-curds later to settle his stomach. But the priest didn't cut corners. It all went off very well, I must say. All the rites done in right royal fashion.'

I suppose we must take our comfort where we can.

She makes no mention of further outbursts from Lilamami.

At about 1 am, when I get out of bed to fetch a glass of water, they are still talking in the verandah. When I pass the door Meenakshi is saying, 'Lilamami absolutely refuses to immerse the ashes in the Kaveri.' Swift upon that, '*This* is what comes of naming Kaveri after a river! I *warned* you at the time, but did you listen?'

I wait for the logic of this. 'I *told* you naming a girl after a river is inauspicious! River names and too-long hair. Both unlucky for a girl.'

'Kaveri's hair is not long,' says Mani feebly.

'That's because she cuts it. She used to have such lovely hair. She could *sit* on it.'

The discussion, as several others, is veering to a point when I'll start flying. 'Besides,' my mother goes on, 'we don't have any control over her *hair* but we did over her *name*'.

Mani argues that half the women in Coorg are called Kaveri after their precious river. Were they all unlucky?

'Oh *Coorgis*! They don't count. They're not Brahmins.' And, 'All I'm saying is you *never* listen to me! If you had, this wouldn't have happened.'

'*What* wouldn't have happened?'

I stop breathing.

'*All that happened today . . . Lilamami screaming as if she really hated Kaveri. And everybody looking at me as if I was to blame!*'

To my dismay she begins crying—*ark, ark ark*, like a bird in distress. '*If we had given her another name she wouldn't have thought of writing this book!*'

I tiptoe away, climb into bed and draw the sheet over my head.

The next morning the sun is already working its heat into the brick paving in the courtyard when I wake. Meenakshi has shadows under her eyes but she is cheerful, and her cooking sari is as reassuringly redolent as ever. As usual, she is agitating a brew on the stove, and paying simultaneous attention to sesame popping in oil and her radio. Her serenity takes the damp off my mood. 'Rajumama, Bharat and Seena have gone for the immersion,' she says, reaching for a spice bottle. 'They have a long distance to go.' She smiles over her shoulder. 'Thank goodness it's a nice day.'

Thank goodness. All her idiosyncratic beauty shines through that smile, and peace on earth and goodwill to man. It's a smile so innocent of reproach or rancour, and so, well, *innocent*, it knocks me back. The world always makes perfect sense to her. It doesn't let her down.

She puts down a saucer of milk for the cat. 'They're taking a picnic lunch.' It's difficult to reconcile a picnic basket alongside Balumama (the remains of) but in Meenakshi's world everything is accommodated. 'Dosais,' she smacks her lips. 'Masala dosais. Lemon rice, mango pickle, appalam.' Coconut chutney, tomato chutney and the all-forgiving rice-and-curds. My mouth starts watering. '. . . they're immersing the ashes in the Paschimvahini. It's a tributary of the Kaveri, you know? I believe it was Balumama's favourite spot. It's very scenic.' Her eyes glance off mine, but her brow is clear.

Meenakshi is sparing my feelings at no small cost to her conscience. What she's not telling me is that the family is avoiding the Kaveri—the river that is traditionally our last resting place.

During the day the guilty relief of being survivors in a tragedy gives way to anxiety. Death has shown up at our door. At least, a few doors removed from us, but still too close for comfort. Although Meenakshi goes about her chores with her usual serenity I know she is worrying about Mani.

That evening they sit down to watch television together with a plate of murruku between them. At 7.30 pm, 'Half an hour to *Santosh*,' she announces. All day she has been waiting for her favourite soap, all week too—and it's been running for three years. Running helter-skelter. 'Completely unbelievable,' scoffs Mani. 'How even *you* can swallow that rubbish . . .' He fails to see that its implausibility is its fascination. Anyway, for half an hour a week she must regale herself on the tears and tension, the smiles and sleaze of this extravaganza. If you subtract the time taken out for commercial breaks, and the recapitulation and the credits, her fix lasts for twenty minutes exactly.

They have been watching India and Australia play. (Or India and New Zealand or India and South Africa . . . Like *Santosh* this saga of hope and heartbreak, of blood, sweat and tears, has no end either.) The two teams are battling it out in some place where it rains every fifteen minutes. This complicates things because when it rains they replay old matches, and Meenakshi, try as she might, cannot separate the two time frames. 'Check the top right-hand corner,' my father says in exasperation. 'If it says *Live* it is Live.'

But my mother is not really paying attention. She's doing a recap of *Santosh* in her head.

A while later, looking at the clock, 'Ten minutes more for *Santosh* . . .' she intones.

'Quiet now! Tendulkar is about to make his century!'

But there's a commercial break. '*Now,*' says Meenakshi, and '*No!*' says Mani.

Come on, Pa. He bats Monday to Sunday, 365 days in the year. Not to mention replays.

'I don't ask for much,' Meenakshi says, with a pathetic break in her voice. 'Half an hour once a week.'

'Hold on . . . *look at that swing!*' And devouring the screen, 'This is one of the finest innings I have seen!'

Against my instincts I'm sucked in. Too late as usual, for when *I* look, they're weeding the lawn. Or flashing a pair of Gucci shades. 'You're so ignorant,' he grumbles. And in a nicely judged swipe, 'Your mother has learned to appreciate the finer points of the game.'

But, 'It's time,' my mother sounds the knell.

'You know what Sir Gary Sobers says about Tendulkar?' he asks, a little desperately, and takes his eyes off the screen for a second to gratify himself with her amazement.

'Yes, you've told me,' she answers, picking up the remote.

She will not be amazed! She's flipping channels! This boldness could only be on account of me. He makes a last-ditch stand. 'Hold on! There'll be a lot of commercials first.'

'I like those too. They're my favourite commercials.'

Sinking back in his chair, 'There were just six runs to go for his century!' he mourns.

Suddenly, during *Santosh's* theme song, *zap*! We're back on Star Sports. *What* . . .? My mother's flipped! The remote trembles in her hand, she doesn't meet my eye. 'It's alright, Kaveri. Let Tendulkar finish his century. *Let your father have his way. He's old, Kaveri* . . .'

Shoulder-to-shoulder, they settle down to cheer Tendulkar.

The rest of the week passes in a blur. I do not dare discuss Balumama's death with anyone, not for fear of any divine retribution, but something closer at hand. A police investigation. Privately (and basely) I hope that if Jana's theology has any basis, Balumama's soul should transmigrate to an innocent girl's, with a relative such as he. But would she be chaste anymore? Would he be punished through her? More imponderables. Meenakshi says do not speak ill of the dead, God rest their soul.

We don't light a lamp in the puja room. Meenakshi doesn't make sweets. A sad deprivation, for this is more a time of waiting than mourning. We are waiting for the soul to depart. A body can be dispatched without much ado, but the soul cannot be rid off so easily. It must be placated and eased out so it will not return to haunt (and harass) the bereaved. This process takes all of twelve days. By the tenth day the *sutaka*, death's defilement of the house and all who live in it, is reduced, and the soul (now ravening for worldly pleasures) is served a salt-free meal as a not-so-subtle way of informing it that it should tarry no more. And, insulted to be so rudely treated, it leaves—in the person of a Brahmin priest, who takes the meal to throw into a river (or pond). He has to make this journey alone and it bodes ill luck for anyone who sees him on this mission. Hence the superstition that it is unlucky to see *any* single Brahmin priest, for, who knows where he's going? Finally, on the twelfth day, the Feast of the Forefathers, after a ceremony with rice, grass, water, earth and firewood, the soul at last joins its forefathers'.

The only significant happening in this time, or non-happening, is that there are no emails. I haven't had one in the fortnight I've been here. I feel like my execution has been stayed.

On the tenth day is the Daughter's Feast, paid for by Balumama's daughters, Tara and Uma. '. . . *spare no expense for our dear father,*' writes Tara, who cannot come on account of preparing for her FRCP exams. And, '*Please remit any leftover cash to my Indian Bank savings account.*'

Ever her mother's daughter.

They've done him proud however, the daughters. All his favourite food has been cooked—bitter gourd and drumstick stew, fried yam, pickled sarsaparilla, and his favourite sweet—jackfruit-and-coconut milk payasam. Brahmin food laden with Brahmin taboos. But, who knows, three years from now (if Jana is to be believed) he could be living in the land of steak-and-kidney pie. Shiva! What a fate for a double-dyed Brahmin!

As we file into the pandal for lunch—the smaller pandal has been kept on for the funeral ceremonies—Bharat tells me the police are sceptical about the suicide theory. Devimami overhears him. 'Between you and me,' she says (and the whole world, mutters Bharat), 'all is not as it seems'.

In my experience it never is.

After lunch the plebiscite, the flat-owners that is, gathers in the pandal. Who and what is to blame for Balumama's accident? Now that the tragedy has receded they are anxious about their own safety. What dangers lurk behind the building's smiling opulence? Are the electric cables safe? Has the roof garden been considered in the load calculations? There are no grilles in the windows. There is no fire escape. And shaft ventilation is a fire hazard. They shake their heads, pondering over what would be a decorous time to march upon Rajumama for explanations.

Lilamami is examining the folds of a silk sari in a Nalli Silks box, her eyes lost in some secret speculation. Her brothers have given her a new sari for this occasion—another mystifying tradition Mani deplores. It appears to comfort her though, as does her new role of Abandoned Bride. She has no one to shoot coy glances at, no one to hold on to. Although Balumama had offered her but a slippery grip. The diamonds have gone, leaving her curiously more dignified-looking. Ash, replacing the vermilion pottu, pulls her eyebrows together in one uneven line. All this is unnecessary in these liberal times, especially when her marriage hadn't exactly been a bed of roses, but Lilamami has decided to flaunt her state. She looks sequestered. Already. 'So Meenakshi,' she says, a little crossly.

'So Lilamami.' Meenakshi blinks, clearly at a loss. 'How are you?'

'How do you think anyone will be after something like this?' retorts Devimami. And, by way of comfort, 'Impossible to recover from such a blow.'

Lilamami tightens her jaw as if to convey she would recover too, and without Devimami's help, thank you.

'At least he didn't suffer, Lilamami,' Meenakshi says softly.

'How *you* know he didn't?' says Lilamami. Something tells me she's already on the road to recovery.

My poor mother looks crushed. 'It rained last night,' she says nervously.

'What?' Lilamami cups her ear.

Meenakshi raises her voice. 'Did you hear the thunderstorm last night?'

Lilamami's chin wobbles. 'I didn't hear a *thing*. I've grown *deaf* with weeping! Karma, karma.' Her eyes mist over. '*He* used to growl like thunder. Such a temper! Once he threw a book at me! Pavam, pavam.'

Once the pavam broke a stick on Bharat's shoulder, but this wasn't the moment to mention that.

By and by she composes herself to address the gathering. 'Thank you all for coming.' Her reddened eyes dart about. 'But where is your sister, Neela? And I cannot see your mother—wasn't she staying with you?'

Lilamami is counting the house.

Jana's attendance isn't of account but she's there—silent, shadowy and full of dangerous potential. Like the building. She bumps about on useless errands—moving a chair from here to there, tweaking the cushions, fetching glasses of water nobody wants. She turns from one to the other of us with a smile that begs to be taken in and given a home. Jana, just stick by me. And she does—sticking her hip into mine. But when I ask her what she meant the other day when she said that I was safe now, she unglues her hip and slips away, and after that she completely avoids me. I know from old this means she will not answer the question. Not if I beg, bribe or threaten to push her head into a bucket of water. Thus do witnesses turn hostile.

Of Ramu there is no sign. Perhaps he dared not ask his rascally MD for leave of absence twice in as many weeks.

Uma does not speak to me. She does not even look at me. Bharat does, but not through his camera lens today of course. 'So Kaveri, how is your conscience bearing up under the strain?'

Oh we're doing fine. Thanks for enquiring.

Astrologer Joshiyar is back, with his belches and his bogus advice. He's holding forth about the *time* of Balumama's death. Hadn't he said this was an inauspicious period for him? Balumama should have been more cautious and not gone poking around places where danger lurked. Forewarned is forearmed. Mani raises his eyebrows. What precaution can you take? You could put a railing around your bed and still have heart failure. 'If you remember I suggested a shanthi puja,' says the Joshiyar. 'Nonsense,' mouths Mani, but Meenakshi nods sadly.

Meenakshi is keeping me under surveillance. Uma is very attentive to her mother. Devimami follows Rajumama with her eyes. Everybody is watching somebody. But when I look around for Jana, she isn't there.

Devimami picks this of all times to act skittish. 'I hope,' she turns a soulful face to Bharat, 'that when my time comes *you* will perform my funeral properly. My dearest wish . . . you know what it is?'

'No,' mutters Bharat. 'You have so many dear wishes.'

'My dearest wish,' she says plaintively, 'is to depart with dignity'.

'Don't worry, I shall send you off in style. To begin with, let me know if you wish to be washed in cold water or hot. I don't want to be callous.' Devimami bridles. But Bharat is incorrigible. 'You shall be polished with that face cream you're hoarding. The one Uma brought you five years ago. The fungus won't affect you.'

Devimami's eyes fill; we hide our smiles behind our fingers. It doesn't appear as if Balumama will be mourned much. Or missed.

Then I chance upon Rajumama. He's in the tarpaulin shed, hunched over scraps of banana leaves. The scent of resin is achingly familiar. As before, the holes in the tarpaulin glitter like stars in the firmament. When he lifts his head I see his face is puffy, his nose is raw. He draws his arm across his eyes. I touch his shoulder but he flinches. 'Venda,' he croaks. 'Please.' After a bit he gives me a watery smile. 'That business of him being a freedom fighter is just a bit of family mythology, you know.'

He wants to talk, and by and by the tale unfolds. He and Balumama were playing truant from school to join a march of Congress workers protesting the trial of 'traitors' of the Indian National Army—Nawaz Khan, Sahgal and Dhillon. They were having a fine time waving flags, knocking down the English street signs and shouting Bharat Mata ki Jai! Mahatma Gandhi Jindabad! Which was the only Hindi they knew. In the fullness of time the police descended, scattering the marchers. They ran to their truck, piled in even as it began moving, and drove off. Balumama, lumbering even then, got left behind. He tried to hold on to the back of the truck, but fell off. Hurt, although not badly, he was picked up by the police, borne off to the local lock-up and kept there for a day and a night. Their grandfather, the British Government colluder, got him out on condition he kept away from revolutionary activities.

'I don't know what happened to him,' Rajumama finishes forlornly. I don't ask what he alludes to—Balumama's prison experience of that long-ago time, or the larger prison of his wretched compulsions.

The next day Meenakshi sets off bright and early to go and 'sit' with Lilamami, whose flat has become a kind of club, with people in and out all the time. (And drinking coffee and tea!) Having got this opportunity to reinstate herself with the Family, Meenakshi is sparing no effort to step up the momentum. How hard it must have been for her to be threatened with expulsion! How nearly it happened, too, but for this! Death does not always part us. Before leaving she gives me a detailed drill for the day—she doubts my competence to give Mani lunch on time and worries he'll fill himself with junk food.

'And Kaveri,' she adds anxiously, 'watch his cholesterol'.

How, Ma?

'Oh, in the usual way. Make sure he eats his carrots.'

Mani doesn't want to eat his carrots or his low-cholesterol lunch. 'Let's go to the club, Kaveri. Drink some beer.'

Oh Pa! The food's so bad there! And Amma's cooked such a nice lunch!

He waves aside my protests. 'Oh, stop going on about food! You're as bad as your mother! We'll eat the carrots for dinner. Or for tea!'

The clear gold of the morning has given way to a leaden

noon. The sky is like whey and the clouds like greasy rags. The stupor has clipped the wings of the sparrows and hushed the bickering of the crows. We drive through a nave of peltophorums, which have paved the road with gold. Our progress is stately, as if our bucking Fiat is a royal elephant in the Mysore Dussehra parade. This is as much for deference to the ancient car as for enjoyment of the flowers. Also, Mani's peripheral vision is deteriorating. I do not moot taking the wheel, however, because that will be an infringement of his rights.

Five kilometres on we are in the centre of the city, which at this hour, is relatively quiet. But in a few hours, when the schools and offices give over, it will be mayhem. Bangalore's much-vaunted peace and quiet is a memory now, thanks to its pioneering vantage in information technology. Mani says it has reinvented itself so fast it's lost its identity. And we old residents are being pushed to the edge by the capacious purses and aggressiveness of the invaders. History, which had spared us from the invaders from Mongolia and Eurasia, is catching up with us now. And, thanks to history again, we've grown too flabby to fight. We will protest our marginalised status (but mildly), we will shake our fists (but weakly) at the despoiling of our city. And do nothing. Because we've sold our soul for a microchip, says Mani. Become a city puffed up with vanity but without an iota of self-pride. A futuristic city with no future for us, its first citizens. This club, he says, driving through its gates, is an example of desecration in the guise of gentrification. He points at a banner announcing a Rain Dance. 'Dancing in the *rain*! What are we—*savages*?'

Come on, Pa, move with the times.

'No, thank you. I shall keep to my own beat.'

It doesn't improve his humour to have to park between two new cars. The proper inheritors of Bangalore took their chances with beasts like ours. As if to test us, the beast balks and stalls, so we have to push it into its slot.

In the verandah, 'What are you grinning into the mirror for?' he growls. 'The receptionist is staring.'

The Mixed Bar keeps the old faith. The sofas are spotted with age, the varnish on the teak tables (too low for comfort) is scuffed and stained, as is the timber wainscoting and the picture rail. Blackened rafters support a high roof, arched windows give to a stone-paved, myrtle-shaded courtyard. A skylight lets in soft, bemused light. The prevalent mood is that of pre-invasion Bangalore, of the pre-lunch cocktail and roast (not tandoori) chicken, of damp and decay, as if it rained all night and will rain tonight and every night forever and ever—no matter what the weatherman says. This defiance restores Mani's good humour. It evaporates, however, when he sits down and surveys the other occupants. 'All nouveau riche, all johnny-come-latelys,' he complains, put out that he cannot recognise anybody.

I thought you liked anonymity, Pa.

'Yes, but not to be swamped by strangers. Who *tip*,' without lowering his voice, 'so we have to wait on the waiters' pleasure. Anyway, this is not too bad a room to do it. Look at that painting—the horse reminds me of the one I used to ride. I really miss riding.'

But you haven't ridden in forty years, Pa.

He pretends not to hear and continues to study the painting. At last the waiter—the bearer, that is—approaches, looking as if one more of us today will finish him off. After another wait our order arrives—a bottle of Kingfisher Lager, a plate of potato chips with tomato and chilli sauce, and one of peanuts with chopped onions and green chillies and lemon juice.

'Cheers.' He takes a long pull, wipes his mouth. 'So. What do you make of this business of Balumama's?'

I dunk a potato chip in the tomato ketchup and chilli sauce and swirl the red and green around.

Well, frankly Pa, it *is* shocking but hardly shattering. Of course I'm sorry at the way he died, but not, well, about the fact of his dying.

Since Mani makes few allowances for the family, and indifference usually rules the day, I believe I'm well fended. And, arguably, Balumama's life hadn't exactly done him any credit. Although nobody will say so, his departure is going to liberate Lilamami.

But Mani is grave. 'I wish his last weeks hadn't been so unhappy.'

Huh?

'People were giving him odd looks, Kaveri. And whispering. People who lived through . . . that time.'

But Pa . . .

'Kaveri, that man couldn't walk in the park in peace!'

My father at whose feet I worship, whose slightest praise is my spur, whose barest nod is a bidding, whose merest smile is my reward . . . My father, whose touch is a healer's grace, a palmer's blessing, the sword that bids me to rise, go forth and conquer . . . My father, my personal god, is withdrawing his hand. The chips turn to corrugated cardboard.

But Pa, surely you don't believe . . .

'I don't know what to believe!' He wipes his mouth with the back of his hand. 'Balumama was nobody's fool—you know that—and his eyes were not that bad.'

The air whooshes out of the room. Unable to look at Mani I focus on the window behind him. Pink crepe myrtle litters the grey stone floor of the courtyard. On the opposite wall, the white entasis billows in a refulgence of noonshine. So normal, so sane.

The air has gone out of him too. He looks crushed and, somehow, wizened. 'He seemed so normal . . . that day. (*What is normal?*) Not like a potential . . . I don't know what to believe,' he sighs. 'All I know is, it's all so . . . destructive. Death is an escape only for the dead. And revenge is not an intelligent means of righting a wrong. As you must have realised by now.'

We are interrupted by our wheezy bearer, who has suddenly remembered to bring us napkins. Mani prods the contents of the plate. 'Bearer, these chips are *hygroscopic*.'

The bearer beams at him. 'Ama, saar. First-quality chips.' Mani shoots me a see-what-I-mean look. Nobody understands plain English anymore. 'Anyway, as I was saying, dying doesn't solve anything.'

Pa, *he* destroyed himself. In fact he died long ago. He was *spiritually* dead.

Mani rubs the side of his head to summon the words to his aid. 'Then you mauled a corpse.' The word *corpse* jumps at us, and we gaze at each other in horror. He touches his glass with trembling fingers. A sour belch froths in my mouth.

But Pa, I couldn't have foreseen this. *You* taught me effort is what matters, not the result.

'I doubt your motives.' He holds his glass as if he needed to hold something. 'I doubted them from the start. I can't say my worst fears have been confirmed because I, nobody, could have foreseen this, but . . .'

But you taught me a goal must be achieved at any cost. Perhaps I had a selfish motive, but how much of what we do is not selfish? I do feel a bit deceived, you know.

The fingers around the glass tighten. Ch-ch-ch. 'Your delusions deceived you. Always, always I told you to check your premises.'

I don't have your keen ESP to help me, I mutter under my breath. Perhaps I shouldn't have written this book then, Pa. I should've been in a laboratory, killing government-issue mice.

This is rather underhand on my part, and I know he knows that. He examines the contents of his mug as if deliberating this alternative, although it isn't an alternative at all—he and I know that too. At last, 'That is so insincere,' he says.

Sorry, Pa.

I'm not entirely forgiven. 'You know that I meant you should have been more circumspect. If you had to use this plot.' He climbs down further. 'Consequence is implicit in a goal, Kaveri,' he says mildly.

He has me in a spot—as he has times uncountable. All at once I am depressed. Our conversations never seem to lighten up. We take a topic, beat it senseless and then sink it. Even this dead issue.

'I'm not so sure it's over yet,' he says, as if reading my thoughts. 'Things have a way of coming back to one, you know.'

Beer-and-onion swill backs up in my throat and I press the napkin to my mouth. Somebody laughs at the table next to us, somebody else squeals. Glasses clink, plates clatter. I remind myself we're here to have fun. At least to let up. There is no letting up with us.

'. . . fate is so susceptible—there's no point tempting it. You should stop shooting off your mouth, for one. Your mother tells me your attitude has been rather, um, cavalier.'

I'm stung by my mother's treason.

But, Pa!

'No, no buts, Kaveri. From now on you will show some respect. Show some charity to the poor man.'

It wasn't because of *charity* that you swept the muck under the carpet! It was convenience! Okay, you didn't *know* the truth about Balumama. Not fully. Not about Jana. Now that you do, you still say *poor* man? Pa, how can you be so, so *sanctimonious*?

To my surprise he grins. 'Because I'm old. Sanctimony is an aging disorder, you know. It dignifies senility.'

Our mood lifts, the skylight glitters. The mirror behind the bar picks up its frosty light and sends it back through the bottles (green, gold and blue), whereupon it scatters on the walls. I swallow my frustration. Heaven knows neither of us has the energy (or the stomach) to keep on at each other. Together, hilariously, we blow foam off our glasses.

You know what, Pa? Pulin Grover would have dismissed this stuff as plebeian. He'd have us drink Puilly Fuisse. At least a Nuit St George.

Mani looks puzzled. Wine, Pa. *Aged* wine, I believe. Very dignified.

'You won't get that here. They are not,' he chortles, 'that sanctimonious yet in this club. But if you lay your hands on a bottle, remember your old father.'

The bearer creaks by, on the verge of collapse now. Mani asks him to fetch another bottle of beer. 'Make sure it's *cold*!' And, 'We want it *now*, not tomorrow!' he calls after him unfeelingly.

A thin shaft of sunlight breaks through the skylight, probes our table. Bright and brazen, it triggers an awakening, an instant of extreme clarity. Of foreknowledge that this afternoon is both charmed and doomed. Unremarkable in itself and indistinguishable from a dozen others, it will mark the divide between one time zone and another. Nothing will add up after this. I will not be able to look at sauce in a saucer without a wrench in my gut. I try to commit to memory this space and time that hold such a special regard for me. And this man, just the way he is. This and this and this. But the light and the bottles, the room, the man, all the loveliness and the preciousness and the pain of transience, are too fragile for my febrile memory.

Mani is regarding me with fuddled sentimentality. We are getting maudlin on our fourth beer, which neither of us had any business to broach. 'Perhaps you should get away, Kaveri. To the hills—Coorg or the Nilgiris. You need a break.'

I *have* got away, Pa. Being here is the best break for me.

'Of course,' he smirks, 'where else would you go?'

The complacence smothers me. The kind suggestion of a break strikes me as an unnecessary solicitude. Why *me*—the least affected by the tragedy? What can he be thinking of?

Well Pa, it is free board-and-lodge, and the catering is of the best.

Why do I do this to him? But he is smiling—an eager smile. 'When will I see you again, Kaveri?'

But I'm *here*, Pa.

'But when *again*?'

In his eyes I see there will not be too many agains for him.

The bearer brings the bill for me to sign. Above the gay necktie, Mani's face crumples. Hastily I push the bill to him.

He examines it as if it's the quarterly report of a company he's invested in, and signs it as if the bottom line doesn't please him.

'The insolent blighter! Giving *you* the bill! *Ch-ch-ch.* What did I tell you? This club is going to the dogs!'

Perhaps he wanted to spare you the effort, Pa.

'Nonsense! He wanted a tip, third-rate fellow. You tipped too,' he accused. 'I saw you put a note under the ashtray. Once,' he continued grimly, 'you'd be blackballed for it. But today! These bearers have been spoilt by new upstart members, that's what.'

Stalwart and upstart file into the dining room.

We order the 'set vegetarian meal', which consists of three greasy puris, thick-grained rice, two mushy vegetables, a cup of angry-looking sambar, one of angrier rasam, and an indeterminate dessert that looks like laundry starch flavoured with mosquito repellant. *Lemon custard.* I give up after a puri and a spoon of rice but he works doggedly through everything. Perhaps it is remembrance of long-ago scarcity and a continuing obligation not to waste. Perhaps it is consideration for the bearer who is hovering at a solicitous distance. Whatever it is, it moves me to tears. (That stupid beer!) He doesn't have to eat this vile stuff. He owes nobody the price of this meal—in money, dyspepsia and principles.

It's all right, Pa. You don't have to finish the custard. You won't be punished if you don't, haha. Unless of course you like it.

He clatters his spoon as if caught in an improper act. 'I *like* it.' He picks up his spoon.

After lunch, when I take his arm to help him down the steps of the verandah, he disengages himself not too gently. 'I can manage!' Then, stopping on the bottom stair, he grunts, 'Don't go making faces in that mirror!' And marches off without a backward glance.

Oh, Pa. Ignore that bearer. Ignore the whole bunch. Not one of them is worth your little finger.

Long fingers of sunlight bless our faces through the windscreen. The clouds are still loitering aimlessly—there's no sign of the rain promised by the Met this morning. (The Rain Dance is going to be a washout.) We rattle along in the middle of the road, unfazed by the uncouth impatience of the traffic behind us that the beer has muted. Mani decides to make a detour to drive through Cubbon Park, the large central green named after Bangalore's longest-serving and long-forgotten commissioner, Sir Mark Cubbon. We circle his statue outside the old State Central Library and go past the red High Court buildings, which, thanks to Bharat and his preservation group, have evaded demolition. At this time of year, as at most times of the year in this city, the trees are a riot of colours. Orange, purple, pink, yellow . . . massed showily against the sky.

Everything is still in the afternoon torpor. Stray dogs lie coiled under park benches on which the gardeners sleep. Even the birds have hushed. But not for long, the lull. 'What're your plans now, Kaveri?'

Nothing special, Pa. Just live abundantly—as Pulin Grover advises. Travel, I expect. I'm planning to resign from the bank. Watch that cow, Pa!

He grips the steering wheel. 'And Arya? What are *his* plans?'

This is an annual question. The answer is unvarying and unvaryingly unsatisfactory, but we go through the routine all the same. It's a part of our oral tradition.

Oh, nothing in particular. Carry on doing what he's doing. He has been chasing a moving target ever since I've known him.

Mani frowns. He can suddenly turn old-fashioned, like a dead programme reactivated.

Actually, Pa, I was hoping to spend some time here. A year perhaps.

'*Here*? In Bangalore?' The car wobbles. 'But you'll be away from Arya!'

So? Oh, that cyclist! You just missed him!

'Hah!' He rights the steering wheel. 'But you're still young and . . . you need . . .'

I am amused and embarrassed. For him as much as for me. But he is unable to get over the hump and he cannot spell out my need. 'You cannot,' he continues firmly, 'hang loose, as you people call it, for a year. Your mother and I,' sidestepping the hump, 'haven't been apart for a *day*.' No, nor hung loose either. 'I want you to have a normal life, Kaveri. A *natural* life. What sort of life is it for a woman without a husband? A woman must have a home of her own.'

I am diverted by this new usefulness of Arya. It is his duty to naturalise me.

But you always say *this* is my home, Pa.

That stumps him. We exit Cubbon Park, leaving behind the green and the quiet. He noses around for an opening in the fast-moving traffic, annoying several drivers with his manoeuvres. After a harrowing five minutes we make it to the road that will take us home.

Pa, don't worry. I'm happy as I am.

But *he* is not happy at all and his distress erupts in a cascade of *ch-ch-ch*. 'What do you know about happiness? Thirty-two years old and so naïve!'

Perhaps it's not the happiness *you* would choose for me, Pa. You would have me do a regular job—with a monthly cheque. *And* be with Arya.

'For *his* sake, too, Kaveri.' He clenches his jaw. 'Are you,' he thrusts out the jaw, 'have you been living . . . a . . . normal married life?'

This is intolerable. But, uncontrollably, I giggle. Is all this getting too much for you, Pa? Shall I just go back to Delhi?

'Yes . . . no, Kaveri.' He turns his head for just a second. His glance is pleading. 'I mean, that's not what I meant at all.' And taking his hand off the steering wheel to pat my knee, 'You're right,' he says. 'This *is* your home. Stay. Stay as long as you like. You know we love having you.' At a traffic light he turns to me again, his face wrinkled with distress now. 'But I must not keep you from your husband!'

Pa, I cry silently. There *isn't* a husband. There *isn't* the life you imagine. There is nobody, nothing. Only you and Amma and this moment. I'm living from moment to moment. For the present that's all I can do. That's all I have.

'You're crying! You're feeling torn! People will say *I* pulled you apart!'

I wipe my eyes and put my hand on his. Forget people, Pa. You and I know better. We know you *put* me together.

He calms down although he isn't entirely convinced. Worn out, we are silent for the rest of the journey.

As we near home we exchange guilty looks. Meenakshi is going to be so mad! All that unconsumed food! 'We'll have it for dinner,' Mani says feebly. He and I know he will not eat dinner after such a late lunch, beer, ice cream and all.

As it happens the uneaten lunch turns out to be the least of our problems.

Meenakshi is standing by the verandah window, obviously on the lookout for us, and obviously very agitated. She flings open the door. 'The police are back! Asking questions again! And Jana has disappeared!'

'What do you mean, *disappeared*?'

'She's gone to Chennai,' she says sheepishly.

'Tcha! How is that relevant anyway?'

'It seems she was the last person to see him alive.'

This is news to him. However, 'So what?' He yawns. '*Someone* had to be the last to see him alive.'

'She's been *saying* things.' But he just closes his eyes. Dismayed by this behaviour and yet unable to distrust his judgement, Meenakshi folds her lower lip with a finger and thumb. Perhaps she has missed something again. I put my arms around her. Don't worry, Ma.

But she does worry—she sneezes and sneezes with worry. 'They're not ... *choo* ... satisfied with the ... *choo* ... accident verdict. It's that Inspector Menezes. *Achoo!*'

Mani says, 'Oh so, it's *suicide* now. Is that what Jana's putting about? Really. Everyone talks too much in this family. And even if it *is* suicide, nothing can be done about it.'

'It's not suicide. That's what I'm trying to tell you. They suspect ... *achoo* ... he may have been pushed into the pit!'

Mani has the presence of mind to sit up. 'I've never heard such nonsense in my life! What gave them the idea?'

'The lift company remembered Balumama had called to complain about that lift door just the evening before. That the outer door on the fourth floor opened even when the lift wasn't there.'

My blood runs cold. Really and truly—just as they say in novels. I can vouch for it. It feels like your skin is shot with hot icicles. Even Mani appears shaken.

'. . . he was told the mechanic would come within the day and that he must switch off the lift and put up a sign. Or there could be an accident.' Her breath judders. 'He was *warned*.' She looks to him for an explanation, for assurance—he's never failed her.

But he just shrugs! 'Perhaps Balumama forgot,' he says, without any especial concern, at least none that I can see. 'Or he may have tried to fiddle with the door and lost his footing. It could have been plain and simple vertigo . . . it's ridiculous to think anything else.'

Meenakshi tugs at the safety pins strung on her necklace. She does not look at me.

Suddenly, the lines on Mani's face slacken. Taking off his coat and tie in a leisurely way he settles in an armchair and stretches out his legs.

I get it. If the suicide theory is kicked out I wouldn't be morally responsible for Balumama's death. This new complication might implicate another, but what of that? His daughter would be beyond the pale. A pyrrhic victory—but for Mani it is a rout.

Ma, stop hurting your lip. They won't get anything out of Jana. *We* can say Balumama suffered from temporary insanity. Because of the book.

Mani starts up. 'Why are you bringing *that* up?' A vein pops on his forehead. '*They* aren't.'

But, Pa, it's better than exposing Jana! They will bully her. And who knows what she . . .

'*You* don't get involved in this—either of you.' The vein retracts. He lies back again.

Meenakshi, bless her, has tears in her eyes. 'The police questioned the people in the building. Jana told quite a few of them she believes it was meant to happen. The police want to know what she means by *meant*. Whether she's mentally sound. They don't believe in karma.'

Ma, did anyone refer them to . . . my novel? Tell them about the, um, parallels—Balumama's, um, crime, and trial and the one in my story?

'Illey. Rajumama said that would be,' her brow wrinkles, '*social suicide*. "All sorts of things might come out in the papers," he said.' She swallows and looks away. 'They've had enough as it is.'

I think it's time the police are told about the novel, Ma. They can go off on that track. *Anything* rather than Jana dragged in.

She nods and blinks back the tears. 'Ama. I see your point.'

Mani jerks up. Another vein pops. 'Are you both crazy? Don't drag in the book!'

I turn away, sick and ashamed. My love for this man is the single reality, the centrality of my life. To doubt it is to doubt my existence. But he's testing it in a way I wouldn't have thought possible. *Don't, please don't. I believe in you. Don't let me down.* I don't know who I'm appealing to—him or my Maker. Once the two were the same. My head begins to throb.

Meenakshi touches my arm. 'She needs our help, Kaveri.' She dabs her eyes. 'Thank goodness they don't know anything . . . they won't find a motive.' But her eyes are afraid, and her lip is raw. They only had to dig a little to find the motive. Not so thank goodness after all. I have to lighten her mood, and mine.

Think of this as an Agatha Christie, Ma. (Meenakshi loves Agatha Christie.) Where was everyone when it happened? I can swear Jana was in the kitchen cutting onions, God knows why. She was *reeking* of onions. I wish she was more like a Christie suspect, though. Glamorous, charismatic, *something*. She's so, well, so *Jana*. The good news is that nobody takes her seriously.

Meenakshi brightens. 'She *does* seem a little unstable at times.' Although that was no reason why anyone could be exempted from committing a crime. There could be Motive in Madness. I don't voice my doubts, however. Heaven knows Meenakshi is rattled enough. 'They won't pay attention to her then. Thank goodness.'

She's never long in the dumps, my mother. All the world conspires to pull her out. The grass springs under her feet, the cobwebs part to let her through. Thank goodness indeed. Thank *whose* goodness I'd like to know.

Mani sits up again. 'How can anyone suspect Jana of this dastardly act? Such a heinous crime? A *woman*, that, too?'

Dastardly. Heinous. Murder most foul. Agatha Christie *and* Shakespeare. Oh, my paws and whiskers. Crispin too. Father dear. Omnipotent, omniscient as you are, you have no idea what it is to be a woman. *We* know that the dubiety lies not in Jana's womanly frailty but her womanly unpredictability. Stemming from womanly rage. Our concern is not the motive but the mode. If she'd sprung the mind to do it, it wasn't difficult to do it.

He puffs out his cheeks. 'It was an accident. They should accept that. We should insist on it. Anyway, there's no proof of suicide. No note or a diary. Anything like that.'

I'm too bored to argue it's only in books that people keep diaries, meticulously and copiously filled—and conveniently found. In real life dead people remain the unsolved mysteries they were when alive. Nine times out of ten.

He hasn't finished. 'And if *you* have these doubts, you might leak them to the police. Accidentally.' He wags a finger. 'Be careful, is what I say. They have ways of tripping up people.'

Tripping up people. She could have stuck a foot out—accidentally. Meenakshi looks as if she wishes she could bury her head in a cooking pot. She goes into the kitchen, takes out the coffee saucepan, heats the milk. The headache is beating a tattoo behind my temples.

'Kaveri,' she says miserably—her lip is bleeding now, 'is it possible . . . that the book . . . because . . . the book brought back what . . . happened and . . .' Her face is clayey. 'Kaveri, what if she . . .' My head lands with a thump on the window bars. 'Kaveri! They cannot prove anything. Nobody saw anything.'

No, there were no witnesses. I don't believe it will come to anything, Ma. It's only that . . .

I feel like I have blood on my hands as well. *Indicted for incitement.* But I don't say anything—my mother has had enough.

It's only that I *wish* she'd gone home after lunch, Ma.

'We must have faith, Kaveri. Everything will work out. Trust in God.' Her hands flutter to her chest, rest there prayerfully.

I'd sooner put my trust in people, Ma. Come to think of it, not even people. I'd rather go with a guide dog than trust some people.

'I do wish you and your father were a *little* bit religious.'

A lamentable old failing, this, and I reply as I always do. We do have a religion, Ma. I believe in him and he believes in me.

But it rings hollow today.

Just before dinner Bharat calls. Rajumama has spoken to the Police Commissioner—to complain of harassment. He's told them the family has accepted it was an accident and wish to close the case. 'I'm going to call Jana in Chennai and warn her not to talk to anyone.'

Do, I say distractedly. You'll probably catch her cleaning her house. There's that comfort for her at least. It must have got into a terrible state in her absence.

The minute I put the phone down, two heads pop up like twin cuckoos. 'Who was it? Bharat? What did he say? Is Jana alright? Are the police . . .?'

'Quite right,' says Mani after I give them the news. 'It *was* an accident. There's no need to bring up irrelevant angles.'

You mean Balumama knowing of the lift's malfunction is irrelevant?

'What do *you* propose instead? That the police continue to ask awkward questions? Browbeat Jana?' (Whose side are you on, anyway?)

I'm merely trying to understand the process of law. How we help, I mean, *direct* it to take its course. I hadn't realised there would be so much . . . public involvement.

The corners of his mouth droop. 'Let me tell you, when it comes to the crux you will not play so high-and-mighty. For all the noise you made, I *am* worried about Jana.'

You are afraid for her. You have reason to be afraid.

'Because nobody should get mixed up with the police.'

Or with family, for that matter.

'The Governor's nephew is a good friend of mine,' he says carelessly.

In case the Police Commissioner route doesn't work? I'm surprised at you, Pa.

'Well, there *is* no case. As I keep saying. Let the police save their energies for real crimes.'

What if this *is* a real crime?

He stares me down. 'Loose talk,' he begins heavily. 'Loose talk . . .'

. . . is the genesis of revolutions, war and genocide. I know.

His eyebrows bristle. Ch-ch-ch. 'This isn't a joke.'

I never thought it was, Pa. Of course you should talk to the Governor's nephew. I mean, absurd to be done in by the *law*!

But he doesn't hear me. He's already dialling.

The day is not done yet. Just as we are going to bed the telephone rings *again*. Meenakshi calls me out. 'Someone from Delhi,' she whispers, her hand covering the receiver. 'It's a *man*. But it isn't Arya.'

From Delhi! A man and it's not Arya! The blood sings in my head.

Slow down, heart. Where's the fire? It could be Pulin. But it's not! It won't be! It's *him*! *He's* called! At last! To ask me to hurry back! To tell me he misses me, and do I miss him too? To tell me the African violets are thriving but not their keeper. He is wilting. Once a week would do him too. It's woefully inadequate but if those were my new terms he would accept them. Only come back! *Look my collar, my watchstrap, my belt, all of me slips loose when you leave . . . everything gives me away.*

And I, what would I reply? I'm coming back. It's finished. It's stopped. No more emails. A new life . . . And I feel such a burst of freedom when I pick up the receiver, such ecstasy of release, that a bird's first flight is nothing to it.

'At long last! I must say you're reclusive—or should that be elusive?'

It comes to me in the instant I hear the voice. The who in the what-and-why. The surprise of it is I don't drop the receiver.

'. . . you don't recognise me? I *am* offended. We talked for quite a while.' And when I still don't answer, 'Let me jog your memory. Bhasin's the name. Vinod Bhasin.'

Vinod. The vital word that had got lost in the music. That I hadn't—insensibly—cared to retrieve.

'I believe you know what this is about,' says Mr Bhasin, Vinod, *V*, the yakkety-yak Beard-and-Sandals at Gita's party.

Decree

I drowned in that moment. I died in that moment. My life flashed by in that moment, all my lives, this, the last, the next, and the next.

I wanted to say, I don't know what you're talking about, I haven't a clue, and what makes you think I want to play guessing games? Or talk to you at all? And where is the urgency in it that you have to pursue me *here*, at *this* hour, startling my parents, stealing my sleep, whatever little sleep I can gather in these nights of prickling wakefulness? I wanted to say, *no*, and to hell with you, and all those who plunder my peace of mind . . .

I wanted to say no, no and no!

But . . .

'I . . . I . . . Yes,' says Kaveri. Oh folly! Then, idiot, she asks, 'How did you get this number?' In such a mouse-like squeak that Vinod Bhasin, in that faraway dusty city, that dreams-to-dust city, says, 'I beg your pardon? I said I wanted to talk to you about your novel. Actually, about this other book.' He named the book with, it occurs to her (even at this moment when the distant rumble she is hearing is not a truck's but an earthquake's), the eager triumph of a master of ceremonies on awards night. *And the winner is* . . . 'You know it, I believe,' he continued. 'Know it rather well, I may add.' There is the familiar teasing in his voice, but with an edge to it, as of velvet brushed the wrong way.

'Hrr.' The country mouse cleared the squeak from its throat. The hairs on its neck rose. The cat was pawing the hole.

'Yes, I've read it,' she says briskly. 'So what?' In effect, a toss of the head and a *so bloody what?* But it's the bluster of one who has nothing and everything to lose. Who, in fact, knows she is about to lose everything, even though what she has, as she's suspected all along, is fool's gold. A dream, in other words. What she is discovering now is that dreams are all you can call your own. Dreams *and* nightmares. Only dreams are inappropriatable. Reality is subject to scrutiny and audit and seizure. But what has really shaken her is the disproval of the myth of miracles. That yet another innocence—the mind as the perfect hiding place—has been debunked. Her secret has been winkled out and now, along with her dreams, is slipping downstream. In a paper boat.

So what?

So it's happening, that's what. The carpet's been pulled from under her feet, that's bloody what. And it's not such a long drop to the dirt.

'Do I have to tell you what?' The cat is playing with the mouse. 'You admit you've read the book.'

Again it is her cue to say, no, I don't admit to anything,
I'm not talking, and is this any time for a literary discussion?
But, 'It's an old book,' she says, struggling to steady her
breath. 'Ob-obscure, obscuran . . . tist.' And in a rush, 'Actually
I read it a long time ago. Years ago. It was part of an uncle's
collection—he's dead now. As dead as the book. Haha.' And
now that they're into a literary discussion, 'It was interesting.
From what I can remember. A thought-provoking take on,
um, morals and mythology.' As if this bit of information could
be traded for something else. Peace and quiet preferably.

'Take, eh? That's a good one.'

He's found out. He's going to prove to her the world is
smaller than she'd imagined. Than she had cast it. With a lot
more people crowding it, a lot less ignorant (or stupid) than
she had deemed them.

'Obviously it made a deep impression on you.' And, his
voice a fingernail scratching satin now, 'A *lasting* impression,'
he qualifies.

Waves of panic crash about her head. She can be reached
here from *there*? From the bottom of the dust bowl to this
3,300-foot-high plateau of sanity and safety? She eases the
receiver, that treacherous instrument of miscommunication,
from her stinging ear. Doesn't he know that bearers of bad
news are put to death? 'Who gave you this telephone number?
Pulin?'

But the dealer of death wasn't to be deflected. As if he'd
been rehearsing the line for just such an occasion, he reels off,
'Art imitating life makes good fiction and life imitating art
makes it *great* fiction,' a rehearsed pause, 'but art imitating
art . . .' Another rehearsed pause. Her ear is on fire. *Stop!* Stop
thief! But he doesn't.

He fires his mortal dart.

'There's been a mis . . .' she begins in a strangled voice, and then *she* stops. Miss what? He hasn't missed a thing. Not the point, not his aim, not a beat. As her heart had. Missed several beats.

It misses another when, 'I'm afraid there's no mistake,' he says. 'No doubt at all.' Is there an executioner's compassion in his tone, or a sadist's sinister thrill? A dentist's steely detachment? *Shut your eyes, it'll be over soon . . . Open your eyes, look what's coming . . . Hold on, this'll hurt a bit.* It is hurting a lot—the phone is a burning ingot. 'Those quotes I sent you,' he's getting down to business, 'there's no argument about those.' Oh, but who's arguing here? Who is opposing your findings? Finding's keepings, so keep your wonderful findings and good luck to you. 'Are you there?' I'm right here. Right there with you. The phone's a poultice on raw flesh—I can't peel it off. So I'll hark, heed, *you* holler. 'The third line in the second paragraph in Chapter 2 and two lines in paragraph 3 on page 18 . . .' It's hearsay! A heresy! The heretic continues to itemise, '. . . the last bit on page 5, and in the fourth paragraph on page 19 . . .' All right. There's no need to labour it. You're telling me it's over. You're the Voice Over.

The Voice Over warms up. With stylised diction, as if it's a citation (or a charge), it declares, 'Mainly it's this man's guilt and justification and atonement before his suicide. Of course his *physical* description is different. That counts for nothing.'

That counted for everything, she whispers. As it happened. 'They're just a few lines,' she brings out hoarsely. 'Here and there. It's just superficial . . . the . . . the . . .' The word snags.

'Similarities.'

'Similitudes.'

'Exactitudes, actually.'

'Exactments. To be exact. Exactly . . . only somewhat.' She's a little hysterical now.

'You can't be somewhat pregnant. And they're more than superficial.' There is heft in his tone now. Quit the thrust-and-parry. He isn't fencing here, thank you. 'Did you say something?' No. Just that you're getting on my nerves now. 'Hello? *Hello*?'

Well, *hello* makes a nice change. Hello there, too.

There is a brooding quiet as if they are hatching eggs. She cracks one open. 'It was not deliberate. They must have . . . stuck in my mind. I wasn't thinking, I must have been abstracted . . . I didn't *abstract* them.' She utters what sounds suspiciously like a laugh. This was becoming a comic sketch. She was the half that got the rotten tomatoes. Don't you have any higher ideal than this cheap wit? It would appear I don't have ideals at all, Pa.

Mani was fond of an old Tamil saying: When a thick-skinned man falls down, the mud will not stick to his whiskers. The mud is not sticking to her whiskers now. Not yet. So, 'We're allowed *some* artistic licence, surely,' she says, a little condescendingly.

The phone crackles. 'It was artistic licentiousness. And don't suggest borrowing is a literary tradition.'

'It was there in the subconscious! We talked about it at Gita's . . .'

'It was there in a *book*.'

'Writers source stuff from books. They just add value and package . . .'

'You packaged without adding. Or subtracting. Value, or anything else. And don't suggest it was research—one book is not research. Besides, your book is a novel, not a self-help manual.'

Red-hot pincers claw her. She's skewered in a barbecue pit! The Defector is wielding the skewer, his hand encased in a blacksmith's glove. Behind him hovers Uma. *You were my childhood friend.* She's losing her mind!

The receiver slips from her fingers. She wipes it on her thigh, holds it there for a bit before raising it. 'That book was out of the copyright period.' A hollow logic but she's beyond logic now. 'The author's dead. He ought to be. He wrote it ninety years ago, haha.'

There's no answering haha from the other end. Suddenly she is angry. 'I don't have to explain myself to you.'

'You prefer to explain yourself to the newspapers then?' She went numb. 'I thought so. You wouldn't want the shit to hit the fan.' Question to the jury: Aren't clichés a form of plagiarism?

More to play for time, for it is of little relevance now, she says, 'Anonymous email! That's just so . . . theatrical. So . . . *juvenile.*'

Now he laughs—his hearty party laugh. 'Worked though, didn't they? I got the idea from Hamlet. I'd love to have seen your face.' He laughs again.

'Haha-ha,' she echoes miserably.

'Anyway,' he says briskly, 'the point is I've bought the rights to reprint the book.' She grits her teeth. 'And I've thought of something that will work in both our, um, interest. Which I want to discuss. Soon.'

She closes her eyes. Her head begins pounding. Open up! *I can't! Shit is hitting the fan out there!* She chokes back the hysteria.

'. . . so you must come to Delhi. *Soon.* That means yesterday. We'll need to talk with Pulin Grover as well.' And, as a parting shot, 'You were crazy, you know, to think you could have pulled off a stunt like this. Crazy or conceited.' There is a tiny pause. 'Some gumption.'

'So,' Mani hails me with his toothy grin, 'what prize have you won *now*? It must be important to be woken up.'

We weren't asleep, I reply drearily. And it isn't a prize.

'But what *was* it? *Who* was it?'

Meenakshi, whose feelers can penetrate concrete bunkers and span continents, intervenes. 'It was a *business* call. *Private* business.'

Mani's mouth turns down. 'At *this* time? Anything wrong?' It might turn into coal, your gold, so have you invested wisely? *There may not be any investments to make after all, Pa.* '. . . don't let them diddle you out of what was agreed upon. You are too timid sometimes. Outside our home, you don't assert yourself enough.' No, Pa. You used to do all the asserting for me. But this needs more than assertion.

'Are you talking to yourself?'

Meenakshi shushes him. 'She's tired. Kaveri, go to bed. And,' adds this saviour, 'sleep late tomorrow morning'.

The morning brings no relief—mornings seldom do. If anything, sleep—even the roiling unrest of the chronic insomniac—sharpens the pain of waking to a fully connected reality. Dark gives way to darkness. For once, the eternal rhythms of the House-by-the-Road threaten to throw rather than restore the balance.

'Quiet,' Meenakshi hushes someone in the courtyard. 'Kaveri is still sleeping.'

That she is not, for sure. Kaveri's sleep is a luxury of the past.

Mixing decoction and milk (full cream), spooning sugar, heating (not boiling) the brew requires a powerhouse of concentration. I am giving it my all when Meenakshi comes in. 'Coffee-a? Make some for your father. And make him a toast—the Marie biscuits are finished.'

Any news of Jana, Ma?

Right on cue, the phone rings. Meenakshi is out of the door on the second ring.

It is Bharat—to tell us the police are asking for Jana. They still want to question her. Just officiousness, I tell Meenakshi, but she begins to worry her lip. Desperately, I try to focus, to stave off my other anxiety with this one, keep *those* yapping dogs at bay.

I shall go see Inspector Menezes, Ma. Tell him about the book—I'll *show* it to him. Get him back on the suicide track. In fact, I'll call him right away.

There's an interruption from the door. 'Don't be stupid. Why're *you* sticking your neck out now?'

He is spanning the opening with his arms, crucified on the light from the pantry window. There's carelessness in the disposition of limbs and torso, and, in the way the hair springs from his armpit, a disdain for the sensibilities of his audience who might not enjoy the display. Not for the first time does the disloyal thought occur to me that other people's misfortunes touch him only as classified news, as a moral lesson, sometimes, more damningly, as mitigant for his own troubles, and even, in a perverse way, be life-affirming. 'It's all inconclusive, anyway,' he says with a wave that is supposed to be reassuring. 'If at all it goes to court, it will be dismissed as frivolous.'

You don't really care, do you? Because you think I am not involved any more! Well, if you must know, I am! I'm neck-deep in shit! And the shit's about to hit the fan, so you're going to get splattered too!

He raises his chin and sniffs. 'Who burned the toast?'

My nerves snap.

You *know* who burned the toast! I did! I'm *famous* around here for burning the toast! Why can't you ask me straight? I'll confess to it! I BURNED THE TOAST!

I slam the mug on the counter. Meenakshi winces but doesn't dare examine the mug. Mani puts on his you-hurt-me-but-I-forgive-you expression.

Dawn dilates to noon. When Meenakshi happens on me making a fourth cup of coffee and it becomes clear to her that I am not going to eat the idlis, or the banana blackening by the plate, that I am not going to eat anything, 'The phone call last night,' she says hesitantly. 'There is a problem, isn't there?'

She is standing by the flaking stove, as she has for years, decades, aeons. Waiting for me to come unto her. Waiting for me to fetch up against her. Waiting with the ladle poised in her hand—the feelingful hand—to scoop up the mess that I am. The light from the window blocks all design but one—that of smashing with the ladle whatever it is that dares to harm me. For this deadly purpose it is ever at the ready. On a bad day, on a day, that is, when she feels with all the feelings in her hands, her shoulders, neck, every bit of her, that her child is in trouble, she can absorb all the light of a noon sun. She can turn day into night—to hide me.

She is standing there, calm and invincible, shining like a beacon. Under the doughy softness she bristles with a vigilance that never leaves her. Not for a moment, not for the world.

Sleeping or waking she watches over me. Sitting or standing she looks out for me. Her nearness, my despair, swells and bursts, and my heart plummets like a felled bird. Down, down, down to where seething clouds crash upon boiling sea.

Wave upon wave of misery break on me. Breasting them, I stagger to my rock-haven.

'Kanna, kanna. What is it?'

It's the book, Ma, my book.

'What about your book?' I lift my head from her shoulder. Her calm eyes meet my drowning ones. She dips a spoon into a pot, tastes. 'Mmmm,' she consults the ceiling, 'a little too much salt . . . what about your book?'

They have . . . I have . . . there are . . . it's been found . . . bits of it . . .

'What has been found?' She attends to her immediate problem of rectifying the brew with a squeeze of lime.

Similar to another book!

'That's all?' She tastes the rectified brew. 'Someone had the same ideas as you. Great minds think alike.' She puts down the ladle, considers me with her still-tranquil eyes—and oh Lord, is there a hint of pride in them?

You don't understand! You don't understand a *thing*! You never have!

That's right, Kaveri. Pick on the first object in your flight path. Just because your mother does not possess your forked tongue, your gift for backchat (and thank heaven she doesn't), she's an easy target for you. Now accuse her—and all mothers and fathers, for that matter—of not keeping an eye on the pot. For not checking how their young are brewing. Or fermenting. Or rotting.

A bewildered Meenakshi is asking, 'What don't I understand?'

You really want to know? I'll tell you. I'll tell you exactly what has happened.

That's right. Initiate them into your dirty little world. For too long have you kept your parents in the dark. Dispel their darkness now, with your black brilliance. Educate them. Explain that crime is not the exclusive preserve of criminals. That there's an entire human history of corruption contained in a single cell.

Corruption.

Edging my head closer to hers, God forgive me, to flatter her with my confidence in her understanding—a confidence reserved for Mani—and deploying dull pedantry to impart the tidings, I disgorge the contents of my sooty heart. In a further show of confidentiality—God forgive me—I gaze into her eyes. She falls for it. Looking excited and eager, even grateful—God forgive us both—she lowers her head to mine. Forehead knocks on forehead.

Meenakshi's brow clears. 'Of course you're exaggerating. You're imagining things.'

Ah. So imagination strikes again. Imagination, that snake, that seducer of virgin minds. Poisoning reason and clouding clarity. Such is her force of conviction that, for just a brief moment, I'm actually carried away. But the belief transference peters out, and I'm back to my wretchedness.

She smiles indulgently. 'I know what must have happened.'

You do?

'Yes. You remember the time in junior school when you brought home your arithmetic test papers? Because you wanted to show them to us? You didn't mean to cheat or anything—you were just showing off. Everyone laughed.' She essays a laugh.

No one laughs with her. Not the oleander, not the crows, not the sun.

Where is the connection, is the question hovering on my lips, when I see it. *In the car I corrected two sums*, errors Mani had spotted—he could spot errors even if the page was upside down—but would never have thought, not at his cynical worst, that I would correct.

As for Meenakshi, she couldn't have known. But being a sorceress as well as being altogether all the time, the most consolidated person in my ken, perhaps she guessed?

She's completing her analogy. 'So this—you weren't to know that . . . that . . . Did . . . you?' she asks in a small voice.

This is my cue to say, no Ma, I don't know how all this came about. Truly, it is a wondrous thing that the left side of the brain knows at all what the right is up to. This was a sleight of hand.

However.

This isn't quite the same, Ma.

'But the *principle* is.' Too long has Meenakshi been married into this house of principles and laws, equations and derivations, not to see an out there. And then she spoils it. 'Don't tell your father. *He* will not understand.' Her eyes send me a we-stand-together signal, but we don't connect. Disappointed, she returns to the stove.

He will understand only too well, Ma.

Now we do connect. She clatters the spoon—the rasam jumps, splatters the stove. 'You acted to the best of your knowledge, Kaveri.' My mother is appealing to me.

I acted in my best interests, Ma.

Tears start in her eyes. 'You did it for him,' she whispers. The deceitfulness of love. We're none of us immune, it would seem.

I did it for myself, Ma. (At least let's right one wrong here.)

Mopping her face with her all-purpose towel, 'I'm going to lie down for a while,' she says wearily.

Yes, cry, mutters cruel Kaveri. Cry like you did when I took a bow, when I cut through the finishing tape, when I marched off with the Class Prize! All those wasted tears! All those wasted years! Is *this* why you cried? Because you knew that all those honours, those firsts I took (never second, never third, oh no, never the bronze for Kaveri), was a mock show? Were you crying for *you* then, or for *me*? Who're you crying for now?

Resting her head against the cold bars of the kitchen window, she gazes into the courtyard. Rules are made by men, broken by men. Men are ruled by their decisions, and damned by them too. Men make errors of judgement and then errors on errors of judgement.

She'd borrowed the accursed book from Balumama's library in the Big House a long time ago. Then, wretched fate, she discovered a copy in College Street in Kolkata, in a stall on stilts, with the city's waste swirling under it. The stall-owner had informed her it was a rare book, out of print for seventy years, and not so popular in its time either. Shortly after that she began writing *AFL*. 'Wonderful,' Pulin's editors declared—unanimously. She'd suggested (weakly) there were some revisions she had to make, but, 'No changes,' they said, 'if it has to make our spring list'. For a moment she hesitated, then the moment carried the day. The qualms (definition of qualm:

disease of the conscience) were put down. *Out of print for seventy years, and not so popular in its time.*

She stares at the oleander with eyes of stone. Find the logic, Kaveri, and reason will follow.

Here it is, Pa. Creation has no beginning and no end. Adam and Eve is a sweet fable. *Is this one of your arbitrary ramblings? Because if so . . .* No listen, Pa. All that exists was in existence before the concept of space or time came to be. We know that. That makes innovation a derived truth—a derivative. *Really, Kaveri this is so woolly-headed . . .* No, wait, Pa. So, in effect, in cause and effect, there *is* nothing new. New is only a transmutation of old—going around in circles. Old wine in new bottle and all that. *But what are you getting at?* The con, Pa! Imitation posturing as invention! Or as original, as the case may be. *Now, really . . .* Don't you see? Regurgitated art fed to a gullible audience as tribute to its intelligence! It's a conspiracy between the unscrupulous and the snobbish! *Well tried, Kaveri. But . . .*

No, no more *buts*, Pa. I have heeded too many of them.

In the afternoon I visited Inspector Menezes. He gave me a courteous hearing, flipped through the book, marked the relevant passages, promised to give it his due consideration.

He promised nothing.

On my return I apologised to Mani for the morning's rudeness and mooted a walk to make up for it.

The road was crazed with homebound vehicles—cars and buses from town and from the new IT park in the opposite direction. In the trees crows were engaged in violent domestic quarrels. Below them stray dogs fought over choice spoils from the garbage dump. The wedding hall was blasting Bollywood music way above the allowable decibel limit, pulling out all stops before the policemen landed up for a bribe. The combined din was scratching the evening sky so raw it was like a butcher's window.

What's the point?

'There's no need to shout. I can hear you perfectly well. What do you mean, what's the point? I asked if you were going to Delhi in connection with your foreign tour. Visas and such.'

Pa! What are you *doing*?

He stops in his tracks, drops the hibiscus he had picked from a passing bush, inadvertently I'm sure, he's never done a thing like that, but, *it isn't like you to pinch flowers from the park*, I cry out before I can stop myself. We're both trembling, he with shock, disbelief, confusion, and I with cussedness, wretchedness, hopelessness, I don't know what, and the sky is trembling too, and the earth, the trees, the very air, because I have frightened and shamed an old man for picking a flower that is dead (for it is a poor specimen, fit only for the compost heap), for deadheading a bush, and doing it unthinkingly, considerately, tidying up as he would his own garden. He was only trying to help.

I'm sorry, Pa.

The road has become a tightrope. The tension grows so intolerable that I am thinking of calling off our walk, although this would mean calling attention to my presence, which I'm hiding behind the silence. And behind the lamp posts, the railings, a child, a cat . . .

All of a sudden he stops. I think he's going to turn back but it turns out he's spotted something. Flowers. Knocking on a creeper like a bunch of luscious grapes. The colour of litmus, of a summer sky, of a very young girl's silk sash. He pulls the bunch towards him, examines it with fretful intent. Then, releasing it, he wheels around. 'What do you mean, *good, very good*? I said, why hasn't *our* petrea bloomed yet? This one isn't even *watered* regularly. *Ch-ch-ch*. And I asked you if this Delhi trip is absolutely necessary. Who's paying for it?'

I am, I answer, irritated that even now he must ask this. Without thinking I add, we have to pay for our sins.

'*Sins*? What do you mean?'

Nothing, Pa. It's not a whole lot of money.

He frowns. This is exactly what he had feared. The old fecklessness is turning to recklessness. I've started to fling my new wealth about. With no thought of the morrow. Today it is flying to Delhi on some extravagant whim, tomorrow some other caper. Circumventing an anthill, 'It may not be much for *you*,' he huffs, 'but for us it's a month's pension'. I feel small. I feel sick. I feel like running. I am trapped. And when, suddenly, he takes my arm, I know I am shackled too. A life sentence. 'I'm worried, Kaveri. No, there's no reason, I know, but still.'

Meenakshi may have feelers, but Mani has a sixth sense. He has a third eye, this Shiva.

I have to discuss something with Pulin Grover, Pa, I say as calmly as I'm able. Nothing very important.

The sun ducks behind a sodden cloud. A wettish breeze sets up, that whips the loose leaves off the hedge. He raises his head and snuffles. 'Coffee blossom showers!' His eyes light up. 'It's going to be a good year for coffee!' The pleasure is short-lived. 'What is it you can't discuss on the phone?'

Something's come up about copyrights, Pa.

'Hmmm. I hope you know your rights. Is your contract watertight? The law protects you from charlatans, you know. Nobody can print your book or parts of it without your permission. In this country the copyright period is for sixty years after a writer's death or the date on your contract, I forget which.'

Look, Pa! The trumpet tree still has flowers!

'*Tcha*! That's *Tabebuia rosea*! Don't interrupt. I was going to say you could go to court if there's a violation. There's a steep penalty for infringement of your rights.'

Violation . . . infringement of rights . . . penalty . . . A needling light pricks my eyelids. Hundreds of tiny suns whirl around. You're infringing on *my* rights! Get out of my head!

Tabebuia rosea, eh Pa? Well, well!

He stares. 'What's the matter with you today? Didn't you hear what I said?'

Let's not talk, Pa. Let's just enjoy our walk. Please.

Immediately he's contrite. 'I expect too much from you. Far too much. But if I didn't, would you be here?' He smiles deprecatingly. 'Here, as in what you are today?'

I can't even smile. There's a familiar tug in my chest.

'I tried to anticipate as much as I could. I tried to *arm* you. But one can't cover every eventuality, can one?'

No, Pa. Life comes in too many shapes and sizes for even you to accommodate all of them.

'Still. I was . . . I *am* here to protect you.' He mulls as over a mouthful of wine. 'But sometimes I can't see beyond my nose. You see this nose?' He pinches it. 'My obstacle. It was my mother's nose too, your Pati's. I see it even now in the corner of my eye—*her* nose. Poking into my life. An infraction.

And now,' he flicks the offending proboscis, 'it is getting into *yours*'.

Oh Pa, I think. How you protected me! From falling into the water. From falling down the stairs. From catching cold. From catching ideas. You protected me from every conceivable danger, and every inconceivable one too!

Parenting *is* intrusive, Pa. You mould a piece of flesh into a likeness of yourself, flaws and all. If it isn't a good likeness, you haven't tried enough. So you go back and hammer it shapeless.

He laughs—what a happy sound—and resumes walking, bobbing along the pavement like a birthday balloon. At our gate he stops, turns around. 'Look Kaveri,' he says soberly. 'About this Balumama business. I know you've been brooding over it. But you're needlessly assuming responsibility for what happened. It's a conceit, you know, to imagine you have such influence. People have a free will. They take their chances with their choices.' He unlatches the gate. 'You took a chance yourself when you wrote your novel.' I shut the gate behind us. 'I shall get hold of the Copyright Act tomorrow itself. I don't want anyone to take advantage of your naiveté in these matters. You're just too trusting.'

Next morning Meenakshi cons me into going with her to the temple, to pray for the success (!) of my journey. Although we—Mani and I—always make fun of this ritual I don't protest now. In times like these you need all the help you can get.

Outside the temple door she rings the three-foot-high bronze bell to announce our arrival to the black granite Ganesha waiting inside, in the *garbha griha*. The room within a room. *Hear us! Grant us! Save us!*

Today Ganesha is the Abominable Snowman—they've

plastered him with white butter, a popular practice in this temple. He's a pockmarked snowman—the butter is studded with raisins. (Butter and raisins will be given away to the poor.) On the forehead glows a ruby four times the size of Meenakshi's vermilion pottu. But the foreheads of the widows lined up beside us are blanked out with ash. They flutter like truce flags as they nod at each other. 'A *son-in-law* now? A granddaughter too! Happiness, happiness!'

A young priest comes around with the offerings plate. The camphor flame throws up the flat planes of his cheeks. Day-old fuzz, a tender green, covers cheeks, jaw and shriven head. In the thin light his veshti is innocently translucent, exposing his meagre shanks. Vedic chants roll out of his mouth, like paper chattering out of a printer. *Of the mantras I am the Gayatri* . . .

The young priest stops, holds out the plate. Meenakshi drops a coin into it, and I, after a second's hesitation, put a fifty-rupee note beside the coin. The priest's eyes widen—this is wholesale bribery—but Meenakshi doesn't say anything. We take turns to wave our hands over the flame, touch them to our eyes. Once, twice, three times. Then we dip our middle finger into the ash-and-vermilion, daub it on our foreheads. Lastly, we cup our right palm in the left to receive the holy water.

Meenakshi tucks a flower into my hair. The scent of jasmine mingles with burning camphor. Pungent smoke threads its way to the blackened ceiling. Nobody effects a reverse transaction. How did Jana do it? *Of things secret I am the silence.*

As he glides away, 'God has a hand in everything,' the priest murmurs shyly. 'Good and bad.' *Of the deceitful I am the gambling* . . .

A gamble. That's what it was. That's what it will be. In the evening I leave for Delhi.

He answers the doorbell as he did four weeks ago. This time she is expected because she has called him from the airport. The door flies open before the bell stops chiming. *My door will always be open for you* . . . He holds his arms out. *My arms too . . . and my heart.*

And, as if she has come back for this very purpose, she clings to him, the stuff and substance of her dreams.

It is late night and they are back on the terrace, back where they had begun, back where—the apprehension sears his stomach with acid burns—they will, soon, end. He's also thinking, with something more than disappointment, more than dismay, more than humiliation—an iron-knuckled punch (in the teeth) would come close to it, he is thinking: *All the time we made love this was in her.*

'Well?' She is offering him her shame as wantonly as she offered herself. 'You despise me.'

'No.' A tiny hesitation there. It's a *no* that clearly means *yes.* 'I'm just finding it hard to understand . . . I'm sorry for you actually.' She looks away. 'Alright then, I'm just sorry. What now? Will there be a legal suit?'

'Not if I can help it.' The city is smothered in ethereal dust that makes haloes around the streetlights. 'It's an obscure book, fortunately. Not in circulation. Out of the copyright period.'

'Still, I don't suppose anyone can make free with it.' (She grimaces.) 'There must be regulations. Intellectual property rights.'

'Yes, that's a bit of a nuisance.'

'Then you'll have to take it off the market, of course.'

A streetlight ejects a stream of insects. 'No. At least, that's not what this man was hinting at. I guess . . .' she studies her hands, 'it has a price now. To begin with I'll have to pass up the Bayswater flat.' She laughs shortly. 'I mean I'll have to write off some money. A lot of money.' The insects swirl in the phosphorescence.

'Pay a fine then? Legal fees? Pay to change future editions or something?'

She looks at him as if levelling with him. 'I mean I have to pay Vinod Bhasin. Buy his silence.'

So calmly, so ingenuously, he thinks she's pulling his leg, and begins to laugh. Who did she think she was—Donna Corleone? He cups his ear comically. 'Did I hear right?'

But she is not smiling. 'He hinted at an out-of-court settlement.' And, with a sound between a snort and a laugh, 'It won't look so good for me if any of this comes out, will it?'

She means it. She really means it! Still, 'I don't believe you,' he declares. 'I can't. Not of *you*.'

He believes in her! She's just confessed an enormity, shown herself in some pretty lurid (false) colours, and he can still believe in her? Manipulative flattery, she concludes. She wasn't going to fall for it. 'I'm serious,' she says, more roughly than she intended. 'My novel means everything to me.' His chair creaks. Everything? What is everything? 'It's why I've come here,' she continues in a colourless tone. 'To talk terms with him.' She looks at him with a stranger's eyes. 'I expect he wants to do a deal.'

Comprehension breaks through, like a dark dawn. Urgent words bubble to his lips but, 'You c-ca-ca . . . you won't agree,' he stammers, merely, meagrely. 'You can't p-possibly.'

Oh, can't I, mock the stranger's eyes. I can see through you, he had teased. You're transparent as glass. And I am dense as a brick. He scrapes back his chair, almost overturning it in his haste to go and peer over the parapet. 'I suppose,' he says dryly, 'you could argue a kind of straightforwardness. In not compromising on your standards. You didn't change or scramble the stuff you took from that book.' Her heart does a flip. He does understand! 'But,' he shrugs, 'to me that is like committing suicide to find out that what you really wanted was to live'.

A plane hurtles out of the dark, drones off, a pencil torch probing the clouds.

His touch is gingerly. As if in finding his way about her, retracing his steps, that is, he has discovered a new dimension—in himself. Friability. He is also wary of pressing an alarm button somewhere. (All of a sudden, she's studded with alarm buttons.) And, frankly, he is repelled by the thing beside him. Truth to tell he is afraid that what it has, what it is, could be contagious. His body shrinks with the strangeness of her, the coldness of him. There was no pleasure in this touching-without-touching. Or touching with rubber gloves, which is the same thing. And, let's lance the truth here, he was finding it impossible to function.

When this last cannot be ignored any longer their nakedness becomes an abomination. She sits up, pressing her knees together, pulling at the sheet to cover herself. 'It's all right,' she mutters. 'You don't have to try so hard.'

He strips his end of the sheet off—strips *her* off, it seems to her—and dresses with quiet efficiency, buttoning every last button as if he finds it unbearable to expose even an inch of himself to her. That little detail tells her more than anything he could have said. Or not said. It said he is on his guard against her, against all women with a nifty turn of phrase, deep-set eyes and an attitude. Against their barefaced guile.

Averting a face hot with shame, she pulls on her kaftan.

In wordless accord they make for the airless, breathless room of her first visit. As before the sofa chairs squat on their haunches and the tables stand on their toes and the beatific Buddha smiles and the inquisitorial ceiling light shows up everything and illuminates nothing.

Silence descends, a nervous anticipatory silence, disagreeable prelude to the leave-taking that is inevitable now. The future they had trusted to is fading fast. Yet hope persists, a tormenting after-image. You were wrong, she wants to tell him, about living in the present forever. But a kernel is stuck in her throat, his face is as tight as a red salute, the silence is life-threatening—death to the one who breaks it—and the minutes are speeding on.

At last he stirs, walks to the window, parts the curtains, opens the window a crack. A pre-dawn lightness leaks into the room, and the night's hangover of cityrot, effluvia, graveyard humours. When he breathes deeply, eagerly almost, of this putrid air, the shaft goes home. The future, the future. This is our future.

Under her kaftan her breasts rattle. Like scraped-out gourds.

She toes the carpet with a moody foot. 'This isn't going to work, then.'

'Yes,' he says ambiguously.

'Ask me, oh, whatever.'

'No.'

'Ask me why.'

'No.'

'Ask me how!'

'No.'

'*Ask me!*'

'No!'

A stomach growls. They tense, scrunch their bellies. 'Have you,' her voice trembles, 'have you never felt you were driven by something . . . out of your control? Something happening before . . . before you could do anything about it?'

He ponders this for a bit, shrugs. 'No.'

'Bloody prig,' she mutters, uncaring of whether he hears or not. (He does but doesn't let on he does.) 'What's so bloody *fascinating* out there? *I'll* tell you what! Greed! Sleaze! Those in the know putting it out for those who can *pay*!' He continues to stand by the window, leaning on the wall in an attitude of utter repose. She gives a small scream and rushes at him. '*Stop lounging*! Don't you care? Why're you making such a big deal of this anyway? Things are only as big or small as we make them out to be!'

He shakes her off. 'But *this* was big for you, Kaveri. Big enough to do what you did. Perhaps you wanted to do the best by your readers. You must certainly have a high regard for them.'

She hated him then. Really hated him. 'The irony is,' his voice cools, 'that if you really had you wouldn't have done it. But you don't really respect them, do you? Or any of us. Even yourself.' She doesn't answer. She hasn't an answer, he thinks, not very kindly. He isn't feeling kindly.

The air conditioner gurgles, another rude intrusion. She returns to her chair, sits down with a bump. 'A liar by definition then. As well as by profession.'

Outwardly disdainful, but inwardly she's screaming, *I didn't mean to*! Crawling on knees and elbows, pleading with time to back up. Back off. Go back three years. To the first word on the first page. 'I didn't lie,' she says in a small voice. 'At least not lie as in *lie*. I just didn't . . .'

'No. You just didn't. Justifying yourself with disclaimers as usual. It's chronic. *Pathological*.' He folds his arms, gives her an appraising look.

'Arya was right,' she says dully. 'I'm only a specimen for you. You should pay me for this. Endless bloodletting—at 500 bucks a throw. You're doing a thorough job of it, I must say.' She utters a snort of a laugh. 'Putting me together and then taking me apart. Even my father couldn't have done better.' He looks at his wristwatch, angering her afresh. 'This is not just about *me*.' The *me* ricochets off the walls. 'You're angry because you think *you* made a bad judgement!'

'Yes, I thought you were what you appeared to be.'

'And that turned out to be a virtual reality. What a shock.' But the stuffing has gone out of her. 'Don't look at me like that! And *don't* bother to tell me I'm going to wake up one morning screaming. I've already been told that, and I assure you I'm not the screaming kind. Whatever else I am.'

'I wonder just what you are, Kaveri,' he says slowly. 'What you stand for, live for. Whether you regret this.' He pushes his glasses back. 'Whether you have any regrets about anything.'

'One.' She pulls her mouth out with her fingers. 'I jumped a traffic light with a cop watching.' She releases her mouth.

Silence again, immutable silence. Daylight leaks into the room through curtains that hang like flags after a storm. The furniture has sat too long in the store and no one will buy it now. She hopes he will moot tea—she is parched—but he has climbed on a peak. She is consumed with jealousy—she wants to be on that peak with him. She is jealous of all the places he will be in without her, all the times he will spend away from her (days, months, years), all the people he will share his person with. Waiters in restaurants, shopkeepers, the milkman who greets him every morning, even the payphone operator across the road. She is jealous of his chair, his clothes, the water that will run over his body in an hour. She has so little time left to breathe his air.

Of his own accord he goes to make the tea. She doesn't offer to help him—she cannot presume on even this small intimacy now—and she suspects he will not want her to.

Scent of burning leaves and autumn mist and wet grass. Unthinkingly she gulps. Her tongue jumps. 'You put in too much sugar,' she gasps. Dashing the tears from her eyes, 'I never expected it to be a success,' she whispers, 'or anything near it. I have,' studying a point over his shoulder, 'this habit of . . . of . . . copying things down from books, magazines, anything. Stuff that interests me. To read later, digest, *ingest*, I suppose.' She sighs, looks up. 'I was going to . . . work on it some more. The book, I mean. But it all happened so fast. Then it was too late. It . . . it was too far gone.'

He squints into his tea mug, as if checking the level of its contents. Then, lowering it to the table, he covers her hand with his. 'It isn't too late,' he says gently. 'And *you* aren't too far gone.'

She stares at his hand, at the four-phalanged fingers, every dear detail of it, willing it to fuse with hers. 'It had seemed so *real.*' And almost to herself, 'And yet not. Before I knew it, it was out there. And I was in here,' she bunches the cloth on her chest. 'I couldn't get out. No,' her eyes glaze, 'that's not true. I didn't want to get out. I didn't want it to end. Only it did. I was so afraid,' she catches her breath, 'it would end'.

He takes her hand again. 'You needn't be afraid now.'

'*No!* Don't you start that!' She leaps up, spilling his hand. Spilling her tea. For a moment she looks as if she will cry. She sits down, palms her eyes. 'All my life. All my life I've been told what to do. It's a family occupation.'

'All I meant was there's a way out, Kaveri.'

'Same thing.' The air conditioner whirs and judders. 'You want a commitment.' Her voice is surly. 'But you won't get it. I'm not going to commit to *anything.*'

'Then we've reached an impasse.' He smiles at her. 'An impasse, you know, is what you get into when you try to cross the Himalayas without a map.'

She doesn't return his smile.

The tea has been consumed. The room has grown too light to ignore the immediacy of a new day. He stands up, stretches. 'Well, Kaveri.'

'It was too good to last,' she says glumly. 'As the boy said when his ice cream cone melted.' After an awful pause, 'This is goodbye, I suppose,' she says even more glumly.

'Let's say it's a point of departure. For now.'

'But what am I going to *do?*'

'Go on as before, I expect.'

'But what about . . .?'

But he is already leaving the room. Us? She finishes

silently. She utters a snort of a laugh. Well, I could get a Labrador, I suppose. Keep a diary. Take the veil.

It is high morning when they emerge. Refusing his offer of a lift, she has called a taxi. He does not press the offer, and though she has no intention of accepting it, the non-insistence depresses her. Now, the shabby taxi and its shabby driver—such a chariot and such a charioteer—is a further humiliation. And he glances at his watch while opening the door for her! Things are going downhill very fast.

The taxi begins moving and, I'm drawing away, she despairs. It stalls—to change gears—and he rushes forward, thrusts his hand into the window. 'It's *not* too late, Kaveri,' he says, squeezing her hand. His eyes walk along with hers. 'I shall . . .' There's a fearful grinding of gears and black smoke pours from the taxi's underbelly. When she strains out of the window she can hear nothing, but his lips are still moving. Then the taxi leaps forward, pulling her hand out of his.

Her voice rises to a scream. 'Shall what?' Shall *what*? *Shall* what?

But the taxi is rolling down the street and the sun is torching his head, and the light, full strong on her face, blots him out.

Too late, again, she remembers her African violets. Please be kind to them. They had no part in this. Then, jumping up, *fuck everything*, she yells at a billboard (advertising a holiday package in Spain). The driver almost knocks down a hawker who has darted into the road with a tray of, of all things, clothespins. Brakes scream. Voices shrill. Pink and blue plastic spill on the road. The hawker snatches the banknote she holds out to him, giving her a baleful glance as his thanks. The driver spits a curse at him, his mouth twisted with hate—the hatred of the poor for the very poor. Her head aches. Effortfully she hoists herself up from the broken springs to give him fresh directions.

Before I can reach its handle, my door is wrenched open. Next I'm ushered through the entrance. The doorman, at least, is sure I have come to the right place. So is the bellhop. And I wonder briefly if they have sniffer dogs to gauge the guests' bonafides, if they have specific methods to deal with intrepid, young(ish) women who have homes in the city but stay in hotels for inexplicable (probably nefarious) reasons. If they took in just about every homeless body that tumbled in or risked turning away a millionaire-in-disguise. Or a Joseph-and-Mary.

Walking across the marble floor I find myself praying: Please God, don't let me meet anybody I know. Please, please, above all, not Vinod Bhasin or Pulin Grover. By the time I reach the reception counter, I am wrung out.

The lady is not in the habit of checking into fancy hotels. The receptionist's manner, professional politeness bordering on patronising, communicates this verdict. 'Do you have a reservation, Madam?' she enquires in a posh drawl.

Um-uh. No. Do you have a room?

Which just begs the answer, 'Rooms are just what we have here. Rooms, rooms and more rooms.' The reception clerk is serious-minded, however. She scrolls down her computer screen, goes through her routine. Address, telephone number, identification, credit card, etc. etc. And all is through in minutes, and I am in my room and ordering brunch.

By and by a wagonload of silvery dishes arrives, so enormous they could have secreted babies. Spinach-and-mushroom lasagne, Greek salad of grape leaves and goat cheese. A basket of warm rolls with curls of dewy butter. Mango ice cream cunningly concealed in a bucket of ice and decorated, improbably, with a fig. I eat every scrap, feeling sad Meenakshi isn't here to share it. She'd have loved the room too, every tired opulent detail of it, especially the four complimentary chocolates in a satin-lined box. I feel so sorry for both of us I eat all four of them. And the complimentary grapes and peach. And drink coffee (well-sugared) from the dinky coffee-making apparatus over the mini-bar. Then, done for, I sink into the bed. Vinod Bhasin will have to wait my pleasure.

At five o'clock I rose from my digestive stupor to take stock. I was in no hurry to meet anybody and I had visited the Qutab Minar only about fifty times. Bath, then a drink. Half an hour later, the more optimistic for the bath, I stepped out. En route to the lift a floorwalker (valet, butler, whatever) materialised out of a wall, smile in place and correct to the crease. Do you never rest? But the lift door closes on his answer.

Thirty minutes later in the bar—empty at this hour but for an executive type engrossed in a bunch of executive-type documents, a terminally bored bartender, and a waiter who, like a minor deity, is there yet not *too* there, and can be summoned by mere thought—I think of how much disillusionment there must be in our unhappy earth, how much dishonesty, dishonour, disgrace, such a dismal prefix, *dis-*, and feel profoundly sad. Then I think of its great, unexplored vaults of possibilities, and feel happier.

But for the background music—Pavarotti ripping out his heart—the room is absolutely quiet. It is romantically decadent to be drinking alone (if you don't count the executive type) on a tropical evening, with the sun going down on the ramparts of the old city (although you cannot see them) and the birds twittering (although you cannot hear them). There is a fin-de-siecle grandeur to my present situation, an end-of-the-empire poignancy.

Well, things looked better after the first drink, when confusion morphs into a spurious clarity and every emotion stands up to be counted but none count. When the moment has passed what *was* the moment? What *is* a moment? Love, anger, hatred, laughter. Things looked better still after the second, when sordor acquires the gloss of glamour and problems begin floating away. And soon I became quite euphoric, upon entering the state of weightlessness, alertness and forgiveness one generally does after three drinks or thereabouts. It would all come right with money. I've never much of it anyway. It wasn't the end of the world, although some people were doing their damnedest to take me there. And once it is sorted out, once all the loose ends are tied, I can start over again. He'll come around. What we had wasn't ordinary. Not for me, and, I can bet my life on this, not for him. What we had was a mutual, an inalienable truth. And we haven't really parted, not in the final sense. Only distanced ourselves from each other. To see things in perspective. You need distance for that. This isn't the time to think of how distance can close in—face upon face . . . Then I hear someone call out my name. It seems to me, in my state of partial dissolubility, that it's a voice from the heavens.

But no. The hail is from ground level. And the second 'Kaveriji!' is a peremptory summons, not the fluting of a divine salutation.

It isn't, it couldn't be . . . It *is*. It's Ma Grover. Bhabhiji in person. In the flesh. All one hundred kilos of it. She is standing by the door on the far side of the bar, wearing her suit of lights. She must have eaten her way out of her cocoon and flown out.

I do the first thing that pops into my head. That is, I obey an animal instinct, nominally a rabbit's. I dive under the table.

How I imagined I'd get away with it, I don't know. It must have been a dim hope she'd think I was a hallucination just as I thought she was one.

Of course it doesn't work. *She* isn't on her fourth vodka or, for that matter, any vodka. I hear my name called out again—closer this time. And pretty soon a pair of gilt pumps heaves into view, supporting two sturdy pillars. (Doric, is my informed guess.) They appear built to withstand flood, fire, earthquake and war. In other words, they're here to stay.

'Is that you, Kaveriji?' wheezes the familiar voice.

It is one of those unreal situations whose very absurdity dictates that you continue in the farce. You can't end it because you don't believe it's happening. You don't know *how* to end it. You just hope for a natural calamity (flood, fire, earthquake), at least a *cut to* in the sequence. Presently, there is a creaking of bones, a mutter that sounds like *bleddy basket* (although I can't swear to this), the tablecloth is lifted and a face appears, inches from mine and startling both of us.

There is nothing for it but to come out.

Hello! What a nice surprise! Excuse me, I was looking for my hairpin.

She doesn't bother to acknowledge my alibi or offer to look for it. 'Not so surprising,' she puffs—those knees must have taken a beating. 'It is the first Tuesday of the month. My ladies' tea. It is okay,' she inclines her head, 'you can't remember everything'. Then, with the self-assurance of one who's sure of a welcome wherever she goes, she throws her bead purse on the table. 'Have you seen Pulinji? He's also in the hotel.' That sends a shiver down my spine. 'In fact I am looking for him.' She peers about the room as if it's a crowded railway station. 'Meanwhile, I will give company to *you*. Till you go home.'

Really, don't trouble. Anyway, this is home. I mean, I'm staying in the hotel tonight.

'No problem. I will also stay.'

But what about Pulin . . . ji? Don't you have to find him? '*He* will find *me*.' She draws semicircles on the tablecloth with her forefingers, to demonstrate the earth was round and you can't escape this circumstance.

I think, I think I . . . Then I forget what I wanted to say. The trouble with drink is one forgets what one wants to say halfway through saying it. It makes for interesting half-turns in the conversation but it doesn't win one popular votes. I think, I try again, shaping the words carefully, I have lost my hairpin. She folds her arms on the table and looks at my glass. A little desperate now, I raise my voice. I really did lose a hairpin, you know. She refolds her arms on her stomach and continues to intimidate me.

I give up after that, and sit back to finish my drink. It isn't much fun with Bhabhiji watching—and marking—my every move, and it must be pretty boring for her too. Although it isn't I who invited her to this party. Then, since another drink is out of the question in the glare of publicity, so to speak, I get up to leave. She gets up too, and follows me out.

I manage to negotiate the tables quite well but after that I am walking on the edge of a precipice. In the uncarpeted marble corridor outside, the precipice gives way.

Bhabhiji's fingers are surprisingly strong—claws, really. Shooting me a now-you-understand-why look, she leashes me to herself. As though I am a toddler and this is my first day at school. 'Don't worry yourself,' she says, giving me a slight push into the lift, 'I will take you to your room'.

The valet-butler rushes up the instant the lift doors open, marches us to my room. Really, nobody trusts anyone any more these days.

Dear faithful. Do they ever let you out or will you die in custody?

'Hehe,' he says uneasily and presses himself against the wall as I pass.

Watch that man, Bhabhiji. He's dangerous. He's from the KGB.

Bhabhiji's lips grow stringy. 'Nowadays there's no KGB. And no Stasi too.' With that she shuts the door and propels me into the bathroom.

Decades of tyrannising her household have imparted to her a raw authority that is hard to contest. But at this point a bath seems the most sensible, the *only*, solution to my problems. I strip, shower and get into the terry bathrobe hanging on the door.

She is sitting on a chair by the bed, clearly containing herself, because the second I put my head on the pillow she is out of her chair and bending over me. 'You must know your limits, Kaveriji!' And like a statistician, or a wife practised in keeping track of such accounts, 'How many?' she demands.

I shut my eyes and pray that she will realise her escort services are no longer needed. But she is nothing if not conscientious. She was going to sit this out. And she was not going to sit it out in silence.

This is the secret of the sages, then. This intimation of death-in-life. The end doesn't come in flashes of glorious recall of life's prouder moments, but in a scratchy replay of its antic ludicrousness. We're all brought to book by a Bhabhiji reading aloud a list of our foolish transgressions. 'Is this the behaviour for ladies, Kaveriji? Drinking alone and all such things? Falling down also?'

I manage to block out the voice at last. Or perhaps the litany has come to an end and she has a) gone away b) let me sleep. Or perhaps I am in a coma. I do not dare open my eyes to find out.

When at last I do she is still there. Watching television in mute mode. 'It is *eight-thirty*,' she reproaches. 'Dinner time! I think so you must be hungry. Chicken tikka ho jai?' Before I can tell her I don't eat chicken she picks up the telephone and dials Room Service. Over her shoulder, 'Pulinji is coming,' she informs me smugly.

What?

My robe flies open. She withdraws her eyes. 'Better you change,' she says primly. 'He will be here just now itself.'

Why did you invite him here?

'Better you speak to him, I think. Hellohellohello? Room Service?'

Better you go, I mutter, but climb out of bed.

I smell the Calvin Klein cologne before I open the bathroom

door. 'So, my dear! Living abundantly, eh?' His mouth flips up like a piano lid, a smile plays on the ivory keys. 'Why didn't you tell me you were coming?' Bringing his hands together, 'I hear you have been enjoying yourself!' The hands part with a squelch. 'What have you been doing? It's been less than a month but it seems like years! What is it about you,' hooking his eyes to mine, 'what is it *in* you,' he goes on hardily, 'that makes a man *miss* you? I really missed you, you know.' The satyric mask gives way to a self-conscious leer. Pulin Grover, the gay dog-about-town. Mercifully, Bhabhiji's absorption in the television screen is utter and involute. 'I have finalised your itinerary . . .' he slams his forehead, 'but what are you doing *here*? *Now*? Your Bangalore reading is scheduled for *tomorrow*!'

I'm not up to it, Pulin.

'Not up to it? Not up to *what*? Please tell me, just what are you up to?' The gay dog had begun to snarl. It would have been funny at any other time. 'You leave suddenly! You come back suddenly! With no word of your comings and goings!'

There may not be any more comings and goings, Pulin. *I got bad news, baby. Your wig is about to blow.*

'What?'

There's a problem, Pulin.

His eyes bulge. 'There are similarities you say? Between this book and yours? But how? *Why*?'

A rash and ill-considered move. I deeply regret it.

He interprets this as an appeal for help. 'Do not distress yourself unduly, my dear! After all, the world is not perfect! A sunset is made with thousands of motes of dust!' Then, rubbing his hands briskly, my knight in shining armour, he fires off,

'Who is this man and what sort of man is he? What are his resources? Does he have political connections? Has he bought legal rights for this book?'

Yes, he's bought the rights. There's no question of piracy.

'Hmm. I wonder now . . . what it would take to keep this, um quiet. Eh? My dear?'

I don't know, but my guess is it will be a lot. Considering *AFL*'s popularity.

He regards me with dislike. *He can't touch me, he's in this thing with me.* This brings small comfort.

Unexpectedly he relaxes. 'But you said the other book has been out of print for a long time. There won't be too many people familiar with it then. Not enough to create a fuss.'

Vinod Bhasin has threatened to make a fuss.

All of a sudden I get an unconscionable yen to make Pulin Grover suffer.

'I wish I'd never entered this publishing business! It is too risky!' His features twist with anguish as he computes money, man-hours—and the returns. Oh, the waste, the loss! 'I don't have an instinct for it!' *Actually, it requires aptitude, Pulin.* 'Although my instinct *warned* me you would be trouble!' *If you live by instinct, not inquiry, Pulin, you deserve all you get.* He glares at me balefully. 'There was *something* about you right from the start, but I couldn't put a finger on it.' The trace nastiness takes my breath away. 'You always acted so damn superior.' *And here I thought you liked me, Pulin! Well, in adversity the truth comes out. That's one place you're sure to find truth—in tight corners.* He clenches and unclenches his hands. 'I am not responsible! I will *not* be blamed for this! What were the editors doing, the fact-checker? They're supposed to spot these things!'

It's funny how fast people will run from a stink—it's no

longer *my* editors and *my* fact-checker. But I cannot smile. Auxiliary forces are being rushed to my headache.

'. . . I *knew* in my bones that things would go wrong with this book.'

Then it was very generous of you not to let it get in the way of our relationship, Pulin.

'That's all right,' he says, in a surprising turnabout, which, knowing him, could only be impelled by a profit motive. And with a magnanimous wave, 'Let us look ahead now.'

'Yes, listen to Pulinji, Kaveriji. He's a very good capitalist.'

'You keep out of this, Kamal!' And creamily, 'So Kaveri, tell me. What is he like? Some of those fly-by-night operators can be pretty unprincipled.'

He seemed pretty unprincipled to me.

'Ah! Then there's our solution! All we need to do is pay him a little more than what he's paid for the rights and what he will make from reprinting this book. Which won't be much, I guarantee you. Will he be open to the idea? Eh? My dear?'

Something hits me—on the head. Cold water. A bucketful of it. Dousing the fires, and drowning me, for I'm over my head in it and I can't breathe, can't see, can't hear, and *let me out, let me out*, but the water is gagging me and the tears are flowing behind my eyes, because I am lost and I am found.

The room stills and settles the right way up. Nothing has changed—Bhabhiji is still watching the television screen on which the same two fools are cavorting, Pulin is still punching his cellphone, I'm still holding my coffee cup which is still gently steaming, and in the mirror across I see that my face hasn't changed at all. I suppose an answer to a koan comes to you like this. Some Zen thing anyway. I put down my coffee cup, take a deep breath.

He may, Pulin. But I'm not.

'I beg your pardon?'

I'm not (my head's still fizzing), I am not open to the idea of negotiating with Vinod Bhasin.

He switches off his cellphone. 'You mean you want to call his bluff? Tell him where to get off, eh? Take it or leave it? I *knew* you were tough! So what's the top line?'

What top line?

'*Tcha!* The bottom line then! How much shall we offer Vinod Bhasin?'

You misunderstood me. We don't offer him money.

'But he's not going to settle for anything else! What do *you* have in mind? What deal?'

I'm not going to deal with him at all.

'But . . .!'

Pulin, we must withdraw *AFL*.

It is 11.30 p.m. The room has been cleared of the coffee tray and Pulin Grover and his wife. Ideally, I would have liked to rid it of the last hour too but it is one of those things, like the smell of earth and the taste of water, that will stay forever in nose and mouth. In all degrees of subtlety.

On the TV the veejay is tugging at her spaghetti straps. There is, in addition to the bosom cleavage, one squeezed out under her arm. A third shows under the thin material stretched across her rump. She is two halves joined by a seam. All at once there is a contretemps. She has missed a cue. Her preset speech and the action on stage are completely at odds. The tugging stops, the mouth falls open, the act falters.

I laugh. Laugh and laugh and laugh. *I got bad news for you too, baby. Your wig's about to blow.*

He had been angry, so angry. Poor Bhabhiji was so frightened she hardly touched her chicken tikka. Her eyes were glued to the TV screen as if taking them off for even a second would destroy the room and its occupants.

'But this is a business transaction! Not a bribe!'

Whatever it is, the answer's still no, Pulin. The stores must return their stock. You'll pulp what's in the warehouse. No tour, no readings. '*No!*' Yes. '*But we'll lose so much!*' That's alright. I'll make good any losses. I've hardly touched my advance. '*Did I bring up paying back? Did I even mention money . . .?*' No, but it will surface sooner or later. '*Alright then, since you have brought it up, what about my investment?*' Pulin, before you sue or anything, let me make this clear. I shall pay whatever expenses you and anybody else will incur. If it takes the rest of my life to do it.

'My dear, my dear! I'm your *friend*! Listen to me . . .'

'Listen to Pulinji, Kaveriji. He is your elder brother.'

'Be quiet, Kamal!'

No, *you* listen to me, Pulin.

'*Don't* do this, my dear! Just think how *AFL* is transforming lives! You must not deprive the poor people!'

I agree it is very selfish on my part. Nevertheless.

'Selfish? It will be downright *immoral* . . .' He checked himself.

He reasoned, he argued. 'Give it a cool thought,' he implored, 'give it a chance, give it a go! Why, *why* are you so stubborn? We haven't discussed anything with this man! He's looking to reprint it? Perhaps it's just a ploy to extract more money . . . I mean, why *this* book? If it's so obscure and forgotten for so long?'

Because . . . because it's a worthy book.

He called me a thief then. And then, seeing that got him nowhere, began wheedling. '*We could cut those lines for future editions.*' It *was* suggested, Pulin, in another context. I refused then and I refuse now. '*Perhaps if you made a public apology for the lapse in acknowledging the source, put in an acknowledgement in all future editions. Sort of like, you know, credits.*' Nobody would believe such a transparent ploy, Pulin. '*You could say it was unintentional . . . that you had absorbed this other book so much that . . .*' I'd be a laughing stock, Pulin. '*We will seek refuge in the Specific Relief Act—I'll find out about the Copyright Act . . .*' Pulin, this is not a legal dispute. Let's keep our dignity. '*Dignity? You speak of dignity? You can look me in the eye and say that?*'

'My dear, my dear! I didn't mean that! But there's so much one can do if you would only hear me out!'

'Yes, Pulinji has very good ideas, Kaveriji.'

'*Kamal!*'

Pulin, this book wasn't meant to be. And, my lips feeling as if I'm kissing ice, it was an unlucky inspiration, Pulin.

He hit the roof. 'You call this an *inspiration?* Then *suicide* is an inspiration! Homicide is God's command, genocide is positively visionary!'

I couldn't help smiling—the reversal was sublimating *him*. The smile inflamed him. What was there to smile about—did I think this was a deliverance or what? Was this, a new doubt struck him—he was clutching at doubts now—a joke?

No, I said wearily. It's not a joke.

'You have absolutely no scruples!'

No, not a single one. I burst out laughing. Not . . . one . . .

single . . . scruple . . . left! The scruples, wire-stiffeners propping up my weak flesh, had been pulled out one by one till at last I collapsed. A moral wreck.

'*Stop laughing*! Is this the time or place to laugh?'

When it finally sank in I was not going to budge, he turned brusque and businesslike. 'I will contact the British Library in Bangalore. And Kochi. Reschedule,' he caught my eye, 'cancel the readings. I will call Vinod Bhasin in the morning. Negotiate,' he caught my eye again, 'for time'. And here, his manner implied, I had just fixed up a four-ball for tomorrow. Suddenly he brightened. 'Perhaps we can get some mileage out of it after all! Flood the market now, people will rush to buy! The book would be a collector's item!'

I cut through the tide, dragged the surfer ashore.

No, Pulin. We're remaindering the remaining stocks.

I thought he would hit me then. But he just made a fist and pushed it into his pocket. 'Are you,' he glanced around censoriously, 'planning to stay here for long?' The first indication of cracks. 'You haven't bought a new flat or anything? No? Good. Better not make any investments. There will be,' heavily, 'expenses. *Lots* of expenses.'

The future, the future. There wasn't going to be one. It was the full wakening from the dream.

After that, as if he couldn't bear to be in the room a moment longer, he rushed out. At the door he wheeled round as if he'd remembered something. 'Come on, Kamal,' he barked. 'Sari duniya gir jayegi aur yeh TV nahi chhodegi.'

Which, though accurate, was unfair. His wife *had* been watching TV while the world, his world, was falling apart, but she had done so in good faith—to avert its annihilation.

Bhabhiji patted me on the shoulder. 'Pick up your heart, Kaveriji! All is not lost!'

I felt as though I'd swum into an atoll.

On the TV the veejay hasn't succeeded in wriggling out of her dress. She is wooing the singer now. 'Here's a number for the girls in black!' *Yes. Sing the Charnel-House Blues, Baby.* I choke it off and go to the window.

The traffic fumes have drawn a smokescreen over the city, tarnished the few visible stars. Neon signs and searchlights have liquefied the sky to molten pewter. A plane is making a meteoric descent through the glowing darkness. The moon rises like a lump in my throat. We should have been sitting watching it on one of the invisible terraces out there. Him and me. He and I.

By and by I pull the curtains together, remove the quilted cover on the bed and slip into the cool, buttery sheets, thankful for their antiseptic unfamiliarity. The bathrobe (I'm back in it) rides up as I flail around in the too-yielding mattress. Uncaring of a chance revisit from Pulin Grover, I wriggle right out of it.

From behind my eyes the stars go out, one by one.

There is an early morning businessman's flight to Bangalore. It offers a choice of eggs or idlis for breakfast, and a no-choice orange juice carton that the businessmen leave untouched, and the airline unmoved, for I see it on every flight I've taken. I cannot eat any of this however—I just drink the coffee that is so watery it could have come from Lilamami's kitchen. I feel as if the bottom's dropped out of my world. But perhaps that's just the effect of jet travel. I will not be affected by jet travel after this, though. I will not have this luxury of starting and arriving in the same day, or in the same hour, or even the day before.

No itineraries, my dear, no destination. And definitely no living abundantly.

They are standing by the myrtle, examining a scraggly patch of impatiens, which, despite all their efforts, is more leg than head. Like a Bollywood starlet.

Parijata pays obeisance at their feet. A bunch of grapes is knocking on the verandah door. Blue as litmus, as a summer sky, as a very young girl's silk sash. The petrea. It has bloomed at last.

Behind me the traffic pounds away. Fingers prod, voices whisper, *open the gate*! But I don't. I can't. Because through that gate I have glimpsed the rest of my life. A short driveway, stopped by the garage. A chicken-neck ingress to a courtyard. A house rocked not by a society of upstarts (and johnny-come-latelys) but a renegade that it has loyally sheltered. And a man and a woman who will, with every lift of eyebrow and turn of neck, crook of finger and curve of shoulder, shape their impossible eternal question: *Are you happy*? And I will never be able to give them the answer they want. Neither will I be able to turn their question on its head: Tell me, please, what is happiness? What is its aspect, what its taste, smell, *feel*?

They look up. 'Kaveri! You're back! Did you finish your work?'

'Kanna, you look so tired.'

'Thank God you're here—we were wondering what to do!'

Do?

'Tcha! Have you forgotten? There was a call from the British Council just after you left! But it's alright now. (*What's* alright? What's *alright*?) You're back in time for it.'

For what?

'*Tcha!* Your *book* reading!'

There will be no book reading.

'*Yenna* Kaveri! It was in the papers! The invitations are out! All the arrangements have been made!'

They've been cancelled.

'But . . .!'

I have something to tell you.

Mani turns away without a word. But his back cries that it's been whipped. His gait has a labourer's end-of-the-day drag—his feet are dredging the ground. He pulls the dead weight of his body up the verandah steps as if ascending a cliff to jump off.

Meenakshi is committing the impatiens to memory. But it has lost its significance. She turns to the petrea. But that has lost its moment too. She gives up, takes my arm. 'Come in out of the sun, Kaveri.' And when I continue to stand, 'Va, kanna,' she says softly. Foot by foot she inches me into the sanctuary.

After an hour of sitting by myself in the verandah, I pick up the courage to peep into my parents' bedroom.

He is lying on the bed, arms under his head, staring at the ceiling, wondering—I can read his thoughts—whether there is, in this that's happened, a higher plan. Whether it was for this he was granted his 'bonus' years (that started after his sixtieth birthday), preserved intact and alert, all faculties humming and receiving loud and clear. Much better if there had been a partial shutdown—so he could still see, touch, hear his daughter, but not make sense of her. In a single stroke she has negated plan and purpose, reason and will. Has *he* failed her? He is struggling to find a way not to fail her now—that *is* a struggle! What words can he find that can comfort too? We box up our children, secure them in airtight, watertight cases, but the maggots get in anyway. We believe we've plugged all the holes but the woodlice were already in residence. We protect them from worms, germs, rogue sperms—for *this*?

His best suit hangs on the cupboard handle, brushed and pressed, his best (silk) handkerchief stylishly folded in the breast pocket. His best shoes are polished to a wink, ready to walk him to the book reading.

Faith and surrender, Kaveri. It's all you need to succeed. But when the doubts came, you surrendered your faith. I kept mine.

The house is creepy, as if a beast is prowling around. We tread carefully, Meenakshi and I, to avoid bumping into it, keeping our conversation minimal and our voices low so as not to attract its ire. This is a period of indeterminate waiting, as after a death. There are so many matters to settle but where to begin?

'Kaveri, come for lunch,' Meenakshi whispers. Hesitating, she tiptoes to their bedroom. From the door, 'Lunch,' she calls in a strangled voice.

The figure on the bed doesn't stir. 'You all eat,' it says tonelessly. 'I'm not hungry.'

She retreats, looking beaten. 'He will not eat,' she mouths to me, her eyes dull with misery.

Why is he punishing her as well? She doesn't ask, as I know he is dying to, *now what*?

In the afternoon we withdraw to three separate rooms. I can concentrate on nothing but a *Biggles* book, a childhood favourite that marked a period in my life when I wanted to turn into a boy, to rectify the sorry mistake of my conception with boyish preferences (including maths over history) to convey to Mani that I was as much a disappointment to myself as I believed I must have been to him, not knowing then that there were other blows in store for him, that would make my femaleness a happy accident. Which it had always been anyway.

That evening Bharat calls with the news that the 'case' is to be dropped—thanks to the helpful offices of the police commissioner, or a nudge from the governor, or intervention from the home secretary—I didn't get which. Maybe a combination of all three. What is relevant is we shall hear no more of it. At this rate we'll get quite a reputation for fixing the law. For Balumama, twenty-five years ago, and now again for him. Bharat also informs us Lilamami's UK/US visas are through—she'll be off soon to Uma and Tara.

Before he rings off Meenakshi informs him of my return. 'There's a problem with her book,' she reports with sad relish. I make frantic gestures to stop her, but for Meenakshi news is news. Trouble must be strewn about, posted on every street corner. A family that cries together stays together. 'Yes, it *is* serious. Some legal issue. (*Ma!*) Wait, she'll tell you about it herself.' (*Maaa!*) But the unbelievable lady is holding out the receiver with a now-you-handle-it expression. There is too, it takes my breath away, a pucker of anticipation on her rosebud mouth.

Sometimes, no, *often*times, I have doubts about my mother. Grave doubts. Disgusted, I take the receiver from her. And masochistically—there must be something of my mother in me, but, truly, there comes a point when you just don't care any more—I tell him that I have withdrawn *AFL* from the market. That I was going to tie a stone to it and drop it into the Sankey tank.

'Has this anything to do with your conscience?' Then, 'I'm coming over tomorrow,' he says firmly. 'You can tell me about it then.'

Later, I summon the courage to go to Mani where he sits in the verandah reading *The Pickwick Papers*.

A short walk, Pa?

'No, my dear. There's too much traffic just now.'

A wee drink, then?

'Hmm. It's a little too early.'

You must have read that book a dozen times at least, Pa. (The word *book* makes me shudder.)

He smiles and continues to read. He does not say, as he once would have, as I silently beg him to now: *I can never tire of it, Kaveri. Here, listen to this.*

At last he lifts his head. Our eyes meet, our lookalike eyes. Their millionth meeting since mine began to focus. My lying young eyes and his besotted—now bewildered—old ones. (*Paar*, Meenakshi, she's making eye contact! Well, *hello!* Who's that? It's me! Me, me, me! Crossing another milestone! Aren't I clever? Aren't I smart? You are! *You are!*) 'It's so funny,' he offers, uncertainly, as if he can't quite trust his judgement any more. 'These characters are so full of gentle humour.' And extruding the words through a pipe too narrow for them, 'They're so full of life.'

But the pipe squeezes the life out of his words.

I know of old what will follow. He will tell me the story— gently humorous—of the punch-drunk Mr Pickwick trundled off in a wheelbarrow by fat, lazy Jim. *Jim! Jim! Drat that boy, he's asleep again!* (sic) Or another favourite: *What is your name?* (sic) *Pickwick. Oh. Peek—Christian name. Weeks—surname; good, very good.* (sic, sic) *Peek Weeks. How do you do, Weeks?* (sic, sic, sic.) Then, touchdown. He will burst into hilarity quite incommensurate with the humour. I will follow suit although the humour is too gentle for my coarse sensibilities.

And so it happens. He reads out a page. We laugh. It is as bizarre a way as any, I suppose, of condoling with each other.

Condolence. The laughter fades. I hold my breath, to quell the last of its offensive intrusion, here in this room of shifting shadows and sweet-sour memories.

Well Pa, consider the upside. We won't have to agonise over how much to disperse in mutual funds and real estate and tax-free bonds. There's that comfort at least.

He doesn't look comforted at all. Perversely I persevere. Watch my lips, Pa. *No new taxes.*

There's no answering smile. The devil digs me with his spur. How about this then? When you aint't got nothing, you ain't got nothing to lose.

He stiffens.

I know you don't like Dylan, I press on (although less sure of myself) but he does get it right sometimes. In this instance absolutely spot on, don't you think?

His silence is getting irksome. I raise my voice. Back to square one, eh Pa? At least it isn't a square *minus* one. I only lost what I never had. Perhaps—let's try some Vedanta here—it was never mine. (Haha, good joke that.) It never *was*, period. Trust our good old sages to not only bring us down to earth but also grind us into the dust!

Still he says nothing. But his cheek twitches. He is removing himself from me!

Say something! Anything! (Feel something, why don't you!)

'What do you want me to say? What is there to say?' The forehead puckers, the glasses slide down. Through the evening traffic his distress screams like a siren. And then nothing. He's gone!

Say you're angry! You're disappointed! You're ashamed! That I'm not worthy of you any more! That I never was!

'Oh no, Kaveri. It is not for me to say or feel any more. It is over to you.' He pushes up the glasses—but not fast enough. Oh Pa, you're . . . you're . . . oh God. Please. Please don't . . . I'm so . . . but it sticks in my throat. Why can't I say *sorry*? Why does my tongue stumble over *sorry*? If there's anyone I must say sorry to, it's him!

He ducks to wipe his eyes with the edge of his sleeve, holding the book up to shield his face. When he straightens up the old assertion is back. It's a great comeback, his greatest yet. A performance to bring the house down. It brings *me* down. 'Actually, I *do* have something to say. I've finally decided there is *no* Grand Design after all. So we shouldn't look for one. All we can do,' he blinks, 'is muddle along as best we can. Adapt or perish. In any case,' his voice drops, 'cause-and-effect hasn't yet supplied a satisfactory explanation for first cause.'

Oh Pa. OhPaOhPaOhPaOhPaOhPa. *Oh Pa!*

He is back in his book, furiously reading, or so he would have me believe. With ostentatious busyness he turns a page, then a second. A third. *Flip, flip, flip*. He's racing round a racetrack. Then he chuckles. It's such a strange sound—an echo from the caved-in belly of a starving refugee. And for one savouring the antics of four jolly gentlemen and a platoon of picaroons, a tale set in small, close print, with overlapping

nuances and arcane cross-references, isn't he going too fast?
Even if he has read the very same a dozen times?

I reach out to stay the current page. He tugs back the book
and shuts it, carefully marking the place with a used envelope.
Then, adjusting his glasses, he thumps the cover dismissively.
'It's all much of a muchness. This Dickens and all that. Literature
was dictated by the humanism of the period. Humour was a
kick in the seat of overstuffed plus-fours; disgrace the debt
prison. And tragedy was youth dying of consumption.
Essentially punitive plots. Not much breaking ground.'

My father-the-littérateur has spoken. He's thrown me a
line to climb out of my moral sinkhole. Such perfidious love!
Listen, my father. You mustn't make excuses for me. You
mustn't compromise your ideals.

But here he is, about to do just that—again. In the angle
of his head there is the familiar authority. It's his stance for a
wavering conviction. The shiftier his premise the firmer he
looks. Now he is about to accommodate me again—as he has
done countless times. 'Literature is a derivative art. A derived
religious art. Originating in the scriptures. In the Bible. And the
Upanishads. Everything stems from those roots.'

Now Dickens is a Biblical romance. Where is the
connection? My book wasn't derived from the scriptures. I
haven't *read* the scriptures! But the face raised to mine, the one
that puts in its daily claim of a walk, is so trusting. Hopeful but
not entirely confident. Stern but crossed with doubt. Distant
but so very connected. Unable to take it any longer I jump up
and cross to the window.

In the trees pattering on the window I look for a cue, in
the sky squeezed out by the roofs, and the blue and yellow
windows across the street, behind which ordinary people are

savouring the peace of the evening. In the cracks of the ceiling, even. Give me a cue!

He has got up too to stand behind me where I stand at the window. There's a creak and a rustle, then a hoarse whisper. *Why?*

I cannot answer, I don't have an answer. I cannot even turn around. I just stand there, temporarily blinded and winded. His *why* has me spreadeagled on the glass.

I needn't have worried. For he has the answer. He has *all* the answers. He always did.

'You wanted instant gratification.' *A-hum.* 'You were in a hurry.' *Aha-hum.* 'But you are young. The young have little patience, much less wisdom. So. However. Anyway.' He clears his throat a third time to signal he's finished.

But he hasn't finished. He's still labouring to find a way out of this. To match feelings with facts, perhaps, and plot a graph. 'It is these unrestrained times we live in. The lines have been redrawn so many times they've blurred. So many compulsions, so much confusion. On the other hand,' his mouth quivers, 'in the large, *larger* scheme of life this is insignificant. A drop in the ocean,' he adds ambiguously. Then, with a touch of the old spirit, 'Put this behind you. Put it down to experience. Look at me, Kaveri.' And I'm back in my crib, crossing my eyes, drooling on the pillow. 'Any fool can learn about the world from a mistake, but the wise learn about themselves.' The glasses slip down again—his nose has lost mass, or perhaps his head has lost girth. He tilts his head up and wrinkles his nose to balance them. 'And don't . . . do anything . . . stupid.'

I already have, Pa.

'Well, then, don't do anything more stupid.' His eyeballs swim up to the glasses.

Huh? Then I understand. That he should even think it! To cover our confusion, he hugs me to him. "You've given me so much happiness, Kaveri,' he murmurs. 'And to your mother too.' Squeezing me tighter, 'My daughter,' he says fiercely. '*My daughter.*'

At midnight I'm roused by a frantic shaking. 'Kaveri, *Kaveri*! *Wake up!*'

Whawhat . . . What is it, Ma?

'It's *Appa*! Your *father*! Get up! *Come now!*'

A million stars explode in my head. For a second, in the instant of the Big Bang, in the time it took to make the Earth, draw up its laws, write its history, in that moment of eternity, I think, *he's dead.* And, oh God, please not. Not another death. Not another . . . suicide. My body is a wet sandbag.

'*Hurry!* He's sick . . . he's vomited . . . *come*, Kaveri!' Meenakshi's words are the breaking of twigs under a heavy tread. The creature that's been prowling around has caught us at last. 'I think it's his pressure! I'm calling Dr Rao!'

The relief of these tidings unlocks my legs. His blood pressure is an old, old menace from which he lowers his guard now and then. But what is the scale of the present attack? I jump out, catch my foot in the mosquito net, rend it, tumble to the floor. Then, my heart in a lather now, I pick myself up and rush to his room.

The smell of vomit overpowers the scent of jasmine. He's lying very still, eyes shut. All of him is shut. This is the stuff of nightmares, I see it now, of *all* my nightmares. His was the figure on the slippery cretonne in the green room, under the blinding fluorescence of reckoning. His was the shadow moving across me. That dusty-grey city—the nowhere place—was his virtual residence. And the terrible silence was his. I know exactly how it must be for him. I have known it for years.

His face is the colour of cement, his breathing stertorous, adenoidal—like Jana's. His jubba has ridden up, his veshti has come undone. Averting my eyes from his humiliation I straighten his clothes before attending to the rest of him. Carefully, as if his bones have been broken and not his spirit, I wipe the drool off chin and mouth, lifting his head to wipe behind his neck, his ears. Then I sprinkle talc and tuck in the sheet, to make him decent for the doctor.

Meenakshi returns from her phone call to Dr Rao. 'He is coming as soon as he can. Meanwhile he said to give him two Valiums. Where to get them *now*, Kaveri?'

As a matter of fact I have a supply of them.

I spend the next ten minutes cleaning the bathroom of vomit and urine. 'He had no control. He just . . .' Meenakshi squirms. This man, this model of rectitude, couldn't aim straight into pot and sink. 'He complained of a terrible headache before . . . this. I . . . I gave him an aspirin.' Her hands grope for each other, fearfully, as if they had administered arsenic.

I take the clasped hands in mine. It's alright, Ma. You did right.

Tears well out of her eyes. 'He said his head was bursting.'

It wasn't his head Ma, I cry silently, it was his *heart*.

Mani is admitted to Dr Rao's nursing home, three kilometres away. Meenakshi and I wait in the visitors' room for the reports, and the treatment being discussed inside. We avert our eyes from the stains on the floor, the contents of the (open, flowing) dustbins, block out the frank nose-blowing and the hawking. Nobody checks our numbers (fathers, mothers, aunts, cousins, brothers-in-law of sisters) or the noise we make. There are not many rules here, for this is a cheap commercial hospital of which there are many in the city. But we are stuck with it because it belongs to Dr Rao, our old family doctor and we are afraid to go to some slick new facility which will hustle us into invasive tests and useless X-rays—and then ignore us. We are afraid of being left to die.

Meenakshi says, 'Kaveri, get some coffee. There's a hotel next door. And get idlis too.'

Our coffee comes in stainless steel tumblers, with a davara, the plate-bowl provided to cool the coffee. The idlis, soft, white as jasmine, gently steaming—poetic idlis—come in a banana leaf wrap, the coconut chutney packed separately. We eat and drink guiltily—it is Mani's coffee time. He loves idlis. Meenakshi wonders again and again what will be his diet, what will be his life. Our anxiety grows. Suddenly she clutches my arm. 'Kaveri! We haven't informed the family!'

This is indeed a serious breach of protocol.

Relax, Ma. All in good time. We don't have to report all our movements. We're not on bail, for heavensake! We'll call when we have a clearer picture.

This unnerves her even more. 'At least phone Bharat. Please, Kaveri. They'll be so offended otherwise.'

Not for the first time do I think it is an abomination—this compulsion to share our fortunes (or mis-). This firing of distress flares. Even in trouble we must seek approval. Give us leave to worry. Meenakshi is actually looking to this crisis to ingratiate herself with the family! She is biting her lip now, a faraway expression in her eyes. Who is she, this woman, who would give her life for the man inside, for the woman sitting beside her, but who would use them as a means and ends too? Who is this opportunist?

The sleeping mound beside us grunts. Annoyed, I pour the last few drops of coffee on the bare foot nudging me. The sleeper gives a little snore. Meenakshi frowns. 'Yenna, Kaveri!'

Mani's blood pressure has stabilised although it is still high. They are assessing the damage to the parameters. Dr Rao is taking his time to do it. Meenakshi worries, 'Why is he taking so long?'

At last Dr Rao beckons us in. Mani's eyes—two part-blown lilies floating on greyish scum—flutter when we speak to him. He can hear us! Half his face is slumped against the pillow, and, I think, that pillow isn't positioned right. It is scrunching his cheeks. Meenakshi tugs at the skin as if it's a crooked sheet. Dr Rao restrains her hand.

One side of Mani is paralysed. He has suffered a stroke.

We spend a nightmarish week in the nursing home, not knowing from one day to the next when his diastolic would shoot up, rush his pulse and blow out his brain. We try to get adjusted to this new Mani, strain to understand his eye communication, his tongue-knotted sounds, even imitating the nurses' cheery optimism-bordering-on-the-idiotic. 'Let's make you handsome-a! Oh, nutty, nutty! Eat your soup! Then only I will give you mango!'

Such indignities! His face is olive in the night-lamplight, motionless in a sleep that isn't a sleep but a hushing of organs. His eyes, unreflecting pools, have the clarity of a glacial meltdown. His senses have fused into a white purity. He has turned into a Buddha—transcended and gone to walk barefoot and empty-handed in the land of shadowless light.

Meenakshi stands by his pillow, smiling, grimacing. 'Can you hear me? *Can you hear me?*'

He's not deaf, Ma, don't shout at him.

But she's unheeding. She ministers to his unspoken needs, stumbling and fluttering, clumsy and wristy. She apologises, smites her forehead in self-reproach and yet she cannot leave him alone, ravishing him as he sleeps, muttering and casting god-knows-what spell.

We take turns to sit beside him, stroking his unresponsive hands for hours, willing the machinery to repair itself. I try massaging life into the poor dead muscles of his face, pulling up the corners of the mouth, patting the cheeks. Meenakshi catches me at it once. 'What are you *doing*, Kaveri?'

Many years ago he had a brief illness, perhaps just the common flu, but an epic suffering in which Meenakshi and I were panicked participants. At the height of the fever he beckoned me to him, and I bent over him, ear to mouth, heart in mouth, to hear what he had to say. His breath was foetid with the fever (Mani, so fastidious that he would inspect my 'Binaca right, Binaca bright' teeth every day) and saliva was gumming up the works, but he got it out. 'Not until we have lost the world do we begin to find ourselves, and realise where we are . . . and the infinite extent of our relations. *Thoreau.*' Then he grinned, a contortion of muscles, as if his bowels were giving him trouble. A smile from the bowels. To tell me he might be going but was not yet a goner.

Hold in there, Pa. You're not yet a goner—despite a world that's slipping away.

The family rallies around. Bharat fetches medicine, brings newspapers, and sits with Mani when we go home for a bath or a meal. Devimami and Rajumama visit every evening. Lilamami came once, looking a little aggrieved as she made her enquiries. How come we were spared and not she?

After a week we come home. At home, we are sure, the recovery will be faster.

The recovery is not going to be faster.

There is to be no recovery. At least not in entirety. The parameters have been irreparably damaged. And the prognosis is not hopeful. He is stiff and unmoving on one side. On the other there is a partial, jerky movement. His speech is a transposition of the marks a baby might make on a slate.

He will not walk again.

He will not talk again.

He will not turn up his empty-dinner-plate face to ask, 'How about a walk, Kaveri? How about some draft beer at the Club, Kaveri? Is there any soda, Kaveri?'

A few days after his return I find *The Pickwick Papers* in the verandah, his glasses alongside, a used envelope to mark the page he'd been reading. Pa, look! Here's your *Pickwick Papers*! Shall I read it to you?

A full-blown sigh rustles the pages. 'Arraraagaa.' One side of his face begins twitching wildly, the other is still.

Does that mean yes? Or no? Blink once if yes, twice if no. It's a game, Pa.

He blinks once with his good eye. The knavish one glares. I open the book at the marked page.

'Missus!' shouted the boy.

'Well Joe,' said the trembling old lady. 'I'm sure I have been a good mistress to you, Joe. You have invariably been treated very kindly. You have never had too much to do, and you have always have had enough to eat.'

'I knows I has.'

'Then what can you want to do now?'

'I wants to make your flesh creep.'

This sounded like a very bloodthirsty mode of showing one's gratitude; and all her former horrors returned.

Um, ah, umm, uh . . . wait. Okay. Here.

'What do you think I see in this very arbour last night?'
'Bless us! What?' exclaimed the old lady.

'The strange gentleman—him as had his arm hurt— a-kissin' and huggin''

'Who, Joe? None of the servants, I hope.'

'Worser than that.'

'Worse than that, Joe? Who was it, Joe? I insist upon knowing.'

'Araarar . . .' He's blinking away furiously.

What? Oh, I just thought I'd skip the irrelevant bits, Pa.

The good hand comes out of the sheet, and scrabbles with the energy of a hundred threshing ants. *'Araraaraa!'*

The *'Araraaraa'* could mean one of two things. Or both. 1) You think you can fool me? 2) You cannot take liberties with art! It's inviolable!

A judgement. At last.

Of course it could mean one more thing. Finishing is not the goal. It is the journey that matters. It's not a lesson you ever taught, Pa, but I'm told that is the world view. Of course you and I wouldn't submit to something so crass but perhaps it has a rationale? It certainly has its adherents.

His eyes are anguished. He has nothing more to teach me. Nothing more to give me. Or it could be that he sees the same in my eyes—I have nothing more to give him. Not even beer, that once, in an attempt to resurrect the past, I bring to his bedside.

Well, cheers, Pa. For the good times, such as they were.

His eyeballs, boletus floating in white sauce, fix themselves on mine. Under this unswerving but impassive attention,

which is like talking to one of Meenakshi's gods or her cat—
I grow garrulous.

What I want to know, Pa, is if *this* is what you meant by
a Grand Plan. And if it is, are you an instrument in it? *I* think
you had a major role. You came on, early, in Act I, and you
stayed there right through. Bring me, I try to keep the bitterness
out, the Golden Fleece. On penalty of banishment. The question
now is, was it in *my* mind, the quest for the fleece and all, or
was it in yours? Are you going to tell me now that you asked
for nothing?

The figure on the bed looks as if it would never again ask
for anything.

You once said that one should enjoy the good times, but
not too well because of the certainty of their passing. You
didn't let happiness intrude on your worries. You *insured*
yourself against happiness. Tell me, Pa. Are you ever right?

The figure on the bed looks as if it doesn't care if it was
right or wrong. It never did, never would. *If* anything was at
all right in the world it had so recently occupied. (Occupied so
absolutely.) But the sauce bubbles, as if the flame has been
turned up under it. And then it flows over. From one eye it
trickles along the side of the nose and drips down the chin, and
from the other it runs behind the ear to a red poinsettia on the
bedspread.

The poinsettia deepens to a bloody stain. Carefully,
wrongfully, I cradle the poor head and feed beer, a teaspoonful
at a time, into the gasping mouth. He slurps, then begins to
choke. I turn away. What's the point? *What's the point?*

The fire in the peltophorums is dying but the pink mohur
is flourishing—*Cassia nodosa*, excuse me Pa. There's a brilliant
one in our secret garden. Like candyfloss. You shall see it, I
promise you. If I have to uproot it and bring it to you.

Meenakshi has finished Mani's Aran sweater but I have a long way to go. After Dickens there's Austen. And Thackeray, H.G. Wells, Wilde, Bronte—Charlotte *and* Emily. The burden of his boredom is lighter than that of my guilt.

His room has become a nursery and his bed a crib where we tend him as if he is a newborn, an exotic plant. An African violet. Pati's equations and principles are of no use here, nor his own bristling intelligence. It is Meenakshi's household hints that rule the day. How to get the coffee stains out of his jubba, how to cook porridge in six exciting ways. I, neither expert on Newton's laws nor proficient in sponge baths, just hover around.

Bharat wants to join our little circle. But I don't let him. I sense, rather than see, the distress in my father's face. The pool of light can only accommodate the three of us. Bharat sits on the edge, hoping. I know he still hopes although he hasn't spoken. It's why he lingers in the penumbra, a region of uncertainty, where hope thrives. I know because I'm there too, hoping. *Look, my bangles, Slip loose as he leaves* . . . I wish though that just once in a while Mani would let him in. Although I dread what it might set off. Intimacies, renewed pledges, reminiscences of our tenebrous childhood—oh, insupportable to be trapped in *such* a time warp! And of course he will offer me his forgiveness along with his heart. That is his present hold. He has forgiven, the other has not, and in the perverse way things work, it makes me resentful rather than grateful.

One day he brings me a package—something that showed up, it seems, when they cleared out Balumama's effects. 'Thought it might interest you,' he says. There's a lively light in his eye I don't trust.

The pages are frail and jaundiced and flutter like moths. I'm surprised at their insubstantiality, considering how they've rocked our little world. There are pencil marks, scholarly, in the margins of some of the pages. *The third line in the second paragraph in Chapter 2 and two lines in paragraph three on page 18 . . .*

My father prefers the English classics actually, I say as steadily as I am able. (For I'm in a daze—more accurately, a fug.)

'Talk straight for once. Admit this does throw a new spin on the case.'

That you've marked . . . those passages?

'Are you being deliberately stupid? I haven't marked them. As you very well know. Nor could anyone else have.' He paused. 'The book never left his shelves.'

So now I owe him a karmic debt. Because he knew and he didn't let on.

'I mean a third possibility now surfaces.'

You don't use a riddle to solve a riddle, fool.

'*Think*, for a change. Look.' He arranges a cup and a spoon and a pencil on the table. 'Imagine the scenario outside that lift. This is Jana and this Balumama, standing by the lift *here*. She says she's going to spill the beans, as it were. First possibility, which I never believed: He can't take that, and jumps. Second: He says he will deny it—nobody will believe her anyway. So she, maddened with frustration, jumps—on *him*.' So what's new, I say, but he sweeps on. 'Now here's the third possibility. He doesn't jump and she doesn't jump but he tells her about this,' he thumps the book, 'and your novel. He says *he* will expose *you* if she exposes *him*.' He looks at me. When I don't respond, 'Kaveri,' he says patiently, 'she's devoted to you. She must have been in an intolerable bind. She wasn't going to let him ruin another life. *Yours*. She must have felt an additional moral justification—it was the last straw.'

Quite the Sherlock Holmes, aren't you? Alright, put *this* in your meerschaum. Someone's been skimming the roses off the bush by our gate.

But I'm more than a little shaken. *We're safe now*, she'd said. *You too, Kaveri*.

'What I don't understand,' he muses, 'is why he never confronted you with it'. He flips the pencil in the air and catches it. 'Perhaps he was planning to do a little blackmailing himself?'

We'll never know, is the classic answer. Anyway, here's *my* take. All of what you said did happen, the arguments, whatever, in front of the open lift door, and then Balumama, agitated, angry, just ... stepped ... back. And the silly girl decides she's responsible—she believes that wouldn't have happened if she hadn't been there. She *rushed* at him—not pushed him.

Bharat shrugs. 'If that works for you.'

It does. There was no intent, okay? Nobody is to blame! It was an accident! An *accident*!

He put his hands up to field me off. 'Ah, easy,' he says softly. 'Take it easy.'

But it isn't easy. It's never easy.

Mani does not improve. At least, I console myself, he has been spared some of the goings-on. For one, the brief notice in the papers that the Dharma Ratna has been awarded to another novel. Pulin Grover has sent me a terse note to conclude the death duties, as it were. My contract had been cancelled, fresh terms drawn up forbidding me, on penalty of a lawsuit, to publish *AFL*, or parts of it, ever again. He had to deal with a lot of awkward questions from the press, since, as he put it, I'd gone underground. (Actually, I'd barricaded myself behind Mani's wheelchair.) My supporters, of whom I actually still had a few, made me out to be something of a martyr—a victim of the 'system'. It was a representation I could have done without.

Pulin also had some explaining to do to Chris and Claire. Claire had been sharp in her censure—overly sharp for a Buddhist. Perhaps she'd stopped measuring her life in breaths. 'I'm more shocked than I can say,' she wrote. 'But there's no call to go round ringing a leper's bell. Self-mortification is so medieval. Misplaced, too, in these times, when morality has become a question of interpretation. Personally, I do not care for stories without redemption.' Nor do I, Claire.

I didn't hear from Chris at all. In retrospect he had often looked as if his worse doubts would be confirmed one day. Well, he'd have had that satisfaction at least. He, the inside trader, privy to information denied to a world quaffing cocktails and wolfing cheese as if there was no tomorrow, had always suspected there *was* no tomorrow. Perhaps that was what he and the British Council director had laughed about. It wasn't as much that it was too good to last as it was too *bad* to last. Brazening out Chris's reaction (in my head) was hard—it brought centuries-old humiliations to the fore. *These lying, thieving natives are all the same.* Not all of us, Chris.

Now that I have not heeded his good advice, Pulin Grover has become a fanatical convert to the opposite view. 'Stealing public property is what it amounts to,' he told me once. I could have replied, in that case, Pulin, all our politicians should be indicted, and quite a few of our bureaucrats, and the police and the judiciary . . . 'No good can come from bad,' he said another time. There he was wrong. If he weren't, every evil mission would explode before countdown. But I hold my peace. In any case I would have been worsted in *this* battle. So I let him have his day—his last. And did he! Possibly he had always sensed and resented my disrespect. How bent I had cast him and his ilk—and here I was, twisted as a hairpin!

'That book was doomed,' he said sadistically. There at least we were in perfect agreement.

There was a phone call too from Jana. Jana was in Chennai, fighting her demons there. New and old. There was not that much to separate us now. Privileged and abused, our separate destinies had crossed at last. Two parallel lines met in infinity by the same law that split the once indissoluble atom. We had each known a truth, grotesquely, hubristically. We neither of us was excepted by fate.

Jana's phone call was to announce she was pregnant.

Jana is pregnant. And Lilamami will bounce about on three continents. First she will go to Tara in the UK, where her two grandsons (in knee-stockings and striped ties) will say, *Please* and *Excuse me* and *Thank you* all day long, in a choppy, bitten-off accent that she finds impossible to comprehend. Lilamami has often suggested to Tara that the boys are free to take liberties with her, that their extra politeness makes her feel like the driver of their school bus. Only to have Tara retort, 'Thanks, but I don't want them brought up the way *we* were.' After Nottingham, Lilamami will go to Endsville, Arkansas, where Uma's baby must be diapered for another year, so Uma will have little time to spare for her mother. And the Defector, who has gone completely native, will not be grateful for his mother-in-law's elaborate Tamil Brahmin menus, improvised with zucchini and broccoli (marked down in a sale), and will churlishly order in pizza. She will not touch it because she once made the horrific mistake of eating a pepperoni one in a mall where she wandered alone while Uma was with her baby at some activity centre that teaches yearlings how to blow spit bubbles. Discovering it was *pig* meat and not the stuff that makes you sneeze, she stuck a finger in her throat and confessed her sin to Uma's pink toilet bowl, chanting the thousand names of Vishnu afterwards for good measure. In time she will learn the new strange ways, but she will continue to feel like a spare nappy pin—sought only in an emergency. Sometimes she will feel like Balumama's soul, suspended between two worlds. Karma, karma. We are *two* lost souls.

But she isn't thinking of all this in Bangalore's tacky international airport which, despite its constant upgrading activity remains depressingly like a mofussil bus station, and where Meenakshi, Devimami, Rajumama, Bharat and I, nursing our aching knees (because, as always, chairs are in short supply), are gathered to see her off. Three Mamis, one Mama and a couple. A couple that hasn't coupled and never will, although the airport can't guess that.

Dressed in a non-crush sari and a plain white blouse that neither matches nor clashes with its shower-curtain print, Lilamami is a typical figure of widowhood, pure extract of Brahma. Her face is unadorned but for the small dab of colour on her forehead, a pottu which is not crimson but brown. Not a flaming sun but a dim satellite thereof. The diamonds too have been downsized. Her suitcase, newly purchased from Commercial Street, is smart and gimmicky, but has a faulty lock—discovered too late. For her return journey Uma will loan her the red American Tourister, which she will fill with the flotsam and jetsam of her travels—odd lots of cutlery, free-size T-shirts for Rajumama and Bharat and the neighbour who pays her electricity bills, and shiny China silk saris—buy three, take one free—for Devimami, Jana, Meenakshi and me. Meenakshi will implore me to wear mine, 'to show Lilamami. Once, just *once*, please Kaveri. Then you needn't wear it ever again. Don't hurt her feelings.'

For what are people but a collation (or a cess pit) of feelings, and what is more important to people than other people? And their feelings? So I will wear my shiny magenta (or oily mustard) China silk, picked by Uma to spite me, despite what my sweet mother thinks, and model it for Lilamami.

'It's a beautiful sari,' Lilamami will declare in her unchallengeable way. 'I picked a purple but Uma's right—she said this would suit you better.'

Uma is as wrong as wrong can be, but what of that? Feelings have been spared. My mother is happy.

But all this is in the future—a future foretold by me, not Joshiyar who, because he looks at the grand picture, the solar system, that is, misses out on Earth's little dramas.

A modest drama is being enacted now in the panicked moment following the departure announcement of Lilamami's Air-India flight. Clutching her bag—containing her passport, some dollars, some pounds, Amrutanjan No Pain Balm, and a picture of Ganesha to watch over her in her new life—she bids everyone one last desperate goodbye. 'Poitvarain.' *I will go and I will return.* But she doesn't look at all confident of doing either.

'Poituvango, Lilamami.' *Go but come again.*

'*Ummmmmm*,' murmurs Devimami. The water in the rusty pipe advises courage. Courage and endurance.

Lilamami, who has never lacked either, quivers. 'So-oo Devi. S-oo Meenakshi.'

'So Lilamami. Bon voyage.' My mother's eyes are misting over as usual. 'Happy holidays! Have a jolly time!' Her hand flies to her mouth. 'I mean, forget this, forget us . . .' She gives up.

Have a safe journey, I help out, and she gives me a grateful smile.

'I will,' says Lilamami in a grim voice that bodes ill for drunken co-passengers. 'So Kaveri,' she turns to me. There's a teeny-weeny pause. Then, fumbling at the clasp of her handbag (Lilamami fumbling!), 'I hear you had some trouble with the book people,' she says.

Devimami is all attention. Bharat is giving the Nescafe dispenser his unwavering attention. 'I'm an old woman,' Lilamami continues mournfully. 'All I have to give anyone now are my blessings.' She has shrunk, I think. She has shrunk to fit herself into her closed-in circumstances. '. . . I don't understand how all this happened. (Tears are running down Meenakshi's cheeks now.) It was all too much for me.'

She's afraid, afraid I may curse her on her way like some disgruntled medieval mendicant. I pat her shoulder.

It was too much for all of us, Lilamami. I'm sorry it turned out the way it did. You look after yourself now. Don't worry. Don't believe everything Oprah Winfrey says.

'I've stopped.' She frowns at a sign advising travellers not to leave their bags unguarded. 'She's a beef-eater.'

It took me a minute to parse this extraordinary indictment. It was an olive branch. Ordinarily she would have said meat-eater—a dig at my marriage and the muddying of our stock. This new classification is a nod at Arya's Hinduness which is usually overlooked because, not being a Brahmin, he is lumped with the other carnivorous subspecies.

It is time.

Rajumama escorts her to the glass wall of Security Check where she joins a queue of hopefuls whose stories are about to end and begin too. We wave till her back disappears behind the security screen.

On our return from the airport I make a call to the meat-eater—shutting the door to my parents' room as a simple precaution. Straightaway, I ask him for a divorce. There is a brief, gratifying silence. Then, 'I knew it,' he says smugly. 'I *knew* something was going on! So when's the big day?'

What big day?

'Your wedding day, of course. You're marrying that fucker, aren't you?'

Who?

'Who else? My erstwhile client, damn the bastard. Your *lover.*'

After I regain my breath, I'll wait for a decent interval, I say. After the divorce.

Quick as a bullet, he demands that the flat—the sale deed—be made over to him. Since he is sole occupant at this point, since I am a home-breaker, since I have other—vast—sources of income. And since I was off to a brave new world. He will pay the balance payments (of which half is left) and obtain sole ownership. I could have the furniture and whatever money there was in our joint account.

That isn't a fair exchange, Arya, and you know it. I get to own a piece of the home I broke.

'I should get *compensation*. For the years I wasted on your fucking artistic temperament.'

He's worked out the cost-to-self of our marriage. Opportunity cost. Frictional losses. Emotional drain. You ungrateful bastard, I say, hoping the phone will amplify the hiss, you bloody calculating bookkeeper.

'Not a single decent meal,' he complains, *now*, for Godsake. Isn't it a little too late to rake up my cooking? 'Not *one* word of comfort.' He goes on to describe with dreary, unhurried passion just how much I have deprived the inner man all these years. 'A cooked breakfast was a glass of hot milk!'

I point out *he* has deprived *me* too. And feeling a little low-life, I remind him that the promise, or premise of a marriage was more than hot breakfasts and soothing words. And in case he didn't get it, there are conjugal rights, I qualify. Not too much conjugality between us, was there?

'You *would* think of that. Base instincts. What about mutual support?'

Well, we didn't have much mutuality either. And come to think of it, *you're* the one who mentioned deprivations.

'You didn't stay deprived for long.'

That's true. (Make what you will of *that*.)

'*Those* are grounds for a divorce!'

You need no grounds (I'm working myself up into a familiar fury), *I* want the divorce.

'Well then, this makes me the wronged party so I claim ownership of the flat as damages. You were cheating on me!' And mistaking my silence for denial (or acceptance), 'You *deserted* me,' he mewls. 'For another man.' Well, shouldn't you thank God it wasn't for a *woman*? 'You left the flat. That proves you have no interest in it.'

Using the tone I reserve for dim housemaids who soak the underwear in hot water, Arya, I say. Hear me out. There's no legal implication to my going away for a month. I haven't been away long enough for you to claim I have no intention to pay the rest of the instalments. So don't talk rot, Arya.

'I didn't know *when* you'd come back. *If* you'd come back. I still don't.'

If you remember, Arya, the loan is in our joint names. And we've been making payments from our joint account.

Suddenly, that miserable flat means a lot to me. The one objective reality in my life. How does one halve a flat?

'We'll get a lawyer for the divorce,' he concedes grudgingly. 'You get one and I'll get one.' As if we're recruiting seconds for a duelling match. 'They can work out the terms and conditions. The settlement.' He sounds almost cheerful. There were lots of calculations he could look forward to.

Fine. I'll have the divorce papers drafted.

'Oh no, you won't. *My* lawyer will draft them.'

Oh have it your way, silly fellow. And I bang down the receiver.

Arya will spend the rest of his life taking revenge in dozens of annoying ways. Even now he must be plotting to change the front door lock. Throw out my first editions. Empty out our bank account. Well, it will give him something to do.

The Family is now a depleted chessboard. It has run out of moves too. To her resentment, Devimami finds that with Lilamami gone, she doesn't merit a visit all to herself. So she clings and complains everlastingly to my obliging mother. The complexities of loving, or, for that matter meddling, have been reduced to a litany of whines and woes. There's nothing left but leached blood ties.

Bharat continues to visit us. Meenakshi always asks him to stay on for whatever meal is going. Sometimes she also asks him to give Mani a decent shave, which neither of us can. And Bharat always obliges.

Manoeuvring a stubbly jowl once, he asks, 'So what do you plan on doing, Kaveri? Didn't you say you're going back to work in a bank?' From behind Mani's chair I flap my hands and scowl at him to shut up. But, 'Will it be in Bangalore?' he continues, all innocence.

If I get an opening. I've applied to the Canara Bank. *As* you know.

Mani's head wobbles like a top. *She is going to stay here.* He will be tormented by shame, the shame of keeping a daughter from a normal woman's life. But only for a while. Then he will be tormented by the shame of the relief of having her here. That too for a while.

It's alright, Pa. It's what I *want* to do.

Then I break the news that I am unhooking myself from Arya.

The top goes into a dying spin. '*Divorcing* him?' squawks Bharat, leaping a foot—fortunately away from Mani. You'd think India had won the World Cup, the fool.

'*Arraraa?*' Shock bristles on Mani's chin.

Meenakshi sneezes dolefully. 'History is repeating itself. Your grandmother's marriage wasn't happy either.' She clutches her brow. 'Kaveri! I see my mistake now! Take off your diamond earrings. *Immediately.*'

I oblige, and then ask her to please supply the logic for this?

'Some diamonds bring bad luck, you know. Those were

your *grandmother's.*' She gives me a significant look. 'Oof, you *know* how unhappy she was.' She starts unscrewing her earrings. 'Here, wear mine. Give me yours. Nothing is going to affect *my* marriage.'

That is too correct. So your earrings are going to be like a divining stick, eh, Ma? When they flash I'll know I've found Mr Right.

'You have no faith. That really is your problem. Shall we have chapatti or rice for dinner? Cauliflower or beans? Dry or gravy?'

But Meenakshi is wrong. I do have faith—although, admittedly, not in the almanac, not in the full moon, no-moon, fourth quarter of the moon that she ritualistically observes to secure a place for her in the afterlife. What else can it be but faith that makes me scan my email first thing every morning and last thing every night and several times in between? That makes me do an Olympics dash to the telephone each time it rings? It has to be faith that hinges my life on two words. *I shall.* After all, I deflected its course for those words. For which I hated him, hated, hated, hated. At first. But there's no turnaround with hate. It's the end of the road. *As* Mani once said. Faith, on the other hand, is the beginning and the middle.

Where Meenakshi is right is that she expends her faith, not banking it as Mani does. Meenakshi fritters away her faith, and that's how it should be.

See her expend some one sunny morning, on a recipe for tomato preservation she read in *Bangalore Beat*—a rag that runs on boundless faith in its readers. She's pottering about in the courtyard in her tarty lavender slippers, moving buckets of tomatoes around, humming along with her Bhakti Geet. Now she tips a bucket onto a plastic sheet, her face showing no murderous intent, not the slightest indication of the bloody spillage her knife is meditating. It is, in fact, the old tranquil face. Her husband has been struck down, her daughter is greying, anchoritic and consortless, but she continues to believe that rape, murder, the Holocaust and Hiroshima are all the sport of an insuperably magnanimous being.

Bloody juice squirts on the yellow straw. The smell, redolent of a long-ago corruption that even now makes me nauseous, spikes the scent of freshly watered earth. She looks at me with shining eyes. 'Tomatoes are two rupees a kilo! *Two rupees!* How can one go wrong!' From his wheelchair under the oleander tree, Mani gives our activities his sardonic attention. An umbrella is propped against his chair. The sun is pumping away in the sky, but who can tell? It may burst into tears any time. This is Bangalore, after all.

I think I hear a chuckle. But it's only the cat.

A giant frond detaches itself from the coconut tree, crashes to the ground. We don't take note although it has fallen dangerously close to Mani. The coconut tree is governed by a natural law, Meenakshi once told me, which prevents its fronds and nuts from harming anyone. They fall just before or just after one passes under the tree. This isn't her usual sentimentality for I've never heard of anyone being brained by a coconut. (Or a frond.) One could extend this decree into a philosophy. The world shelters under a coconut tree atop which sits a maniac who flings down fronds and nuts as capriciously as he goes about his other business. But we always escape them. We always escape *him*.

No coconut or coconut frond falls on Mani but an oleander blossom does. It falls on his head and stays there, making him look like one of the lesser gods in Meenakshi's puja room—

impassive, inflexible and impossible to please. He is not about to grant any boons, but he will allow himself to be worshipped. That is the way of gods.

In a week Meenakshi's tomatoes become a heap of seeds and dead skin. She is hard put to hide her dismay—kilos of succulent bounty reduced to this bathos—but she will not acknowledge her failure. 'It's *dehydrated* tomato,' she says, as she feeds the stuff into the mixer. Spooning the resultant dust into the rasam she exclaims, 'Tomatoes are fifteen rupees a kilo now! *Fifteen rupees!*'

The rasam looks and tastes like mud. Mani dribbles his disapproval on the towel tucked into his collar. 'Perhaps it isn't good for rasam,' Meenakshi says doubtfully.

After some months Meenakshi will throw away the fruit, rather, what was once fruit, of her industry. It will dawn on us that our mistake lay in not skinning and de-seeding the tomatoes. Fresh tomatoes are fine—skin, seeds and all. But in trying to preserve its earthly qualities, that is, its substance, we lost its essence. We meddled with a natural law. Evidently our intelligence has not yet been fully secured. There's a pointer in that if I care to probe.

My faith was rewarded one fine day in early autumn, although I didn't check if my diamond earrings flashed. I had returned from work (yes, I did get the Canara Bank job) and we were sitting in the verandah as we did every evening, after coffee and before television—a routine that has acquired a ritualistic dimension. I was reading to Mani, Meenakshi was knitting and listening partly to me and mostly to the pulse of the house, specifically the whistle of the pressure cooker in the far-off kitchen. The smoke from coffee beans roasted that morning had settled in the curtains and cushions and would stay there for days. (Yes, it had been a good year for coffee.) Light from the garden, deepening from citrine to chartreuse, deposited secrets in the corners and under the chairs, secrets that would be resolved when the lamp was switched on. (Which wouldn't be till Meenakshi dropped six stitches and I glued the book to my nose.)

Anyway what happened was I came to a paragraph break just when there was a lull in the traffic. Into the second's silence the telephone shrilled. Meenakshi said she'd get it—I guess she was getting a bit tired of Mr Pickwick.

'It's for you, Kaveri! It's long distance, I think. The line's not clear.'

It was a long call so the light was on in the verandah when I returned. She looked up from her knitting. 'Who was it, Kaveri?'

I continued to stand by the door, not replying, not moving even. I *couldn't*.

'Who . . . why Kaveri,' she said wonderingly. 'You . . . you look so *happy*.'